# Admissions

### A Novel
### by Eric Sasson

*Admissions.* Copyright 2018 by Eric Sasson. All rights reserved. No part of this book may be reproduced in any form or by any electronic or mechanical means, or the facilitation thereof, including information storage and retrieval systems, without permission in writing from the publisher, except by a reviewer who may quote brief passages in a review. Any members of educational institutions wishing to photocopy part or all of the work for classroom use, or publishers who would like to obtain permission to include the work in an anthology, should send their inquiries to braddockavenue@gmail.com.

The characters and events in this book are fictitious. Any similarity to real persons, living or dead, is coincidental and not intended by the author.

*Printed in the United States of America*
10 9 8 7 6 5 4 3 2 1

FIRST EDITION, June 2018

ISBN: 978-0-9989667-6-2

*Cover image by Ryan Bradley*
*Book design by Kristina Yarberry*

Braddock Avenue Books
P.O. Box 502
Braddock, PA 15104

www.braddockavenuebooks.com

Braddock Avenue Books is distributed by Small Press Distribution.

# Admissions

A Novel

# PART ONE
## FALL 1999

# 1. WELCOME TO GABRIELLE LEVY

They could scoff at her, bemoan her aggression, deride her shrillness, question her taste—well, maybe not that—they could call her a slew of names but no one, ever, could deny the steadfast devotion that Gabrielle Levy showed to her daughter.

Society was on the verge of crisis. Another school shooting on the front page. Children killing children—was this becoming acceptable? Were we to cry for a few days each time and, sooner or later, sit comatose through the nightly news, the tears replaced by a vacant silence, a cruel lack of outrage? Would we glorify the statistics, tally the similarities and point out their idiosyncrasies, collect and swap the killers' life stories on glossy trading cards, invite them to freshen up our news magazines and dinner parties, buy the shampoos they endorse?

Not on her clock. While the rest of the world was being snowed under an avalanche of dysfunction, her Arianna would surely be safe, in the well-insulated igloo of her mother's careful nurturing.

Gabrielle tossed aside the morning newspaper. She didn't know why she bothered; there was never any good news anymore. Her family thought she was crazy, the way she popped up at 5:30am. What pressing matters jolted her out of bed? They wouldn't understand. Sitting in the silent museum of her apartment, making her own coffee—it gave her time to think, to prepare.

At 6am, she scanned Arianna's schedule on her Palm Pilot. She had met half of Arianna's teachers in person and had spoken to the other half on the phone. She knew that Madame Reeve was a sharp wit and that her meticulous attention to detail intimidated Arianna. Still, she felt an affinity for the woman—preciseness would make Arianna stronger.

Mr. Gluckman had never been married. His beard suggested a lingering nostalgia for 1971, and his vocabulary confirmed it. He taught calculus in what he believed was a more practical, user-friendly way. She knew this approach annoyed Arianna, and it annoyed her as well. Arianna had received a 78 on the last test, and while the median grade was a 74, she knew Mr. Gluckman was one of those teachers who considered a B-plus to be perfectly respectable. A few weeks prior, she had called him for a progress report and mentioned in passing that Arianna seemed worried about the midterm. The man had the nerve to tell her that Arianna seemed to worry about a lot of things. He asked questions about Arianna's schedule which she entertained at first, until she realized she was being snookered by his amateur psychology. Wishing him a good day, she vowed never to let this man get the better of her again.

Grey-haired at forty-two, Wendy Williams, or "Kumbaya" as the students called her, would have been the perfect People's Ambassador under Mao. Instead, she was the English teacher, or Professor, if you will, since she wouldn't hesitate to remind you that she'd taught five semesters at Hunter College. Kumbaya insisted that all the students feel like they "have a voice." The fact that someone had something to say, no matter how ignorant or poorly articulated, was reason enough to listen and thank the person for his tremendous insight. Arianna would come home with horrible stories: "She *never* calls on me, Mother, and when she does, and I give the right answer, she frowns and says, 'well, I guess you can see it that way' and then she'll call on someone else who'll say the most stupid thing, and she'll whistle and clap and tell him he's brilliant."

That her daughter was chided for her intelligence—it was appalling! If everyone's opinion was equally valid, what was the purpose of having one? She tried talking to Williams about it, but every time they spoke Gabrielle felt as if the woman had a string coming out of her hips—she'd pull on it and out of Kumbaya's mouth would come some canned platitude from the 1969 Soviet teacher's manual. She finally suggested to Arianna that she go to class one day in a black wig and peasant's dress. Perhaps then Kumbaya would show her some respect.

But Gabrielle reserved most of her bile for the odious, perfidious, jaundiced she-devil known as Carlotta Piper. Could someone be less equipped to be a guidance counselor? The woman did not even have a Master's in Education! So she was a Rhodes Scholar. This was supposed to convince people of what, exactly? Arianna and the rest of the kids at Valhalla weren't ordinary students at Mediocre High. They weren't a gorgeous mosaic of intellectual diversity. They were the *future*, had been prepared for their positions since birth. This woman's haphazard suggestions were going to affect the course of history, do untold damage to their children's psyches and, in the long run, have consequences so far reaching that New York City would one day scratch its scalp and ask, what in the hell happened to our progeny?

Freckle-faced Carlotta Piper (Why did people find freckles cute? Even as a child, Gabrielle found them grotesque: a permanent case of measles. Spots, after all, belonged on *felines*) was guiding Arianna on a course of second-best, full-of-regrets housewife martyrdom. She had convinced her daughter to apply to several safety schools in order to assure a "soft landing." She spoke highly of NYU, Brandeis, and George Washington University. She said other students dreamed of attending those schools, and that Arianna would likely be accepted to all three was "nothing to shake a cinnamon stick at." She said Columbia was possible, but not definite. When she mentioned Brown, she disparaged its elitism. She called Yale a crap shoot and Harvard an arid desert of uncertainty that Arianna dare not traverse with much hope of finding an oasis. Any mention of Princeton was done in hushed whispers, as if Arianna's chances were so tenuous that any conspicuous discussion might make them disappear. She spoke of 1600 SATs and 4.2 GPAs as if Arianna were a tourist to such exotic destinations. She asked Arianna if she really enjoyed the endless competition at Valhalla—asked *her* daughter, her *only* child, to sit down and think about what she wanted most out of the next four years of life and make a list of her expectations. *Not the things that others want for you, Arianna. The things you keep inside, that you truly wish for yourself. I'd bet peace of mind would be high on that list.*

Who did this woman think she was? Like a sand beetle, she had clandestinely dug into Arianna's skin, found a warm spot in her daughter's insecurities and laid her eggs there. Gabrielle suspected that if Carlotta Piper had asked Arianna to throw together a little bag and take off to an Ashram in central India with her, her daughter would hesitate only briefly. Hers was a poison pill in a pretty orange capsule, one that promised peace and contentment like those ecstasy drugs the kids were taking at clubs, only far more dangerous. Smooth and reassuring on the way down, this pill would undo years of careful preparation by forcing Arianna to reconsider her destiny.

But Arianna had to realize that even an ounce of second-guessing would be fatal. As soon as alternatives were given a place at the table, all the prominent guests were sure to leave. Getting into the Ivies took absolute conviction in today's environment, an *a priori* acceptance of the certainty of the outcome. Not a single mitigating circumstance could be expected to swing her way. She was white, wealthy and Jewish: the iceberg lettuce of the Ivy League salad, an ingredient so redundant that it is left in the recipe only for the sake of tradition. She had neither the deep hue of radicchio, the zest of goat cheese, the unexpected nutty flavor of watercress—these were the minorities, the disadvantaged, the strugglers who had overcome disease and famine and suspicious looks on the Q train. No, Arianna could only be the freshest, crispest, healthiest Iceberg lettuce out there, and hope that her luster would not be overlooked.

And after all they'd gone through narrowing down the list! Sure, each school had its qualities, but Princeton was the one. Arianna *had* to see it. Columbia was too urban. And staying close to home: *frightfully* bourgeois. To send Arianna there would demonstrate a lack of imagination on her part, a refusal to allow her daughter to grow. Harvard? Sure, its graduates were the movers and shakers of the world. But Harvard was too obvious; there was simply nothing interesting about it anymore.

Brown? Full of "creative thinkers." In other words: freaks. Graduates from Brown end up sharing such a distinct world view that it became hard to invite them to dinner parties. She wanted Arianna to be independent, but not fiercely so. The University of Chicago? *Boring.* Honest to God, did anything interesting ever originate in Chicago? Chicago existed so that Midwesterners could pretend they're in New York. NYU? People kept insisting that the school's reputation had grown by leaps and bounds, but considering all the construction downtown, it seemed evident to her that they were fast becoming the Kmart of higher education. Aside from not having a campus, how could Arianna possibly get any individual attention in a school of 50,000 also-rans?

Berkeley? Not a chance. Everyone she knew who went to Berkeley had given up their lives for Greenpeace or some other terribly earnest charity. As if donating money and hosting events weren't enough. Unless you personally breast fed a starving child in Mogadishu, you hadn't really ponied up to the cause. No, Arianna was far too vulnerable to expose to a band of brain-washing zealots, which also ruled out Sarah Lawrence and Wesleyan, where she would come home a lesbian, and Vassar and Amherst, where Arianna would meet a painter, get married and live in a house with two other couples in a rustic townhouse in rural Vermont. Stanford was out—all those raves and dot com cults. Worse: Arianna might become a *liberal*. Duke or Dartmouth would turn her Presbyterian. Jews from Manhattan did not send their kids there and expect them to stay Jewish.

Really, there was only one choice: Princeton. There could be no other. Yes, Princeton. A grove of intellectual poplars fragrant with ivy-scented tradition. Arianna would sit by the fireplace in Clio Hall, drinking spiced tea with her professor of linguistics. The four other students and she would listen, argue, and have profound life-altering conversations under the aegis of a man whose expertise on life was matched only by his impeccable taste in 18th century furniture. Mathey College would house her for those delicate first years. She would have to be selective about her eating club; it was crucial to find the right mix. Luckily Arianna knew all about cliques from Valhalla.

This was Arianna's destiny. The marathon ran straight down the I-95 to Exit 9, following the US 1 to the finish line in central New Jersey. She had a sworn duty to see Arianna through this race. She would be there, at every mile, rabble rousing, holding out the towels and the cups of water, pressing her daughter to never give up. Arianna would clutch her providence like a baton and go forth into the world, her head held high, beholden to no one, a life without regret. A life of her own making.

That is, if Piper didn't ruin it. Gabrielle imagined her daughter attending the interview at Princeton unprepared or recklessly cavalier, convinced by Piper that she had other, more adorable schools to fall back on. But the truth of the interview process is this: you are not being judged on whether you are an acceptable candidate; when you are the expected valedictorian from Valhalla, you are simply letting them know your time has come. You must *know* that you are in, and the interview is only to let *them* know that you know. It is the difference between saying, "I'd like to attend" and "When I attend", "If I get accepted" and "During my second semester I will..." She must approach it as more of a coronation than an evaluation. As soon as there is doubt, the possibility of error occurs. The admissions board will smell the ambivalence. *She does not know that she belongs here,* they'll say, and then they'll wonder if she actually does, and someone else more convincing will take her spot. All because of Carlotta Fucking Piper.

Gabrielle put down the Palm Pilot and took a deep breath. She was summoning up far too much bitterness so early in the morning. Her last therapist told her the reason she woke up so early was because she never allowed herself any time off from her grievances. They were the roosters cockle-doodling in her subconscious, forcing her out of her slumber. *You aren't Atlas,* he told her. *The weight of the world won't fit on your shoulders.* She stopped seeing Dr. Orlando two weeks later. At $200 an hour, she expected a more creative analogy.

At 7am the Levy household snapped into life. Everyone had to be tended to in the next forty five minutes. Myklos, Arianna's trainer, came every other morning. The salon-tanned Greek waited for Arianna in the gym downstairs.

"Go easy on the legs today," Gabrielle told her daughter as she thudded down the stairs. "Your calves look swollen."

Arianna rolled her eyes. "My calves are *fine.*"

"They're perfect, dear. What are we having for breakfast this morning?"

"Ugh. I can't. A glass of water."

"Egg white omelet then. I'll tell Tatiana."

"Why do you bother asking, Mother?"

"Protein, Arianna. Do you want to pass out at school? Besides, you'll be ravenous after the workout."

She brushed her daughter's hair out of her eyes, kissed her gently on each cheek. Arianna sighed and headed to the front door. As soon as she left, Gabrielle rushed to the kitchen. Tatiana would need to be watched over, lest she put capers in Arianna's omelet. How many times had she explained to the woman—in Spanish—that capers made Arianna queasy?

Morty would be next. Her other child, this husband of hers. Mr. Easy Going liked his suits laid out for him, his oatmeal perfumed with nibbles of skinless peaches, his newspaper rid of all sections besides finance. He liked all these things, but what he liked even more was being perceived as Mr. Easy Going, Mr. Don't Go Out of Your Way For Me. The staff adored him—every morning he came down the stairs with a kind word and a Santa

Claus smile. All the dirty work was left to her.

That morning was no different. He hummed his way down to the dining room table. He was every synonym of chipper. She stared him down until the last nib disappeared from the bowl.

"Delicious," he said, smacking his lips.

"You're not leaving without giving me a list for next Friday," she said.

"Darling, it's always the same people."

"Not *again*, Morty. I'll invite a dozen oils and half a dozen waters and we'll end up playing charades to make up for the excruciating lack of conversation."

"Gabrielle, not a single dinner party you've thrown has ever lacked conversation."

"Because I *plan*. I force you to make *choices*."

"Your choices are always perfect so please don't oblige me to make a mistake."

"Very well. Your daughter wants permission to attend a party."

"Would you like my permission to refuse her?"

"It's a Thursday night. At a nightclub. In the East Village."

"Gabrielle." He kissed her on the cheek as he lifted himself from the table. "Let's not pretend you're asking."

"So I'm wrong for setting ground rules?"

"Tell her what we've decided, dearest. I'll be late for work."

By 8am she had the day to herself. She would go shopping later; Arianna needed a stronger calculator, knee pads for volleyball, a Hermes scarf to go with her new cashmere Inverness. She had to switch an orthodontist appointment with an optometrist's; Arianna claimed her left contact was foggy. But there was something else she had to do. What was it? And what was the purpose of a Palm if she didn't use it religiously? Well, she couldn't worry about it now. She absolutely had to call Sebastian. The tiles he'd sent over for the upstairs bathroom were hideous.

"Monique? Gabrielle Levy. Is Sebastian in?"

How she detested being put on hold. She paced the living room, counting the seconds in her mind. On the mantel by the fireplace, housed in a large antique frame, sat the sepia-toned photograph of the newlywed Levys of 1980. She picked it up. What a lost look her young eyes had, so unprepared for the fairy tale. She'd been an uncommon beauty. A recipe of angels, Morty had called her. No doubt he'd read it somewhere, but at the time, it had charmed her.

And what a day it had been. Her parents' happiest moment:

her father's unsuspecting grin as well-wishers hoisted him up on a chair at the reception, her mother's gluey Slavic accent suddenly lost, a New World confidence surfacing in her r's instead. Crimson petals would be scattered down the aisle of their daughter's life from this day forward.

Gabrielle replaced the photo on the mantel. She looked up and the woman of today stared back at her in the mirror. Was there that much of a difference? The years had done little to corrupt her features. Her skin was still youthful and resilient. Her green eyes had only gotten greener.

Sebastian came to the line. She entertained his Italian excuse-making for a few seconds before sealing her point. "I expect you at four. You'll have three minutes to convince me I'm wrong. Goodbye."

She hung up the phone. What was next? She flipped through the Rolodex in her mind but couldn't remember where to stop. The house was too still. She went to the den, hoping some TV would jog her memory. Flipping channels, she saw nothing but a swarm of television talk shows about girls gone bad. If only she could dismiss the lot as vaudeville, freak show diversions for the common denominator. But there were so many, their stories all pointing to the same problem, a disgraceful neglect by parents who did not do enough, care enough, discipline enough. What were these children rebelling against, if not the total disregard of their parents? Too many people having too many kids they couldn't afford. As if bearing children were a right and not a responsibility. A 24-hour responsibility.

Her one child — the sole extension of herself. When she looked at Arianna she saw the smudges her fingerprints had left on the pieces of an unfinished jigsaw puzzle. The finished product looked promising, but if she wasn't careful — if she didn't choose properly — a new picture could easily emerge, and her daughter could end up like the girls on Sally Jesse Raphael.

She sat and watched for a while. It wasn't like she didn't understand these poor girls' needs. Neglected by their selfish parents, these young women would resort to anything to slake the thirst in their lives. When a kind hug or strong hand would have sufficed, instead they turn to these slick Lotharios, boys who project an uncomplicated if hollow strength, boys who will look at them with desire and need. Not knowing what true love is, they allow themselves to be manipulated, deceived, disregarded. They tolerate the violations, the unkindness. They disregard the sporadic phone calls that only involve appointments for sex, the abrupt cancellations and vague explanations, the suggestive looks at other girls, the forgotten birthdays, the lack of tenderness.

Gabrielle turned off the TV. It was unlikely she'd need to shield her daughter from this particular brand of misery. The need to center your life around a man had become an anachronism that Gabrielle was only too happy to see disappear. There'd be none of the expectations her mother had thrust upon her. Instead she'd provide her daughter with the greatest gift a mother can give: the opportunity to realize herself, through a life packed with activity, enrichment and self-actualization. Arianna's inner diamond would grow solid, impenetrable by any boy's needs or caprices. Her mother's tough love may have stung hard at the time, but it had left valuable scars on Gabrielle's temperament. *She* would do things differently.

It was nine o'clock, and there was no time for lollygagging. A mother's work was never done. If only she could remember what it was she needed to do.

Only then did it occur to her. Of course! She had to cancel her yoga appointment.

## 2. RANDALL MILLER

*You are more than just a tutor.*

Scribbled in purple crayon on the back of a page torn from his teacher's manual. Stuck onto his refrigerator, where it was held up by bleary-eyed penguin magnets his parents had gotten him on their trip to Sea World back in '96. He would see these words, every morning, right before he took out the Egg Beaters, the whole wheat, the skim. Or the Cocoa Puffs, the bagel, the two percent. He wasn't very good with diets.
 It was true. He was more than just a tutor. *Way* more.
 Randall Miller yawned. He had no right to yawn. It was eleven in the morning. Pretty much everyone else he knew had been awake for over three hours by then. Then again, they didn't go to bed at 3am. They got up for their nine-to-fivers. He was more of a five-to-niner.
 He dragged himself around his cubicle of a kitchen. If Mr. Coffee didn't hurry up, he'd miss the first ten minutes of *The View*, and everyone knew it was all about the first ten minutes, when the ladies did the Hot Topics. He walked into his living room and turned on the TV. At least he'd hear the women if he couldn't see

them. He remembered the time he'd gone with his friend Dana to see *The View* live. It had been Lisa Ling's first day. Sheryl Crow performed two songs. God was it awesome.

He put the coffee and Cocoa Puffs onto a tray and sat himself down by the TV. Tutoring had its privileges, one of which was a leisurely stroll into the day. No scrambling for starchy pressed shirts. No rush-hour commutes in trains reeking of cheap cologne and morning breath. No, he worked for the Center for Advanced Test Preparation for Entrance Examinations, teaching the high-profile SAT classes, tutoring the most promising students.

He was damn good at his job, too—so good he didn't plan on sticking around much longer. His own client base was secretly building up quite nicely, and pretty soon, it'd be time to say Adios. He certainly didn't plan on being a tutor forever. It was just an easy way to make money and still have enough time to write. Because that's what he really was, a writer. It had dawned on him a couple of years ago, after crisscrossing through several dead-end jobs that did nothing but suck the life force out of him. His degrees, in philosophy and economics, were so far no more than congratulatory calligraphies on sturdy paper, housed in attractive wood frames, taking up what precious little wall space he had. Yet through all his schooling years, he always seemed drawn to writing. He admired writers. They seemed to have something to say.

He'd been dabbling in several forms for a while. In a few months—or a year, at most two—he'd complete his screenplay, or novel, or Broadway musical. By then he'd have a supportive boyfriend. Someone who understood him, someone who liked Star Jones as much as he did. Mr. Right—he'd be named Wilder, for Randall had a thing for kooky surnames-turned-first-names—would be just as successful as he was, but not right away, so Randall could bask independently in the limelight. Wilder was twenty six; two years his junior. He had a honey-infused accent, large compassionate hands, a Canadian disposition. He played REM covers on his pawn shop guitar. Quietly landing in New York from a petite yet progressive town on the left side of Vermont, he did not know the ways of Gay New York, and once he did, he'd reject them as thoroughly as Randall did. Randall hoped Wilder would show up soon; his love life was growing moldy.

Forty minutes into *The View* Randall turned the TV off. Once they reached the makeover segment, he knew it was time to plop himself in front of the computer—which sat on a stack of crates in his bedroom—and create. There really wasn't any room for a desk in the painfully cramped room, but that was New York for you. If space was a priority, he could have stayed in Fairlawn, New Jersey, found himself a two bedroom with parking and built-in washer/dryer units on a quiet, elm-lined block a stone's throw away from the house he grew up (and his parents still lived) in. His mother could Volvo over on Mondays with ready-made dinners for the rest of the week: lasagna, meatloaf, tuna surprise. He shivered. Better if he ate runny Thai from the dive around the corner every day for the rest of his life than subject himself to the cloying hospitality of Sylvia Miller.

He had just turned on his Compaq, a birthday gift from his parents four years ago, when the phone rang. Why did people insist on calling before noon? Randall didn't recognize the number on his Caller ID. 717. An Upper East Side prefix. He decided to take the bait.

"Hello?"

"Is this Randall Miller?" A snappish voice demanded.

"Speaking."

"I understand you do SAT tutoring. I got your number from Pamela Welton. She says you're the one."

"Well, one should never argue with a lady."

The woman didn't laugh.

"I have a daughter, Mr. Miller."

"Please." He tried to lighten the tone. "Call me Randall."

"I need a fearless tutor, Randall. Someone without equal."

"Well, Mrs..?"

"Levy. Gabrielle Levy."

Randall paused momentarily. Should he know this Levy? There were so many Levys. The Levys of Sutton Place? The Levys who were shipping tycoons? Surely she was of a certain family. Surely, if she'd gotten his number from Pamela Welton, she'd be willing to pay a fancy price.

"I don't have the time, Mrs. Levy. Would you like me to recommend someone else?"

Of course he had the time. But the more he hesitated, the more she'd salivate, and the more money he could squeeze out of her.

"I didn't call for someone *else*, Randall. I'm calling for you. It *will* be you. In two years Arianna will be attending Princeton. Will you help us see to that?"

The woman had already picked her daughter's school. Randall was intrigued.

"Arianna just entered her junior year at Valhalla with a 97 average," Gabrielle said. "She got a 1300 on the PPSAT. She's already taken several AP classes and she's up to her neck in extra curricula."

"I see. Still, I'm not sure—

"Listen here, Randall." He hadn't met the woman, and already he felt like her secretary. "I'm a very convincing woman. With a tremendous Rolodex of names."

"Let me check my schedule and see..."

"This Friday, just after five. A half hour getting-to-know-you. We'll discuss the game plan. You'll be paid for the full hour, of course."

How could she possibly know that his last appointment on Friday ended precisely at five o'clock?

"We're at the Minotaur on Central Park West. Tell the concierge Levy on thirty-three. One of the doormen will escort you up. Did you get all that?"

He did. She repeated it anyway.

"We'll see you Friday, Randall."

"Yes, Mrs. Levy."

"*Gabrielle*, Randall. Call me Gabrielle," she said. Then she let out a most unnatural chuckle and hung up the phone.

Randall felt groggy, as if he'd gulped down a slushie too quickly. She hadn't even asked him his fee. Even if Pamela Welton had given her a ballpark figure, he could easily charge thirty or forty an hour more without raising a brow. A handful more of these and he could tell the minions at CATPEE where they could shove their #2 pencils. Then he'd have more time to himself. More time to write. More time to pick out the perfect end table. More time to search for Wilder.

He just didn't want to keep everything on hold anymore. Somewhere, not too far away, sitting patiently at a swanky French bistro, sipping Pinot Noir, was his Life, this Life he was supposed to be living, his New York dream, full of breezy, *Sex and the City* moments, dinner soirees with dynamic, successful friends who laughed at his jokes and made toasts in his name, rascally boys who flirted with him but only mildly because he was with Wilder, and Wilder was such a loving, supporting guy, such a teddy bear, and they had such a divine relationship—the envy of all, really.

He had to gather the courage to approach this stranger. Buy him a drink, compliment his tie. *Don't be afraid, Randall; your Life isn't that intimidating. When he asks you what you do, remind him, you are more than just a tutor. Way more. Tell him you're ready for your close-up, prepared to seize your destiny.*

Miriam, resident grouch of CATPEE's downtown hub, snapped her fingers at Randall as he walked in five minutes late. "Not so fast, cowboy. Cha-Cha and the Plague want to see you pronto."

"What do they want?"

"To fire you? How should I know? But you probably won't be so lucky. They'll probably give you a raise instead."

They looked at each other and laughed.

Randall headed to the back, where "Cha-Cha" Cheryl, the center manager and Harry "The Plague" Prague, the new center director, shared an office. Given the amount of money CATPEE paid its managers, Randall figured the Plague would last six months, Cha-Cha an additional three. Randall had seen eleven directors come and go in the four years he'd been at CATPEE. The last one, Sheila Morningsong, had been a fellow teacher who'd gotten the job simply because it was available and she had asked. Plus they'd cut the director's salary by ten thousand dollars, which essentially meant they were paying her the wages of a Honduran schoolgirl sewing buttons on the Kathie Lee Gifford clothing line. But Sheila didn't mind. She walked in that first day as if she'd been chosen for the President's Cabinet. She had *prestige;* people would *respect* her. Last Randall heard, Sheila was doing secretarial work at a discount law firm in Flushing. Somehow prestige and respect had forgotten to pay her rent, so she decided to suffer the Anne Klein rip-offs and the endless OT, because *Sopranos* talk was *de rigueur* Monday morning by the water cooler, and how the hell would she get ahead if people knew she couldn't afford HBO?

Randall knocked on the door before entering.

"Randall!" Cha-Cha called out in her backwater Georgia twang. "The man of the hour!"

Randall took a seat. The Plague looked up from his computer with a perplexed grimace. "New haircut?" he asked.

"Not really," Randall said, refusing to elaborate. He was going to hit a few bars after class, and had done himself up accordingly.

"We're in a situation, Randall. Remember that guy you tutored six months ago for the GRE? Abdul?"

"Forget it. Don't even ask."

"Be a sport, Randall," Cha-Cha continued. "He requested you. He wants forty-five more hours."

"You've got to be kidding." Randall was shocked. Was the

man as stupid as his test scores indicated? Randall never understood why some of his former clients would contact him through CATPEE when he'd specifically told them to call him directly. Did they enjoy paying more money for nothing? There was no way he'd agree to it now.

"We know it's a bit much." The Plague was the smooth talker, the deal closer. "We told him it'd be impossible to have you tutor him exclusively."

"Absolutely not. He needs to be dropped off by one of those specialized vans. Then they pick him up two hours late. I can't exactly go about my business with a wheelchair sitting in my kitchen."

"Please," Cha-Cha begged.

"Why don't we just tell him the truth? He isn't getting in anywhere."

"But that's not what we're here for!" Cha-Cha said.

"What *are* we here for? To suck up his money? He has a 960 combined, guys. Out of 2400. I can't perform miracles."

"Come on, Randall." The Plague's mouth sagged, like a wounded dog. *Here it comes*, Randall thought. *Kiss up time.* "He said he really likes you."

"I bet he likes me. He *came on* to me, that's how much he likes me."

"Oh stop it." Cha-cha rolled her eyes.

"He did. He touched me. Repeatedly."

"Is that even possible? I thought he was paralyzed."

"Only his left side is paralyzed. He touched me with his *right* hand."

"He was probably just seeking validation," Cha-Cha said. "I understand those people need to be touched a lot."

"Touching is not a part of my job description."

"Randall." The Plague's voice dropped an octave. He took off his glasses and set them down on his desk. "We want to find a way to make both you and Abdul happy."

"How about a raise, Harry? That would make me happy."

Silence.

"You know we can't do that, Randall. You're already in the top bracket."

"Oh well. Rules are rules. Anyway, my class is waiting."

"Thanks for your time," Cha-Cha said, dismissing him with her dimples.

He left their office with little regret.

\*

Dating in New York was hazardous to your health, and several times more so when you're gay. The same men seeking long-term relationships on Match.Com were the ones trolling the parks and the steam rooms at New York Sports clubs. Pipe dream pretenders. They all thought a boyfriend was a nice idea, like a goat cheese omelet was a nice idea, but sex, sex was more like salt—you weren't going to go too long without it.

Even when something did start, it never lasted. Some people thought the *Seinfeld* episode was an exaggeration, the one where Jerry broke up with his girlfriend because she liked the Dockers commercial. He'd heard of guys breaking up with their boyfriends for much less. Why suffer with some flavorless flounder in a New York aquarium overflowing with exotic, tropical fish?

He'd had enough of the modem addicts and their crystal-clear delusions. Why was it that every guy, no matter how old, was a "boi" online? Why did so many eyesores describe themselves as "hot" just because they had a few well-placed muscles? There was a reason these guys didn't have pictures of their faces, and it had little to do with discretion.

So that night Randall decided to stay away from dial-up love and give live human interaction a try. This would require some courage. Not for the faint of heart was Chelsea. Flamingoes on parade in snug kitschy muscle tees and Diesel jeans. Eyebrows plucked, faces scrubbed with Kiehl's, cheekbones of Nordic models, military buzz cuts or choreographed tresses, smiles like access-restricting velvet ropes concealing the fabulous beyond—fragrant gardens where go-go boys frolicked naked sipping pomegranate juice under cloudless skies. These smiles saw right through you. They saw your lack of pecs through your shirt, the puny bulge in your pants. They knew who you were wearing and why you weren't wearing better. The judgment was quick and it was merciless.

How he hated the shallowness of it all. But was he really any different? Would he go home with someone more than a few years older than him, more than a few pounds overweight? Of course not. He was just as shallow, only quieter about it. As if this somehow legitimized his feelings and impugned theirs.

Less than fifteen minutes at Splash and he was already getting antsy. At least online, getting sex was as easy as ordering a Big Mac, and just as quick. But at a bar, he blended in with the Cosmopolitans. Which was not to say that no one looked at him—just the ones that did were so much lower on the totem pole that he couldn't possibly return their gaze. It was simply unacceptable! He was always careful to stay within a certain range of physical attractiveness. Men who were too attractive would get a casual nod of acknowledgment. Men far uglier than he would be ignored. What troubled him was how many men that were certainly within his range overlooked him. And the men several levels beneath them—how could they gape at him so lasciviously when surely they knew he was far too attractive for them?

Still, he couldn't leave without trying. Not tonight, not again. Wilder could be there at that very moment, circling about. He looked around. Anyone of these men could be Wilders-in-Waiting. Any one of them could have profoundly complex psyches buried beneath their waxy, youthful exteriors.

Lurking about the room, he settled on a dark corner not ten feet away from a scruffy, post-*Growing Pains* Kirk Cameron type. Corn-fed and plucky, this apple-cheeked boy. *A graduate student,* Randall thought. *Still in touch with his New York dream.* He'd always had a thing for lost boys. Guys who looked like they were in constant need of directions. Not an easy look to come by in New York, where credulity was to be expunged from your face like a bad case of acne.

Randall stared politely. Grad-boy was drinking a blue drink, which somehow completed his bouncy look, much in the way the orange wedge completed his drink. He'd wait for some sort of acknowledgment first. Something that would let him know that in ten seconds he wouldn't be limping away with his head stuck up his ass.

Not a minute later, Grad-boy sent the opening smile. Randall tensed; he knew he'd have to act quickly. If only he had a foolproof line—Gay men weren't easily hoodwinked by awkward but sincere bumbling.

He moseyed over casually. The boy's smile widened. He was sipping his drink through a straw. He looked ready to blow bubbles. Somehow this gave Randall hope.

"Hi," Randall said.

"Heya," the boy replied, his eyes fluttering about, looking for a safe place to rest.

"I'm Randall," he offered, along with his hand. Grad-boy responded tepidly, as if shaking hands was reserved for board rooms or other lethally straight places.

"Steven."

"Nice to meet you. Here alone?"

"Looks that way."

"Your drink is very blue."

"It's a Blue Iced Tea."

"It brings out your eyes."

"My eyes," Steven said, "are mocha brown."

"It's a dark corner." Great, now he was explaining himself. "So, come here often?"

Steven put down his drink and let out a sexy little laugh. "You can do better than that."

"Don't be so sure," Randall said. He stared at Steven's lips during the awkward silence that followed. Luckily Cher came to his rescue through the speakers.

"How much do I love Cher!" Steven pronounced.

"I don't know," Randall said. "I mean, is that a question?"

Steven rolled his eyes. "You're funny. Seriously though, there are moments when I just know I owe Cher my life."

Randall nodded. He didn't worship at the shrine of the sanctified divas; still, he wanted to keep Steven laughing.

"Do you go to school?"

"I'm done with learning," Steven replied, tossing the idea in the trash like a pair of chinos three seasons old. "What about you?"

"Me? I'm not that young."

"Really? You look young. And confused."

"Well, we're all confused, aren't we?"

"About what?"

"Everything. The weather. Directions. Life."

"Tell you one thing I'm not confused about." Steven shook his empty glass in the air.

"Let me get that for you."

Randall walked over to the bar and with a grim face ordered two Blue Iced Teas. He watched the bartender pour seven different liquids into each glass. He was liking his chances. But was this what he wanted? Should he go for a number or a fuck? It was hard to tell. Most guys at bars wanted a quick fix-and-forget. Still, a lot of meaningful two month relationships started as one night stands. Some guys dismissed you as old-fashioned if you only asked for their number; at least if you went home with them, you'd have gotten laid.

Steven thanked him when he returned with the drink.

"So what's your take on bars in general?" Randall asked.

"They're great places for drinking, don't you think?"

He didn't appreciate the sarcasm. The drink was good,

though. Strong and sweet at the same time. "Is this how you like meeting guys?"

"Some ways are better. Some are worse."

"Yeah. Not exactly easy to connect with someone at a bar."

"Yeah," Steven said, acquiescing nothing.

"So what kind of guys do you usually go for?"

"I don't know. Cute. Easy to talk to."

Randall felt his mood deflate. Steven was being pat, dismissive. Was it because he ordered the same drink? Did it show a lack of character? What was he supposed to say now, I'm sorry? He hated the uncertainty. "Are we getting along?"

"Excuse me?"

"I'm sorry. I'm not very good at small talk."

"We could always try no talk then."

"Ouch. I guess I'll leave you alone then."

"Sweetie, I was *joking*," Steven said.

Randall walked away before the sting got any worse. He should have just stayed at home. He could have worked on the novel, or the screenplay—anything that would've made him feel less worthless. It was silly to have come. But then he thought: it was silly to be so fucking defeatist all the time.

He bought himself another drink. Within a few minutes, he was feeling happier, the room now suggesting all manner of possibility. He was giddy. His teeth tingled, like they were ready to yodel. So began the ritual of forgetting: losing himself in the ear-splitting house music, the rainbows reflected off of disco balls, the phosphorescent smog of cigarette smoke and sweat. Lost in the rapture of his drunkenness, he could finally tell those synapses in his brain to shut the fuck up and relax.

He had no idea how late it was when a certain mustached someone sidled up to his left side. A man of many layers: layered hair, layers of clothes, layers of innuendo in each of his prickly comments.

"Hey hot stuff," the man said.

"Hot stuff?" *Surely he's not serious,* Randall thought.

"You have a sexy aura about you."

"Cue the cheesy music." Randall laughed. The guy was like a refugee from a 70's porn video, the kind where men in chaps picked each other up at construction sites. Still, it felt nice to be approached.

"Having fun, baby? Want another drink?"

"The room is spinning at just the right speed, thanks."

"So tell me what you want then."

"I think I want to go home."

"So soon?" The mustache raised an eyebrow. "You're not ready to go home yet."

He admired the man's confidence. "I'm not?"

"You came here for a reason, baby. Tell me what you want."

"All right," Randall said, thinking: *You asked for it.* "I want to connect with someone. On an intensely chemical yet ultimately post-sexual level."

"We're connecting right now."

"Do you ever wonder why it's so hard to meet stable men in this city?"

"Is it hard?" the man asked, reaching down for Randall's crotch.

Randall rolled his eyes. But he wasn't ready to swat that hand away just yet.

"Sometimes I think we should all take a long look in the mirror and start seeing the truth. Because this is bullshit. I mean, I feel great now but in the morning it's the same jar of lube sitting on the nightstand."

"So you wanna come over?"

"Did you hear anything I said?"

"My hand is speaking to your dick. It's hard to carry two conversations at once."

"Jesus H. Christ. I gotta go."

"But your dick wants to stay," the man said.

Shit, was he really getting hard? "Kinda old, aren't you, to be acting this way?"

"Old enough to go after what I want."

"Old enough to not care when you don't get it?"

"It's late, Pumpkin." The man winked at him. "Make up your mind."

Randall stared at the ogre, weighing his options. So this was his choice now: He could take up Burt Reynold's offer, confirm for him and all other gold-chain-wearing playboys that sleazy come-ons actually worked, thrash about on a waterbed, Jovan musk candles burning, his eyes scolding him in the overhead mirror as he got acquainted with premature ejaculation and his cousin post-coital indifference, get handed a bottle of Jergen's—*oh I'm sorry, did you want to come too?* — leave reeking of cigarettes, get lost in the bowels of Brooklyn praying a cab will take pity on him, arrive home in the shallow light of dawn and lose his keys along with his self-respect in a gutter outside his door.

Or he could go home alone.

*Forgive me Wilder,* he told himself.

He took hold of the mustache's hand, which was still rubbing his crotch, and placed it in his own.

"My jacket's in the coat check downstairs."

# 3. EXCERPTS FROM ARIANNA LEVY'S JOURNALS

September 25th

I know I'm not supposed to complain. Everyone says the grass is always greener on the other side of the fence, to which my mother would reply, they should buy better fertilizer. Water more often. Hire a gardener. Whatever it takes, but for goodness sake stop yammering and do something about it.

I'm not saying my grass isn't lush. *Verdant,* if you will. (PSAT word—I'll be sprinkling these in, at least until the test.) And I know I have it good. But still, life is stressful. Sometimes I'm super into my insane schedule and other times I just want to jump the hell off this ride.

Today's events:

Weaver's macroeconomics quiz. Aced it. *Slight* chance of a 95, but likely a 100.

Guess who was named Junior Managing Editor of the Yearbook! SO psyched, but UGH! The amount of work is going to be excruciating. Last year's yearbook was lamer than a two-legged dog, and I'm not going to let our class come off all dorky this time. Besides, if I play it right, I'll be Editor-in-Chief next year. Which would be awesome. And SO HARD. But awesome.

Penelope told me—although so far it's just a rumor—that the Drama Club is seriously considering switching to *Streetcar* after my speech yesterday. I mean, how tedious is *West Side Story*? It's about as square as our yearly abstinence seminar. Hispanic chick sleeps with White Boy—yeah, that's scandalous. Somebody suggested we do *Rent*. Loved the show, but whose parents would allow their daughter to don fishnet stockings and tell the audience she has the best ass below 14th Street while searching for a vial of crack? Besides, my heart is set on Blanche. I will *so* do her justice.

What else? Kumbaya continues to plague me. This morning she could barely contain the resentment seeping through her chapped lips as she called on the only person in class—me, of course—who could accurately recite Desdemona's soliloquy in Act Three. There I was explaining its significance to the overall plot when suddenly, mid-sentence, she says: "Why don't we give someone else a chance, Arianna?"

That socialist bitch! Is it my fault I'm diligent? While the rest of my classmates are out living *la vida loca* (Ricky Martin!! Do they get cuter? Shame he's an Elton), I'm doing my assignments, organizing after school activities, preparing for my future. Which isn't to say I don't have a social life, unlike *some* teachers I know. She's so uptight, she really needs to just let somebody pleasure her. Studies show that middle-aged women who don't have some form of sexual outlet for long periods of time tend to become emotionally imbalanced, possibly leading to depression and/or schizophrenia. It's true. I read it in a legitimate magazine.

In any event, I will not resort to *obsequious* gestures just to appease her *capricious* personality. It's not like I haven't tried that already! She seemed to love the "homemade" raspberry truffle cookies I brought her on the first day of homeroom. (Actually, Payard Patisserie. Not that she'd know.) If I just hadn't gotten an 89 on that surprise quiz (*so* unfair) I wouldn't even need to concern myself with getting on her good side. Think of something, Arianna!

Last but certainly not least: I'm getting a new SAT tutor. Mother called Samantha last night. Poor Samantha. I could practically hear her tears on the other end of the line. She's so sweet, but as Mother put it, sweet's not getting me into the Ivies. Mother's kept a running tally on my latest diagnostic PSATs, and after seven months with Samantha, I've only broken 1300 twice. She's not-so-subtly suggested that I needed to step up my game, insisting that she's *very concerned*. Great, one more thing Mother is concerned about.

I'll miss Samantha, though. She had great fashion sense. On top of that, we could dish, and she wouldn't feed me the straight-from-the-parents-manual bullshit about boys. Mother thinks I tell her everything—I pretty much do—but sometimes I don't want to get lectured. Sometimes I just want to shout out loud that I want Matt Damon to fuck me into tomorrow and have someone agree with me instead of tell me to watch my language.

Anyway, the new tutor's name is Randall. Supposedly he's some hot shot. Mother isn't eager to "switch horses mid-stream," but she says we have no choice. More likely she isn't eager for me to have a male tutor under the age of 40. At least I hope he's under 40. Guess I'll see Friday…


October 9th

After *meticulous* consideration, I've decided to go Princeton Early Decision. Well, more like Mother decided, and I've decided she's probably right. I still pine for Amherst, but Mother has made a very convincing case for Princeton. Sometimes I think she secretly wants to go there with me. Yes, Mom as my roommate: Neil Diamond posters on our walls, Metamucil in the mini-fridge. Lights out at eleven. Boys given questionnaires to fill out—in duplicate—before escorting me to the dining hall. We could pledge Sigma Ima Pruda together—NOT!

Still, I can't deny her logic; Princeton is the cream of the crop. Plus Mother insists that God forbid I don't get in, then other schools will chase after me like rabid wolverines. And Randall's convinced I can get a 1500. He's *very* encouraging. Here I was worried the guy would smell of talcum powder and a lifetime's supply of celibacy. Meanwhile, he's like 23, if that, tallish, narrow, with hair that's thick and blacker than midnight. Not unattractive. He's got this swarthy Mediterranean peasant look about him, like he's just come back from picking olives. Also, his eyes haven't grown up yet; I bet he still gets carded at bars. He has questionable fashion sense, but at least he doesn't sport a beard and wear corduroy shirts. His one concession to style is his glasses. In fact, his glasses are so stylish he might be an Elton, but sometimes his hair is disheveled and his face is scruffy, and Eltons tend to be neat and clean cut. Besides, when I wear my baby tees and I stretch I've seen him check out my belly button, and Eltons only look at women's belly buttons if they're attached to Madonna or Britney.

But all this is academic. It's not like I'm going to scam with my tutor. Imagine the scandal. Mother would simply die!

I can just see it now: I purposefully shut the door one day, instead of leaving it slightly ajar as I'm supposed to. Randall and I are discussing geometry when I hear mother "pass by." (Mother has an annoying tendency to loiter outside my room. I wonder what satisfaction she derives from walking past a closed door.)

I will have teased him for weeks, but just then I turn it on even more. He'll flirt back, innocently at first. Then I'll be forward. He'll demonstrate a problem and I'll refuse to understand. He'll be forced to inch closer and explain it to me again. We'll redraw the diagram together, my hand upon his. He'll say, *Arianna, we can't* and I'll say, *Can't what?* and he'll turn away, embarrassed by his overwhelming lust.

Then I'll draw him closer to me. We'll embrace, his tongue plunging into my mouth, his fingers drawing circumferences around my nipples. And just when things are about to get illegal I'll hear a distinct cough, from right outside the door.

She won't enter; instead she'll ask how things are going. I'll sigh, and then softly say, *Everything is under control,* to which Mother will anxiously say something like "Oh good" and then walk away. By this time Randall will have jumped up to stuff what little dignity he has left back into his pants. For the next few days she'll stare at me funny; then the insinuations will begin. I'll pretend not to understand. *Mother, what exactly are you suggesting?* Before long Randall and I will be conducting our lessons in the den...

Ugh! I love my mother, but she dissects my life so relentlessly I feel forced to protect something from her, even if I'm just making shit up. Yes, that's me: Lolita Levy. Arianna the tutor slayer. No time to mess around with real boys so I guess I'll have to settle for being a slut in my mind. Well, there is Karynne's party next month. Who knows, maybe her older brother will show up with two friends, and they'll just happen to be Italian exchange students majoring in Psych at Princeton. Ha. More likely they'll be X dealers at SUNY Stonybrook. Even that would be better than the boys at Valhalla.

God do I need a distraction. Anyone, just please no dweebs or stoners or future frat boys chugging Alabama Slammers and barfing on me not three seconds after "Hey baby." Just a nice, normal, hot, complicated, fiercely intelligent boy. That's all I ask.

## 4. GABRIELLE

San Domenico was packed to the rafters. At a table by the window, Gabrielle was toying with her cell phone. The gadget kept beeping, sending her brief, tantalizing messages such as "home heating oil prices send consumers into a rage." She pressed every button, hoping to stop the noise.

Her mother tapped the phone with a scarlet nail. "Big Shot. Spend hundreds of dollars but you still don't know how to use it."

Earlier that day Gabrielle had taken the woman to Bergdorff's. Selma Lowenstein had wandered the aisles sporadically clipping swatches of scarves and blouses between her well-manicured fingernails, only to summarily discard them. *Seven hundred dollars? For this? They've got to be kidding.* Gabrielle had endured her gripes all morning. The Right Honorable Mrs. Lowenstein seemed to have an answer for everything. When Gabrielle told her she wanted to buy her a new dress, it was: *Who do I need to impress?* When she said Bergdorf's: *What's wrong with Macy's?* When she mentioned lunch at San Domenico: *But Au Bon Pain is just up the block.* When they took a taxi: *For three blocks? What are we, the Maharajah's concubines?*

"You'd think they sprinkled it with gold dust," her mother kvetched, after the waiter set down her twenty-two dollar orecchiette.

"You could have ordered the prix fixe if you wanted a deal," she replied.

"I should spend ten more dollars when I won't even finish this?"

"Try to enjoy the meal, Mother."

Selma sighed. Gabrielle looked out the window to hide her smirk. Her mother's foolproof method for accommodating all that was conferred upon her: first protest, then reluctantly accept, then pretend she hated the fuss to justify her secret delight in it. And what a fuss she'd made when Morty moved her to the apartment on Park Avenue! The greater the prize, the more resistance she put up.

She had far too much on her mind that day to enjoy lunch. But if she cut the afternoon short Selma would never let her hear the end of it. She was about to take a second bite of her salmon when her mother grabbed the fork from her hand.

"Let me taste." Selma rolled the fish around her daughter's plate to soak up more of the sauce. Her tongue made a smacking sound as she chewed, before her eyes glazed over with indifference. "Give me twenty minutes, a nice slab from Feingold's, some thyme and fresh lemon juice, and I'll show you salmon. All this fancy *narushkeit*. I went to D'Agostino's yesterday. They had bottles of water — *water* — for five dollars a liter. It was from *Antarctica*. Like penguins know something we don't."

"Mother, enough." Thank God she had told the waiter to put them by the window. Even there, Gabrielle could feel the lords and ladies' eyes weighing mercilessly upon them, these two gypsies from the Lower East Side, playing dress up uptown. It was how she always felt around her mother.

"You remember Shmookabernstein's on Essex? The way you'd scarf down that pastrami when you were little. I couldn't steal one piece! Nowadays you eat sushi. You know what festers inside raw fish, Gabrielle? Microscopic worms. If they're off by one degree, the worms come out. And they sit in your stomach forever."

"You want me eating pastrami, Mother? Because then I'd get *fat*."

"You don't look so fat. Just tired. You always look tired. The whole family. Like Irish zombies. Leprechauns could hide in the bags under your eyes."

"Gee. What a perfectly pleasant thing to say."

"*Bubbe,* don't mistake my honesty for petty insults. I'm just worried, the way you run around like a headless chicken. And my granddaughter! She looks like a broomstick. Are you sure she doesn't have that disease? Basilica? That girl from the *Alan Thicke* show was on *Oprah* last week. I understand it's very common."

"Don't be ridiculous. Arianna is not bulimic."

"And I'm forced to communicate with her via email now?"

"She has yearbook meetings and Model UN and God knows how many other projects to coordinate by Friday. You'll see her next week."

"So now she's Kofi Annan. Does she ever have time to be sixteen?"

Gabrielle's phone rang to signal the end of round one.

Selma scowled. "God forbid you should turn that off while we eat."

The Caller ID revealed Morty's office. No doubt it was Tamyra, one of the secretaries. She had asked the woman to research local Princeton alumni. One of these people might welcome a new intern soon, someone they could then write a glowing recommendation about.

"Talk to me, Tamyra."

"Mrs. Levy? Councilwoman Walters from Tribeca said she'd be thrilled to have Arianna on board."

"We need to do better, Tamyra. I want a judge. And none of those outer-borough hacks. Either that or some big wig at *Vanity Fair*. Did you call the Alumni Society?"

"I did. They said what I was doing was *highly unusual* —

"Now you *didn't* tell them who you were calling for."

"Of course not, Mrs. Levy. But they told me they never release any names."

"Please try harder, Tamyra. My husband thinks the *world* of your abilities. Did you get the Aveda basket I had sent over?"

"I did, Mrs. Levy. It's very kind of you."

"It's for a job well done, my dear. It's not too early to congratulate you, is it?"

"I'll get right on it, Mrs. Levy."

"Gabrielle, dear! You know you can call me Gabrielle. Take care."

She hung up the phone. Selma's hands were holding her cheeks in disbelief.

"Such a *fashtinker*. So now you're putting your daughter to work?"

"Things are different nowadays, Mother. Arianna wants to go to Princeton. If this is what's required, so be it."

"All this to get into a school? Of course she should go to college, but really, she should be allowed an ounce of fun at her age."

"Has it ever crossed your mind that Arianna enjoys this responsibility?"

"Whatever." Selma brushed aside the comment with a wave of her hand. Gabrielle wondered why she tortured herself like this. Every week the same browbeating, and every week she'd come back for more, like a dog returning to its own vomit.

"The one consolation—there'll be truckloads of nice Jewish boys at Princeton."

"How could you say that? That is *not* why she should go to Princeton!"

"Why not? You don't remember how you were at that age? I had to practically padlock your door. Luckily, I knew early on to put you in a room with the right one."

Gabrielle sighed. "Once again, Mother, I owe it all to you."

"Please, Gaby, if I hadn't pulled some strings you'd have never gone to that social, you'd have never met Morty, and where would we be now? Such a smart cookie you were but *oy*, what a dreamer. You forget those downtown *shnorers* you were cavorting with? Artists, they called themselves. Pretenders more like it. They haven't changed the world, Gabrielle. Most of them are probably still shacking up with roommates in a converted studio on Delancey. They're not eating lunch here, that's for sure."

How she wished her father was still alive. He had been so much better at handling her mother than she was. He would brush off her comments like lint off his tweed jackets, hum a catchy tune, defuse her word bombs with his diplomatic smile. He was the lubrication between their two rough joints. She missed him. She had to remind herself that her mother probably missed him too, and she had no other way to show it.

She smiled stiffly and pushed the fennel emulsion around her plate. Her appetite had drifted away a while ago, along with her energy to fight back. It would be over soon enough. She just had to keep reminding herself.

## 5. LEGION CARTWRIGHT

September light flooded through the windows of the office in the rear of the 3,000-square-foot Classic Eight on the Park as sixteen year-old Legion Cartwright sat squirming in his father's Argentine leather recliner, in front of a custom-made mahogany desk imported from England, ready to shit his DKNY gym pants. Sweat dribbled down his cheeks, making his crisp young stubble glisten. He looked delirious, his eyes fixated on the giant plasma TV that hung on the far wall.

CNBC. Another lousy day, capping an extraordinarily lousy week. The Nadsaq tumbling a billion more points. Semiconductors down eight percent. Biotechs down eleven, and internet—forget about internet. The correction had not fully corrected. The bubble was still being burst, the air oozing out in a painfully slow high-pitched wheeze. The great big grizzly bear was circling about, hungry for some tasty bull meat. But first he was going to fuck the steer up the ass a few times.

He should just give up and go to school. He should be in school, where he could be learning the law of cosines, polishing up his conversational Italian, discussing how *The Invisible Man* made him feel. *Sometimes, Mr. Kelp, I feel invisible too. I think we teenagers often feel invisible.*

But how could he be in school? It was bad enough Monday, having to feign sanity through seventh period Anthropology when just minutes before he'd dialed up his portfolio tracker on his cell, scrolled through his holdings and watched as thousands of dollars of his net worth disappeared. What was the point of going to school, if his college money was evaporating like the hydrophilic gases he'd experimented with last week in chemistry lab?

No, he had to stay home. He had to stay home, get on E-Trade, and save his fortune. He had to be patient, wise, ready. Wait for the right moment and strike.

Jesus. Rambus dipping below 70. The guy from DLJ called 70 a support level. This was fucking idiotic. How could people behave this way? Millions of previously rational investors all across America simultaneously deciding to commit collective suicide. It was at 275 last month! Two *hundred* seventy five. Does he buy on the dip? *No.* He bought on the dip last week. Three times. Two hundred shares at 170, then two hundred more at 126. All on margin. Jesus Fucking Christ! Why did they let him buy on margin! He was *sixteen*, for God's sake. Didn't they know?

Of course they didn't know. His father had opened the account. It was supposed to be his father's account, not his. But it *was* his. *His* money. From fifty thousand to over a hundred seventy five thousand in eleven months. It had all slipped away.

It all started last December, when Ken Cartwright had sat him down in the office one evening. Closing the door behind them, Ken took out a Cuban from his stash in the "secret" compartment, kicked his Wingtips onto the desk and stretched his hands behind his neck.

"In a couple years, son, you'll be going to college," Ken said. "And like most parents in America, I'm more than a little pissed at how much those four years are gonna cost me."

Legion watched as his father chomped on the cigar, took it out of his mouth to stare at it, and put it back in, all while adjusting his crotch with his left hand. "Now don't get me wrong. I have the money. It's just that, well, you and I know your grades aren't exactly four-point-oh and I'm not so sure I'm ready to lay out a hundred and a fifty grand so you can get shit-faced and poke your pecker into some sweet sorority ass from Kentucky up at Syracuse. Now it may sound like I'm being a jealous old man—and let's face it, I am a *little* jealous—but I'm also your father and if there's one thing a father should teach his son, it's to stand on his own two feet. So this is what I propose."

Ken's feet dropped to the floor. The man switched on the IBM, and for a few moments, while the computer warmed up, Legion and his father sat silently. *Fuck you, Dad*, Legion wanted to cry out. *Fuck you because I can get into way better schools than Syracuse and who are you to talk, considering you went to Indiana State?*

"Son, have you heard of online trading?" the man had said, his eyes glazing over. A brave new democratic world, without busy signals, or secretaries who couldn't take messages, ridiculous turnover times and expensive brokers who'd push what their bosses told them to push. Instead, they were just a point and click away from 5000 shares of Yahoo at a real time price. His father explained to him how to navigate the site, taught him the lexicography, the differences between limit and stop-limit orders, when and how to sell short. He told him about thirty day moving averages, price-per-earnings ratios, betas. He told him which analysts would make them rich and which were about as reliable as the Psychic Friends Network.

Legion could not remember he and his father ever having such a long conversation. His dad usually had a way about him. Where other dads might just yell at their kids, Ken's style was one of deliberately low expectations: *You can fix yourself a bowl of cereal, right, Legion?* or *You know how to post and mail a letter, right, kid?*

He tried to understand the implications of what his father was doing. The guy was giving him *fifty thousand dollars*. He trusted him enough, believed in him enough, to give him *fifty thousand dollars*. There was no way his old man would risk giving him that kind of cash just to prove what a good-for-nothing jackass his son was. Maybe the comments over the years were masking a deep love and respect that his father just didn't know how to express.

The first few weeks were the toughest. He'd turn on the computer like a clumsy virgin, the market, his gorgeous blind date, a lady rumored to be fast and impatient with little boys. He fumbled with the keyboard to type in the website, tip-toeing into this and that blue-chip large cap, ten shares here, fifteen there, like dry, hesitant pecks on the cheek. If the market price went an eighth higher than his limit price, he would balk, refusing to push, always respectful, lest she not want to take it any further. Still, he could tell she wanted more; he'd watch as stocks he was tracking kept rising to ridiculous heights, and his lust grew, his money eager to go further. So he let his hands explore, first in safe places, then in mildly risky crevices, then in the most speculative areas that promised hotter returns. He started selling short, placing stop-limit orders with a broker. He read the analysts, joined chat rooms to talk about takeover targets, subscribed to the Motley Fool and Robertson Stephens Internet Index. And no matter how hard he'd thrust, no matter how dirty he played, she'd keep begging for him to go deeper.

Soon he couldn't stop thinking about her. He had to be with her every day, for hours at a time. It all came down to her. She would afford him everything he could desire: not just his college tuition, but the car of his dreams, the loft in Soho, the vacations, the hot sex...sure, the hot sex. She wouldn't be jealous. She'd want him happy.

Did he have reason to think otherwise? For so many months, barring a few moody days, she had treated him oh so well. And every time she did, he'd gradually drop his guard, expose himself to her even further. Their relationship thrived on him being dangerous. Soon he was borrowing money on margin. What could he lose? She had seduced him with two hundred, three hundred percent returns. What harm could there be in riding the greatest bull market in the history of bull markets? At seven and a half percent interest on his margin account, he could be making an extra fifty thou a year. But just to be safe, he promised to wait for a dip before overdoing it. Then the dip came, and in he went. Five thousand. Ten quickly became twenty, then fifty...

In seven weeks he'd lost one hundred and seven thousand dollars. Since June, another twenty-two thousand more. She had tasted his blood and it was very sweet. He could hear her twisted laughs in his head as she sucked him dry. For months he watched and did nothing; he was far too involved, far too addicted to cut the ties while he still had some dignity left. *No, she will return. And she will love me that much more when she does.*

He pleaded with her, promised to treat her with more care, be less demanding. But she'd changed. Her heart had turned black; she had no use for him now. He had taken her for granted, bored her with his naive expectations. She had left him for raunchy times with reckless short-sellers, cagey bondsmen, blue-blooded blue chippers.

And now, *now*, he was fucked. Discounting all his holdings on margin and subtracting all the interest on debt would shrink his portfolio's net value to a paltry twenty-eight thousand dollars. That wouldn't even cover first year tuition at Harvard.

He didn't even want to think about what would happen if Ken found out. Luckily the old man rarely pressed for details. Or maybe it wasn't luck, maybe the asshole was laissez-faire on purpose. Last year he still believed in his father's good intentions. Now he wasn't so sure. It wasn't Ken's fault the market went south, but it was certainly his fault for giving him the money in the first place. Who tells their kids to play the market for their college money? Sick fucks, that's who.

The worst part was that Ken Cartwright wouldn't get mad. He'd just laugh. He'd nod his head, sigh, tell Legion he knew it all along, really—here was his fuck-up son indulging in yet another fuck-up. Yet another nail in the coffin. Yet another four years of living at home—or would you like Daddy to bail you out again?

No. *No.* No *fucking* way.

He just wouldn't tell him. He hadn't, for months now. He'd find some other way to pay for his tuition. Some other way to get into Harvard. Show the motherfucker he wasn't such a jackass. But he'd never, *never* tell Ken Cartwright the truth.

4pm was closing in. Qualcomm was flirting with 75. CDMA was supposed to take over the world. It *would* take over the world, markets be damned. Technology was changing the face of the future. Should he buy? Was this the one? The one stock that would make tomorrow seem brighter, that would signal the end of the bloodletting?

Yes, this was it. She wouldn't lie to him. Not again.

# 6. RANDALL

Fate had it that CATPEE had run out of SAT books for Randall to purloin. The company had recently declared a new policy of mailing the lesson materials directly to students' homes, in order to "institute a more efficient allocation system" and "counteract against the misappropriation of company material."

Thus fate had required he drag his ass to the local Barnes & Noble, where he'd be forced to pay retail. Then Fate decreed that his local branch would be out of the books he needed, forcing him to head uptown, to Sixty-sixth Street. Had, with its magnetic and unstoppable force, drew him to the study-aids section, where standing there with six different SAT books resting in his sinewy arms was a site of such undeniable beauty that if it weren't already busy chewing Juicy Fruit, Randall's jaw would have dropped open.

The recipe for his lust: a ruddy lad, scruffy brown hair falling into his dewy hazel eyes, tank top over short-sleeve T which barely concealed his obvious swimmer's build, sweat pants rolled up to expose taut calves sparsely coated with fine hair. The boy was sweaty, almost goofy with bewilderment. All that was needed for Randall to complete his fantasy was a skateboard and a series of short whispered breaths in his ear—an offer by the boy to sell himself—followed by a humiliating if somewhat liberating session where Randall licked the sweat off the boy's body.

Drunk with lust, Randall dropped his cell phone. Little girls were skipping down a road in his head. The sun was oh-so-bright and the girls had lollipops, sporting matching N'Sync T-shirts. "He is *so* cute!" they kept saying. He wanted so much to let them speak to this boy.

But he could not let these vixens flirt. Still, he had to say *something*. After all, he was an SAT tutor. It was his business to do so. Besides, the boy had the Gooser's New SAT, for God's sake—a 1700 page behemoth that was less than worthless. He had to intervene.

Retrieving his cell phone, he watched the boy put the books down on the floor and squat next to the bottom shelf to add a seventh to his collection. Randall hovered over him, admiring the tension in his calves.

"Need some help?" he asked, with a pleasant, blank smile.

The boy looked up, sliding the hair away from his eyes with his right hand. "Uh... I'm okay, thanks."

"No, you're not. Are you planning on buying all those books?"

"Maybe?"

"If I may offer some advice. The two on the top?" Randall reached down to grab them, holding them up like a '50s housewife advertising dishwasher detergent on TV. "Terrible. They could actually decrease your score." He put them on the top shelf. "Now this one." He picked up the next book. "Great for verbal, plus the flash cards in the back. A nice added plus. But the math doesn't resemble the math on the test. For my money, I'd go with either the bottom one, or..."

He began to scan the shelf. The boy scooted over to make room for him, his eyes following along with great interest. Finding the book he was looking for, Randall pulled it out. "This is what's missing from your collection. The absolute best in my opinion."

He handed the book over to the boy, who looked down at its cover.

"Thanks."

"No problem. So when are you taking the exam?"

"Oh, I'm just a junior. I'm taking the PSAT next week."

*A junior! Shame on you.* Randall's brain chastised him. But the little girls in his head weren't having it. *Don't be silly. It's OK to look.*

"An early bird," Randall said. "Good for you. Never too soon to start. Are you taking any prep classes?"

"Don't have much of a choice. I want to go to Harvard."

*Aha,* thought Randall. *His way in.* "Harvard. Very ambitious. Have you thought about getting a tutor?"

"Wait, do you, like, work here or something?"

Randall rolled his eyes. "Christ, no. I'm a test prep specialist. Where do you go to high school?"

"Valhalla."

"Really. Some of my students attend Valhalla. Do you know Arianna Levy?"

"Yeah. You tutor Arianna? Shit. You must be good. Arianna's, like, *really* motivated."

"She is. And I am. Damn good, that is."

"Cool," the boy said. "Pretty lucky I ran into you then."

"One could call it *fortuitous* even."

The boy widened his smile, expressing either confusion or utter disdain. *Nice going, dweeb, break out the SAT words, real smooth.* Randall ran his hand around the sides of his neck. His flesh felt clammy. He could feel his heart beat in his throat. If he wasn't careful, the little girls were going to start to scream.

"Let me give you my card."

"Thanks."

"Don't worry about it!" Dear God, he was yelping. "I mean, I'm *extraordinarily* busy but if your schedule is flexible I can manage to find some time. Why don't you have your parents call and I'll discuss it with them."

"No," the boy said. "I mean, my parents have decided to let me take care of these things."

"Okay. We can talk about it then."

"Don't worry about getting paid, I've got the money. It's just my dad wants me to learn responsibility. That whole 'you have to learn from your own mistakes' bullshit."

*Pay attention, Randall. You can't just stare at his crotch.* "What?"

"I said you have to learn from your own mistakes."

"Yes, of course. I'll help you do that...once we set up some appointments."

"Sounds great. Nice bumping into you, Mister..."

"Call me Randall."

"Sure thing, Randall. The name's Legion."

The boy extended his palm. Randall quickly conjured up a firm handshake in his mind before shaking the boy's hand. The effect was one of an advertising executive thanking the CEO of a fifty million dollar company for giving him the exclusive rights to their next campaign: too enthusiastic, too eager. Still, Randall felt an electric surge in his body. Surely the boy must have felt it too.

"Great to meet you. So you'll call soon?"

"Yeah...gonna need that card first."

"Oh! Of course." Randall fumbled through his pockets for his sterling silver card case, a graduation gift from his mother. As soon as he opened it, several cards fell out, and Legion rushed to the floor to pick them up.

And thus was the image that burned into Randall's memory: the boy, kneeling on the ground, his taut arms moving briskly to pick up the scattered cards. Oh, the humanity!

# 7. EXCERPTS FROM ARIANNA LEVY'S JOURNALS

October 8th

Why is it that no matter how hard I try to do a good job something always manages to backfire? Case in point: Today's poly-sci debate. Of course we won. It wasn't even close. And *why* did we win? Because *I* organized the team, *I* made sure the research was done and *I* thought through each and every possible question that might be thrown at us. We were prepared and we were *on*. My arguments were *pithy*, *cogent*, and *methodical*. The class voted for us overwhelmingly.

So why am I filled with melancholy? It seems that winning has its drawbacks when your opponents happen to include one smug überdork by the name of Mandela Robinson.

The topic: affirmative action. The two sides debated whether it was still necessary or was now outdated and unfair. Last week I volunteered for the "pro" team. Personally I side more against the concept, so I felt it would be a learning experience. Mrs. Grunfeld had scarcely finished writing my name down before that pretentious shithead Mandela stuck his hand in the air and volunteered for the other side. Gullible Grunfeld smiled — her cheeks swelling with "my, how far we've come" pride  — and thanked him.

The fact that he joined "con" only after I joined "pro" only confirms my suspicion that he has it out for me. Well, if last year's *arriviste* thinks he's gonna win over friends by challenging me, he can think again. It's not my fault that nobody hangs out with him! OK, I did suggest to Lauren not to invite him to her sweet sixteen, but since when is it my job to bake a pie and be the welcome wagon?

In any event, I knew I'd have to take it up a notch with Mandildo on the other team. No doubt some of the P.C. losers in our class were going to find it so courageous for one of our precious few African American students to argue against affirmative action. But that, dear diary, is *exactly* my point: Mandela wasn't being noble; he's just a poseur! I can see right through his cynical strategy: take the side of the white establishment, win the debate, and two weeks later write an article for the school newspaper explaining that the only reason he got to debate *against* affirmative action at Valhalla was because affirmative action got him in in the first place.

An ingenious plan, had I let him get away with it. Ever since he came to Valhalla, he's been nipping at my heels for academic ranking. And while he doesn't have a 4.0, he's *black*. A 3.8 is more than enough to make him a serious threat.

But getting back to the point. Knowing full well that Mandela was going to use himself as an example, I decided to do a little snooping. Amazing what you can find on the Net if you know what to look for. Turns out Deidre Walters, a.k.a. Deidre Robinson, attended Harvard in 1975. Deidre Walters from Union, New Jersey. No doubt an exceptional student, but how many black girls from Jersey got to go to Harvard in 1975? Exactly one, in fact. Part of the "Open Doors" scholarship program. Which is just a fancy name for you know what. So as soon as Mr. Perfect finished his speech on how diminished expectations have perpetuated a cycle of under-achievement among African Americans and affirmative action has only fueled the fire of white stereotyping against blacks, I brought up his *mother*.

Right away the class sprung to attention; they could smell blood in the air. But I knew I had to be careful. I made sure Deidre's story was dignified, uplifting. She was a pioneer and a success story, I told them. And then I went in for the kill, asking one simple question: should today's young girls from New Jersey be denied the same opportunities that your mother clearly benefited from twenty-five years ago? *Isn't it you, Mandela, who wants to perpetuate the cycle of disenfranchisement and white dominance in today's society?*

Bam! A lethal blow. He tried to recover, going on about the past being the past, yada, yada. He pointed to some sleepy statistics. But he was a deer struggling for life. Feeling bad for him, I did what must be done in these situations. A quick shot to the head to end the suffering: *Why don't you tell those statistics to Rashanda in Newark? Or the Hispanic college student from Corpus Christi. I'm sure they'll understand why they should sacrifice their potential for the sake of so-called progress.*

He didn't say anything. He couldn't even look at me, so he turned away from the podium and sat down. For ten seconds, the silence kept us hostage. Then Grunfeld began the vote. As expected, I was vindicated. I left the class high-fiving my debate partners, ready to savor my victory for the rest of the day. Until *he* pulled me aside.

"Superb performance, Arianna. Congratulations."

I smiled and assured him that the more challenging opponents brought out the best in me. He thanked me and we continued the round of compliments. Then he asked me what colleges I was planning to apply to, and, my defenses down, I told him of my singular desire to attend Princeton.

He smiled. Lucifer smiled at me and said, *You know what, Arianna, you've really persuaded me. Perhaps affirmative action isn't so bad. I think I'll apply to Princeton too. Maybe I'll see you there.*

That asshole! Of all the *pernicious* things to do to a person. I mean, he obviously had no intention of applying to Princeton before I mentioned it. Now he's going to apply just to spite me. What kind of twisted freak would do such a thing? I'm so screwed. God knows what will happen if Mother finds out. She'll have a breakdown. She'll hire a hit man like that crazy cheerleader's mom from Texas. She's researched my entire grade to scope out my competition, and Mandela has *never* been on that list. He's artsy and weird. He'd never consider Princeton. Or so we thought. I can hear her now: *If Mandela applies, then you're toast. Why take the spoiled JAP when they can have the black success story?*

I know I have to tell her, but I'm seriously afraid she'll hurt me. For the next eight months she'll be on my ass about every single 90 I get. *Why not a 95, Arianna?* If I don't kick his ass on the PSAT, I'm a corpse. Might as well just drop me out of a plane over Burma and I'll go dwell among the pygmies. At least with them I won't have to study the whole fucking dictionary and do two hundred math questions a day. In fact, who am I kidding? I can't afford the luxury of writing anymore. Later.

## 8. RANDALL

The striking Hispanic man asked him which Cartwright was expecting him.
"Legion Cartwright," he replied, softly.
While the doorman dialed up Penthouse B, Randall inspected the lobby. Antique gold leaf chairs, a sofa of ochre and royal blue stripes, an exquisitely refined cedar wood coffee table. Very *Louis*, Randall thought, although he couldn't remember which dead Frenchman favored this particular pattern. In the corner, an intimidating arrangement of orchids rested on an end table. A fetor of superiority oozed from every pore of the room.
The doorman hung up the phone. "Please follow me," he said. *Where? To a bathroom stall?* Jesus, how did Randall expect to tutor the boy with nothing but sex on the brain? Inside the lift, the doorman placed a key into the slot above the keypad. A button marked "B" lit up. He then tipped his hat at Randall and stepped out.
The elevator opened to a floor of Italian marble. A second and third bouquet of orchids rested on identical end tables to each side of the imposing door. He knocked. A gaunt butler-type opened the door.

"This way," the man said.

The pomp and circumstance of the lobby quickly dissolved into a different sort of intimidation once Randall stepped inside. The vastness of the main room was astonishing, its sleek, minimal decor making the room seem even larger. The few pieces of ornament were so precisely placed Randall imagined himself inside an exhibit at the Met. It was both beautiful and chilling.

By now Randall had adjusted to the conspicuous wealth of his clients. Still, he felt uneasy. The rooms were so silent, so empty. He felt like he was preparing to meet a head of state. Perhaps the boy was trying to intimidate him. They had discussed price over the phone and Randall had preemptively discounted his rate, figuring teenagers in charge of their own tutoring decisions wouldn't be willing to pay his usual hourly. But now, seeing how Legion lived, Randall felt cheated. He could have asked for double.

The butler tapped twice on Legion's door and quickly retreated. Randall held his breath. He had forgotten the specifics of the boy's loveliness and was eager to recollect them. Exhaling slowly, he simultaneously hoped and feared Legion would be half-naked. Instead he sported a backwards baseball cap, a mock black turtleneck, khaki cargo pants and Adidas cleats.

Legion greeted him with a full set of teeth. "Hey. Come in."

Randall did as told. He canvassed the room, figuring it was at least the size of his own apartment. Immediately in front of him were two leather love seats, resting in front of a cast iron coffee table. Beyond that was a king-size bed. Both bed and sofas faced a mammoth wall-unit, housing all the trappings of affluent adolescence: flat screen TV, BOSE stereo, DVD player, PS2. Past the entertainment unit was a computer desk upon which rested a neon-blue iMac, completing the collection of luxury toys. Posters adorned the walls, most of rock bands he had only a passing knowledge of. And, of course, one of Bob Marley. Bob Marley was King among teenage boys, because he was the godfather of Jamaica, and Jamaica was Weed Paradise.

Two doors toward the back caught Randall's attention. He imagined the first would be the walk-in closet, the second, a private bathroom, fashioned of Peruvian marble, a five-speed Jacuzzi, heated floors, anti-steam mirrors. The boy's underwear coquettishly poking out of the hamper. He'd need to confirm this later.

Most outstanding were the floor-to-ceiling windows, which looked out to a breathtaking view of northern Manhattan. Randall walked over to them. He imagined, as he gazed out into the night, that it would be hard to maintain one's humility with a view such as this. Looking down upon pedestrian traffic so many stories below, Randall found the heavens much easier to empathize with.

Legion was placing some books onto the coffee table when Randall turned around.

"Nice view," Randall said.

The boy, who had his back to him, turned his head. "Thanks."

"This is one heck of a room."

Legion smiled. "No complaints." He nodded towards the sofas. "So I thought we'd study over here."

The boy plopped down on the right love seat. Randall took off his jacket and placed it on the left. He opened his messenger bag and timidly took out his notebook. He was not accustomed to studying on love seats. He figured he should sit on the opposite sofa, but how could he demonstrate the Triangle Inequality Theorem from several feet away? Still, if he sat beside the boy, they would be immoderately close, their limbs inches apart. Sitting there would be a purposeful invasion of personal space unless... unless he just sat down and started talking. They wouldn't have time to ponder the implications.

Which is exactly what he did.

"So, the PSAT is coming up..."

Randall kept his speech going, staring the boy flush in the eye. The boy stared back with equal force. The sexual energy felt palpable, here in the boy's inner sanctum. Legion was crouching down so that his back was almost flat against the sofa's seat. His knees were bent and his sneakers were up on the coffee table. He seemed remarkably at ease with the whole situation. *Was I ever at ease with myself at seventeen?*

"...Look at it as a practice run. Don't panic or rush. Just think clearly and confidently."

"Give it to me straight. Do I stand a chance for Harvard or Yale?"

"Those are tough schools. You'll need the grades first. And AP classes."

"I have the grades. They're not Valedictorian material, but they're pretty solid. And I'm taking Psych this year."

"Take another. And at least two more next year. Preferably three."

"Christ." Legion sighed, putting his feet down to the floor. "And what about the SAT score? It's gotta be phenomenal, right?"

"If you don't break 1400 they won't even look at the rest of the application."

Legion pulled himself up, his body tensing.

"Can you do that? Can you get me that score?"

"If you put in the work, yes. I've had several students go up 250 points or more."

"And you've gotten people into Harvard before."

"Sure. Princeton, Columbia. Penn. You name it."

"I really want Harvard. But Yale would be cool too."

"I have a good feeling about you. I think you're willing to work for it."

"I'll do whatever it takes," Legion said.

*Whatever it takes.* The boy spoke the words with an Olympian's conviction. There was something in this shift of tone, an urgency that belied his previous self-possession. Randall had heard these sentiments before, and yet this time, they struck a chord.

And so they began. Problems were explored, strategies explained, methods reinforced. Randall enjoyed watching Legion's eyes light up when a particular problem—something which previously seemed impossible—suddenly became as clear and simple as a nursery rhyme. His approach, like most of Randall's other students, was too textbook, lacking in simplicity or elegance.

On several occasions Randall would lean in to explain a problem on paper. His arm would brush against the boy's, causing the bristles on his arm to stand erect, his desire like a static charge. Spontaneously, the boy kicked off his sneakers, as if in response to a challenging question that was pestering him. He peeled off his socks, and soon afterward, his scent permeated the air—a tart, buttery bouquet of sweat which invaded Randall's nostrils.

Within seconds, Randall was hard. He'd never given much thought to a guy's feet before, but now they were driving him wild. Just a pair of feet, and yet...the boy was exposing himself with his scent, sharing something intimate with Randal. Randall tried to focus on the material but the feet kept distracting him. He'd watch as the boy would rub them together, flexing his long toes. He wanted those feet. He needed to touch them.

"So it's $2\pi r$ then."

"Yeah," Randall mumbled.

"I thought you said Pi-r-squared a minute ago."

Randall averted his eyes to the boy's face, where he found a cold, mocking stare awaiting him. The kind of stare you give to someone telling you an elaborate lie, one you find so amusing that you wait to hear how it ends. Shit, he'd been found out. It happened so quickly, one gratuitous glance, a fraction of a second too long. What was he to do? Should he not react? Apologize? Laugh it off? Jesus, this was preposterous! His relationship with the boy was preordained. Or was it?

"Actually, it's Pi-r-squared. But getting back to my point. You see how much faster it is this way." Randall coolly went through the problem. Legion nodded along, the smirk melting from his face. "Now you could do it the long way, which is exactly what they want you to do. Or you could save yourself some time and frustration and look for the simpler method."

"Wow. I never would've seen that," the boy said.

"That's why I'm here." Randall glanced down at his watch. Shit, they'd gone over by fifteen minutes. "Well, that's why I *was* here. Time to call it a day."

The boy stood up. He wiped the few strands of hair that had slipped in front of his face back underneath his baseball cap. "Let me get that," he said, grabbing Randall's jacket. Randall lifted himself from the sofa. His right hand started trembling; he held it down with his left. The boy helped him into the sleeves.

"That's very kind of you," Randall said. No doubt his face was turning several shades of pink. He looked down at the ground while the boy fitted the jacket on him. And there they were again: those damn sexy feet. The scent still frolicking in his mind. He'd have to cover his erection with the messenger bag.

"I don't know how to say this," the boy said, once Randall gathered his things.

"What?" Randall blurted. His heart jumped. He was going to be reprimanded. Dismissed. Accused of moral perversion.

"I had a really good time. I mean, this really worked for me."

Randall was dumbfounded. "I'm glad you feel that way."

He wasn't sure what to make of these comments. Was the boy being sarcastic? Was he just generous with his feelings? At that age, emotions, like hormones, swell up and bounce around so indiscriminately that it's hard to keep them under control. But what if the boy was coming on to him? What if this was the only way he knew how? Randall wanted to grab him. He wanted to hug him and tell him everything would be alright. OK, kiss him too. And... No. Just a big hug. To reassure him. Quell his doubts.

"So I'll see you Thursday?" Randall asked.

"Yeah. Is cash okay?" The boy had removed a wad of twenties from his pocket.

"Sure. Listen, if your parents need to speak to me, just give them my number. I'll be glad to talk with them."

"My parents are divorced." Legion's eyes narrowed. "This is my dad's place. I haven't told him about you yet."

"Oh. Okay. That's cool."
The boy extended his hand and Randall shook it.
"Let me show you out."

# 9. EXCERPTS FROM ARIANNA LEVY'S JOURNALS

November 21st

It's been three hours since I've locked myself up in my room. I feel like a Mac truck has just run over my future. Even my worst case scenario did not prepare me for this score. I'm too ashamed to commit it to paper. Once it's written down it will become true, and then I'll have to believe it.
1250!!!!!!!!!!!!!!!!!!!!!!!!!!!!!!
TWELVE-FUCKING-FIFTY. Pardon the obscenities, but it's either swearing or throwing myself out a window right now. Could I be any more fucking average? Sure, just give me a chance, and maybe I'll start pulling B's and C's.
640 Verbal, 610 Math. Six *forty* verbal, when I'd been scoring 700s on my practice tests with Samantha. Six *ten* math, when I've never (never!) scored less than a 640 since late freshmen year! I honestly expected a score in the low 1400s. How could I have been so off?
I haven't even examined the answer sheet yet. I don't think I can bear it. When I came home the envelope was waiting for me on the dining room table. My oh-so-subtle mother had sectioned

it off like a celebrity behind a velvet rope; she might as well have hired paparazzi to take pictures. With a magic marker she had circled the return address, just in case I was too stupid to notice whom it was from. She gave me all of three seconds before she came into the room. *Oh, you're home,* she said, as if her antennae hadn't been buzzing the millisecond the elevator had landed on our floor. I grabbed the letter and ran up the stairs, feeling her white hot stare on my back. In a short moment she expected me to skip downstairs, screech the results into her ear, and jump up and down with pride. *I knew you could do it!* She'd say. *Only with your help, mom,* I'd tell her.

Well guess what: tonight's episode of *The Brady Bunch* has been canceled. Instead, I held my breath, tore open the envelope, found the score in the upper left hand corner and literally gasped. I dropped the paper as if it were contagious. My mind was playing tricks: surely it couldn't be! I picked the paper up and there it was again: 1250. I added the numbers on a calculator. 1250. Three times. Still 1250. Then I checked the name on the front: Arianna Levy. The social security number: mine, to the last digit.

I scrunched the paper up and threw it against the wall. Then I picked it up, scrunched it some more and threw it again. By this time Mother was already holding vigil outside my door. *Sweetheart,* she said, softly. Like she already knew. I didn't respond. I thought about lying, but it would be useless. She was my mother; she'd want to see proof.

"They could have made a mistake," she said, throwing me a bone.

But they didn't make a mistake. I made mistakes. Several of them, apparently.

I can't tell *anyone*. No one can be trusted. The junior class intelligentsia have all assumed I'd get the highest PSAT score in our grade. And now I won't even be close! Asshole Mandela probably kicked my ass so I can kiss my Princeton dreams goodbye. There's *no fucking way* he's going to find out. I can't even tell Penelope or Sharon or Karynne. They'll promise never to reveal my score but by lunch period the very same day everyone will know. *Everyone.*

"This is getting ridiculous, Arianna. Open the door and let's talk about it."

Mother keeps passing by my door, repeating herself every half hour. I imagine her with a candle in her hand, looking up at the sky, trying to decide the appropriate passage of *Tehilim* to recite. That's Gabrielle for you: when nothing else works, get God on the line. A thirty second chat with His Holiness and suddenly

I'll come to my senses and fling open the door. You know what? She can wait. I don't want to hear her comfort me now, because I know what's coming tomorrow. Tomorrow I'll have to try harder. Tomorrow I'll have made careless errors, spent too much time with friends and not enough with my flash cards.

A dozen things run through my mind: I envision myself at community college, or worse, working at the GAP, folding cheap acrylic sweaters with Jolette from the Bronx. She's wearing hoop earrings. She loves her boyfriend's Jetta. She's thinking about having his baby. Flash forward ten years. I'm at my high school reunion, still single, working downtown as a legal secretary, sporting an off-the-rack cotton dress on my flabby physique and a moderately cute office assistant on my right arm. I've promised him he'll get lucky if he pretends he's made partner and dotes on me all evening. We sit down at a table and I find out that half my grade has won the Nobel Prize while the other half have started the top twenty biggest IPOs of the past five years. Everyone pities me, but their spa-whitened teeth glisten as they cover up their secret delight in my failure. Some of my former gal pals suggest we do lunch sometime; I'm forced to tell them I only get an hour because my boss is a hardass.

Dear God, just kill me first.

## 10. LEGION

Today's lesson: Don't mess with natural resources. Selling Halliburton short two weeks ago has added another 5K to his margin debt. That asshole Henry Blodget had promised, nay, *guaranteed* that oil couldn't sustain $37 a barrel. Ha! Try $44 and rising. For two months on CNN the overpaid wunderkind had been heralding a return to high tech, a resurgence of chips, a tapering off if not a downright erosion of utilities and energy. Thanks a lot, shmuck. Oh, and by the way, Henry, have you seen where Amazon is trading lately?

He feels like smashing something. A Baccarat vase would be empowering, but it would upset Veronica. He could toss his laptop across the room and blame it on the maid. But Ken Cartwright would just tell him to buy himself another one. *Imagine she broke my computer, son. Would I ask you to buy me another one?*

"Ready to retire yet?"

Someone was talking. Legion looked up from the screen. "What?"

"Shit, dude. You're fucked up. You start without me?"

"What? No. I didn't start without you, man."

Legion had completely forgotten Mandela was over. They had been watching TV around 3:00, downing a few Red Stripes.

He looked down at his watch. Shit, that was two hours ago. How the fuck did time pass so quickly? He remembered excusing himself to go check up on his lady Lucinda NASDAQ, leaving Mandela in the living room with Ken's "hidden" porn collection at his disposal.

Mandela looked worried. "You're not bailing on me just because the market's down."

Legion turned off the computer. "Dude, Malaysian Jane will be fucking your mind doggy-style in a matter of seconds."

"Well then, why don't I get shit ready."

Mandela went over to Legion's walk-in closet and, using the clothing rod as leverage, hoisted himself up to reach for a blue knapsack resting on a high shelf. He took down the knapsack, unzipped it, and took out a well-used water bong.

"Speaking of fucking, how's your right hand doing?" Legion smirked.

Mandela looked up. "I'm sorry, did you say something?"

"Just don't leave any milk stains on the sofa."

"Why, you worried your dad's girlfriend might get hot for the smell?"

"Ouch, Dude. Nice one."

The two boys high-fived one another.

"So did I tell you about the debate? With Arianna Douchebag?" Mandela said. "After she won I went up to her and asked her what her first choice is..."

"Princeton. Everybody knows that."

Mandela smirked. "Let me finish. So she says Princeton and I say 'Isn't that funny? I'm leaning towards Princeton myself.' Then I wished her good luck and walked away."

"Oh shit." Legion chuckled. "She probably pissed her panties."

"She put on one of these big shit-eating grins but I knew what she was thinking."

"You're not really considering Princeton."

"Hell no." Mandela looked at him as if Legion had just told him to apply to Yeshiva University.

"Do you picture me at Princeton?"

"Dude, you gotta go to Harvard so we can hang out."

"You plan on taking the bus from B.U.? Cause you're not getting into Harvard."

"We'll see, Dickhead." Legion reached into a nearby drawer and took out a small wooden box. Inside, underneath a stuffed dead tarantula, was a sheet of aluminum foil; and underneath the aluminum foil, his stash. Sweet shit. He'd found the dealer's number in his father's office.

He passed the bag over to Mandela, who brought it up to his nose.

"Fuck does this smell good."

Mandela was filling the bong when the phone rang. He jumped and put the bong behind his back. Legion wheeled his chair over to the Caller ID box. He didn't recognize the number.

"Who is it?" Mandela asked.

"The cops. They're watching from across the street. Better turn yourself in, dude."

"Just pick up, Dickhead."

By the fourth ring the answering machine picked up. *Hey, Legion. It's Randall. I was just wondering if you got your PSAT....*

Legion quickly reached for the phone. "Randall. Hey man. Sorry. I didn't recognize the number."

"Oh, well. It's me. Randall."

"Yeah, I caught that."

Mandela was gesturing to him: *Who is it?* Legion gestured back: *Just fill up the water.*

"So, you should have gotten your results this week."

"Yeah."

"Well? Are you pleased?"

His scores sucked. He got them yesterday. But he didn't want to get into it. "Yeah. They're not great."

"Well, don't worry about it. I promise things will only get better from here. We can move ahead with SAT tutoring whenever you're ready."

"Let me give you a call soon and we can set something up." Legion felt a pause on the other end of the line. He knew he had to get back on track, but right then he just wanted to get fucked up. He didn't want to think about the stupid SAT.

"Sure...you could do that, but my schedule is swamped so I'm thinking we should set something up now. I wouldn't want to have no time for you."

"To be honest, I'm not sure I have the cash flow right now."

"What about our usual time, say, next week? We can discuss cash flow then."

The guy was being pushy. "I guess that's okay. I'll call to confirm though."

"Great!"

"Later, man." Legion hung up the phone. Mandela was loading up the bong.

"Who was that?"

"My SAT tutor," Legion replied.

"You're already starting with that shit? The SATs aren't until May."

"Einstein, you *aced* the fucking PSAT. Us fuck-ups have to start early."

Mandela laughed. "That's *we* fuck ups."

"Asswipe. Put away your MENSA badge and pass me my shit."

## 11. GABRIELLE

It's not that she didn't respect her daughter's privacy. Simply put, she was left with no other choice. Arianna had been moping for days. The color had been drained from her cheeks, her skin resembling the brittle hue of refrigerated brie.

Certainly the PSAT score had been unpleasant, but it had to be more than that. Despite several attempts to speak with her, Gabrielle had uncovered nothing. Arianna was resorting to forced smiles, vague replies like, "It's nothing, Mom, really." But this was not the Arianna she knew. Her daughter told her *everything*. She never held back.

Morty chalked it up to adolescent angst. "All teenagers are moody," he told her. "It's biological. Their problems are magnified 1000 times by their hormones."

*Don't overreact,* he said. Easy for him to say. The one time of day he'd see his daughter was right before bedtime, when her nerves had succumbed to fatigue and she was his little baby doll, perfect, not a care in the world. He didn't see the changes. He wouldn't even recognize them if he did.

She had suggested a visit with Dr. Carl two days ago. Arianna had rolled her eyes without comment, her silence more consent than condescension. She was reaching out for help by refusing to ask for it. She wanted Gabrielle to dig deeper. She needed Mommy to prove her love by uncovering the problem, even if she herself was too proud to admit to it.

Because if this wasn't the truth, Gabrielle reasoned, then why had Arianna left her journal out in the open that very afternoon? Right on top of her vanity table, as conspicuous as a canker sore, or a note written in scarlet lipstick on a bathroom mirror. Arianna *never* left her journals out in the open. She hid them, locked, in the bottom shelf of her sweater chest.

Yet here it was. Naked. Irresistible. Begging to be fondled by a mother's concerned fingers. A map of her daughter's heart, the legend to her mind's secret passageways.

*Desperate measures need to be taken,* the journal whispered to her.

But what about my daughter's trust? I cannot violate her privacy.

*Ignore me and you violate a different trust, Gabrielle. I was not left out in vain. Your daughter is giving you a sign.*

Gabrielle struggled. She wanted to believe the voices inside her head, but her instincts told her otherwise. She went over to the table. The temptress' pages were open, her daughter's smooth rounded letters splayed before her. No, she could not give in. She reached over to close the book, but it seemed the vixen had one more trick up her sleeve. Her clumsy fingers shook and the book dropped to the floor, face up, with a new set of pages lying open before her. Even from a distance she could read the date on the upper right hand corner: *October 8, 1999.* Just over a month ago. Right before the PSAT...

Minutes later, Gabrielle was in a state of panic. This was not to be believed! Contingencies had been made for every student in Arianna's grade. Parents had been spoken to. Piper had been coaxed into divulging the probable competition. Never once had the name Mandela Robinson come up.

Mandela Robinson! That crafty ingénue. Eve Harrington in *All About Eve.* Jacob tricking his blind father, stealing Esau's inheritance. And Princeton! Never in a million years did anyone think Mandela Robinson would apply to Princeton. Mandela Robinson would attend an African American college like Howard. If he went Ivy League, surely it would be Harvard. His mother went to Harvard, for God's sake! But Princeton? Good Old Boy Princeton?

*How* could Arianna keep this from her? Did she not understand how important this was? The poor child. She must be delirious with anxiety. *Oh dear, you can tell Mommy! Mommy under-*

*stands. Mommy will know what to do. Why didn't you talk to Mommy?*

Gabrielle placed the book back exactly as she had found it on the vanity. She'd have to pretend not to know. She'd have to put an end to Mandela Robinson and his foolish notions. But how? She'd start with the Robinsons. Perhaps they could be coaxed into seeing things differently. She would find a way. It didn't matter what had to be done; she would do it. It didn't matter if things got ugly; things were *already* ugly.

That peasant would not steal her daughter's destiny. So help her God he would not!

## 12. LEGION

The laughter from the living room hit him as soon as he opened the front door. Half a dozen voices, but the same laughter. The yipping of hyenas.

They still hadn't left. Worse than that, they had company. Asshole company. He'd be forced to pass by the assholes on the way to his room, make small talk, and listen to their fucking jokes.

He could slip on his Walkman, wait for just the right moment and...*Motherfuck.* Too late. Ken Cartwright at twelve o'clock. In a monkey suit. A glass of scotch in his right hand.

"Lookee here," Ken shouted. "Veronica, call the media. My son has returned from captivity."

Ken put his arms around his shoulder. Time to fake Daddy for the guests. Legion smelled musky cologne, cigar smoke, panther piss breath.

"I thought you guys had an event."

"We're knocking some back so I can get through the evening. Opera, for Chrissakes. One of Veronica's charity functions. Feed the Blind or whatever."

Legion smirked. "When are you leaving?"

Ken stopped short, looked his son in the eye. "What's the rush, Leeg? Got some girl coming over? Come say hello to my crew."

*Crew.* Ken Cartwright was styling. He was down with the lingo.

"Listen, Dad, I've got serious homework..."

Ken pushed his son along. The living room was filled with familiar faces. Fake smiles. Real smiles, on people too drunk to fake smiling. Jeffrey Ronson, billionaire. Very tan. In his late forties, but you'd never tell. No regrets to crease his skin. No stress to gray his hair. A model type in a tight dress sitting on his lap. Nineteen? Twenty? Great breasts. She fed him champagne while his fingers kneaded her exposed thighs.

John and Linda Deavre. Still married. Now that was novel. Old friends. Touchy-feely people. Mr. Deavre liked to talk football and punch Legion in the arm. His wife liked to squeeze cheeks, above and below. *You're getting so big, Legion!*

Patty Smith Samuels, some guy massaging her shoulders. Ken liked to say, if Valium doesn't work, then call Patty Smith Samuels. But she was invited, everywhere. Don't fuck with Patty Smith Samuels. She was important. She was connected. Smith Samuels could clear her throat and suddenly you'd be washing dishes at McDonald's. Ken liked that. Ken probably fucked her regularly.

Legion surveyed the room. His throat was dry. Warriors preoccupied with tales of victory. Wives and mistresses exchanging pleasantries, eyeing each other for imperfections. He tried to breathe. He smelled sulfur. The room was larded with their arrogance.

He should have gone to his mom's. He wondered if she called. She had promised him some time over the weekend, the last time they spoke, a few days before. She sounded sincere. But his mother didn't like surprise visits. She might have company. Or be in one of her moods. She could be working on a piece, and then she'd have to stop, and fix him a sad sandwich, with her blotchy painter's hands. She'd ask him questions about school, questions he'd answered weeks ago, with her faraway look, her eyes squinting, as if searching the skies for a star too distant to see. Then she'd talk about herself. Her friends. Her projects. Her goals. At one point, realizing she was hogging the spotlight, she'd tell him how good he looked and ask him about his father. And then she'd hug him, because what else could she do? She'd talk about a Saturday brunch or a weekend in Vermont. Right after she got back from the retreat. Right after so and so's show in Santa Fe. Right before he left, she'd open up her purse. Hand him a twenty. *My young man. So grown up.* He'd leave the money on a table by the door.

"Ladies and Gents, I present my firstborn," Ken said.

The crowd turned to greet him. He forced a smile.

"Hey, sport." Mr. Deavre punched him in the arm.

"Look at you!" Mrs. Deavre grabbed his face. "Every day you look more like your mother."

"The eyes," Patty Smith Samuels said. "Absolutely Celine's. And the *chin*!"

"There's gotta be some of me in there somewhere," Ken said.

"Don't be so sure," Mr. Deavre quipped.

Legion turned to his father. "Where's Veronica?"

"Probably putting on her face," Ken said.

"Speaking of faces." Mrs. Deavre once again squeezed his cheeks. "Take a good look, Jeffrey. Can't you use this puss in one of your commercials?"

"I bet the girls are crawling all over him," Ronson replied.

"If they are I sure haven't seen them," Ken said.

"He knows better," Ronson said. "I wouldn't bring a high school girl around you either."

More asshole laughter.

"You can't blame a guy for looking," Ken said.

"John, remind me never to speak to this man again," Mrs. Deavre said. "And lock up our daughter until she's thirty."

"I've seen your daughter, Linda," Smith Samuels said. "Probably a good idea."

"How about it, Leeg?" His father winked at him. "A nice sorority girl. Plus, I hear her dad's *loaded*."

The hyenas were hysterical.

"Can I go now, Dad?" he asked.

"What's the matter, son? Can't wait to get on the web and download some porn?"

Legion looked at his father. The bastard was drunk enough to say anything. He felt his jaw tighten. He wanted to tell the motherfucker off. But he wouldn't. He couldn't let it faze him. He remembered being eight years old, taking a trip to Mexico City, when he, his mother and Ken were still a family. He had come down with a horrific throat infection and the Mexican doctors, not used to antibiotics, had prescribed a week long daily vaccination involving a needle of mad-scientist proportions. His mother was supposed to administer it herself but couldn't stomach it. So Ken hired a nurse, a plump, flat-nosed Aztec with a mole on her cheek, a woman who hummed ghostly tunes while holding him down flat against the bed. The sting of the needle was excruciating, but after a while, the pain dulled, until he didn't even realize it was there. When he had to do it all over again the next day, he just didn't see the point in screaming. Screaming didn't bring in his mother, who jacked up the Spanish soap operas to drown out his tears. Screaming didn't summon his father, out closing deals with Mexican oil magnates.

He wouldn't scream now.

"Gotta hit the homework, Dad. That OK with you?"

"Sure thing, kid. Hit those books hard. Did I mention my boy wants to go to Harvard? No Indiana State for this one."

"Can you blame him? Look how you turned out," joked Smith Samuels.

"Yeah, look at me, a regular underachiever," Ken said. "Used to be balls and hard work got you ahead in the world. Now it's all about fancy degrees."

"Well I think it's great, Legion," Mrs. Deavre said. "Never mind your dad. He's three scotches past making sense."

"I'm not saying he shouldn't go," Ken said. "I'm all for bringing a little prestige to the family. Who knows? Maybe he'll make it happen. I gave him some change to play the market, and that's going well, right, Leeg?"

Legion forced a grin. "Real swell, Dad."

"Just be careful." Ronson said. "We've all been losing sleep these past few months. Put it somewhere safe for the time being."

"He's not a *moron*, Jeffrey," Ken said. "If the kid's bright enough for Harvard then he's bright enough to handle a shaky market. Right, Legion? Everything's kosher?"

His father looked at him with a fat smile. He hated this. Why couldn't he just go to his room? Was Ken doing this on purpose? Whenever Ken asked, he lied. Told him everything was OK. He even paid his brokers to keep quiet. Had Ken found out? No, he was just drunk. He gave him the money. Yes, he was an asshole. But he gave him the money. Gave him an opportunity to prove he wasn't a fuck up, and Legion had failed him. He was a failure.

"Like matzo ball soup, Dad," he said. "Are we through here?"

In his room, he found a blue rubber ball. He threw it against the wall, caught it, threw it again, harder. Sometimes he'd throw it so hard it would fly past him, ricochet off the opposite wall, and knock something over. He liked that. It didn't matter. They couldn't hear.

But someone heard.

"What the fuck, Legion?"

Veronica was twenty-six. She was almost as tall as he was, standing in her Jimmy Choos, a good inch taller than Ken. He was supposed to hate her, this Joanna-cum-lately, this Marla Maples—she even looked like Marla Maples. Problem was, Veronica was cool. Veronica was smart. Smarter than Ken.

She had a black dress on that was going to piss off the other women.

"What's with the ball?" she asked.

He didn't respond.

"Did Ken say something?"

"Ken always says something."

"What do you think? Too much? It's the opera, but at the same time, it's City Harvest and I don't want to look, like, freakishly over-dressed."

"You look great."

"The makeup? The hair? Ken's going to lie so tell me the truth."

Her makeup was perfect. Her hair too. "One of your eyelashes is lopsided."

She approached him, grabbed the ball out of his hand, and took his hands in her own.

"You wanna talk about it?" she asked.

"Nothing to talk about."

"You know I can stand those people about as much as you can. I holed myself up in the bathroom for the past twenty minutes catching up on back issues of *Vanity Fair*."

He smiled. "Why do you sleep with him, Veronica?"

"Who should I be sleeping with, Legion?" she said. "Wait, don't answer that."

Legion laughed. He liked playing with Veronica. He liked the way her small hands fit so easily into his. "It's not like any of those cretins care about the opera. Or homeless people," he said.

"They care enough to write ten thousand dollar checks."

"So it's all just give and take? Is that what life boils down to?"

"Legion, I'm not going to even pretend to lecture you about life. But I will say this. It gets a lot different after high school. What you care about now, it doesn't always last."

"That's just way too *Dawson's Creek* for me, Veronica."

"Then I owe you a moment when I get home. Right now I gotta jet." She brushed her cheek against his, kissing the air. "Can't fuck up the makeup."

"Have a memorable evening."

She turned around, blew him kisses from afar. "Don't polish off the Courvoisier. I need my nightcap."

He threw himself onto the loveseat. Fucking Ken. Making fun of him for trying for Harvard. He had to get shit off his mind.

But how? He turned on his computer and went online. He hadn't checked up on Lucinda in a while. He could no longer track his portfolio every day. It was too painful.

Fuck it, that wouldn't solve anything. He needed to be productive. No, what he needed was to get *fucked up*, that's what. Or get laid. Something to drain all the vinegar from him. He turned off the computer. What he needed to do was study. But what good would studying do? Randall said without a 1400 they wouldn't even look at his application. His PSAT score was light years away from that.

Maybe he should call Randall.

The laughter was growing dim; the hyenas were heading out. Finally, he could exhale. He could take out the bong. Take out the bong, do a few hits, and then study.

Maybe he should call Randall. Randall liked him. He could sense it. Randall gazed at him with twitchy eyes. Randall stared at his feet. That was weird. Randall was OK, though. Randall wasn't bad. Randall would listen to him. Randall would tell him what to do.

Randall promised to help him. Randall promised.

Shit, should he get fucked up? No, not totally fucked up. Just a few hits.

He looked out the window. It looked like it would rain soon, a hard, unforgiving rain. He was glad. He hoped the hyenas would get soaked.

He had to call Randall.

\*

He was a comic sight, his jacket and hair both flattened by the rain. The thunderstorm had clearly caught him by surprise.

"I guess it's pretty bad out," Legion said.

"The news guy said midnight." Randall wiped his feet several times before entering. "You can never trust those people."

"I'll get you a towel."

In the bathroom, Legion noticed his squiggly eyes, the mushy clown-lipped grin plastered under his nose. Giggles sputtered out of his mouth, but he quickly stifled them. He had to focus, affect poker-faced sobriety. He thought about his approach. What if the guy turned him down? That would be awful. But what were the chances? Randall's eyes were upon him at every moment. It was like being on an airplane and turning around in your seat, and there, staring at you between the cracks, was someone eager to catch a glimpse of anything: an arm, a leg.

Adults were funny.

When he entered the bedroom, Randall was observing some pictures on the wall. The man spun around like a jackrabbit.

"The towel," he said, handing it to him. Randall wiped his face.

"I'm really glad you came," he said. "Sorry about the rain."

He took the towel from Randall's hands and tossed it on his bed.

"It sounded important. On the phone."

"Not really. I just had some free time. Thought it'd be good to do some SAT stuff."

He sat down. He remembered the first time, how Randall had sat on the sofa beside him, forgoing the other. He opened his math workbook. When he looked up, Randall was still standing.

"Are you gonna sit?" His eyes shifted to the empty space beside him.

Randall sat, timidly. He looked uneasy. But he had agreed to come. He sounded so eager when Legion had mentioned no one would be home on the phone.

"So where's your dad this evening?"

"At the opera," he said. "Do you like the opera?"

Randall smiled, sheepishly. "I'm no expert."

"Ken hates the opera. He always gets shit-faced beforehand. Then he just falls asleep anyway. He only goes because Veronica makes him. It's her form of revenge for all the fucking he does on the side."

He watched Randall's face turn pale. This was necessary: he had to be intimate, destroy the space between them. It could scare the guy away, but that was the risk he had to take. He had to allow Randall to be honest. Let him know what he'd be open to.

"I'm sorry. That's way too much information."

"No," Randall said. "I mean, go ahead, if you want to talk about things. I'm happy to listen."

"Thanks. I feel comfortable around you, like I could talk about shit I wouldn't talk about with my parents."

Randall broke into a smile. "I'm glad you feel that way."

"Yeah. Ken's a first class shmuck. And my mom, well, let's just say the shmuck got custody."

Randall nodded but said nothing. He had to move quickly. If he didn't, he might over-analyze, lose his courage. He looked into Randall's eyes. They were darting around the room. Soon would come the nervous laughter. He needed to pounce.

He lifted his feet onto the sofa. Randall's eyes followed his nervously. There was barely any room between them.

"I've had a long day. My feet are really tired."

Randall's eyes remained on his sneakers. "Phys-Ed class?"

"Listen, do you think...forget it."

"What?"

"Do you think you can massage them for me?"

The silence confirmed everything. Exposed to his own lust, Randall was left speechless.

"Forget I asked." Legion shifted his feet back to the floor. "It was stupid of me."

"No, it wasn't, it's just..."

"I've freaked you out."

"You haven't freaked me out at all," Randall's composure was returning to his face.

"So you'll do it?"

"If it will help you relax for the lesson, sure."

He placed his sneakers on Randall's lap. Whatever way the guy chose to justify it, the hard part was over. Gingerly, the man began to rub his ankles, as if he was still unsure how much permission he was being given.

"Would you mind taking off my shoes?" Legion asked. "And you might want to put that book on the table."

He watched the man silently fold the book off his lap. He smiled; Randall smiled back, nervously, but could not hold his eyes on him. He shifted in his seat, and Legion could sense, in that shift, the meltdown of reason, the acquiescence to desire. Randall fumbled with his laces. He looked like those heroin addicts in the movies — low on cash, they see the shit right there on the table, praying their dealer will take pity on them.

The sneakers came off and the scent of his foot sweat filled the room. He didn't say anything, and neither did Randall. He wondered if it bothered him. Perhaps he enjoyed it.

Randall took hold of the bottom of his right foot with his left hand, massaging the toes with his right. Legion closed his eyes, let out a breathy sigh.

He opened his eyes again. "You can take off the socks," he said. Randall nodded. He watched the slow precision of Randall's hands, peeling the socks off his feet. It was only his bare feet, but he might as well have been removing underwear. He wondered what Randall wanted to do with him. He thought about how far he would let it go. Just as far as he needed to.

Randall worked his left foot, grasping gently around the ankle. He kneaded the heel. His large hands were softer than expected. Their caresses sent messages of desire through the arches of Legion's foot: the docile slave, eager to please his host. Having this power felt strangely enjoyable. It relaxed him. His right foot sat motionless on Randall's lap. He pretended to be too absorbed in the massage to notice the awakening only centimeters away. He closed his eyes and pushed his right foot into Randall's crotch, dead against the stiffness.

He kept his eyes closed. He did not budge. Randall said nothing. He said nothing. He pushed his foot harder against the man's cock, rubbing it with his toes. He did not open his eyes. The massage continued, the caresses a bit more forceful. Legion's foot began a steady back and forth. He would not open his eyes. Within a few seconds, a warm wetness enveloped his toes. Randall was sucking on them. It was getting hard to concentrate. He felt pleasure now. An indescribable weightlessness, like the first thirty seconds of a skydive. He let himself fly.

He rubbed his foot faster against Randall's crotch, creating an unbearable friction. He did not open his eyes. He could hear nothing; only the rubbing. His left foot felt gooey. Randall was chewing on his heel, devouring his toes. He was shivering; he had gotten hard, so hard. His mouth was dry. The back of his head started to throb.

He did not open his eyes. He only knew how to rub. Randall's hands began to shake. He felt a sudden constriction, his big toe pushing deeper into Randall's mouth. He only knew how to rub. He kept it up until, suddenly, a death grip on his right ankle, a muffled moan, a tremor of release. Randall's cock grinding frantically against his foot. A yelp, a desperate yelp, the sound a bystander makes the split second after seeing a car crash.

It was over. He kept his eyes closed for several more seconds.

When he opened them, Randall's hands were unbuttoning his pants.

## 13. RANDALL

The space around the computer was cluttered: bills, Post-its with random phone numbers, CD-ROM games. He opened Word and stared at the blank page. A hazy sun intruded onto the screen from the naked window beside him. He didn't know what to write. He knew he should be honest: it was his journal, after all. With everyone else, he'd have to embellish, construct, couch in acceptable terms.

*Yesterday I had sex with my student,* he wrote. A catchy opening line. His future editors would like that. His Barnes and Noble space would be secured, his book tour sure to attract thousands. He can hear the narrative voice-over in the Miramax produced film...

*I shouldn't have sex with my students,* he continued. This was the right answer. The only problem: He did have sex with his student. Not only had sex with Legion, but masturbated three times thinking about it in the fifteen hours since. He was a child molester. A chicken hawk perpetuating a stereotype about gay men, one that personally offended him. *He* was the responsible one, the one that was supposed to know better.

*I could have stopped it.* Even if Legion came on to him, he didn't have to go through with it. There was a line. Society's norms weren't arbitrary. They made sense. He should have never offered to give the massage. Once it was clear what was going on, he should have stopped it.

*I took advantage of him.* It was only natural for a teen to want to try something new. But what was *his* excuse? He couldn't even fathom the emotional stress the situation might put on Legion. The boy could mistake their sex for love. He was crying out for attention, and instead his sleazy tutor exploited him.

*He could have me arrested.* Worse, Legion could tell his father, who'd hire a hot-shot lawyer to bleed him dry or a Mafioso to break his legs. Ken Cartwright was Saudi sheik wealthy. He could take out a full page ad in *The Times* branding him a pederast. And then who'd talk to him? He'd be a pariah. His family would disown him. His few sympathetic friends would suggest clandestine meetings in Polish restaurants in Queens. His neighbors would give interviews to the local media: *He seemed like such a normal guy.* Congress would be outraged. Court Orders would put him on lists of sex offenders. He'd never be able to tutor again. He'd have to leave the city, maybe even the country. He was Roman Polanski, or Michael Jackson—except they had money or talent or the French to fall back on.

Randall turned his swivel chair away from the screen. These thoughts were good. He needed to take responsibility. Face up to the facts. When he turned back to the computer screen the phone rang.

"Hello?"

"Hey, Randall," the boy said. No inflection, no subtext. Just *Hey Randall.*

"Hi...How are you?" He didn't know what to say.

"It's all good. I'm finishing up lunch."

Then there was the pause. A pause he was supposed to fill in. The boy was waiting for...what? A declaration of love? A mea culpa?

"Listen, I was thinking," Legion continued. "We didn't really get much accomplished last night."

"No," he said. "I guess not."

"You live in the East Village, right? I'm going down to St. Mark's to buy some CDs. I was thinking I'd pop over when I'm done. To make up the lesson."

"Oh." So the boy was going to invite himself over now. "I don't think that's a good idea. I think we need to talk."

"I can get there sometime after three. Just give me your address."

"How about we meet at a Starbucks or something."

"Starbucks." The boy sounded unconvinced. "You want to have a talk at Starbucks."

"I think it would be wiser." His voice was cracking. This wasn't going well.

"*Wiser,*" Legion repeated, in a high, mocking pitch. "Chill out, Randall. Just give me your address."

He was at a loss. He didn't want to give the boy his address. He didn't want him to know where he lived, to *see* where he lived. But did it matter? Legion could easily track him down. There was no point in resisting. He told him the address.

"So three o'clock?"

Randall knew he had an appointment at four. He'd just have to push it back. This was too important. "Sure."

"Gotta run. Fourth period starts in five. Ciao."

He put the phone down, staring into space for a good moment. He looked back at the computer, unable to reread the lines he had written; the sun's rays were shooting into his eyes. He wanted the words to give him courage. He wanted to see things the way he ought to. He brought his fingers to the keyboard. *It's all an outrageous lie,* they typed. But as soon as they did, he deleted it.

Hastily, he saved what remained of the document, and shut off his computer. He had to deal with his depressing and cluttered apartment: magazines piled up on the "dining room" table, dishes overflowing the sink, empty cereal boxes playing leapfrog on the floor. What would Legion make of all this modesty? He seemed to lack the neat gene most gay men carried.

He wanted the apartment to show off his style, but at the same time, not look too fussed with. Some things would be strategically left where they were: a pair of pants draped over a chair, a half-eaten bag of chips on the coffee table. But the framed posters on the wall were too obvious; he doubted Legion had even heard of *The Pajama Game.*

So much for a productive afternoon. He was supposed to be revising his screenplay, the comedy about the female Mafiosas. Now writing would have to wait, again. He scuttled about, rearranging as necessary. He didn't worry about the bedroom; that door would remain shut.

He thought about their earlier conversation. The boy seemed unfazed. Still, Randall wondered how much of it was an act. If *he* didn't know how to deal with his feelings, how would the boy? He'd have to choose his words carefully. He'd start with *People made mistakes.* He had made one. Then he'd give him Melissa's phone number. She was an expert, even better than he was. That was it: make him believe it was all for the best. Legion might throw questions at him, and he had to be prepared to answer them. He had to keep his cool. Avoid arguing. *Remember*, he told himself. *You're the adult. You have to know better.*

Did he know better? Earlier, when he'd hung up the phone, his dick got hard. The scene flashed back in his mind. He couldn't avoid it—his Zapruder film, an endless seven second loop, the painfully sweet frames rolling over and over in his head: the boy's eyes closed, his lips parted, the flesh of his neck turning pink. The short pants of breath, Legion grabbing the back of his head with both hands, his fingers clawing into skin. He wanted the boy to draw blood. He yearned for scars.

How was he going to get this Purple Elephant out of his mind? He tried to coax it out, but his voice was shaky, his peanuts were stale, and the elephant was unconvinced.

At twenty to three, he poured himself a tall shot of vodka.

At a quarter to, he gelled his hair and put on a fresh shirt. He took out his *L'eau D'Issey* from the medicine cabinet, then thought twice about it.

At ten to, he had another shot of vodka.

At five to, he stuck *Moby* into the CD changer.

At ten after, the doorbell rang.

## 14. LEGION

Interest rates falling, weak dollar rising—it was hard to give a shit anymore. Lucinda was such a well of desperation lately. He hadn't visited her in over three weeks. All the investor services were cutting the prices of online trades, offering digital cameras and other incentives for account transfers. But who wanted to lie down with a crack ho? Thirty day moving averages were like the track marks on her arms, and his needles were dry.

At least he wouldn't have to pay for tutoring anymore. He'd just spent ninety dollars on drum-n-bass imports from England. Goddamn expensive, but fuck if Roni Size wasn't the shit. All the cool music was from overseas. Except for hip-hop. That was fly. Jay-Z was the shiznit.

He was listening to *Hard Knock Life* when he rang Randall's doorbell. He put his headphones around his neck. He hoped this "talk" wouldn't take long. Randall had sounded weird on the phone. He wanted the guy nervous, but not *that* nervous. He needed to be tutored, after all. Bringing up his GPA would be tough; the SAT score was key. Plus these schools expected him to be involved in "extracurricular activity." He'd have to join the chess club. Write haikus for the yearbook. Get one of his mom's boyfriends to hook him up with a job at a gallery and then write a gushing recommendation.

Because he wasn't going to ask Ken. Fuck no. The asshole would probably buy a dormitory in his name, but only *after* he saw the rejection slips. Super Shmuck to the rescue. How great would it be to turn the fucker down. How amazing if he got into Harvard all by himself, without his father greasing palms or trading in favors. He wanted to look the man in the eye, hold up the acceptance letter and say, *How about that, Dad? Turns out I'm not such a screw up after all.*

Randall greeted him at the door. "They disconnected our buzzer," he said. "Something about keeping us safer."

"Uh-hunh." Legion took Randall in. The guy was dressed for Saturday night dinner on Park Avenue South. He looked good. He wasn't bad looking. They'd probably mess around again at the end of the lesson. Randall gave good head. Older guys always gave better head, especially compared to high school girls. Girls did it because they thought you liked it. Older guys did it because they loved sucking cock.

He followed Randall up three flights of stairs. Jesus, what did these East Village buildings have against elevators? He was out of breath by the time they reached the door. It was a small place. Definitely a gay guy's place. Super clean, plus it had that gay-guy smell, which basically meant it didn't smell like beer and armpits. Movie posters on the wall, Moby on the stereo. Moby was kinda over. A fancy wine rack. He thought he could use a drink. He hoped Randall had something stronger.

Randall stood by a table in the living room. He obviously wasn't up for a house tour. Legion didn't see any SAT books anywhere.

"Take a seat." Randall pulled a chair out for him. "Can I get you a Snapple?"

"Sure," he said. The guy was tense. He'd have to play it cool. It was like a game of *Operation*. He'd have to go slow, hold the tweezers tight and not flinch.

Randall pulled two bottles out of the refrigerator and handed one to him. The man sat down across from him and folded his hands, looking down at the table solemnly.

"Do you think I can get into Harvard with a 1450?" he asked. Randall's eyes were restless and distant. He didn't want the lecture to begin. "I know I fucked up on the PSAT, but I think a 1450 is totally doable."

"We need to talk," Randall said. "Last night I...behaved irresponsibly."

"You mean because we didn't use condoms? It's OK, man, I'm safe. Plus you can't really get anything orally, can you?"

"No," Randall said. "*No.*" He got up, took a short walk around the room, and then sat down again. He breathed in. Then he looked at Legion. "You're my student. I should have never let it get to that point. I know it's kind of stupid to say this after the fact, but I'm sorry. I can't even begin to tell you how sorry I am."

Legion frowned. "Why exactly are you sorry?"

"Because I should have known better."

"Forget it. I'm not sorry, so why should you be?"

He popped the Snapple cap. It was a diet peach iced tea. Not his favorite. He considered asking Randall to spike it with some rum, but decided against it. The guy was not in a party mood.

"Listen, Legion." Randall was summoning up his reasonable voice. Legion had seen his teachers do this before. "I think it's great you're so calm about the whole situation. But we have to come to an understanding. I don't…How do I put this?"

The man was gesturing with his hands. It was amusing. He had obviously prepared this speech and now couldn't get himself to say it.

"I'm flattered. That you find me attractive. And I understand—"

"You don't find me attractive?" he asked.

"And I understand that at your age there's a lot of curiosity…"

*Here we go,* Legion thought. *The at your age speech.* "You don't find me attractive?" he repeated. He wanted the question answered.

Randall looked him dead in the eye. "Don't make me answer that."

"Then what? Oh, I get it. You think you were my first time with a guy."

"That's not the point."

"You weren't. I've been with other guys. And girls, for that matter."

"That's really none of my business."

"Then what's your point?"

"My point, Legion…" Legion hated the way Randall kept repeating his name. It was like he was six years old and his mother was explaining to him why he shouldn't cross in the middle of the street. "My point is that you're my student. And what we did was wrong. *Very* wrong."

He had no idea the guy was going to pull so much drama. It was weird. At the bookstore, Randall was obviously checking him out. Their first lesson he stared holes through his pants. Now Legion had given the guy what he wanted and he was acting like a born-again Baptist.

"You didn't enjoy it?" he asked.

"Certain boundaries need to be respected."

"I think you enjoyed it."

"I crossed a line I shouldn't have crossed."

"I enjoyed it," he continued. "It was pretty hot."

"Please hear what I'm saying. You're not listening."

This was getting tiresome. He wanted to start the lesson already. "OK, so what you're saying is you don't want to fuck around anymore."

"Absolutely. We should try to forget the whole thing ever happened."

"That's not likely, Randall."

Randall's eyes darted at him. He looked terrified. "Please, Legion. If anyone were to find out about this I'd be royally screwed. I could get arrested."

*So that's it,* Legion thought. People never really felt bad about what they did. They just didn't want to get caught. He could understand that.

"First of all, I'm seventeen," he said. It was such a small lie. He'd be seventeen in a couple of months. "That's legal in New York. Second of all, I don't kiss and tell. Especially with guys. You think I need people knowing my business?"

"I'm glad you feel that way." Randall looked relieved.

"Great. So can we start the lesson now?"

Randall shook his head. "I think that's a bad idea." He reached into his shirt pocket. "I have a number for you. Her name's Melissa. She's fantastic. The best, really."

"Fuck that, Randall," Legion said. Things were getting out of hand. Why did Randall have to make such a big deal about it? *"You're* the best. You tutor Arianna Levy. That girl is psycho about getting into Princeton and she wouldn't settle on just anyone."

"You're gonna love Melissa. She's a total pro."

Randall handed him the phone number. Legion sighed. At what age did the brain shift into overdrive and analyze all the fun out of life? He wasn't going to tell anyone. He didn't want another tutor. He liked the guy. He needed the best, and he couldn't afford anything less. It was *expensive,* two, three times a week. Where the fuck would he get the cash to pay someone else?

"I have some supplemental materials that should prove useful. I'll be right back."

Randall left the room. He knew the guy liked him. Why couldn't they just work something out? He didn't want to have to beg. He didn't want to have to play hardball.

"I'm not going to tell anyone, Randall," he said, when Randall returned with some pamphlets. He looked up and smiled. He wanted Randall to relax. Should he come on to him? Kick off his shoes? Randall might want to suck on his toes again. But that might only make things worse. Then again, Randall had put on nice clothes. And the apartment did look pretty clean. It was like examining a box of eggs; some cracks are small, but they're there, if you look hard enough.

"These are some tests from '97 and '98. You can't buy them anywhere."

He didn't see any other way. "I'm not going to tell *anyone*," he repeated. He grabbed Randall's hand. It was soft. It wanted to be touched. The man stood over him. He looked up. Randall was staring down at him, panicked and bewildered, his hand trembling in Legion's own. But he didn't pull away.

"I can't..." Legion watched as the icicles of Randall's logic and good intentions melted away. What a pain in the ass it was, putting on a show for your moral code. It was like a bad television sitcom, where Buddy takes the car out while his parents are away and of course gets into an accident *that one time,* and right before the last commercial he learns to be responsible and not disobey his parents. What bullshit. In the real world, Buddy takes the car out even with his parents home, does E with his boys, fucks some random chick in the back, and brings the car home with nary a scratch or a cum stain. Parents don't know shit. They're too busy fucking up their own lives.

With his left hand he held onto Randall's right, while his other hand explored elsewhere, around the waist, grabbing hold of Randall's ass. He watched Randall's cock stiffen in his pants. It was hot, seeing someone's dick wake up right in front of him. He massaged it through the thin corduroy.

"I can't," Randall muttered, under his breath. His own mother wouldn't believe him now.

"Resist?" Legion finished his sentence for him. "You don't have to."

Randall was trembling, his eyes focused on the ceiling. Legion rubbed his cock harder. The man looked down. He looked about ready to cry. He reached for Legion's face, cupping it between his hands. Legion stood up and brought his lips against Randall's eager mouth.

"You're so fucking beautiful," Randall said.

Oh well. He would've preferred the lesson first, but at least the matter was settled. There was no turning back now. They'd both get what they wanted.

# 15. EXCERPTS FROM ARIANNA'S JOURNALS

November 27th

Thanksgiving has arrived. I should be spending this day acknowledging all the things I'm grateful for. Then why do I feel like telling my whole family where they can stick the fucking turkey? I just want to lock myself in my room with pints of Cherry Garcia and eat till I puke. I know I should keep things in perspective. Millions of kids my age are starving in Mogadishu or Chad, suffering from malaria or leprosy, watching their families get gunned down by rebels, and here I am getting all steamed about the PSAT.

But can you blame me? I put so much work into it. I know it doesn't *really* count, but what if it's a harbinger of things to come?

OK, I need to stop. I'm thankful for the grand Thanksgiving dinner that Tatiana has prepared for us, even if my bratty cousins from Westchester will be here. I'm grateful for my mother, a warm, loving woman, once she's taken her pills. I'm grateful for my sweet Daddy, even if he comes home so late at night I barely spend any time with him.

OMG, almost forgot! I'm *so* grateful for my upcoming trip to Aspen for Winter Break. Ten glorious days on the slopes, and no Kumbaya or surprise French quiz or late night meetings with the megadweebs of Yearbook. I'm going to think about nothing. Literally. Just snow, hot apple cider, hotter ski instructors, and shopping. Well, not exactly. I still plan on taking SAT stuff with me. I actually asked mother if we could bring Randall with us. I wonder what he's like in real life. Anyway, she looked at me like I'd asked for an albino hippo to join us. So I pulled a Subliminal Sally: cleared my throat and out came my PSAT score. She raised a brow, told me it wasn't going to work. But honestly, I think she's considering it. Wouldn't that be priceless!

December 3rd

If my life gets any more bizarre I'll be forced to sell my story to *Inside Edition*. Last night, descending the stairs, on my way out to Trevor's party, I run into Deidre Robinson, heading in the other direction. Mandela's mom! In my house!

She can read the shock on my face. *The downstairs bathroom is occupied,* she says. *First door on your left,* I respond. She thanks me and smiles. Neither of us is having a good day.

Needless to say, the party will have to wait as I'll now have to drag my mother into the kitchen to find out what the hell is going on. I locate my mother in the living room, clutching Gladys Pendington in one arm, an apple martini in the other. I know better than to interrupt; Gladys rarely attends Mother's dinner parties, but when she does she's sure to receive the most exquisite ass-kissing. Instead I poise myself within her line of vision and make obscene facial gestures at her while pretending to refresh drinks. When she notices me, she excuses herself graciously and follows me into the kitchen.

*Whatever it is, it can wait,* she tells me, before I even open my mouth. I could tell it wasn't her first martini. There'd be no point in beating around the bush.

"Why is Mandela Robinson's mother in our upstairs bathroom?" I cry out.

"Because someone's using the bathroom downstairs?"

Sarcasm. How charming.

"Don't you have a party to go to?" She puts down her martini, walks over to a cabinet, takes out a large glass bowl and shoves it under the ice maker. The machine makes a grating sound, which Mother hopes will drown out my complaints. Fat chance.

"You know how much I loathe him. I don't feel like forcing

myself to play nice with his parents in my own home."

She places the bowl down and approaches me. "Don't be melodramatic."

"Mandela's applying to Princeton, Mother. He told me a few weeks ago. How's that for melodramatic?"

I expect her jaw to drop, her face to turn even redder. Something. Instead she picks up her drink. Finishes it. She looks around, lifts a goat cheese crisp from a tray, plops it in her mouth, and wipes her lips with a napkin. Then she laughs at me. She grabs my chin with two long fingernails, brushing my hair behind my ear with her other hand.

"Sweetheart, you don't put out a fire by pouring gasoline on it."

"You should have told me we'd be using clichés tonight, Mom. I would've brushed up on my sitcom comebacks."

"Don't be so tiresome, Arianna." Then she rolls her eyes. Again. "If Mandela Robinson is applying to Princeton, don't you think his parents would know about it?"

"Don't patronize me."

She smiles at me. Then she chuckles. She hugs me, kisses me on the cheek. And then I *know* something's up. I can sense it, lurking behind the good intentions of her gestures. I see it: the glint of guilty pleasure. I hear it, past the *blithe* tone of her conversation, a jaguar stalking in the distance.

"You worry too much, Arianna," she says, right before she leaves the kitchen.

Oh, she's up to no good. Why else summon the enemy into your lair? But how could she know? All this time I was terrified of telling her, and she brushed my confession aside like crumbs from the crisp had just landed on her lapel. I guess I shouldn't be too surprised. God knows when Mother needs to know something, nothing gets in her way. I just hope she knows what she's doing.

Anyway, I didn't linger...Meanwhile, Trevor's party was *so* lame. When will high school boys realize a keg of Coors Light and half a dozen joints does not an evening make? They're so immature! Everything's like a fucking dare to them. If you're not going to get wasted, or take your clothes off, or get into a lesbian lip lock with one of your friends, then you might as well be invisible. That is, unless you want to have a somber conversation about Kant with the future linguistics majors contingent. Sigh. So I'm either a prude for not doing the first thing, or a snob for not doing the second. I can't *wait* to get out of here. Nineteen days to Aspen!!!

## 16. RANDALL

Two o'clock always weighed down upon him. Smack in the middle of the day, the office peons kept busy mastering their pretenses of productivity: making copies, writing intra-office memos, nursing that fourth cup of coffee. But he rarely started work before four, and today his first class wasn't until six.

He sat himself in front of the computer. He had to get back to the novel. He tried to edit an earlier chapter, but it was hard to concentrate. The other occupants of his head kept pushing their way to the front, like groupies at a boy band concert. Nothing was coming to him. Non-sequiturs tossed and turned in his head. He tried to empty his mind, self-motivate. *Turn your lemons into lemonade, Randall.* Problem was, he didn't have a juice presser. He didn't have ice, a glass pitcher, Cascade, clean glasses.

After an hour of false starts, he closed the word processing program and went online. He had joined a dating service three weeks ago, and he wanted to see if Wilder had finally replied. The early responses had been dispiriting: a slew of tiresome men, some with graying temples, some with resigned smiles, some from Long Island living in aluminum-sided houses. Here and there, a few piqued his interest. But these guys weren't Wilder. They were over thirty-five; they *looked* over thirty-five. They butterfly-collared through disco, remembered Jimmy Carter. They'd either bore him with their nostalgia or intimidate him with their salaries. Where was his shy, eager twenty-three year-old grad student from Toronto?

He thought about checking out some porn sites before signing off and then stopped himself. Porn was a reward for hard labor. *Brussels sprouts before ice cream, Randall.* So he headed to the living room and grabbed the remote. Like there was anything worth watching at that hour. He switched channels furiously, unwilling to commit. MTV had a *Real World* marathon on, and the guys were often delicious. There was usually a gay one, and doubtless he'd be the hottest, and—wait, what the hell was he doing? Indulging his vices, again. Slouching by the TV. Mentally comparing Legion's nipples to those of the cast of *The Real World: Back to NY*. Shit, these guys weren't anywhere *near* as hot as Legion.

Everything he did was wrong.

Could he even use the word wrong anymore? Wrong was what you said after it happened once. But what do you say after the fourth time? Because it was really wrong now. Wrong because someone would find out. Wrong because this wasn't a relationship. He needed to date someone with a job, someone who wasn't carrying Trapper Keepers in a backpack to homeroom, someone who didn't *live with his father*, for Christ Sake. Wrong because he needed to stop letting his dick make decisions. He was losing out on $400 a week because the little tyrant expected everything for free now. He *needed* that money.

Wrong because it was so draining, this struggle to break free of his routine—Wake up, dick hard, think of Legion, get harder, tell yourself *Not yet, Cocoa Puffs first,* drink coffee, think of Legion's lips, hard again, *Not yet,* take out the garbage, see teenager, think of Legion, go inside, imagine his nipples in your mouth, *Is it time yet? No, be productive.* Productive? How? *Sit down by computer, that's how,* sit down and…imagine what he'll let you do next, dick so, so hard, he hasn't let you do everything, *No, don't go there, think of nuns playing baseball, nuns sliding into home base,* oh God, sliding into Legion's home base, oh fuck, so soft, so hot.

Get off on that. He can't not get off on that.

It was wrong because it wouldn't stop. How could he stop it now? How could he settle for some thirty-something who needed an hour between blowjobs? Legion came *four times* in an hour.

The phone rang. Caller ID revealed his parent's phone number. Great.

"Honey!" his mother screamed. "How's my baby doing?"

She was always so chipper those first few minutes. "Listen, I was looking at that Learning Annex brochure? You should take one of those real estate classes. I hear it's such a hot market now."

"I don't exactly have the time, Mom."

"What about all those hours in the morning?"

"Those are my writing hours, remember?"

"Oh, that's right," she said. "And how's that coming along?"

"Super. I'm back on the novel now."

"Really. How *super*." And there it was: the shift in tone. Her voice had gone from Celine Dion to Toni Braxton in the span of one sentence. "You've been tinkering with that one for a while now."

"Takes time to write a novel, Mom."

"Of course, Honey. Mom knows that," she said. "So are you advertising? You should put an ad in the Voice. I hear people read it now that it's free."

"Can't do that, Mom. Not while I still work for the Center."

"Right." She paused. "Your father and I are sending a check."

"No, Mom," he insisted.

"It's no big *deal*, Randall."

Why did they always have to make him feel like a little boy wearing a bib? "I'd prefer you wouldn't," he said, knowing it wouldn't make any difference. She would send it. If he didn't cash it, she'd call and complain. Then his father would call and complain. Then they'd send another.

"Stop it," she said. "Don't be difficult."

Yes, he was difficult. The difficult son. The one without a career at twenty eight. The homosexual. *That one over there? Yes, he's a homosexual. They're very tortured.* He imagines his mother on the phone, talking to her trophy friends in Boca, trying to come up with excuses. *You know how it is…he's a writer. No, not married. It's okay. You love them anyway.*

"So how's the social life?" she asked.

"Fine."

"You want to talk about it?"

"Do you?"

"I just don't want you to be lonely."

"I'm not lonely, Mom."

"Of course not," she said. "You have friends. *Terrific* friends. But you know…"

"I'm working on it," he said.

"Good. I'm glad."

"I really should go, Mom."

"Take care, honey. You know how much we love you."

"Take care, Mom."

"We *love* you," she insisted, sticking the spoon further into his mouth.

"I love you, too," he said. Only then would she hang up.

So much for his hard on. He supposed he was better off. He got up and paced around the room. He had to *do* something. It wasn't even three o'clock. He could go to the gym; God knows his pecs weren't what they once were. Did Legion notice? Did he care?

In the bedroom, he changed into sweatpants, grabbed his gym bag from the closet. Should he call Legion before he left? *Just confirming our appointment.* Yeah, that wouldn't sound desperate. What the hell was he doing? He had to write. He threw down his gym bag. He was going to plant himself in front of that computer. He was going to pour himself a glass of vodka and be fucking brilliant. Fresh out of lemonade, never out of Stolichnaya. Did Legion drink Stoli?

Christ. What was the point? Inspiration was a moving van waiting downstairs, and all his ideas were boxed up, ready to be taken away to his fabulous new home, except he couldn't touch them, because there was this huge sofa, this really great looking sofa he'd gotten a month ago, that wouldn't get through the door. It wouldn't budge.

He'd have to find some way to get that sofa out. He had to get out of his apartment, get to that fucking bistro, where Life was having his third *menthe a l'eau*, Life was impatiently checking his watch, Life was wondering, *Where the hell are you Randall, I don't have all day.* And wait, wouldn't you know it, who's there with Life but Wilder, Wilder making small talk to Life, hitting on *his* Life, about to take off with Life because Randall couldn't get his shit together, couldn't get that sofa out of his teensy-weensy apartment, couldn't get a stupid boy out of his mind, a *boy*, for God's sake.

But the boy. *The boy!* Imagination was one thing. The boy, however, was real; Reality was sloppy, but it didn't disappear when you opened your eyes. Maybe he was wrong. Maybe Wilder wasn't Wilder. Maybe Wilder's name was really Legion.

He'd never get that sofa out today.

## 17. GABRIELLE

How preposterous of her to have thought she could squeeze water out of the rock-solid Robinsons. Such the charming couple they were, so chicly dressed, such porcelain white teeth, such witty repartee, and such fascinating anecdotes. *Mandela? Princeton? That's the first we've heard about it.*

So they thought she was stupid. Probably did their research too, figured a simpleton like her with no degrees would be easy to fool with a wink and two smiles. Their off-the-cuff denial made her all the more certain that Princeton was now the number one choice on Mandela's list.

A fresh scheme had to be devised. Which is how she found herself in the driver's seat of the Levy's midnight blue Mercedes, stationed down the block from Valhalla at half-past three in the afternoon, hunkering down like a Secret Service agent assigned to stake out a suspicious third world emissary. She would do what she must to secure Arianna's place. She may not outwit the crafty Robinsons, but surely she could take on their son. Surely she could persuade this schoolboy into seeing how wrong Princeton would be for him.

Marinating in her own sweat, she tried fixing herself in the small makeup mirror. She fussed with the radio. She hated driving; there were so many buttons she had no idea what to make of. She didn't know when the boy would come out. Luckily Arianna was off campus, at Model U.N. He couldn't prove that difficult to spot, this chocolate chip in a swirl of vanilla ice cream. Sensing he'd have no car waiting, she positioned herself across from the bus stop.

Everything else was swimming along so smoothly. Only this obstacle remained in her way. She'd remove it with a bulldozer's certainty, a scalpel's precision. Even if he felt strongly about Princeton, she had many statistics to rattle his conviction — this was not a school teeming with African-Americans. The glove compartment was crammed with brochures from other schools that seemed infinitely more appropriate for Mandela. Whatever he wanted to study in college, she was ready with a program that made Princeton's seem toothless and absurd.

Still, these chewy pleasantries might only be the appetizer. No, the snake could have a rapacious hunger. If necessary, she'd resort to other methods of hypnosis. No one would have to know, certainly not Arianna. And Morty never knew anything anyway.

At 3:44, her target stepped out of Valhalla's front gates and headed towards the bus stop. She studied the boy. No doubt it was him. He sported the same singularly opaque expression as he did in the class photo she'd examined. He slumbered across the street, as if the burden of his life was weighing down his backpack. Ha, these kids thought their lives were tough. They should only know tough.

Avoiding the throng of SUVs gathered outside Valhalla, she threw the car in reverse and maneuvered it directly in front of him. Probably not as gracefully as she would have liked, judging from the stares being flung at her. Still, a little intimidation might be just the thing.

The tinted window slid down ominously. The boy did not flinch. He was making an effort to ignore her.

"Mandela Robinson," she said, more a statement than a question.

His eyes drifted slowly to her.

"Mandela," she repeated, this time more cheerfully. "I'm Arianna's mother. Arianna Levy? I was wondering if I could speak with you for a few minutes."

She thought about those survey-takers positioning themselves on street corners, Greenpeace peddlers clawing you to sign their forms. She had to be careful not to seem desperate.

"What about?" A tinge of suspicion began to color his face. It looked rather formidable up close.

"Would you mind getting in the car? I promise I won't kidnap you."

He stood still, unconvinced.

"I could drive you home if you'd like," she said, regretting it as soon as she did. Acquiescing was a sign of weakness. Still, he had inched closer to the back door.

"Come sit up front with me," she said. "If you don't mind."

"Just so you know," he said, getting in next to her. "I live on Ninety-eighth. On the East Side."

"No problem at all," she said. She watched him take her in. The whole situation could quickly dissolve to ludicrous; she had to keep things moving. The less time he had to reflect, the better.

"Your parents are lovely people. They were over for a party last week, did you know that? They're very proud of you. I understand you're doing phenomenally well at Valhalla. And Arianna thinks you're just brilliant."

"Does she."

"Of course she does. I think you spur her on, in a way. So thank you for that."

He didn't reply. She looked over to him. She was happy she was driving, because she wouldn't be able to stand the tartness of his gaze for too long. His mouth stood silent, but his eyes kept speaking. She didn't like what they were telling her.

"Anyway." She took a long breath. "I'm sure you know Arianna plans on applying to Princeton early decision."

And then he tittered. He didn't even stop himself.

"Please, don't laugh. I haven't made a joke."

"I'm sorry," he said, composing himself. "Go ahead."

"If you don't mind my asking, what are you interested in studying at Princeton?"

"I haven't thought about it," he said.

Another politician, just like his parents. She turned left onto Central Park West. She really wasn't sure what the best way to get to Ninety-eighth was. She assumed it involved crossing through the park.

"Please," she said. "Allow me the pleasure of your honesty."

"*Honestly*, I don't know," he said. "I like philosophy. I like to paint."

"Seriously?" She looked at him again. He seemed relaxed now, even amused. He had thrown her. She hadn't thought about painting in so long. She didn't think kids these days gave much thought to it, certainly not the kids at Valhalla, with their enrichment programs and deadly academic schedules. A shame, really.

She turned into the park on Eighty-sixth. "I used to paint. When I was younger. Around your age, in fact." She could tell what he was thinking. "I'm not lying. I was an abstract expressionist groupie. DeKooning, Pollock. My parents thought I was possessed."

"I'm more of a post-modern realist," he said. "Ever heard of Rick Sheppy?"

"Oh, he *is* intriguing. A bit twisted, but he's still learning." What was she doing? She had no time for coffee table discussion. "Getting back to my point," she said. "I don't think Princeton is a sanctuary for painters."

"Painting is not a career. I'll need something to fall back on."

"Of course," she said. "Still, there are far more suitable schools. So many schools will want a bright young man like you."

"*Black,*" he said. "Don't forget *black.*"

She wasn't going to take the bait. "I just think it would be easier for you and Arianna not to step on each other's toes, if it can be avoided."

"This is a *really* nice car," he said. "My parents drive a Camry."

And here it was. She expected it would come to this, although not quite so soon. East Eighty-sixth street was a carnival, a cheap display of handbag hucksters, leopard-striped nail salons, the blood-money din of multicolored beepers. This was not the Upper East she was familiar with. She made a left onto Third Avenue. The further she drove, the thinner the air of her city became.

"Alright," she said. "I think I understand. So do me this favor. Why don't you think about how I can convince you to do the right thing, and then let me know what that will entail?"

"I'm not exactly sure what you mean."

He looked at her strangely, his eyes roaming over her. Was he checking out her legs? Really?

"You're exceedingly bright, Mandela. I'm sure you know precisely what I mean."

Her temples throbbed. She would not let him shame her into spelling everything out. The streets outside were painfully new. Her hands trembled softly on the steering wheel. She needed this episode to end.

"Oh. Wow. Wow. Okay...I mean, are you for real?"

She took off her sunglasses and let her eyes do the talking. "What do you think?"

"I don't know what to make of all this."

"Do the math. You'll figure it out."

She was not going to make any suggestions. Any number he'd come up with would undoubtedly be less than she'd be willing to pay.

They sat silently for ten more blocks. "I can walk the rest," he said when they reached Ninety-eighth. She pulled over on the right side. Her screams begged for escape, but she swallowed them into her stomach. She had chosen this risk, and things remained far from certain. Only a level head could save her now.

She unlocked his door for him. He opened it, then hesitated, turning to look her flush in the eyes. "Thanks for the lift," he said. "This was really interesting."

"I'll contact you when we return from Aspen. We'll resume our conversation then."

He smiled. Or was it a snicker? Was he mocking her? Would he tell his parents? Or Arianna? So many unknowns. She could only pray her poker face was convincing enough.

"You have every reason to take me seriously." She smiled warmly at him before he closed the door. "But you know that already."

"Take care, Mrs. Levy."

She nodded her head. As soon as he turned away, she relocked the doors and shut down the window controls. For several seconds she took deep breaths. She had not expected this mysterious dancing mouse, this stargazer, this ambivalent artist.

Gingerly, she pulled the Mercedes into the uptown traffic. Her eyes concentrated on the road. There would be no accident in that neighborhood. She had to break all the way left, plot her way back across town, to the goose down shelter of her West Side quilt.

# ASPEN

# 1. GABRIELLE

They should have stayed at the Jerome. Instead, they were slumming at the St. Regis because Morty wanted a property he could ski out from. *Casual Mountain Elegance,* the travel agent insisted. Ghost town nostalgia more like it. Rawhide lamp shades. A smorgasbord of leather. Gabrielle felt like she had stumbled into a bar in the meatpacking district. They couldn't even place them on the best floor.

"I'm sorry. The Club Room suites are fully booked," the mousy blond at reception told her.

"Here I thought $900 a night might buy us some privacy," she replied.

The manager was summoned, another Midwest chipmunk, who rehashed the same line, with the same phony flight attendant's smile. "We assure you, Mrs. Levy, the suite we've given you is of the highest standard."

She insisted on filing a complaint. Morty looked embarrassed when the man said they'd send up a courtesy bottle of champagne to apologize for the inconvenience. *You didn't even know about the special floor until we got here,* he told her. As if that mattered. True, they had only heard of it when they had run into the Cartwrights in the lobby and Ken Cartwright had flaunted his club room key.

The model/actress by his side was no doubt the trophy girlfriend. Of course she looked more like the boy's girlfriend. The Cartwright boy went to school with Arianna, and this apparently was reason enough for Morty to invite the couple for drinks later that evening. Gabrielle couldn't wait. In between the business jabberwocky, the two men would ogle the girl's breasts and laugh at her delightfully clumsy comments; the girl, with thoughtless pity, would ask her where she had her eyes done.

She couldn't tell what Arianna thought of the Cartwright boy. His name didn't come up much. There was no denying a certain dewy magnetism to him, but also, something else, something askew; he reminded her of a painting hanging off center on the wall, only you weren't sure which way to tilt it to set it straight. And what on earth had gotten into Randall? The way he kept shifting back and forth like he owed Ken Cartwright money. Inviting the tutor along was such an extravagance. But oh, the twinkle in Arianna's eyes when Morty had told her that Randall would join them! Randall had seemed hesitant about the proposal at first, but a week later, had changed his mind. Perhaps—sly devil—he was tutoring the Cartwright boy too. She'd have to remind him in no uncertain terms who was really buttering his bread.

Upstairs, while Morty settled in the bathroom, she canvassed the room. There was nothing immoral about it, on the surface. The furniture was from the mountain chalet pages of a catalog and the paintings were atrociously risk-free, designed to blend in with the walls. Everything came in various shades of brown, like being inside an assorted box of chocolates. She sighed. At least one piece was worth biting into—the view. While everyone else slacked off, Mother Nature delivered.

In the mini-fridge she found her first problem and wasted no time dialing up reception. "There's Colorado water in our refrigerator. Please send up some Evian."

"By all means, Mrs. Levy," a well-trained voice replied.

"While you're at it, dear, check on the champagne we were promised."

"Right away, Mrs. Levy."

She hung up the phone. Morty's tinny tremolos rode a putrid wave out of the bathroom, his comic homage to Puccini. This was his idea of vacation. Had it been up to her, the family would be sipping mai tais at the Ritz Carlton in Antigua. But at a certain age, men need to be reminded that they are alive. She remembered the way his eyes had lit up on the plane as he spoke about the exquisite terror he felt on Ajax, how death chased him down

Ruthie's Run. For a few seconds, she could see the thirty year old she'd married, the man who once spoke about her with equal conviction.

Arianna came out of her bedroom in her prize Prada and picked out an apple from the complimentary fruit basket. "Do you think Randall's ready to embarrass himself?"

"We're not here to harass him, Arianna. And must you wear that right away?"

"This is my *third* best outfit, Mother. Shouldn't we at least check up on him?"

"We arrived *half* an hour ago."

She sighed. Morty had been the same way on the plane, even suggesting they splurge for a first class ticket until she put her foot down. As if Randall couldn't survive five hours by himself in coach. Maybe they'd throw in some new skis while they were at it? A shopping spree at Paragon, some lessons with the U.S. Olympic team?

"How come you haven't changed?" Arianna asked.

"Not today. You'll go with your father. And don't even think about doing double diamonds. Daddy's hiring an instructor to keep an eye on you. And don't linger. You're seeing Randall at four."

"Are we inviting him to dinner with us?"

"We'll see. He's a *grown* man. Besides, Daddy and I have cocktails with those characters...Sweetie, you never told me what you think about that boy."

Arianna's lips scrunched into a smirk. "Legion Cartwright? Ugh. I mean, he's so opaque, which I guess impresses *some* people, but honestly I just don't know."

Gabrielle sometimes wished she had a teenager-to-English dictionary handy. "I gather you won't be spending much time with him then."

"I seriously doubt that."

And then she noticed it, out of the corner of her eye. High above the couch in the sitting area, hovering on the wall like a centipede. Dear God, was there an *insect* in the room? She approached guardedly. Upon closer inspection, it wasn't an insect at all. It was a splotch. A sickly, sticky, greenish brown splotch. It was vile. Not on the wall, but *part* of the wall, as if the wall had scraped itself and scabbed over.

So this was what they meant by highest standards.

"Maybe I should start a ski club at Valhalla." Arianna was adjusting her ski cap in the mirror over the fireplace. "We could organize trips to Bennington. I mean, when we go on weekends I bump into *so* many people."

"Arianna, come here this *instant*." She summoned her daughter over with a rapid waving of her hands. Arianna turned around and looked at her curiously. Gabrielle pointed at the splotch with a snappish finger

"Look up there, do you see it?"

"That green thing on the wall?"

"I'm calling reception."

"Wow, do you think it's like a leak or something? Does my hair look okay? I think this hat makes my ears look Dumbo-ish."

"I'm supposed to believe they inspected this room and didn't notice that sickness?" She picked up the phone just as Morty strolled out of the bathroom in his silk robe.

"Pack your bags," she said. "Yes, reception?"

Morty came over and pressed down on the receiver. "What's the *problem*, Gabrielle?"

She brought him near the wall and pointed up. The splotch seemed to have changed shape. It was three smaller splotches now, two round balls, one long tube. An upside-down smiley face, laughing at her.

"Look at that thing!" she shouted.

Morty walked closer to it than she would have dared. "It's a stain."

"She thinks it's a leak," Arianna said.

"Not a leak. Just a stain," Morty said.

"It *festering*," she said. "We should leave."

Morty laughed. "Yes, that's it. It's a *virus*. While we sleep it will kill us all."

"So we kowtow to this level of disrespect, do we? They put us on the wrong floor and then they stick us with this...thing."

"Your mother has the most active imagination," Morty told his daughter. "I've always told her she should do something with it."

"You've *encouraged* my imagination, Morty? Is that what you're saying?"

"I'm going to change," Arianna said. "Let me know if we're moving."

Arianna escaped to her bedroom. Gabrielle walked over to the phone.

"I'm not staying here. It's an insult."

Morty came over and reached for her hands. "If that's what you want," he said. "But is it worth troubling yourself so much?

Isn't everything else in the room fine?"

He looked at her with what she knew he believed was kindness. Grabbing her gently by the elbows, he led her to the bed and sat her down. She decided not to resist.

"Why don't you get a massage this afternoon? They have that hot stone treatment here. And then you can go into town, pick up something nice at Fendi."

"I'm not a *child*, Morty," she said, uncertain of herself.

"Of course not." His face was serious. "You're a vibrant, beautiful wife and mother."

He kissed her forehead. The argument was officially over. She felt clammy and exposed, her sweat turning sour on her. She hated that stupid splotch, resting above her.

Watching her. *Judging* her.

Twenty minutes later Morty and Arianna left together to squeeze in a few good runs. She sat on the bed, flipping through channels and pages of guidebooks with equal indifference. Her water and champagne had still not arrived.

She didn't even hear the bell the first time. But then there was a knock, so she got up and slumbered over to the door. A cherub-faced black boy greeted her with a most forgiving smile. For a second she was confused, and thought Mandela Robinson was in Aspen, bringing her refreshments. She wasn't sure if it was his age, his tender eyes, his self-possessed smile—or if there was any resemblance at all, really.

On the cart beside him were three large bottles of water and an ice bucket housing a '95 Veuve Clicquot. She stepped aside to let him enter.

"Apologies for the delay, Mrs. Levy. We were out of Evian and had to send someone to get some for you."

"That's fine. I'm afraid I'm far too particular about my water," she said. She looked around. She would need to find her purse to tip the boy.

"The manager hopes the champagne will be satisfactory."

"It will do nicely," she said. She wondered where the real Mandela Robinson was now. She imagined him in a narrow room, deep in thought, his paint-smudged fingers caressing his chin as he mulled over a half-finished canvas.

She found her purse cowering on the sofa underneath the splotch. Quickly, she took out her wallet. When she turned around, the boy was standing right in front of her. She flinched.

"I'm sorry, Mrs. Levy, did I startle you?"

"No, it's alright." She buried her head in the wallet, searching for a five.

"Is there anything else I can be of service with, ma'am?"

She looked up at him. He had an honest face. A trusting face. "As a matter of fact." She gestured upwards with her head. "Look up there. Tell me what you think."

The young man passed right by her. He brought himself flush with the wall.

"Would you mind if I got a closer look?"

"By all means."

The man removed his shoes and stepped onto the couch. Gabrielle was impressed.

"Hmm. Someone really ought to check this out. I'll tell them right away."

"You're not just saying that to get a bigger tip?"

He descended off the couch and put his shoes back on. "Ma'am, there's no reason you should have such unpleasantness in your room."

Gabrielle felt woozy, as if she had been suffocating, and the air had suddenly returned to her lungs. "Thank you very much," she said, handing the man a twenty.

"That's too much," he said, looking embarrassed.

"It's not. Believe me."

The young man tipped his cap and wished her a pleasant stay. She locked the door behind him and headed to the cart. Normally she was afraid of the indiscriminate trajectory of a champagne cork, but this time she threw caution to the wind. Let the cork leave another mark on the wall, for all she cared. After a few sips she began chuckling out of embarrassment. Soon they'd send someone up to inspect, and she'd have to turn them away. What had gotten into her, getting all worked up over a stain on the wall? She didn't need to leave that room. She could make peace with the splotch. Of course she could.

## 2. LEGION

6am. The morning air was too thin for his stomach. Legion pushed his omelet around his plate, taking the occasional bite. A heaping bowl of fruit sat in front of Veronica; Ken liked to lean over and feed her blackberries one at a time. He'd nestle himself into her neck, making ludicrous noises while Veronica giggled. People stared; Ken wanted them to stare. That was the whole point. They were decked out in their Burberry best. Veronica looked fucking amazing, even for a town full of amazing looking women.

"Do you hear that?" Ken had his competition face on. "I think the mountain is whispering something. Something about someone getting his ass kicked by his old man."

"Dad, there's no snowboarding on Ajax. I'm going to Buttermilk."

"Oh come on, you've done Pussy Mountain for three days now. Gimme a day's worth of runs to show you how it's done."

"Why don't you get a snowboard and I'll show you how it's done."

"Now now, children," Veronica said. "Ken, we have reservations at the Tavern for lunch. Besides we should let Legion hang out with people his own age."

"By that logic I should head to the nearest bingo hall and you should find yourself some strapping ski instructor."

"Pookie." Veronica plopped a berry into Ken's mouth. "You're years away from bingo halls. Until then I'll wheel you around myself."

"Thanks, sweetness. Remind me to change my will when I get home."

"I need to use the little cowgirl's room." Veronica stood up. Ken copped a quick squeeze of her ass as she walked away. She shrugged for a second before forcing a smile.

"She's a keeper, that one," Ken said. "Even you like her."

"She's not an imbecile. It's refreshing."

"Fantastic. Then you won't mind spending some time with her tomorrow afternoon. I have some business to tend to."

"She can go shopping by herself."

"You're a far cheaper date." Ken took out his wallet, removed five hundreds and shoved them into Legion's hand. "Take her to the mountain of your choice and keep her there until the sun sets."

"Can I buy her lessons from some strapping ski instructor?"

"Funny, kid." Ken got up from the table. "Sign everything up to my room. When Veronica comes back, tell her I went upstairs."

Legion nodded his head. Ten seconds later he got up, without bothering to call a waiter. He had enough bullshit and was ready to hit the Drop Zone. Or fuck it, maybe he'd head to the Highlands, lose a few limbs at Thunderbowl.

When he returned to the room later that day, the red light on his phone was blinking: more messages from Randall. So this is what it's like to have a wife, he thought. He was supposed to be on vacation. Maybe—just maybe—he didn't want to think about studying for ten fucking days. Maybe he'd like to hook up with someone else while he was here. Maybe even a girl.

He listened to the messages. The entire day before he had avoided Randall. Hearing the guy's goofy ramblings made him feel sad. Randall could be such a dork. As needy as a golden retriever, but he still liked to pretend it was all about the lessons. If only it was lessons and easy sex, he wouldn't think twice about seeing Randall. But for Randall it was more. He could tell. Even if the guy didn't say anything, he knew.

It would be wrong not to call back. He'd leave a message. Randall probably wasn't in anyway.

"Hey," Randall said. "Come up to my room. I want to play a game."

"Dude, I just got back from boarding."

"Cool. Bring the cards you were supposed to study for yesterday."

"Aren't you meeting with Arianna?"

"Not until later. Come up. We'll do shots. I'll make it worth your while."

He didn't know what to say. He didn't want to piss him off. "I can't stay long."

Inside Randall's room, the TV set was on. Used room-service trays and bottles from the mini-bar lined the wall by the door.

"Jesus," Legion said. "Have you been here all day?"

"I went out for a bit. This city's pretty fucking crazy."

"Why don't you go visit the ghost town or something if you don't wanna ski?"

"Are you going to Buttermilk tomorrow? I can ski there."

"Um. I don't know."

"Forget it. Maybe we can go out later then, see a movie or something." Randall smiled. He grabbed the flashcards out of Legion's hand. "So I have this idea. I test you on the words, and for every one you get wrong, you lose an article of clothing."

"Shit, I might as well get buck naked right now then."

"You didn't study them?"

"I forgot."

Randall frowned. "You can't keep forgetting, Legion. Where's your motivation?"

"Dude, I'm on vacation."

"Don't call me dude. It's so fucking passé."

"The word passé is so fucking passé. And queer."

Randall's lips slanted mischievously. Instead of pissing him off, the word queer had the opposite effect. "That's the way you like me," he said, reaching for Legion's hips. "You like me queer."

Fuck was this getting predictable. "Did you call me here to study or to get off?"

Randall dropped to his knees and pressed his face against the crotch of Legion's jeans. This was the game they played lately, Master and Servant. He wasn't sure how it started, if Randall thought it turned him on, or if it just turned Randall on. Predictable as it was, it still got him hard. He liked seeing the lust foam up in Randall's eyes. He liked the idea of someone worshiping him.

Randall ripped open his jeans. He thrust himself hard into Randall's mouth, slapped it against his willing face. His mouth opened, and out came the dirty talk, the put-downs, the slurs, the bossing around. Randall's head-bobbing sped up, the friction of his hand against his own swollen cock growing even more fervent. He grabbed Randall's hair by the back of his head and finished himself across the man's mouth. Seconds later, Randall let out a series of yelps and shot all over the floor.

In the bathroom, Randall grinned silently as he brushed the viscous fluid off of Legion's shrinking penis. Afterwards, he guided them over to the bed, where they lay down next to one another, spooning. Randall nuzzled his head against his shoulder, kissed his neck, fluttered his fingers against his chest and stomach. There was nothing Legion could say. He didn't understand how this tenderness followed the nasty scene of just minutes before. He didn't know what Randall wanted from him.

Ten minutes later, Randall lifted himself off the bed and shifted into tutor mode. "OK. Get dressed. We have to talk probability." For half an hour, it was like nothing happened. Not the blowjob. Not the little nibbles on the back of the shoulder. Nothing.

"Call me later?" Randall asked, as he was about to leave. "About the movie?"

"Yeah. Sure."

He left the room, lightheaded and spent, like a 7am hangover after too many shots of Tequila. He was going to stop trying to understand, go upstairs and steal some of Ken's weed. Jesus, how did people get through life without weed?

Turning a corner down the hall, a curve ball hit him dead on. Arianna Levy in a miniskirt. Not a girl he could stomach for more than a few minutes. She didn't need to join a pep rally; she *was* the fucking pep rally. Aside from that she had a thirty year life plan or something. Not cool.

"Hey," he said. His hair was all fucked up. He knew it.

"Hey." Her eyes dilated with suspicion. "Aren't you on the special floor?"

He looked around, pretending to be confused. "No wonder nothing looks familiar."

Arianna wasn't amused. He wondered if she could smell it on him. He could always tell when Ken and Veronica had just did the nasty.

"So is Randall in his room?" she asked.

"Uh..."

"Please," she said. "You were just coming from there."

"Was I?" He didn't care for these accusations. Arianna liked to think most people were stupider than she. He could easily play along.

"You realize I'm fully aware he's tutoring you. It's no big deal."

"OK. That's cool."

"So have you seen anyone else from Valhalla? A group of seniors are at the Gant."

"No." He hoped she wasn't going to keep him long. There wasn't enough air on that floor for the two of them.

"So where have you been?"

"You mean today? Snowmass."

"No, I mean, where have you *been*? Yesterday I met this guy on Ajax who said he'd get me on the list to Hades' Kitchen."

"Oh," he said. "I've been there. It's cool. Anyway, gotta jet. Catch ya around."

Her mouth twisted to a smirk. But he had enough of the interrogation. He winked at her and smiled. She rolled her eyes and walked down the hall. So she thought he was weird. Good. The weirder she thought he was, the more reason she'd have to avoid him.

## 3. RANDALL'S LETTER TO LEGION*

*found crumpled in the wastebasket of room 203, St. Regis, Aspen

I always feel such a profound sense of safety in a hotel room. It's comforting how the same things materialize in all of them: *Reader's Digest* lithographs on the walls, factory-fresh Gideon bibles, mini bottles of milky, unscented shampoo — people from all walks of life surrendering to this crushing homogeneity just because they're on vacation.

I'm sitting here by the desk, halfway through the second shelf of the mini bar, scribbling this note to you on hotel stationery, knowing I should spew out something safe and reasonable. But my feelings aren't going to allow for that right now, so I might as well just let my heart grab the pen and write whatever the fuck it wants.

Have you noticed how new the air is here? When we landed I felt weightless. You were already here and I thought, how strange that our paths should join here, in the powdery white. We passed by the Wheeler opera house in the cab, Arianna's determined fingers pointing out every designer boutique, and I wondered: What is he doing this second? I thought about how I'd run into you. I knew I would. You'd be sitting alone at the chalet coffee shop, scarfing down a sandwich, your hair falling lazily over your eyes. I'd walk in, and you'd throw me a grin from across the room. I'd sit with you, and when you were ready, we'd return to the slopes, you the instructor this time, and with great sensitivity you'd show me the finer points of snowboarding. I'd stumble, and you'd laugh, without cruelty. You'd lift me up when I fell, adjust my feet to the board, allow me to steady myself on you before setting off, down the mountain, out into the open, the afternoon sun causing our eyes to squint, the continental divide surrounding us like frozen soldiers of an awesome cavalry, a zesty wind frosting our faces, fear coating our lungs as we thrust into the unknown.

Instead, I saw you in the hotel lobby. Surreal. But more than that. There's a moment when coincidence, no matter how reasonable, loses its ability to clarify. You never told me where you'd be staying. The same city is one thing, the same hotel another, but the precise moment when we arrive? There are footprints only fate can leave.

Obviously it's disappointing to see how things turned out. Of course I knew you'd claim your independence somehow. On some undeniable level you only see me as your tutor. I also know that, at your age, adults seem hopelessly square. Which really isn't true, in my case. I mean, I'm not Capital G Gangsta Fresh, but I can get around the hood without a map. My milk's a few days shy of the expiration date.

Anyway, I wasn't fooling myself. Under Gabrielle Levy's charge, I knew I'd be forced to gallop the course and jump the hurdles like a prize gelding. Still, somehow I thought the time I'd spend with you would make up for the marionette strings the Levys had attached to my arms and legs. I should have known better.

It was one thing when you didn't show that night. But then you disturb me with your excuses. So many legitimate-sounding explanations you could have made up and you chose 'I forgot,' knowing full well that earlier that day you had used the same fucking excuse when I tried to test you on the flashcards. Forgive me for not believing you forgot. Forgive me for thinking you just did what you felt like doing.

So I burden you with tedious assignments. But I also licked your ass for the first time. Why not focus on that instead of my criticisms of your careless methods, your laziness with the Pythagorean Theorem? What about the way I made you shudder? You shouted for God right before you screamed. You swatted at my head like I was a mosquito. You didn't know it could feel that good, did you? My God, watching your eyes, I came without touching myself. Silently. I didn't want to take away from your moment. Because that's the kind of guy I am.

You love the dirty thrill as much as I do. Admit it. Remember when Veronica called? You stayed on script while I licked your balls. You wanted to cum in my mouth while she was on the line. You did. You're not the Scared Nelly type. So why pretend running into Arianna outside my room was such a close call? She already knows I tutor you, so what? It's no reason to avoid me.

I'm trying to keep things in perspective. I *know* I'm overreacting. What do I expect, anyway? You're just a kid. You have every right to act like one. But you see, there's something I understand about you, something you may not understand yourself. I was walking around downtown yesterday, trying to clear my head, sucking up mouthfuls of alpine quietude to store for a frantic day back home, when I came across that public park down by the pedestrian mall. Nothing too fancy. Statues, benches, trees. People basking in the luxury of the ordinary—as ordinary as Aspen gets anyway. (I walked into Mezzaluna yesterday around 4pm in jeans and a turtleneck. The Apresnauts looked at me like I was a janitor from Columbine High.) Anyway, so I'm in the park, and this brawny jock type was tossing a pigskin with his pint-sized son—at least I think it was his son, but who knows, maybe they hire people to do that sorta stuff here. Anyway, this dad—or this Manny, whatever—he's encouraging the boy with this rah-rah sportscaster bravado with every throw, every catch, every miss. *Atta boy, Charlie. You can do it, Charlie. Good try, Charlie.* I watched this kid send the ball spiraling effortlessly into the air, and I realized that even if I tried my absolute best, I'd never throw a ball as well as he did. Twice his height and three times his weight, and I can't throw a football or a baseball because my father never did that stuff with me, he wasn't that kind of dad, the football-tossing baseball-throwing dad, he was a football and baseball *watcher* – or maybe he already knew, when I was nine, and thought, to hell with it, the boy's going to join the drama club not little league, he'll throw a tantrum not a ball, he doesn't care about balls, this son of mine, not unless they're low hangers attached to some sexy auto mechanic.

I think you know what I mean. I think you have the same thing at home except worse because at least my dad loved me in his own risk-free way, he loved me and kept his quiet seething to himself, whereas Ken Cartwright troubles you, he nicks you with his razor, he probably throws footballs just to see you miss.

Believe me, I know what it feels like when the shame strikes. You do everything you can to deny it, build walls, make excuses, assume a new image for yourself, something you've picked out of a magazine or movie and suddenly you're this other person, because no matter how hard it is to pretend it's still easier than looking in the mirror. I just want to help you, share with you the patchy life lessons I've learned. Christ, it's so fucking confusing. What do I mean to you? Do I even know what you mean to me? Of course not. I feel like we're trapped in a room, like those people in Sartre's *No Exit*. Did they make you read that in school? Probably not. Do you ever feel like you're stuck in a room and nothing's really happening? Like the world stopped spinning years ago and we've been coasting on the residual energy?

Such fucking nonsense. It doesn't make a difference; I'm never going to give this to you anyway. I realized that a few paragraphs ago. I just want us to have some perspective. Maybe it's better to stop caring and just flow. You do that a lot, don't you? Turn everything off and float in the dark? I need to try that sometime.

Have you seen that warning by the bed, the one about drinking moderately at high altitudes for seventy-two hours? Lucky me, we passed day five already. So fuck moderation and pass the Tanqueray. No one else here seems to believe in moderation, why should I? I hope you enjoy your last night in Winter Wonderland. I hope you find yourself some excuse, and the two of you get terrifically drunk and pretend to enjoy each other's company. There must be a gay bar in Aspen. Someplace with a password or a secret handshake. Maybe I'll scrape myself off the floor and sample the local cuisine. Hell, it's my last night too.

And when we return to New York, let me guess: Water under the bridge. We have our best laid plans to attend to. I get you into Harvard and you — well, you make my list of references stronger. Because I'm your fucking SAT tutor. When you get into your first choice, then my job is done. Yeah, that's how this works. For a while there I forgot. I better start reminding myself.

# 4. EXCERPTS FROM ARIANNA'S JOURNALS

January 3, 2000

Mother's exceedingly disgruntled every time she steps off a plane. No matter how many Camparis she downs, nothing relaxes her. When we arrived at the hotel, everything was wrong. We weren't on the right floor. The room was claustrophobic. And then she went twelve rounds with a splotch on the wall. Yikes. *Someone* needs a new prescription.

And who do we run into in the lobby but of all people Legion Cartwright—ugh. Legion and I do not mix well together. He kind of reminds me of *The Matrix*: sexy and cool on the surface, but once you really think about it, everything falls apart. And just like *The Matrix*, a swarm of rumors spin around him like bees waiting to inseminate the Queen. All because his dad is Vatican rich. All because he's invited to every party and almost never shows up. As if he's doing something better. Besides, he hangs around with *Mandela*, how cool can he be?

In any case, I think I unsettled him. And Randall was acting all weird around him too. Like I wasn't supposed to know he was tutoring Legion. He *told* me so himself. Besides, if he's going to tutor anyone else at Valhalla, then by all means let it be Legion. I mean, HELLO, *not* a threat.

I don't know why, but I really want Randall to like me. I know he's my tutor, and an adult, but not *really* — like he's not sure about adulthood yet, like he's still weighing his options. He can be so clueless sometimes. When I comment about my preference for watermelon martinis or how I'm totally going to get into Hades' Kitchen this year — which I am — he stares at me like we're in Salem and I just confessed to dabbling in witchcraft. I think he's just deathly afraid of doing anything that would piss off Mother. Well, screw that, he needs to loosen up. There's a naughty little boy hiding behind that professional exterior, and I'm going to tempt him with my cookie jar. I don't mean *come on* to him, I just mean, you know, get to know him.

January 7th

Clearly I've hit that age when my parents have decided they need to suffocate all hints of sexuality and hover over me like owls protecting the nest. At any given moment, someone's been assigned to watch detail. Problem is, Randall's a novice and Mother rarely ventures beyond the bunny slopes — which leaves Daddy as my sole protector, and it turns out his priorities are different than Mother's. Sure, we start the day together, but Daddy's loyalty to Ajax is stronger than his loyalty to his after-dinner shot of Remy Martin.

So it didn't take me long to separate myself and find a strapping would-be instructor to crash into. I locked on my target as he was roughhousing with his friends. He's the second hottest of the bunch. Not the hottest — that guy's usually an arrogant prick who'll expect a handjob in his hotel room just because he bought me a beer in the lounge — but still sufficiently hot. I overheard their conversation and pegged them at twenty or twenty one — perfect, since the almost and just-turned legal are the hungriest to get into the best clubs. Within thirty seconds his buddies dispersed to give him some space to score. Anyway, his name is Brandon, which you have to admit is adorable, even if 90210 is so over. I played clueless while he showed me some pointers. How the boys love the damsel-in-distress routine. And it's not like I minded. His grip was quite firm and his eyes are BMW blue. Plus, he smelled vaguely of Faconnable, which scored major points with me, since most boys never venture beyond Drakkar. Half an hour later I had plans for the night. At eleven, after the parents have turned in, I'm gonna sneak out and meet him in the lobby and we are heading to Hades' Kitchen!! He's *guaranteed* me he's on the list. One of his friends supposedly knows the owner. He better because otherwise the tongue stays in the mouth.

Looking forward to some excitement because Vacation Randall's been a total drab. It's like he's not here. Something's disturbing him. I took a practice test when I got back from the slopes today — scored a *very* bootylicious 1410 — so I thought I'd go down and show Randall the results, and who do I run into right by Randall's door but Legion. He actually tried to pretend he was *lost*, can you believe that? Basically I ignored his excuse-making and asked him if he noticed anything odd going on with Randall, but then I realized that that would be like asking Anna Nicole Smith if she thought Elizabeth Taylor had gotten fat and crazy.

Maybe he's part of the reason Randall's acting weird. It can't be easy tutoring someone like that. How could you even know you were getting anywhere? Three painful minutes later we parted ways. Then I realized Randall might not be in the mood for back-to-back students invading his space, so I slipped the results under his door.

January 10th

Today, Mother and I decided to get in touch with our inner Chanel. First, lemon soufflé pancakes at Little Nell, where OMG Sandra Bullock was sitting two tables away with the most scrumptious hottie this side of the Mississippi. He couldn't have been a minute over twenty-five! I'm telling you, she was showing off. Not that I blame her.

After brunch, we headed to the stores. In Aspen, the shops cluster together like profiteroles. On days like this I absolutely treasure my mother. Sure she can be a diva, but she's absolutely indispensable in a boutique. She has the most terrific sense of color. She'll pair things together that should never work and then you see it and it's like whoa. I think it's because she used to paint. She rarely talks about that though.

Anyway, powder blue salopettes at Stephane Kelian. Cashmere scarf from Marc Jacobs. Ostrich water bottle holder from Lana Mark's — what more could a girl ask for?

A better time than I had the other night, for one thing. Hades' Kitchen remains a dream, since apparently the list doesn't include a bunch of second-rate cabana boys from Ohio who think pawing the bouncer with a fifty would make up for their scuffed-up shoes and obvious fake IDs. Here I thought I was with a swift crowd. One look at the other girls these guys had scrounged up for the evening and I knew our next stop would be the 7-11 in Snowmass where we'd hold up the wall and pass around a couple of duecey-dueces. They didn't even *try* to get in somewhere else. Some Joe kept insisting he had three bottles of Dom in his room and we should just get wasted there. Considering I wasn't about to pull a train with the boys from Anonymous U, I decided to break the news to Brandon that I was jailbait. He didn't say a word as he walked me back to the hotel. He looked so cute pouting the way he did I felt kinda sorry for him. And kinda hot for him too. Oh well.

Tomorrow we go home, and I'm not so sure that's a bad thing. I actually miss my bed and my room and just calling Penelope at any hour of the day and gabbing. And you know what, I even miss school. Sorta. Ugh, I'm such a dork!

# PART TWO
## SPRING 2000

# 1. MANDELA

The streaky orange sirens of double-parked ambulances. Soot grey delivery trucks careening to avoid potholes, multi-hued bodegas, whiskey brown liquor stores, the khaki competence of Korean dry cleaners: this was the palette of his neighborhood.

He was beginning his journey from the apartment to the Guggenheim.

She wasn't serious. It was all about intimidation. Like daughter, like mother. Arianna was well-versed in intimidation. She had mopped the floor with his arguments in the affirmative-action debate. And then he'd made a *joke*, for Christ's sake. He made a joke, and Arianna went running to Mommy to protect her.

Ash-faced Chinese delivery guys on wobbly bicycles reeking of scallions. Patriotic blue Duane Reade fliers advertising discounts on pink Herbal Essence family-size conditioners. Newsstands hawking glossy covers, *Juggs* alongside *Architectural Digest*. Lotto tickets, the fire-engine red of our dreams. Hey, you never know.

How odd their first encounter had been: the heady scent of Mercedes leather, the woman sweating as she tried to hide nerves behind her Gucci sunglasses. She was offering him money! And not just new Adidas money. She wanted him to come up with a figure. *You do the math,* she'd said.

The East 90's: yet another neighborhood in progress. Soon, he imagined, a multiplex. Soon, panini boutiques mingling with Popeye's fried chicken. Soon, a hip new nickname, the product of a resourceful real estate agent with irises shaped like dollar signs. South of East Harlem? SeHa.

It took one titanic set of balls to do what she did. Didn't she realize how crazy the whole thing sounded? No, she wasn't crazy. She was calculating. She wanted to scare him. And then she called him *at home.* To set up a meeting. At 4 o'clock, when no one else was likely to answer the phone.

The homeless: transparent. Conspicuously ignored, along with the headphone addicted Mexicans pushing fliers advertising discounted Italian leather jackets. He always takes one. It's their job.

Cardboard living. Some have signs. *I'm trying to raise $1.2 million.* Some have jobs, collecting aluminum cans. Some have dogs and cats, with just the right amount of desperation in their eyes. He gives when he can.

Banjo wielding optimists keep their dreams alive with songs.

She thought she was calling his bluff? *Lady, I'm about to call yours.* He had come up with a figure all right, and it was a doozy. He was going to savor the look on her face when he said it. See her lips quiver. He had earned the right to see at least that.

Lexington Avenue, the Great Divide. Ninety-sixth street, another divide. East of Lexington, North of Ninety-sixth, there were actual middle-class people in New York. People without cell phones or trophy dogs, like Yorkies or Pomeranians. Normal people. Mutts.

And yet, the way she had looked at him when he said he liked to paint. Like he had come upon the secret password, unlocked the door to her psyche. A crack in the Faberge egg. For a moment, she lost track of herself; she was about to get into a serious discussion about neo-expressionism. The new Richter exhibit had just arrived at the Guggenheim. He wondered if she wanted to see it. He could suggest it. Take the sting out of his request. Make the whole thing seem more reasonable.

Traffic cops affixing tickets to windshields in have-a-nice-day orange envelopes. The asphyxiating tang of shish kebab mixing in with the sweltering steam rising through sidewalk grills. De-Kooning's women are everywhere. A gallery of Lucian Freud's greatest hits, the city air engraving reality like pockmarks into their weathered New York faces.

And then: the tree-lined impressionism between Lexington and Park. Brass-knobbed townhouses. Doormen yawning the hours away. The consulates of esoteric foreign countries. Madison Avenue. Clean, precise. Like Mondrian's lines. Things make perfect sense on Madison Avenue. Boutiques. Dog grooming parlors. Bistros serving bouillabaisse in baccarat bowls.

Because there are no gates in New York, the masses are not inspired to revolt. A welfare mother can live less than twenty blocks away, but she'll still walk down Park Avenue blissful and calm, fully aware that upstairs, behind Ming Dynasty silk screens on hand-stuffed ostrich featherbeds covered with silk sheets, is a lady who has just spent *her* annual salary on a dress for a cocktail party.

What if she agreed to give him the money? Would he take it? What would he do with it? Hide it in a box with his brushes? He couldn't tell his parents. Couldn't pick up the bill for college like they'd just gone for dinner at Uno's. *I'll get that, Dad.* So what was the point?

It was weird. He really was curious to see her again.

She was standing by the doors when he approached: El Greco tall, her sunglasses resting on top of her head. She had a salon blonde perm, a sharp nose, a Modigliani neck. Her skin was seashell smooth and just as white. Her body refused to admit she had a teenage daughter. She wore expensive clothes that were meant to look casual and clutched a designer bag under her arm.

Her face said *I'm prepared for anything.* It was the same face from the car, an icy indifference meant to signify resolve.

"You're ten minutes late," she said, looking at her watch.

"I'm sorry," he said. "I don't have a watch."

She returned the sunglasses to her face. He noticed that even as she spoke to him, she kept a comfortable distance.

"So how was Aspen?" he asked.

"Invigorating. I'm not sure where to do this. Should we find a bench somewhere?"

"I was thinking we'd go inside. There's a Gerhard Richter exhibit going on."

She raised an eyebrow. "You want to see Gerhard Richter. With me."

"Well, I was going to go anyway, but if you don't want to..."

"Right," she said. "The coffee shop then. You can see the exhibit when we're done."

"Would you like a latte or something?" she asked him, once inside the shop.

"I'm good," he said.

He listened as her heels took her over to the counter, heard her fussily order a double espresso, with the formality that rich people mistook for civility. She returned, sat the coffee down in front of her, the purse to her side. She kept her sunglasses on.

"So," she said. "It's pointless to pretend this isn't awkward. Let's just acknowledge that it is and move on from there. I'm ready to hear your proposal."

So she was feeling awkward. "Ok," he said. He'd gone over this moment in his mind all day. "I want you to know that you were right. I was—still am—seriously considering Princeton as my top school."

"I see," she said. "Go on."

"I thought pretty hard about what it would take to strike it off my list. I realized you were making a serious offer and I wanted to come back with a serious response."

She stared, waiting for him to continue.

"OK. So the number I came up with was forty thousand dollars."

God, he couldn't believe he was going through with it. He watched her as her eyebrows crimped and her mouth seemed to stiffen. She pushed herself away from the table, crossed one leg over the other and took a long sip of her espresso. Smart choice, to keep the sunglasses on. To move in slow, deliberate gestures. He couldn't tell what she was thinking. When she finally spoke, the words came out more tenderly than he'd expected.

"I wasn't prepared for that figure," she said.

"I think it's reasonable," he said. "Considering what you're asking me to do."

"It's a tremendous amount of money."

"It would be tremendous for me to give up Princeton."

*How did I just say that without laughing?*

She took off her sunglasses. A locomotive was speeding out of control in her eyes. Here he thought she was hiding a vulnerability. Her stare pierced through him, seized him. He felt a tingle in his groin. "I'm prepared to pay you half that," she said.

*Fuck. She's going to give me twenty thousand dollars.* "Those four years will be very expensive."

"You'll get a scholarship anywhere you go," she said.

"That's not true," he said, a bit wobbly.

"It might be. You'll be wooed by so many schools. Besides, if you didn't want the money, you wouldn't be here."

He was losing the upper hand. It was hard to maintain cool after hearing her offer. Was he supposed to refuse and storm out? No. He had to stay cool. "I don't think that's the point."

"You went high," she said. "Knowing that I would negotiate."

"I'm going to have to think about it."

"The payments will be made in installments, the bulk of which will be issued after the application deadline. I assume you'd prefer cash?"

"I guess. I mean...I don't know. We're not done here."

"We're not?" she said. "I think we are. I'll call you next week to set up a meeting for the first payment." Like a gecko, she had snapped out her forked tongue and swallowed the discussion whole. Resistance was futile.

She got up from the table and extended her hand. "So we have a deal?"

If she said they had a deal, so be it. *Twenty thousand dollars!* He got up and shook her hand, and they began to walk up the stairs. "Can I ask you a question? Because it's been gnawing at me since you first approached me."

"I had a feeling you'd be curious."

"What?"

"The answer to your question: I had a feeling you'd be curious. To see how things would go."

"But you couldn't know. You can't *know* I won't say anything to my parents or Mrs. Piper or anyone else for that matter."

She stopped and turned to him. "I don't *know* what you're going to do, Mandela. I only know that Arianna wants to go to Princeton, and I will do what it takes to remove any obstacle in her way. You are one obstacle. So I had to try something. Is it a risk? Of course. But you *are* curious. I'm not wrong about that."

"Some people might think you're taking advantage of me with money. Buying something for your daughter that she should earn for herself."

"Ha! Arianna has earned the right to *any* school, all by herself. Even you know that. As for the money." She paused, shaking her head, as if stricken by something that was making her laugh and cringe. "By the '70's most of the Jews had long left the Lower East Side for Long Island or Westchester. But I remained there, with my family. So the rich white bitch tag won't stick to me. I have peasant blood running through my veins."

He wasn't going to touch that one. Not yet. They headed towards the entrance doors. He paused. Realizing that he had stopped, she turned around.

"You should come inside." He nodded towards the galleries.

She laughed. "You're serious about Gerhard Richter."

"That's why I wanted to meet here."

"Intriguing." She walked toward him. "I enjoy how he's tweaked with abstract expressionism."

"His photographic simulations? They remind me of dreams. Like the second after you wake up, how it's hard to sometimes recognize where you are, because you still see these images in your mind. That's how I picture it."

"I saw a couple of those at the Art Institute of Chicago. They gave me the chills."

They stood there, nodding at each other for a few seconds.

"Well, enjoy yourself," she said.

"C'mon. You look like you need a distraction. Besides, you already paid."

What was surprising was that she hesitated.

"I really should go," she said, finally. "I have a million things to take care of."

"Maybe next time," he said, smiling.

"Maybe." She smiled back. But then the smile left her face, and she turned away from him, heading out the door.

This was the bizarre thing. He should have despised her, scoffed at her arrogance, and dismissed her pathetic attempt to steamroller him with her money. He should have gone out and told all those nannies strolling past the Park Avenue high rises that it wasn't fair for them to take this lying down. But this was New York, and in New York everyone was painfully democratic about wealth. Everyone was OK with everyone else making a buck.

But it wasn't really about the money, was it. It wasn't about Princeton, or Arianna. It wasn't about blackmail, or bribery, or right versus wrong.

It was about Gerhard Richter and the Art Institute of Chicago.

It was about that Modigliani neck. Those shifting eyes.

*You are curious,* she had said. *I'm not wrong about that.*

Oh no, she wasn't wrong about that.

## 2. LEGION

He'd never fucked a man before. For the handful of guys he'd messed with, jerking off and a blowjob were good enough. A couple of his older tricks had tried to coax him into giving up his ass, but he just wasn't interested. It wasn't the thought of the pain; he knew there'd be pleasure beyond it. He just didn't want to *need* it. Have that kind of pleasure infect him, the lust spotting his eyes like cataracts blurring his vision.

Randall had rolled the condom on him. The suddenness of what was about to happen made his dick very hard, even though he was filled with dread. They started on their sides; Randall said it'd be easiest to enter that way. Randall took charge of the lube, of grabbing onto his shaft and guiding it in. He was relieved to surrender the responsibility to someone else. He watched Randall's face tighten those first few seconds. When he penetrated, it felt squishy and slippery, like entering a pool of moisturizer. He had to concentrate hard to stop himself from cumming. Soon they changed positions, and Randall was riding on top. He'd thrust, first steady and slow, then faster, watching Randall's face for approval. Randall looked down at him and he saw it then, that need, possessing the man's face—this ravenous, desperate need. The girls he'd been with looked pained and uncomfortable. This was different. He couldn't believe he was the cause of such ecstasy. It made him want to push harder. Soon it was unbearable. Within minutes he couldn't contain it, and he released himself. Randall jumped when he sensed it, his eyes widening, his mouth starting to quiver, his grip tight like a falcon's talons on Legion's shoulders, and then, pellets of cum, falling onto his chest.

So this was what it was all about. He knew then that things wouldn't be the same between them. They'd never be satisfied with anything less.

Lying in Randall's bed, he thought about the past few months, and it made him feel itchy and tender. Randall smiled at him with such profound certainty. The problem with this smile, even if there was something pleasant about being on its receiving end, was that this wasn't the bargain they had struck. The lessons had become the side dishes to the main course of their sex. He simply wasn't making progress. The SAT was three months away, and on his last practice test he'd gotten a 1240. He knew he couldn't jump 250 points overnight. But could he really do it in a few months? He wanted to believe that Randall took his ambitions seriously. But he wasn't so sure.

Concentrating on Randall's face, it hit him. Of course. The guy looked *crazy* young. Like a teenager, with his ruddy skin, his eager eyes. Nobody would ever think he was twenty-eight. No way. So why not have Randall take the test for him?

It wasn't that far-fetched. Kids did it all the time, got some crafty opportunist, usually some Asian brainiac looking to lower his college loans by customizing a 1500 for the geometry challenged but financially cushy set. It was a *business,* for God's sake. Nothing more than that. Problem was, the going rate for that kind of job had to be at least five thousand dollars, and that was money he just didn't have.

So why *not* Randall? Put him in the right clothes, spike up his hair—who the hell would know? Randall could pull an *exact* 1500 if he wanted to. It was a brilliant idea.

"Someone just had a happy thought."

Legion shifted his eyes to Randall's amused mug. "What?"

"You suddenly have this goofy smile on your face."

"Do I?" He kissed Randall on the cheek. He wondered what it would take to convince him of the soundness of his plan. "Randall?"

"Yes, Dolphin?"

This was his new nickname. Randall said his skin reminded him of a dolphin's, because it was so smooth, so pleasingly cool and moist. Randall told him that he got hard just thinking about his skin.

He removed the smile from his face. "I'm worried."

"Is it your test tomorrow? I told you I don't remember shit about physics."

"About the SAT. But I think I know a way for me to stop worrying."

"Uh, study harder, maybe? Do what I tell you to do?"

"It's not working. At some point we have to start being honest."

"Leeg." Randall sat up from the bed and ran his hand through the back of Legion's hair. "Sweetie, you're making progress. Now if you want to make more progress, you'll have to step it up a little."

He lifted himself out of the bed. This wasn't the right answer. He found his underwear on the floor and hastily began to put it on. "Listen, I'm working damn hard and I'm pretty much at my saturation point. I can step it up and I still won't break 1300."

"Give it time." Randall stared anxiously as he fumbled for his clothes. "Where are you going?"

"We need to consider a different route." He looked at the floor as he spoke. The longer he avoided Randall's gaze, the more the man would understand how serious he was. Once his shoes were on, he left the bedroom. Randall jumped out of bed to pursue him.

"Christ, Legion, what's going on? Will you look at me?"

He did, finally. But he wouldn't budge. "I gotta jet."

Randall looked stricken. "All of a sudden, in the middle of a conversation?"

"I don't want to get into it now."

"Get into *what*? Two minutes ago everything was fine and now you've gone schizo on me." Randall reached for his hands. "Dolphin, we'll make it work. Trust me."

"There's only one way it'll work," he said. "I need you to take the test for me."

Randall let go of his hands. His face scrunched up like he had just bit into some battery acid. "Excuse me?"

"You heard me."

"That's insane."

"Not insane. Brilliant."

"I'm almost thirty!"

"You look eighteen. You know that."

"Come on." Randall smirked. "You're not serious."

"I couldn't be more serious. People do it all the time."

"I'm an *SAT tutor*, Legion. How fucking stupid would it be for me to take that kind of risk?"

"I don't know, Randall, maybe as stupid as sleeping with one of your students?"

It hadn't come out the way he wanted it to. Randall's face turned white as a sheet.

"So that's how it is."

"I'm sorry," Legion said. "I didn't mean it that way."

"So you're threatening me, is that it?"

"Fuck." He was blowing it. Why the fuck would Randall think it was a good idea? Of course he'd think it was crazy. He had revealed his cards too early. He needed to get out of there before things got worse. He headed to the door, but Randall beat him to it, blocking his exit with two outstretched arms.

"Listen, I'm sorry." He tried to say it calmly. "I mean it. I gotta go."

"So where does this leave us?"

"I don't know. Maybe we need some time off. To think things over."

"What do you want me to think over? Is this like, a fucking ultimatum?"

"Could you please get out of my way?"

"That's it. You're just going to walk out."

"No." Christ, everything was turning to shit. He had lit one of Randall's fuses and now the guy was bursting with a fireworks of melodrama. "It's not like that. Fuck. I just need to clear my head."

"Dolphin, please…"

He looked up at Randall's wounded face. And he realized that he understood this desperation, because he too felt desperate. He needed to explain that to Randall. So he grabbed Randall's head and with great force shoved his tongue down the man's throat. All would express itself this way: his need, his frustration, his anger. He wasn't doing a good enough job with words.

It was an angry kiss. Violence shape-shifting into passion. He could sense Randall clinging to it, trying to make sense of it. Then he tore himself free as swiftly as he had started. He stared hard at Randall. Harder than he'd ever stared at anyone.

"It's not that I want to get into Harvard. It's that I *have* to. I fucking have to. That's what you need to think about."

He untangled himself from their embrace. Randall said nothing. The man reached out for his hands but Legion would not allow him to take hold. This time, when he grabbed the door knob, Randall stood out of his way.

"Will I see you later this week?" Randall asked.

He didn't bother to respond. Down the stairs he went, sensing Randall's hopeless gaze on his neck at every moment. He thought: it's hard when you think things are going well to have the rug pulled out from under you. He knew the feeling well. Lucinda had betrayed him the same way, made him believe the good times would never end.

He didn't hate Randall. He didn't want to teach anyone any lessons either. He didn't know if the man would agree to his plan, tell him to fuck off or what. But he could make an educated guess, the kind you're supposed to make on these standardized tests.

The world was all about give and take, and fuck it, he needed to start taking.

Randall just happened to be the guy giving.

## 3. GABRIELLE

Two weeks of crippling headaches. Without warning, they had seized the back of her neck and wrapped around the sides of her skull like strangling vine around a tree. First, in the bathroom at Fekkai. Then in Saks, on the elevator. And now, in her bedroom. She closed her eyes and rapidly shook her head. She was going to will it away by whatever means necessary.

*Stress. Stress. Stressssssssssss.*

What was she supposed to do, confess to Dr. Carl? Useless. He'd just want to suck more hours out of her and prescribe more pills—Percocet that shriveled her lips, Zoloft that jaundiced her skin, Xanax that gassed her intestines. Ambien to make her forget all the side effects. She was under an *enormous* amount of pressure. Patience was in order. Eventually the headache would tire of her, find someone less headstrong to plague—she simply had no *time* for a nervous breakdown.

Two days before she had taken out five hundred dollars, another five earlier that afternoon. She was going to say nothing. If Morty bought it up, there were a million reasons she could come up with. If push came to shove, she'd blame it on the help. *I didn't want to upset you, Morty. Marisol's mother in Guatemala? Something pancreatic.*

Placing the bills into a sturdy white envelope, she suddenly recalled her father, and his curious habit of stashing small amounts of money in envelopes and taping them underneath chairs, behind appliances, inside encyclopedia volumes. *For emergencies,* he'd proclaim. Nine years old, she had enjoyed trailing him around the house, making a game out of picking the hiding spots, much like the hiding of the *afikomen* at the Passover Seder. Her mother had not been amused. *Nincompoop,* she'd scream. *Put the money in a bank where it can earn interest. I don't trust banks,* he'd tell her. *Instead I should trust your memory?* Selma responded. But her father never lost a single one.

She zipped the envelope up in her purse. Earlier she had called Mandela to set up an appointment, her fingers slipping on the keypad as she dialed. Their previous encounter had gone reasonably well, even if the gold digger had the gall to ask for forty thousand dollars. His serenity was so convincing. It was positively *alien,* the way he swallowed everything with his eyes. What did he see when he looked at her? Was he several steps ahead in this game of chess they were playing? And then he invited her to join him for the exhibit! *A little art with my extortion, thank you.* Like it would be dimly appropriate, host and parasite, mother and someone else's teenage son, strolling up the corkscrew ramps of the Guggenheim, scrutinizing Richter's abstractions and each other's comments. Ridiculous!

*You want to meet in Soho? There's the Guggenheim on Broadway.*

Was this his idea of a joke? All because she indulged him with a two minute chat about art, suddenly they'd have weekly play dates at galleries about town? Still, downtown would be better. There'd be less chance of running into anyone. Plus she had never visited the Guggenheim in Soho. She wasn't sure why she agreed, but she did.

Gabrielle searched her closet for something to change into. Her mother was coming over for Friday night dinner, and Selma would not tolerate slacks. She laid out an assortment of cheerful blouses and skirts on the bed.

"Knock, knock."

Gabrielle whipped around. Arianna stood in the doorway in sweats and a t-shirt.

"Grandma will be here any minute," she said.

Her daughter sat down on the bed. A prize-winning pout occupied her face.

"You spoke to Gluckman today."

Arianna nodded her head.

"And?"

"And…are you alright, Mother? You look unwell."

"I'm fine. And?"

"And he was not convinced by the logic of my argument."

"Really?" Gabrielle picked up a blouse, held it against her frame in front of the mirror. "Let's see if I can convince him of the logic of mine."

They had returned from Aspen to Gluckman's B+ on Arianna's report card, the solitary dandelion in an otherwise immaculate poppy field of A's. She had advised Arianna to politely inquire, but much as she expected, Gluckman liked his weeds; he thought they added character to the garden. She'd have to extricate this one herself.

"What about your session with Randall?"

"Whatever. He's beginning to bore me."

Gabrielle laughed. "He's your tutor, Arianna. Don't fault him for doing his job."

"I suppose. You know, I was thinking. There is the possibility that they'll let us both in. Me and Mandela."

Gabrielle placed an orange silk blouse up to her chest. She felt a sudden jolt, hearing the boy's name out loud. She looked blankly into the mirror. "Yes," she said. "There's also the possibility he won't even apply."

"Yeah, well. I can't exactly count on that."

She put the blouse down on the bed, the headache's seeds once again sprouting in her head. Secrets made her tense. What was she supposed to say, *Oh my dear, you most certainly can count on that*? She couldn't. She wouldn't. "Don't think about him. Focus on yourself. You *will* get in, Arianna. Believe it. You're everything they want. You've earned the right to be there."

"Holy hell, where are the cameras? You're having an Oscar moment."

She gave Arianna a hug to tease her further. "Sweetheart, no leaving tonight before her pound cake or Grandma will be offended. And leave me a number. Then I'll know you won't *accidentally* turn off your cell and have me worry myself sick because then, God forbid, I might have to use that number and embarrass you in front of your friends."

Arianna rolled her eyes. "One day I'll do something worthy of these suspicions." She strutted out of the room. Once the Selma-appropriate uniform had been found, Gabrielle went downstairs to check on dinner. She scrutinized the carefully orchestrated table, trying to imagine what her mother would find fault with.

Well, there was always the menu. The Upper West's finest matzo ball soup notwithstanding, Selma was bound to expound on the glory days in Estonia and the painfully intricate Sabbath dinners her mother would prepare. One could only nod along and smile.

Ten minutes later, Morty and Selma arrived together. Her mother's cheeks carried the rosy afterglow of one of Morty's jackpot zingers.

"I saw this knockout in the elevator," Morty said. "And I couldn't resist inviting her to dinner. You don't mind?"

"Morty Levy, you are incorrigible!" Selma slapped her son-in-law on the arm. Reflexively, she extended her left cheek for Gabrielle to kiss, without eye contact. That would come later, in a full body once-over.

"You look well, Mother," Gabrielle said.

"Where's my granddaughter? Arianna!" Selma bellowed. "*Safta's* here, *mamele*."

"You alright?" Morty tilted his head after he embraced her. "You look pale."

"I'm perfectly fine," Gabrielle said.

"She always looks pale," Selma said. "And that yellow only makes it worse."

Arianna ran down the stairs. Granddaughter and grandmother greeted each other like long-lost friends on *Maury Povich*. Then Arianna traded another five-star hug with her Daddy. Gabrielle stood silent as her mother and husband fished information from their darling progeny about her conquests of the week—things Arianna had already relayed to her as soon as she got home.

Usually this recap soothed her. But at that moment the migraine would allow her no such joy. The longer Arianna spoke the more acute her pain became, the words reverberating like distant echoes in her ears.

Distressed, she excused herself and went to the kitchen. Tatiana looked up briefly from dressing the veal. There was nothing for her to do there; the servants would see to everything. But she couldn't go back, not yet. Just a second to calm herself down. Just a few deep breaths. Her mother's titters resonated from the living room. She looked over at the door; it seemed so far away. She was isolating herself in her own kitchen, afraid of her own shadow. *Stop it,* she told herself. *There's nothing wrong with what you're doing.* Bracing herself, she returned to the dining room.

After an impromptu prayer was recited, the family dug in. Conversation around the dinner table followed its familiar pattern: Selma offering tidbits of gossip, Morty egging her on approvingly, Arianna reciting tales of frustration and joy at glorious Valhalla High with the unbridled enthusiasm of her years. She tried to remain in the moment, but her thoughts kept returning to Mandela Robinson.

Painting! Who'd want to be a painter nowadays? The brush and the canvas were far too confining for today's crop of aspiring artists. She had tried her hand at it when she was younger. Even then artists had all but given up the canvas in favor of more cutting edge forms of art: environmental, performance, body. But none of these interested her. Even the lowbrow populism of Sixties Pop Art seemed too conceptual to her. She wanted to look at a piece of work and have a visceral reaction to it, not just one of puzzling indifference. For this she had to hark back to the more expressionistic painters, to a time before art became an interdisciplinary study and all meaning had been sucked out by those black-hole deconstructionist theories.

Painting! How positively quaint. And a realist no less! It was practically an invitation for ridicule nowadays. It was *radical*.

"Sweetheart, are you listening?" Morty was looking at her with concern.

"Sorry, what?" she answered.

"Earth to Gabrielle." Selma sighed. "Your husband twice asked you a question."

"Mother, tell Daddy you're taking me to Short Hills next Sunday," Arianna said.

"Just go this Sunday," Morty said. "Your mother and I have a function that day."

"Sorry, but no. This Sunday I'm hitting the Met. Some project for my art class."

"Really?" Gabrielle said, a bit too enthusiastically. "What kind of project?"

"Some comparative study. I have to find a modernist and post-modernist work and show how each reflects the ideas of their movement or something."

"Fascinating." Gabrielle clapped her hands together. "I'll join you. Why don't we go to the Guggenheim instead?"

Arianna looked askance. "I'm going with Penelope, Mom. Besides, the Guggenheim is claustrophobic. I may not find what I need."

"Of course you would," Gabrielle said. "You could use Richter as example for both modernism and post modernism."

"Who?"

"Gerhard Richter. He has a retrospective at the Guggenheim. He's an abstract expressionist. I could help you. I know quite a bit about all that."

Selma chuckled. "Gaby, please. Spare your daughter the trip down memory lane and let her enjoy herself with her friends."

"Fine." Gabrielle glared at her mother. "In any case, I'm going Sunday. Perhaps you'd care to join me?"

"Gerhard?" Selma sneered. "Sounds German. I don't need to look at Germans expressing themselves. They've expressed themselves enough this century. Besides, I have no patience for museums."

"Alone it is then." Gabrielle looked at Morty. "Unless my husband would like to come?"

"Of course, dear," Morty said. "Afterwards we'll go to a Knicks game together."

Selma laughed. Gabrielle bit her lip and looked down at her plate. How stupid she was to pass around such an invitation, allowing them to make her feel ridiculous.

Not fifteen minutes later, Arianna excused herself, and Selma announced she was ready to get home. Marisol helped Selma put on her coat, and Morty turned to his wife. "I'm stopping by Saul's after I take her home. He wants to go over a few things. I'll be home by midnight."

Gabrielle nodded. What would be the point of protesting? If he stayed home he'd just watch the game downstairs anyway, while she holed herself up in the bedroom, fine-tuning next week's to-do lists with that morning's Tivo-ed *Martha Stewart* serving as background noise.

She kissed her mother goodbye and sat down on the couch, allowing herself a moment's repose for the first time that day. Whatever happened to her weekends? She seemed to remember having more free time, and now every minute was being plucked from her like feathers from a Perdue chicken. She had to speak with Gluckman at some point. She had to research Arianna's summer acting seminar, make sure these European programs were well-supervised, not simply bacchanalian retreats for the offspring of free-spending Americans. She had to take Selma to lunch, stop by the dry cleaners, run dietary errands for Morty.

But who was she kidding? She didn't have a full-time job. She could work around all these things. So why did she feel so antsy? She needed to see the Richter exhibit. What if it was closing soon? Maybe she'd go on Tuesday. Right before she met Mandela. She could go, and then they'd have something to talk about...

"Is there anything else I can get you, Mrs. Levy?"

She opened her eyes. Marisol stood in her jeans jacket, a floppy bag resting on her shoulder. How long had she been sitting there?

"No, Marisol. Goodnight. See you on Monday."

Marisol smiled and headed for the door. Gabrielle looked over her shoulder. The table had been thoroughly cleared; she had blacked out for a good while. Something else she wouldn't discuss with Dr. Carl. Still, the silence was refreshing. The space others occupied in her life was overwhelming.

She decided to take a long bath. Cleanse the day off her skin. She headed upstairs, ran the water in the tub, tossed in her favorite salts. She shucked off her clothes, lit a vanilla candle, and tested the water with her big toe before immersing herself. Slowly the relief settled in. How liberating it was to hear nothing, feel nothing, become nothing.

She drifted, letting the memories wash over her. Late nights at Kiev, 1981. A year when she still owned the right to each and every day, where she didn't bother with thoughts of a future. She and her friends were just living, breathing in the heady fumes of downtown Manhattan, expressing their minds over borscht and blintzes, improvising rambling poems on the spot.

Then came the whispers of college. Night school, of course. Selma had forbid her from working with her father in the pickle store. *Who on earth will marry a girl who sells pickles?* She begged Gabrielle to be a secretary, dreaming of a tinted midtown highrise for her daughter, where up-and-coming accountants with robust pension plans were eager to meet the Slavic girl of their dreams—someone with a winsome smile, sexy but not too independent, smart but not too feminist, someone who made his balls tingle but would also pass his mother's white glove inspection. Someone Jewish, for God's sake, of course that. But Gabrielle refused. And held her ground, at least for a while. Until Morty.

Morty, and her new, uptown life.

Gabrielle opened her eyes. The migraine was even worse now, creating halos around the track lights above the mirror. She grabbed her face into her palms and squeezed, hard.

"Why don't you leave me alone like everyone else?" she demanded.

That there would be no answer infuriated her. What had Mandela said about the seconds after you awaken, something about the interim images, how they're often more vivid than reality? Ha! Dreams were nothing but the unfortunate by-products of sleep. Memories be damned, she was quite comfortable with reality, and she was going to force that reality back into focus. There'd be no time to entertain these strangers knocking at her door. She could handle a migraine, and the sudden nostalgia for a time she thought she'd not only forgotten but dismissed. She could handle the secrets, and Mandela Robinson with his dancing eyes, mocking her with his kindness. People were counting on her. She had responsibilities. She would take care of everything, just as she always did.

# 4. EXCERPTS FROM ARIANNA LEVY'S JOURNALS

February 12th

Elections are approaching. I remain in limbo over whether or not to run for class president. If it were anything more than a popularity contest—if people voted based on who they thought would actually make a difference—I'd be a shoo in. But tell that to the brotherhood of jocks who secretly conspire to shut out any girl's chances of winning. Sigh. If I settled for second best I'd likely run away with it. But honestly what's the purpose of a VP? First runner up at the Miss America pageant I am not.

In any event I've got to stop dabbling in after school activities like they're free samples at Häggen Dazs. I need to learn how to relax. The thing is—and I hate to admit it—I'm beginning to feel the need for a boyfriend. I know I don't have the time for a full-on romance, but I'm so sick of this 'chill' bullshit that everybody's doing these days. Fuck that! It's not like I'm asking for a ring or a varsity jacket. Am I such a retro dweeb because I want a daily late-night phone call, a note slipped into my locker and my very own tree in Central Park where my sweetheart has carved our initials inside a crooked but well-meaning heart?

At least I'm not the only one with love life problems. The last time Randall came over he looked like someone had just ran over his dog. His clothes had that slept-in look and his beard was several days past scruffy, well into I-just-don't-give-a-shit mode. You know that yellow-green color of mayonnaise gone rancid? It's hard to concentrate on surface areas with someone sitting beside you looking like the poster child for vomit.

So here I am doing level three analogies when suddenly Randall's cell chimes. You should have seen him jump for it, like it was Publisher's Clearinghouse, ready with his grand prize check. Not only does he *not* shut it off, he actually mumbles some undercooked excuse and answers it! Then, for the next thirty seconds, it's Tom Buchanan on the phone with his mistress and I'm Daisy in the boudoir. Obviously *something's* up, especially when he gets off the phone looking even more distraught. Concerned, I decide that perhaps a little feminine concern might be just what the doctor ordered. (That, and some Paxil, probably.)

"So," I say, twirling my pen between my fingers. "Was that your girlfriend?"

No answer.

"Boyfriend?" I offer instead, without batting an eyelash.

He doesn't look at me.

"Do you have one?" I ask, not specifying which.

At some point during our Aspen fiasco, I began to suspect Randall was gay. Why would Mother, who would buy a global positioning system to track me down if she could, suddenly turn all jolly whenever she knew I was with Randall? Mother would be suspicious of a castrated rabbi; only gay men gain her gleeful trust.

"No," he said. "I don't have a girlfriend. Or a boyfriend."

"Do you wanna talk about it?"

He sighed. "You have four minutes to finish the exercise, Arianna."

"I can be very sympathetic, you know."

"There's nothing to talk about."

"Whoever this person is, he's not worth the pain you're putting yourself through."

He didn't say anything, just kept looking at his watch. Which was so unnecessary. I mean, why the whole secrecy thing? If some guy had dumped him for a Brazilian tennis instructor, hell, I'd be all ears. I'm a great listener when I want to be. But first I have to get him to talk. And that just isn't happening.

February 23rd

Whatever weirdo disease that's been attacking Randall has now spread to Mother. They both keep insisting that nothing's wrong, which only makes it all the more obvious that something is. Mother can be a freak, but usually she's easy to read. Lately she's indecipherable. Plus she's skittish—I walk into a room and she jumps like a cornered zebra. When I ask her what's wrong she snarls and tells me to stop being so suspicious. Then she laughs and puts on this Stepford smile and tells me not to worry about her.

Talk about Schizo. It's like she's got her Do Not Pass Go Head Directly to Bellevue card. I caught her watching PBS in the den two days ago. My mother, watching *public television*. Some show on Jack Kerouac. She was *entranced*.

Clearly she's stressing about the whole college thing. I should have never brought up the whole Gluckman fiasco but it's not like I had a choice; she saw my report card. That's the way things are with mother; I don't tell her to intervene, she just does it anyway. And Gluckman may like to emit this Joe-Cool-toured-with-the-Dead vibe but deep down he's a total hardass; an 89 is a B+ and there's just no way around it. It's no secret he has a chip against overachievers. He's the kind of guy who rewards people for creative excuses for cutting his class, no doubt harking back to his high school days when he was the lazy smart ass who toked up on the roof every day and still pulled straight A's.

So two weeks ago he was blathering on about how today's music sucks and how we should all go to a Stones concert like he did the past weekend to see what real music was. He went on about how close to the stage he was, etc. Now get this, two periods later, Aimee Randolph who sits behind me in Jungian Psych tells me how she can't believe her parents had the balls to bitch her out over a bottle of Guinness they found in her room when just last weekend they came home from the Stones concert reeking of pot.

Understand, I told these details to my mother on separate occasions; only a mad scientist like her could manage to see the invisible lines connecting these two seemingly isolated statements. She has me get Aimee Randolph on the phone and ask her what kind of seats her parents had to the Stones' concert and Aimee's like "Duh, my parents know the owners of Giants Stadium, they had VIP passes" and so I say "Oh, I wonder if they bumped into Gluckman" and she's like, "Obviously, Arianna, since they got him his tickets in the first place?"

Bingo.

Mother paid a visit to Gluckman the very next day. She told me he hemmed and hawed, defending himself to the death. But Mother knew that didn't matter. Even the whiff of scandal was enough to turn Mr. Change the System into Mr. Scared Shitless. Looks like I have an A- in Calculus now. The whole thing's sort of shady, but since no one's getting hurt I'm not going to feel guilty about it. Still, much as I love Mother, I don't like to encourage this side of her. Sooner or later she needs to understand I can fight my own battles.

# 5. RANDALL

Motivational fliers, gold-starred performance progress charts, the jerky scribbles of someone's four year-old daughter: Randall sat inside CATPEE's inner sanctum, gawking at the riff-raff covering the walls. Cha-Cha and the new center director, one Roger McGee, had called him in. Within four days, due to a persistent bout of asthma, McGee was forever known as "Wheezy" at the office. Every time Randall heard it, George Jefferson instantly sprang into his mind.

The Plague had landed himself a cushy job with an upstart telecommunications company in Jersey and Cha-Cha quickly commandeered his desk before Wheezy knew any better. She sat behind it with a giddy sense of her own authority, even though she had been offered no raise, no promotion. She was going on about so many things:

"The latest batch of teacher evaluations came back and…"

"A couple of the newer recruits have expressed feeling disoriented after teacher training, and aren't sure…"

Randall was finding it hard to concentrate on what she was saying. Her head bobbed back and forth like a ventriloquist's dummy. If Cha-Cha's head were a jar, he wondered, how many marbles would it take to fill it up? 500? 1000?

"Mrs. Stein called and said you've shown up late the last two sessions in a row..."

And Wheezy. Sitting there with his hands crossed over his belly. And his hair! Apparently not too fond of the top of his head, it found refuge in the bushy areas around his ears. A man who should be selling lawn mowers to confused housewives at a strip mall outside of Columbus. He wore a saber tooth grin on his face and had a tendency to guffaw at only mildly amusing comments. He was even smiling now, when his face should have been saying *concerned*. Where did they find this bozo?

"Then we offered you two more SSHSAT classes at your ideal time slot and you flat out refused them!" Cha Cha's eyes fixed on him with wifely suspicion, as if she thought he was cheating on her with another test prep company.

Randall felt obliged to defend himself: "You stick me with two fourth-tier classes and expect me to sign up for more? Bless their hearts, but not a single one of those kids has a shot of getting in anywhere."

The Specialized Science High Schools Admissions Test: CAT-PEE's juiciest money maker, the cash cow of all cash cows. Thousands—tens of thousands—of students taking a class for schools that were going to reject at least 90% of them.

"You don't know that. Besides, the class will improve their process. They will feel more confident about future standardized tests."

"So you're saying when they *fail* they'll be more confident about standardized tests? At least let's be honest about the scoring process. Parents ask me about the cut off and I have to feed them the same bull about how it 'changes every year.'"

"It *does* change every year."

"Not by that much! No one in the 40th percentile is ever going to get in."

"We appreciate your concerns, Randall." All of a sudden, Wheezy was chiming in. "But certainly you're not suggesting we turn away students?"

Randall didn't respond. Isabel Sanford was running around in his head, yelling at Florence the maid, talking to the dopey English neighbor with the surfboard chin. What was his name again?

"Listen, Randall, you've been with us for a long time," Cha Cha said. "I know you've been frustrated lately. So promise not to tell and I'll share some tremendous top-secret news with you."

*Bentley.* That was his name. *Bentley.*

"We're starting an employee incentive program! A points system. The more points you rack up, the bigger your bonus…"

Why didn't he just say it: Sayonara, Cha Cha. Auf Wiedersehen, Wheezy.

"…since you've been with us for four years, you *automatically* get ten seniority points, which *guarantees* you a $200 bonus. That can go up to as much as …"

He should just bolt out, in the middle of Cha Cha's speech. Say nothing at all, and just waltz out.

Better yet, say one thing. Some total non-sequitur: *Garbanzo Beans*.

"Randall?"

"Garbanzo beans."

"Excuse me?"

"I'm sorry. The incentive plan. Sounds great. Really."

"Listen, Randall." Wheezy leaned in closer. The man looked ready to hug him. "I know this may sound like a load of new-guy horse dung but I'm all about building a strong bond with the teachers. So if there's something on your mind…"

Something on his mind? Wow. For two minutes he actually forgot.

"…and do my best to address them. Because I know how important you are to this company…"

*I have something on my mind, Wheezy. One of my students has stopped fucking me. He won't even take my calls!*

"I just hope we've made ourselves clear."

Now, now, don't worry. He's not a CATPEE student. No lawsuits, I promise.

"So if there isn't anything else…"

Just say it, Randall. Say it: *Hasta la vista*. The words swam up his throat, but the fear enzymes in his saliva would not let them escape. "I'm glad we had this talk," he offered, instead. "I apologize if I've been distracted. I assure you things will get back to normal."

Everyone got up to shake hands. Wheezy's mile-long smile was joined by Cha Cha's more cynical one in a half-hearted attempt to feign that progress was made. Her pursed lips betrayed her. They told Randall she wouldn't have this conversation again. There would be no next time.

He left the office. Christ, how had he let things slip this far? He was going to lose his job. He had to stop being so stupid.

Out of the building, into the damp February evening, the five degree wind-chill only adding to his misery. Not only did no one know about the phlegm congesting his heart, not only could he not talk about it, *do nothing* about it, not only that—he had to *pretend*, pretend to give a shit when Cha Cha did her patronizing two-step, when his mother carped about her lower back pain, when his friends—the few that remained—yammered on about their good-for-nothing lovers/boyfriends/husbands. *Who me? Oh, I'm fine. Thanks for asking.*

At what point does infatuation become obsession? When you start empathizing with Celine Dion songs? When Sabrina the Teenage Witch gets dumped by her boyfriend and you start to tear up? When the most mundane things start to take on a new significance? Take, for instance, the journey home to his hole-in-the-wall apartment:

The elevator down, Muzak version of Biggie's "Mo Money Mo Problems": Legion loves Biggie. Pass by the Foot Locker on Broadway, red New Balances in the window: Legion wears those.

Corner deli on Fourth Avenue advertising a special on persimmons: Legion had told him he was allergic to persimmons, that they made his face blow up like a balloon.

NYU dorms on Third Avenue: Don't get him started. The artless slouch of college boys, their sleepy banter and beginner's guide to stubble, thrasher tees hanging on their painfully young skin: All Legion.

Chinese take-out dive on Twelfth: The last time they ordered from Peking Garden, a cruel rain was falling, and the hapless delivery guy had tripped over his own shoelaces in the hall, causing their wonton soups to spill. Legion calmed the guy down and gave him a twenty from his wallet. *If we make him come back*, he said, *they'll take it out of his pay.*

The door to his building: The way the last few minutes they spent together kept replaying in his mind, but this time he says something different, and suddenly all is forgiven, and instead of his Dolphin walking out that door, the boy turns around and reaches into the cabinet for a box of Pop Tarts.

Legion's favorite: Chocolate Brownie. Raw, right out of the box.

How quickly his apartment had turned into a minefield of memories. Every nook held a hidden Uzi, ready to shoot him with rounds of nostalgia. He couldn't just sit at home again, allowing the placenta of *Nick at Nite* to feed him familiar one-liners. He had to do something. *Move on. You're twenty-eight years old, for God's sake, you're reasonably intelligent, you look great for your age...*

Legion's argument: he could pass for a teenager. Could he? With some hair gel and baggy jeans, maybe. Was that it, he secretly wanted to be a teenager again? Or was he just a victim of that unspoken tragedy of all gay men, desperate to consummate their first adolescent crush, searching for eighth grade Johnny in every guy they date? The thing was, no matter how crazy Legion's request was, he knew it came from an honest place. The boy was desperate to get into Harvard. But why? What kind of fucked up dynamic did he have at home? Did Ken abuse him? And where the hell was his mother?

*Why* was he still ruminating about this? It was over. Kaput. Finished. *Move on. Do something. Write.* Yes. He needed to sit down and write.

He turned on the computer. If he could just finish a project, then maybe he could save himself. But writer's block was a house guest with no return flight home. Everything he attempted was half-hearted and blurry. Everything seemed dishonest, except for his journals. Rereading his feverish words, the moment-by-moment dissections, made him laugh. But it also made him sad. There was no point in denying it. He was in love.

Maybe he could salvage something from this junk pile of emotions. The writing was overheated, but the swelter was convincing. It was sad to admit to such a prosaic truth, but his words had heart. He meant what he wrote, which lent the words a natural power.

Maybe he should dump everything. All the pretensions of his previous manuscripts, the cloying simulations of his favorite authors, the desperate yelps of chapters trying to do something fresh with the form. Dump it all, and start anew. A novel about the one thing no one could ever deny him: a novel about himself.

He'd leave nothing out. It could be therapeutic, actually, and a lot cheaper than a shrink. He'd throw in every sordid detail, every mortifying iota. Exorcise his demons by exorcising himself. Let the world see him for what he truly was.

But this saucy narrative would need a powerful second act, the surprise yet inevitable ending. Indecision and agony could only sustain so many pages. *Something* had to happen. Maybe, just maybe, he had to lead the life less traveled. Maybe he needed to find out what happened next, *experience* this story's end to know how to write it.

Did he really have that much to lose? He looked around his modest hovel searching for any sign that his life was progressing. *Give me a reason to say no.*

A menagerie of wasted opportunities glowered back at him in silence. He could bring an end to his misery with three life-changing words: *I'll do it.* One phone call. So that was it, then. If to nothing else, he had a responsibility to his art.

He picked up the phone.

## 6. MANDELA

Tyrese sat on the floor, a hodgepodge of clumsily folded papers encircling him, unable to make the perfect airplane. Sarafina looked on in gleefully skeptical silence.

He needed to be downtown. Instead he was pacing the apartment. He could not leave. Within two minutes of his absence, Sarafina would make a snarky comment about her brother's ineptness, and Tyrese would then savor the next few hours finding clever new ways to torture his sister. Sarafina would suffer an embolism from crying so hard.

Tyrese was eleven and Sarafina was five. For two hours every weekday they were his kids, two hours he could be out with friends or concentrating on his painting, instead of on Kraft cheese sandwiches, Lego towers, Barbie coloring books. Whenever he protested, his mother gave him that look: *I have a job, your dad has a job, and so do you.*

Normally, he does it. He sits on floors: in the foyer, where the coats droop on a plastic coat rack; in the sepia-toned living room, filled with lace doilies and the painfully arranged mementos of a widow. This dead room that moonlights as his bedroom. His parents had put in curtain rods to give him some privacy.

For the privilege of this apartment they had moved to New

York City a year ago. Had it been up to him, they would've never left Montclair, where they had a house—an ordinary house, but a house, nonetheless. But Aunt Mozelle had passed, and Aunt Mozelle had no children, and Aunt Mozelle had bequeathed her rent-controlled Upper East two bedroom to her favorite nephew. It was a steal. It was *Manhattan*. So what if the apartment was unbearably cramped for a family of five?

He needed to be downtown. Now. He had no time to watch his siblings, no time to look at the college brochures his parents had spent so much time amassing, no time to make the phone calls he'd promised to make to the galleries around town offering summer internships (he didn't want to work at a gallery, he wanted to *paint*), no time for homework (he'd do it on the subway), no time to think about his future.

The present was waiting: Gabrielle Levy, with her defiant stare and intimidating purse, the purse that held the samples of his bounty. He needed to be downtown. To see her again. Chat with her. He'd had so many imaginary conversations already. They could really get into it this time. She could help him. He could use some help with the female form, in more ways than one.

His parents wanted him to understand what a privilege it was, this life he had. They wanted him to understand the sacrifices they were making. He *knew* it was a sacrifice. He could see all the *sacrifice*. He just didn't get why they did it. Why Deidre and Joe Robinson had to work so much harder than everyone else he knew. What was the point of the degrees they hung so proudly on their walls? What could they show for all their hard work? Valhalla?

He didn't have to go to Valhalla. He didn't *want* to go there. He didn't like having to contend with the pixie-dusted boys and girls, the effortless skill they had at being rich and care-free and popular and well-adjusted. *That* was what fancy degrees were supposed to get you. *That* was what it meant to be living the good life.

He found an empty envelope in a pile of discarded mail, and scribbled two phone numbers on the back. Then he sat himself down beside his brother on the floor and picked out one of the more promising specimens.

"This one's not bad," he said. "But it's not even. You have to maintain symmetry."

"What's symmetry?"

"Balance. Before you fold things, line them up. Make sure the sides match."

Tyrese grabbed the paper and started refolding it. Mandela guided him with his hands, sharpening the folds, bending at the proper angles, chipping a piece off the back to make the plane more aerodynamic. *See, Mom and Dad, my skills can come in handy.*

His parents tolerated his painting. They'd say encouraged, but he could read between the lines. Sure, whenever he asked, they'd relinquish him their room and some time. He'd throw old burlap onto the floor, take out his brushes, set up his easel. For an hour he'd scrape off the sticky layers of his life and lose himself in the colors and lines.

But painting was not a career. Not the type of career the Robinsons wanted for their son. Painting meant their son was *well-rounded.* It added dimension to his life like shadowing added dimension to his portraits. Mandela was to join the Fast Track. Become Somebody. Make ancestors proud. Doctor Robinson. Mandela Robinson, Esquire. Never demand, only suggest—that was their way. But when you saw all the sacrifices being made for you, you knew that suggest really meant deliver.

How could he not deliver? He had stellar grades, had aced the PSAT. They'd showered him with praise that week, bragged to every relative from Raleigh to Riverside, had even invited his grandparents up from Jersey for a family dinner to Outback. But it was like the Triple Crown: Clear one race and the next only stared you in the face. There was no end to the expectations—you just had to keep going until you were put out to pasture. But what if he wasn't a thoroughbred? What if the ribbons didn't seem worth it?

He couldn't dwell on this anymore. He needed to be downtown.

A light bulb popped on in his mind. Mandela grabbed Tyrese's paper and raised it above his head. "You can't do anything yourself. You always need my help."

Tyrese frowned. He reached for the plane. "No I don't. Give it back!"

"Oh yeah? I bet if I left you here all by yourself you'd cry your eyes out."

"I would not!" Tyrese was furious. "Give me the plane, asswipe!"

"Asswipe?" Mandela stood up and put the plane behind his back. "Let's see who the asswipe is. Five dollars says when I get back Mom will tell me you cried like a baby."

The bribe worked its charm. Tyrese dropped his arms and his eyes turned gangster-hard. "Go on, Chump. You think I need you here?"

"OK, tough guy, we'll see." He picked the envelope off the table. "Just in case something happens, here's Ms. Walker's number and Mom's cell."

"The only thing happening is you'll be five dollars poorer when you get back."

"Alright," Mandela smiled. "You got it. So when did I leave?"

"Five minutes before Mom got home."

"And I went to the *library*. Got that? And you better be nice to your sister, Runt, because if she talks, you don't get a nickel." He turned to his sister. "Sarafina, your brother's going to be so nice to you for the next two hours you won't even stand it."

\*

Soho was noisy and flavorless, an urban strip mall of the usual suspects. Did New York really need another Banana Republic or Armani Exchange? Carbon-copy galleries plugging trendy minimalism to blend in with the custom-designed couch. How could any neighborhood consider itself hip with so many soft-serve chomping grandmas from Wisconsin strolling down its streets in Bermuda shorts and Harley Davidson tees?

He arrived early, pulling a New York hat trick, switching to a waiting express at Eighty-sixth and then back to another waiting local at Fourteenth. The syrupy smell of caramelized cashews invaded his head.

She'd thought he was joking when he suggested the Guggenheim downtown. He shuffled outside the entrance doors, wondering if he was. He'd really wanted to meet in the Lower East Side. He wondered if she ever went back there. Had she been part of the scene?

He could ask, but he wasn't sure how that would go over. Returning to your roots was like returning to the scene of a crime of which you were the victim — most wanted to forget that part of their life ever happened.

Still, he loved the Lower East Side. Not the northern parts bordering Houston, fast becoming more like Soho every day, but deep into its belly, East Broadway, Delancey and Essex, a neighborhood that time forgot, a place which went about its business indifferent to the fast and furious style wars being conducted about the rest of Manhattan. She *grew up* there. Sort of unexpected, but not if he thought about it; no one was more vulgar with money than the newly rich, no one better at selective amnesia. He wondered how she'd offer him his first payment: A wad of bills? An elegantly sealed envelope?

"Am I late?" she asked, stepping out of a cab. She had foregone the sunglasses. He studied her face: the jumpiness of her owlish-green eyes, the Slavic paleness of her skin, the nose of dissatisfaction, the taut lips more used to frowns than smiles. Hungry was the mood assigned to this face. Forever hungry for something not on the menu. It would be an interesting assignment, this face, if he were to take the challenge.

"No. I was early."

"Good for you. It's a lost art." She took a look around. "What an awful crowd. I was afraid I wouldn't find you. So. Dean and DeLuca? It's across the street."

"How about the museum? They also serve espresso."

She hesitated. "I've never been inside. I assumed it was one of those trendy bistro museums serving *soup de jour* works of art."

"True. But sometimes the soup de jour is good."

She smiled, ran a hand through her hair. She glanced around skittishly, like they were up on a roof and he had just passed her a joint. "Alright," she said. "Let's go."

The climate-controlled stillness of the museum enveloped him. When the crowds were thin like they were that day, the silence paid respect to the work hanging on the walls. It allowed them the space to think and react. But he didn't want to tour the collection in silence. Fine for the first room; they both needed to acclimate. But by the third room they came upon two Rothkos, and no one was neutral about Rothko. Still, she only nodded her head, reserving judgment. By the fifth room, a jumble of all things Eighties—Basquiat, Wojnarowicz, the occasional Haring—he was growing impatient. At the very least, he thought, she'd make a patronizing comment about Basquiat's talents. No dice.

In the last room he decided to test her timidity. Luckily, she seemed struck by two particular paintings juxtaposed on the wall, both from artists he'd never heard of. He read the title cards and looked over to her. She was biting her lower lip.

"Stop holding back. Say it."

She let out a tiny laugh. "It's striking. Seeing these two works side by side."

"Go on."

"Well...purposefully or not, they highlight a problem I have with the newer breed of artists. The one on the left I'd call theory without expression. It's totally detached, and that detachment is supposed to make you think about what it means beyond the physicality of paint on canvas. But I have no gut reaction to it. While this one," she pointed to the right, "is quite the opposite. He's all expression without theory. Or more to the point, his theory is muddled. I can make no sense of it. But I can tell right away if I enjoy it or not."

"You think he knows his theory is muddled?"

"He's unsure of what he wants to say, so he's saying many things, hoping they will gel with each other. But they don't. Yet I can still appreciate it. He's OK with—in fact he may want me to—look at his painting, but not see it."

"And the other guy wants you to see his painting but not look at it."

"Exactly."

"Which do you prefer?" he asked.

She smiled. "Good question. I admire the first but prefer the second. It's messy but it grows on you."

"It's honest," he said. "Life is messy."

"Not necessarily," she said. "But I see your point."

He was happy to see her losing her guard. They headed towards the exit.

"So what about you? Do you still paint?" he asked.

"I never really did. Seriously that is. Just derivative stuff, copying people I admired. I'd bounce back and forth from Miro to Picasso and back again."

"How did you know you weren't any good?"

She seemed taken aback by the comment. "Well I...I just stopped—once I got married there were other things to keep me occupied."

"Sounds like you gave up too easily."

She laughed. "Never mind that now. What about you? What have you been doing lately? I have to say it's surprising. I thought kids nowadays wanted to direct rap videos. Hell, even back in my day, canvas painting was hopelessly square."

"Yeah, I guess it's not very cool. Probably why I think it's cool."

"I'm sure you're parents are proud."

"Not really. I mean, they say nice things. But they don't want it getting past the point of interesting hobby."

"Well, they have their reasons." She nodded her head. "I know the sentiment well. My mother, God bless her. To this day can't say a nice thing about any artist. It's like every day of my life she needs to remind me that she steered me on the right path."

They reached the entrance of the building. Beyond the doors, the din of Broadway awaited them. He was not ready to go outside. He liked looking at her, her eyes, her lips. He wanted to stay with her there, in that protected space, and keep talking. He wanted to say: *Stop. Wait. Not yet.* But how could he say that?

"If you don't mind my asking," he said, instead. "What was it like, growing up on the Lower East Side?"

She stopped walking. Her left hand began to rub the back of her neck, as if the question had given her a cramp. "Wretched," she said. "And ordinary. More ordinary than you can imagine. Except the smells. There are certain smells you can never forget, and I'm stuck on one in particular. The smell of putrid, rotting cabbage. Memories of a summertime garbage strike. That is the Lower East Side for me."

"You must have pleasant memories too. Wasn't it amazing back then? With all those artists around? You must have known some cool people."

"I suppose I did," she said. "I know some cool people now too."

"Not the same kind of cool I'd bet."

"No. But I'm not that kind of cool anymore."

He smiled. "Do you ever go back to visit?"

Her eyes met his with resistance. "No, I don't. I'm happy to stay away."

"I see. Well, I like it. It's like we're all rushing into the future and the whole neighborhood just can't be bothered. There's something fascinating about that. Something honest."

She nodded her head. "Poverty is certainly honest. I won't argue with you there."

"We should go there."

"Excuse me?"

"You could show me around. Tell me what it was like, growing up there."

Her eyes narrowed. Like a summer storm, her features turned stark and menacing. She took out an envelope from her pocket. "Here's the first installment." She swatted it into his palm. "I'll call you when I'm ready with the next."

She pushed against the doors and walked briskly out of the building.

"Wait!" he called after her, scurrying to catch up. "What's with the shut down?"

"I'm not here to learn any life lessons from you, Mr. Robinson," she snapped.

He looked at her, dumbstruck. "What do you mean?"

"Are you accepting the envelope? Because if you are, then you're no less compromised than I am. Unless this is part of the deal, you humiliating me?"

"Say what? I'm just curious, that's all. No harm meant."

"I don't think we should allow ourselves to be so curious. We're negotiating a deal. These conversations are inappropriate."

"So you say. They don't have to be."

"They have to end."

"I was just being friendly, Mrs. Levy. I can turn it off if I want to. I can be cold like you if necessary. But it seems like an enormous waste of time."

"You know what's a waste of time, Mandela? Your naïve sanctimony. You can't afford to be so idealistic when you're accepting twenty thousand dollars from someone just for sitting on your ass."

Her words struck him like a hangover. The return of equilibrium after a glorious spin of vertigo. *This* was reality, not what had happened inside the museum. He stared at the lady in front of him, in her stylish accoutrements. How well she blended in with the sparkle of Soho. How well this bitch knew how to demarcate the boundaries between them. Of course, they were negotiating a *deal*. How silly of him.

He threw the envelope back at her. "Take your fucking money."

He took off down the street. She called after him, but he didn't respond. By the time he reached the traffic light at Houston, she had caught up.

"Mandela," she said, softly.

He didn't respond.

"Mandela, please. I apologize."

"We're done speaking."

She reached for his arm. He jerked back from her.

"Don't touch me."

"I'm sorry. Please, just hear me out. A few more seconds."

He didn't cross the street. People were staring.

"You caught me off guard," she said. "I didn't know how to react to your questions. It's my fault, not yours. Please, take the envelope. You were only being kind."

"You know who Fischl is," he said.

She looked at him perplexingly. "Eric Fischl? Yes."

"And Clemente? Jacob Lawrence? Alice Neel?"

"You're all over the map, but yes. I know them."

"Well, no one else I know has ever heard of them. No one else

I know would meet me at the Guggenheim in Soho, or if they did, it would be to kill some time laughing at stuff before heading to the Puma store. Do you get me?"

"Please. Take the envelope."

"I'm not one more item to scratch off the list, Mrs. Levy. I can refuse your offer. Maybe I'll feel better about myself."

"I'm sorry. Don't do this just to spite me."

"Maybe I want to go to Princeton instead."

"Maybe. But hold on to the envelope. Think it over and hold on to it."

He watched her as she put the envelope into his pocket. He could feel her hands inside his jacket. He thought again about stopping her, but didn't.

"I have to go," he said. "I'm late and my parents are already on my ass."

"Thanks for your time. We'll talk in a few days."

He looked at her, but said nothing. Around them the city continued its march, purposeful and indifferent. She began to walk away from him, just another dot on the grand canvas, blending namelessly into the scene. So many people striding past each other, knowing nothing about one another, caring even less, everyone in their own little bubble. It was ridiculous to try to connect with her. She'd never understand him.

But before she was fully absorbed, something unexpected happened. She had hailed a cab, and even though by then she was a hundred feet away, she paused. Before jumping in, she looked around, searching through the other dots. Searching, through the patterns and seemingly random abstractions of color and space. Searching, like in a three dimensional puzzle book, for a deeper vision, a focal point where a new reality opens up. Searching for him. And when her eyes found his, she waved. She *waved*.

His arm, as if by its own accord, lifted itself up, and waved back.

# 7. LEGION

Ken Cartwright was shouting vigorously on the phone, in that particular tone of voice he reserved especially for his family. He could hear it from down the hall.

"Must you always follow the path of least resistance, Celine? You're the perfect target for a cult...Don't tell me not to criticize you. You haven't called your son in *five* fucking weeks."

Legion grabbed a beer from the fridge and headed to the old man's office.

"There's not a dime in that account. Let me guess, he said it was a loan. Sure...what show, Celine? *What fucking show*...You saw the letter. Oh, it's official then, isn't it? Like any jackass with pirated software and heavy stock paper couldn't forge a letter..."

Ken was pacing around the room like the prosecutor in a made-for-TV movie. Legion slumped down into a seat. He took exaggerated sips from the beer bottle, trying to distract his father. But the script for this conversation had already been written.

"Fuck ups are fuck-ups," Ken continued. "You try to save them but...Celine, if you want me to start talking civilly then start acting like an adult. It's not my job to keep cleaning up after your messes..."

How hard would it be to just grab a paperweight from Ken's

desk and bash the guy's head in? Something to break the stubborn monotony. *Yes, Ken, we're all fuck-ups. Everyone except you, right?* But what purpose would it serve? He had no grounds to defend his mother. His mother *was* a fuck-up, and her blood ran Scarlet Letter through his veins. She was his genetic destiny, and they each met Ken's expectations spectacularly well. Why bother resisting?

"Tough—he *is* in the room. Why shouldn't he know what his mother's doing? Oh, so I'm the bad guy here...Of course you can speak to him, just one last thing, let Bill know that from now on if he wants anymore loans he should come straight to the source. And he won't even have to fuck me first."

Ken Cartwright tossed the phone to his son. "Your mother the artist," he said.

"Thanks for your kindness," Legion replied.

Ken shook his head. "Christ, you're naïve. You know what? Forget it. Enjoy your conversation."

"Legion! I'm in Arizona! Bill and I—have I told you about Bill?" His mother's voice sounded distant and spotty, like the transmissions from remote foreign countries on a short wave radio. "Honey, can you hear me?"

"Barely," he said. "What's going on, Mom?"

"We've been meeting with Bill's people, honey. Bill is Hopi. Native American? I met him last month at Genesis's opening. You remember Genesis. The Wicca woman? She baked those apricot ginger scones you had the last time you came over."

"I haven't heard from you in over a month." He didn't want to sound too critical. There wouldn't be enough time for it. "I mean, it's good to hear your voice."

"Honey, speak up, the connection is awful."

"I am speaking up, Mom."

"I know it's been a while, sweetheart, but I'm just now getting to a place where I can reconnect with people. Right after we last saw each other I had this...emotional blackout. I felt like I was suffocating. Bill rushed me here for an emergency spiritual makeover."

"You haven't been paying your rent, Mom." Inside, he could feel himself shutting down: knobs tightening, spigots drying up, his concern doubling back and disappearing. He wasn't going to listen to these rationalizations, these convenient truths hard won through intense soul-searching. Adults liked to fuck up and then overcompensate with words. But they were just words.

"I can't tell you how inspired I am by this place. These people...there's just this tremendous *primal* honesty about them that I didn't realize still existed in this world."

"Are you hearing *anything* I'm saying?" He was shouting now. It was pointless. Why should he protect her? "We haven't heard from you in a month. Dad's *pissed*. He's getting notices."

The line was silent for a while. And then Celine chuckled. "I'm sorry, honey. I understand you're angry. Your dad, too. I thought I paid before I left. Really, I did. It must have slipped my mind...I'm so bad with time, Legion. Has it really been that long?"

"Five weeks, Mom. A month doesn't just slip by." But he could sense *her* slipping away — her usual retreat, whenever confronted. So he dropped the anger from his voice and continued. "So, are you having a good time?"

"Bill's real chummy with the leader of an organization called Soaring Falcons. They're doing extraordinary things for these poor tribal children. *Orphans*, honey. With no one in the world." She paused to let her compassion sink in. "Plus, it's just a loan. He's going to pay me back once his show opens."

Doorbell chimes echoed throughout the apartment. Legion watched Ken pass outside the office on his way to the front door. Randall would be surprised to see him.

"And what about you, Sweetie? How's life? School? What you been up to?"

"I'm fine." What else could he say? He inched closer to the hallway. He couldn't leave Randall alone with Ken for too long. Given the guy's vulnerability at the moment, Legion imagined Ken Cartwright might be too much ego for him to handle.

"Doing okay with math? Don't be careless with numbers like your mom, honey."

"That's OK. I have a tutor now. He's a big help. Wanna hear about him?" he asked, just waiting for her to say yes.

"When I get back, Sweetheart, I want to hear *everything*. It won't be long. Two weeks tops. There are two shows I absolutely must attend. So how's your dad's girlfriend? What's her name again? She seemed so sweet when I met her."

"I've got to jet, Mom," he said. He had to get off the phone, transfer his fecund lactating teat from the mouth of one co-dependent adult to another.

"Sweetheart." His mother paused. "No one loves you like I do. Take care of yourself and I promise we'll see each other soon."

"Yeah. Take care, Mom."

He hung up the phone. Approaching the living room cautiously, Legion noticed, from his partially obscured vantage point, Ken fixing Randall a drink. Liquid copper on the rocks, the kind that tested your mettle as a man. Randall willingly took the challenge. Which was unusual. He seemed oddly at ease, given the circumstances.

"The way I look at it." Ken picked up a cigar. "One less hour of him smoking weed is an hour well spent. Unless that's what the two of you are doing."

Ken nudged Randall in the arm and Pavlov's dog laughed on cue.

"Hell, it's a lot worse than that," Legion said. He strolled over and took his place alongside Randall. "Randall's warped my impressionable young mind."

"Don't mind the sense of humor," Ken said. "The rotten apple never falls far from the tree."

"Let's not forget your irresistible charm, Dad."

"Witty. So witty. Anyway, just in case Einstein forgets." Ken pulled out a loaf of hundreds from his front pocket, slicing off three crisp bills and sliding them into the breast pocket of Randall's Oxford. "I've seen his nose in those SAT books a few times so you must be doing something right. Who knows, it might even pay off."

"Things are going well," Randall said. "He's making great progress."

Ken slapped his hands together. "Anyway, kids. Dad's gotta run. Enjoy yourselves."

"Oh, we will," Legion said.

Randall followed him down the hallway to his room. A heaviness spiked the air, blending with the cigar and alcohol stench, causing his temples to throb. Their pending conversation would be a tricky one. When he'd received Randall's call two days before, he figured the hard part was over. The man was ready to succumb and just needed the proper hand to guide him through the process. In that short time, Legion had done his best to come up with a blueprint. It was best to make these situations as painless as possible. Like feeding liver to small children, you need to cut the organ into manageable pieces, remind them that it will soon be over, and promise them an enticing reward for their bravery. He was ready on all counts.

Once inside his room, he shut the door behind them. Randall unceremoniously assumed his place on the loveseat. Legion watched the man's eyes canvass the area.

"It's good to see you," he said, sitting down beside Randall.

He wasn't faking. It *was* good to see Randall. He'd realized, in the weeks since they'd seen each other last, how weightless he felt around Randall, how familiar a space the man occupied in his life. He missed looking into someone's eyes and seeing a full range of emotions staring back at him. Randall *reacted* to him, treated him as a real person.

"This is some damn fine scotch," Randall said, polishing off the rest of his glass.

"I'm glad you called," he said.

"You knew that I would."

"You held out for a long time. I guess my charms aren't so irresistible after all."

He winked, but Randall didn't notice. The man kept gazing around the room.

"I've been a little lost. But I'll feel better when we put this behind us."

"We can do that," he said.

His legs brushed past Randall's knee as he lifted them to sit cross-legged on the couch. Randall looked down at his feet, then back up to his face, but the message was not a familiar one, and it made Legion uneasy. The clumsy tics which usually channeled Randall's desire were gone, replaced by an odd passivity, as if Legion were a difficult problem the man was determined to solve. He felt interrogated by Randall's blank stare.

"I've done a lot of prep already," he continued. He began to explain the process, describing how he chose the location, a nondescript public school in the depths of Brooklyn, which boasted upwards of 1000 juniors, many of whom would be taking the test that day. Next week, he'd tell his guidance counselor that the thought of taking the SAT with his classmates was making him edgy; he was certain he'd do better in an anonymous setting. Besides, his mother had promised to be in town that weekend, and as her presence in New York was rare enough, he hoped to spend the weekend at her apartment in Williamsburg and she could take him to the test site.

Some of this *would* be true—he would spend the weekend at his mother's. But Randall would go to the test center, sporting three different fool-proof IDs. He'd dress accordingly that day; he could even borrow some baggy pants and a t-shirt from Legion.

Lastly, Legion's signature was crucial. If there were any doubts about his score, the ETS board might call up Valhalla. The swirl of letters would have to match, so they'd have to spend some time perfecting identical autographs.

Randall took the information in without comment. Not that he expected the guy to jump up and down with glee. Still, he seemed about as curious as a day-old slice of pizza.

"You don't have any questions?" Legion asked, disappointed.

"Not really. It seems pretty well planned. I applaud your ingenuity."

"I know what you're going to say,"

"Do you?"

"I know there are risks. Trust me, they're manageable. I wouldn't ask if I didn't believe we could do it. And I want you to know." He paused, resting his hand on Randall's shoulder and looking him dead in the eye. "I really appreciate this. More than you think."

Randall coughed. His body shrugged to highlight just how unimportant these reassurances were to him. "I've gone back to my novel," he announced.

"Have you," Legion said. "Good for you. Writing is a noble pursuit."

"Teaching is noble," Randall said. "Writing is selfish. I'm starting over from scratch. Do you know what it feels like, to abandon something completely?"

"I imagine it would be very frustrating."

"No...I mean, yes. But not if it means understanding something I didn't before."

Legion cracked his knuckles. Where the fuck was the guy going with this? "And what's that, Randall?"

"It's hard to explain. I'm not afraid of the truth anymore. All the stuff I wrote before...just bullshit."

"I see." Legion nodded his head sympathetically, hoping his silent assent would soothe the man's frustrations. What had happened during the month of their separation?

"Why are you telling me all this?" he asked.

Randall looked at him. "I don't know," he said.

"So what do you think? Are you good with helping me out?"

"I'll do whatever you want."

"Providing?"

Randall lowered his head and shook it, letting out an exasperated sigh. "I don't have any conditions."

Legion smirked. "Come on, Randall. There are always conditions."

"Why don't you suggest some then?"

The conversation was disturbing him. He couldn't understand the signals Randall was sending. What else was left? He didn't want to have to resort to it, but he didn't see another way. When the tiger won't be tamed, just give him the meat.

"I have an idea." He crawled over Randall's body, straddling himself on the man's lap. He could sense, in the crisscrossing of Randall's eyebrows, that the move was unexpected but welcome, that just underneath Randall's cerebral excuse-making was an angry knob of longing begging for release. "Why don't I fuck you silly?"

"Your father's home," the man said. A weak retort. Was this an excuse to stop, or to continue?

"He'll never open that door," Legion said. "Not without my explicit permission."

He removed his shirt slowly, making a game of it. Lifting himself off Randall, he pulled his undershirt out from his pants, inching it up his torso, revealing first his sleek abdomen, then his delicate nipples, surrounded by wispy ringlets of hair. Then he slid his belt free of its loops and wrapped it around Randall's neck. By the time he began unbuttoning his jeans, he expected a smile to pop up on Randall's face, or his temples to break out in sweat. Something. *Anything.* But instead, the same vacant gaze stared him down. An indifference which left him feeling self-conscious. He stopped himself before his pants fell around his knees.

"What is it? You don't like me anymore?" he asked.

"You're being ridiculous," Randall said.

"You're jaded. Found yourself some other kid to play with."

"You really believe that?"

"I wasn't the first," Legion said. "Just one of the perks of your job."

Randall grabbed the belt from around his neck and threw it at him violently. "Fuck you. I *love* you. You know that."

He didn't respond. What could he say? But the violence, instead of provoking him, calmed him down; it was proof that Randall was still his. He walked over to the window. He needed to think. A few seconds, to adjust.

"I know I shouldn't," Randall said. "It's pointless and masochistic."

"Sometimes you don't have a choice," he said. Outside, the skyline of the Upper East Side extended for an unreasonable distance, lights shimmering like glowworms in subterranean caverns. "The things you do you just do."

"Exactly." Randall had gotten up. Legion could feel him approaching, fangs out, ready to strike. "I know you don't love me."

"Shut up," he said. He turned around. Randall was hovering

over him, impatient for a response. Quickly, he reached over to kiss him, but Randall dodged him.

"You don't," Randall said. "You like the stuff I do for you. Not me."

"Look, I like hanging out with you. Honestly. And I need you. That's gotta count for something."

"It's not love."

"And what you feel for me? That's love?" He was raising his voice. He wasn't sure if getting angry was a good idea. But how much could a person fool himself?

"It could be," Randall said. "But it doesn't matter. I'm going to do what you want, no matter what your feelings are."

"Really," he said. He didn't know how to react. Randall's moods had been much easier to translate before. He never imagined things between them getting so complex. Was it wrong, what he was doing? Did it matter? It wasn't about right and wrong. Randall could have chosen to resist his temptations. He could have stopped their affair at any point. He chose not to. *Because he didn't want to.* In the end, only selfish desire guides people.

"You don't trust me." Randall said, his voice calmer now.

"Isn't it the other way around?"

"Neither of us has much choice then. We'll just have to trust each other."

"Look," he said. "I don't trust anyone. Not even myself. But I want to trust you."

"You can," Randall said. "I have a lot more at stake than you do."

The man was finally making eye contact with him. He could sense the frost beginning to thaw.

"I can't afford any surprises," he said. "If I don't get a 1500 I can kiss the Ivy League goodbye."

"May I ask a question? Why do you care so much about the Ivies? Until now I thought there was serious pressure from your Dad. But I don't see that at all. I'm not sure he cares, actually."

"I've fucked up one too many times," he said. "I can't do it again."

"How?" Randall asked. "You get good grades. You've tried hard—damn hard—to boost your SAT score. How is that fucking up?"

"You don't know. You look at me and see someone I'm not. I'm just...a fucking disappointment."

His mouth felt dry, like the words had sucked out all the saliva with them. Blood was rushing to his head and his lips were trembling. Where was this random outburst coming from? He certainly hadn't planned for it.

"Listen, your dad's an ass. You're not a disappointment."

"My dad is an ass," he said. "You wanna hear just how much an ass he is? He gave me fifty thousand dollars for my college tuition two years ago. Told me to invest it in the market. And guess what? I lost pretty much all of it. But you know, *he's* the ass, because who the fuck gives a fifteen year old money to play the stock market, right?" There was no stopping him now. "And get this. Before you got here? He was drilling my mom a new one on the phone just because she hadn't called us in a month. I mean, so what if she falls off the face of the earth for a few weeks. What an asshole!"

He looked down at his hands. They were shaking. His whole body felt foreign to him. What the fucking was going on? Who the fuck was this person, shooting off at the mouth? He walked around the room, picking up socks from the floor, tossing them into the hamper. He didn't want to be there anymore. He was embarrassing himself.

Randall approached and grabbed his hand. "It's OK. Relax. Let's sit down."

"My room's a mess," he said, laughing. "Sorry about that."

"Sit down with me." The man guided him down into the loveseat. "Everything's going to be fine." Legion closed his eyes. When he was a kid, he liked to spin around in circles and savor the dizziness that would follow. If it got too overwhelming, he knew he could always close his eyes, and in a few minutes, his balance would return. Everything would be alright.

"It's going to be fine," Randall repeated, reaching over to hug him, rocking him delicately. He reached his arms around and squeezed back forcefully, shutting his eyes even harder. There was so much emptiness inside him. But it felt right to embrace, to allow Randall to nurture him. Wasn't this what Randall wanted? All this time he had held his cards close to his chest. But he'd been wrong. Mystery had ensnared Randall, but only vulnerability would sustain him now. The guy needed something to hold on to.

But this meltdown wasn't part of the script. Or was it? He opened his eyes. The dazzling radiance of Manhattan stared at him through the window.

"Don't you want to kiss me, Randall?" he asked.

"No, no," the man whispered, hugging him tightly. "We can just sit here."

# 8. GABRIELLE

Your Palm Pilot.
*But where is it,* you ask yourself, fussing through the farmer's market that your once spiffy Chanel bag has become. Who are you without the appointments, the social events, the smoldering errands that give your life boundaries, shielding you from loneliness? You try to remember the routine, dates and times buzzing in your head like bees jostled in their hive. Lunch with your mother, uptown, somewhere. Therapy and Yoga...but which comes first? You'd need the yoga after a session with Dr. Carl—he doesn't care about your needs. You come when his prissy receptionist tells you to.

You have a gift to buy. The Mizrahi boy's bar-mitzvah, in an 18th century Gothic castle, in western Connecticut of all places. Nobody's done a castle in years. People will ooh and aah about it, allowing Caroline to bask in her ingenuity. You could give money, but that would only highlight your prosaic mind. You have to come up with something fresh, live up to the affair you've been invited to.

Morty needs his Prilosec prescription refilled. While this could easily be accomplished with a phone call, he reminded you last night that the past two times the pharmacist had short-changed him. *And while you're there, dear, how about some extra-strength Preparation H?*

This must be it, you tell yourself, these definitions of a life. But the outline of a body is not the body itself. Are you a worker ant or the Queen? No matter; both are defined by their function. Lately, functions bewilder you, like they did in high school trigonometry. You are forgetful, philosophical; you hear ripping noises, seams coming apart, innards seeping through with hideous resolve.

Remember that movie *Pleasantville*, where the blissful citizens of the black and white town were progressively invaded by pockets of color? What if something was happening, beyond the obvious? What if hiding in the cracks of your monochromatic existence was a Crayola box of tangerines, midnight blues and periwinkles, waiting for your rusty fingers to grasp and broaden the hues?

What if? It wasn't a question you liked to ask yourself. What if had no ready answer. What if was hypothetical. What if left the door open for mosquitoes to fly inside, lay eggs in your hair, feast on your flesh.

But what if, passing by a newsstand on Sixty-fourth and Broadway, you found yourself face to face with a copy of *Time Out New York*, a magazine for *hipsters*, for God's sake, for fad victims, now junkies. What if, instead of zipping by without a second glance, what if, for a cold second, the cover were to whistle at you coquettishly, force you to take notice of the emerging artists festival taking place downtown over the weekend—in the Lower East Side, no less. What if you took out three dollars from your purse, slapped them down on the counter and wrested a copy from the slot?

What if: you sat yourself in a corner of a Columbus Avenue café, feverishly fondling the pages of the magazine like a teenage boy with his first *Penthouse*, fingers slipping, pushing past the filler to the art section, your centerfold? You see listings. You fantasize about possibilities. The feeling is overwhelming.

What are you doing, catching a cab cross-town? You have places to be, remember? Your mother will skin you alive. Don't turn your cell phone off! You can't—

And yet here you are, looking out a grimy taxi window. Do you feel brave, my dear? Is this necessary, this acting out? You lower the window and notice things you've never noticed before with your myopic vision: fliers on lampposts advertising guitar lessons, free-standing cabins with brochures from the Learning Annex. What in the world was the Learning Annex?

And the people! So many people, living out the syncopated rhythms of their lives, breathing the same air as you. Can you smell it in the air, the heady aroma of transgression, like the first time you let bacon touch your lips? Remember, you were young, twelve maybe, and Elana, your best friend, was holding your hand? Mischief on her mind, Elana walked you down Essex, past Seward Park where the black boys were shooting hoops half naked, their skin glistening like chestnuts freshly shucked from the shell. She dragged you to your first McDonald's, where with much emphasis she demanded two bacon cheeseburgers. She led you to a corner table, unwrapped the sandwiches with her spindly fingers, and held one up to your nose. *Taste it,* she cooed, the scent raiding your nostrils. Your tongue tingled, your insides shivered as your body adjusted to the alien matter. You were able to imagine, for the first time, the ecstatic power that surrender could offer you.

Is this what you feel, Gabrielle, stepping out of a cab in industrial north Chelsea, where the bombed-out remains of Guiliani's Shermanesque march through the nightclub universe have risen phoenix-like into a new frontier for artists and other Bohos lured by cheap rents? Nothing wrong with taking a break, my dear, but not at the expense of your schedule. Your schedule *is* your life. Would it be rude to suggest you left your Palm Pilot at home on purpose? Even if you allow yourself a cursory tour of this exhibit ("Beyond the Beyond: Art in the *Nouveau* Millenium"), you don't have to dawdle. You don't have to purposefully drown out the little voice inside your head trying to send you reminders of the day you should be leading. You don't have to strike up a conversation with that man—when was the last time you had a conversation with a total stranger? From Luxembourg, he says, his opinions and mustache both excessively European. But he moves you, doesn't he, the way he discusses the death of opinion, the disconnect of mankind, the resurgence of desire as truth...you listen but you know that you must get going, that in less than an hour your daughter will be home—your only daughter!—and she'll ask you about...

The look on her face. Pure mystification.

"But mother, you *never* forget," she says.

"I know," you reply, at a loss for words. "I'm sorry," you manage.

And you are sorry, but you are more shocked now, appalled. Arianna's concerns were usually etched like tattoos into your memory. Or so you thought. Meanwhile, you had forgotten to pick up the vintage Fifties dress for her upcoming audition. You just *forgot*. But how did you forget? *Why* did you forget? And what will Dr. Carl say? How you lie to him lately, throwing herrings at him as red as raw filet mignons. What would he think of the way you fabricate stories like a reflex action, the way you justify your lies with even bigger lies?

"Mother. I'm concerned," Arianna says.

"Don't be," you bark. *Don't ever be,* you mean. *I can handle it,* you think. "I've had a lot on my plate lately. Everything will get done tomorrow."

"*Fine.*" She smiles; the conversation will end here. You want to reassure her, tell her it's not about her. But your thoughts are murky and unfinished, and you're afraid of your own voice, afraid it will come out wrong because you spent an afternoon in an art gallery in Chelsea with a man from Luxembourg. You shouldn't have, but you did and you enjoyed yourself, and you don't want to feel guilty, you don't want to make excuses, you don't know if you can even explain it—you're not sure you understand it yourself. These contradictions elbow each other in your mind and then your thoughts return to the source: Mandela Robinson, troublemaker extraordinaire, coloring outside the lines of your tidy life. You should hate him, shouldn't you, but instead his spirit lulls you. You will call him in an hour.

You will see him soon.

Strange. Aren't you afraid of chaos, Gabrielle? But you haven't had a migraine in almost a week. That's some kind of progress, isn't it?

\*

Avenue A, gateway to Alphabet City, a bedtime storybook of caution impressed upon her by her mother since early childhood: *A is for Alcoholics; B, for Broken Homes. C is for Criminals; D, for Drug Addicts...*

"Whenever you head north, my Strength," Selma used to cluck at her, North meaning anywhere past Delancey. "First go west. Only when you reach Broadway do you change direction. The natives there are still crazy, but not as dangerous."

If her mother knew how little regard she'd paid to these paeans to paranoia. Standing outside the Elias Gallery on East Seventh on that breezy afternoon in March, she remembered how she had held her breath walking the very same street so many years ago, she and her hotheaded friends scampering past an abandoned carnival of storefronts and overgrown weeds, on their way to soak up some atmosphere in the Village. At the immortal age of fourteen, a mother's threats almost require you to take the dare.

So much remained the same. The ghosts of yesterday still haunted the sidewalks, the buildings that couldn't be torn down. But the idea of the neighborhood, that had changed completely. Land of the Freak, Home of the Foolishly Brave had become Land of the Restaurant/Lounge, Home of the Hipster. Times were good, and New Yorkers had grown curious about their frontiers.

How strange the past few days had been, all the surprises she was allowing herself. She would share them with Mandela, if only she could be sure he wouldn't laugh at her. No, he wouldn't laugh. He might even understand. But why was she bringing him here? What did she expect him to see that words could not express? And why did he care? Between contempt and curiosity, contempt seemed easier. Perhaps this was her years of cynicism; she'd have to let some of it melt away. He was an artist, curious about the world. So had she been once, before the world revealed its vulgarity to her, and she lost the will to keep looking.

She would not rush to judgment. A mild gust of air sailed past her face, invigorating her. Spring was seeking to hatch.

Mandela Robinson approached from the north. He wore his hooded parka unbuttoned, a striped sweater underneath, blue jeans: clothes she would have picked out for her son, if she'd had one. All except the shoes: two-toned, scuffed up—the artist refusing to surrender completely. He looked spectacularly fresh. Weren't adolescent boys supposed to be cavalier about their hygiene? Perhaps his tortoise frames lent him dignity. But the dignity was already there, in a face looking for answers but patient enough to wait for them. Arianna's eyes were searching too, but there was an awareness in Mandela's gaze, of obstacles and dilemmas Arianna was unfamiliar with. She and Morty had been careful to shield her from them.

"Sorry I'm late." He looked above her head. "Elias," he said. "How'd you come up with this place?"

"I was sifting through a magazine. And this guy jumped out at me. TJ Volonis?"

"Sounds vaguely familiar." Mandela shrugged his shoulders, still on his guard.

"Before we go inside." She took out the folded envelope from her purse and handed it to him. "Just thought we'd get it out of the way."

He looked at her hesitantly. "Thanks."

The gallery was up a flight of creaky stairs which lead to a room the size of a high school gymnasium. There were fewer than ten works on display. A redhead with a dozen piercings scattered throughout her cherubic face greeted them with a brochure.

Sunlight spilled through the windows, casting patterns on the walls and floors. Volonis had a certain flair for provocation that weeks ago she'd have dismissed, but now found herself scrutinizing more carefully. Mandela, too, had much to say. They'd stand in front of a piece, and one of them would offer a few words, and the other would ask for elaboration, and suddenly they'd be debating. The sculptures, made of burnished copper tubes, were several meters tall and dizzying. She found the endless overlapping loops aggressive, almost sexual, but he thought they were balanced and peaceful. He pressed for explanations, and she admired his refusal to allow her to be vague, his need for responses unadorned with abstraction or generalizations. He forced her to be precise, and even when his responses were naïve, he backed them up with conviction. She hated to admit it, but she was truly enjoying herself.

"So what are your plans for the summer?" They were headed west out of the building. The sun was beginning its retreat from the sky.

"Not sure," he said. "I wouldn't mind taking a class at Pratt. My dad would prefer I do something productive which will look good on my applications."

She laughed knowingly. "I've told Arianna the same thing."

"Yeah, you adults need to chill out. Let us find our own way sometimes."

"What would you like to do instead?" They had reached the corner of Seventh and A. But she was not ready to go home.

"Ideally? Head to Europe and bum around. Scrape by painting portraits in Montmartre. Visit the Prado, the D'Orsay, the Louvre. Eat foods I can't pronounce. Meet astoundingly cool people."

"I remember the first time we took Arianna to the Louvre. She must have been eight, and we were dragging her around like a Kewpie doll. Within twenty minutes she was bawling so loudly I had to rush her out. The Parisians stared at us in horror."

He smiled. "Serves you right."

"So why don't you go?" she asked. "I'm sure it will look very enterprising on your applications."

"Tell that to my parents. Besides, I can't afford it."

"You can't?" she asked. "I think you can now."

He laughed. "My parents aren't exactly aware of the whole

Robin Hood thing."

"Of course not," she said. "Do you have to get home soon? Let's take a walk. This way." She nodded her head. Southbound.

*

Kossar's Bialys. Shalom Chai Falafel. The names seize you like a stroke, paralyzing you. You thought forgetting meant annihilation. You had condemned these places by removing them from your mind, earmarked their territory for new foundations.

Still, they remain. Not even the names have changed. Pickle Guys at 49 Essex. *The Competition!* your mother would furiously scowl, but your father allowed everyone their space. Rabbi M. Eisenbach, Sofer. Weinfeld Yarmulkes and Benchers. Ha'atikos.

Some of your tribe linger here, even now. See the men with their Armani suits, exiting Lexus SUVs. Two women, hemlines brushing their ankles, step into the East Broadway Kosher Bakery, for loaves of *challah,* apricot *rugelach*—the same items your mother sent you there for, handed over to them by the same woman, or her daughter.

They see you, Gabrielle. And they know something is amiss. *"The Lowenstein girl has returned. Didn't she leave us years ago, for the more assimilated pastures of the north? What brings her back to our ghetto? And who's this schvartze boy by her side? Parading around with him, mocking us and our ways. She didn't sufficiently shame her mother the first time, and now she's come back to finish the job."*

You remember, don't you, Gaby? How you stridently resisted your mother's attempts to tame you? You wanted to be free; you were an artist! You demanded to be sent off to college so you could meet bohemian boys from far-off lands with goatees and dirty fingernails. You screamed, you objected, you tried your father's patience, a man whose patience had been richly cultivated by his wife. You almost didn't get married...

"What's that building?" Mandela points to the tallest in the landscape, with a giant fading clock tower and minarets, golden Hebrew letters spelling out its name.

"*The Daily Forward*," you respond. "It's the Yiddish newspaper."

"There's Chinese writing along the side," he says. "Looks like times have changed."

"They have," you reply, because you see this too, in the nail salons, the dry cleaners, the take-out food shops, all with their dripping neon signs. "And they haven't."

"Are you uncomfortable?" he asks.

"Somewhat," you say. "There are memories here, waiting for me."

"We don't have to keep going." He wants to console you.

"Do you have a girlfriend?" you ask, changing the subject.

"No. I'm invisible at Valhalla."

"That's surprising. Most girls your age are prone to be curious."

"The curiosity I inspire is like the curiosity of a freakish reptile behind a glass wall in a zoo," he says.

"That will change," you say, chuckling. "Be confident, you have a lot to offer."

"What about you?" he asks. "What was dating like back then?"

What about you, Gabrielle? Stop this before it gets out of hand. What on earth are you trying to prove with this stroll down memory lane?

Your mind floods with memories. You imagine yourself confessing to him.

\*

*When I was nineteen my mother took me to a doctor on Park Avenue who told me I was pregnant. I felt so exposed, sitting in his Thirtieth floor office. We had dressed up in our best fabrics and still I felt like an interloper. This uptown world, with all its untroubled glamour, made me feel even more ashamed of what I'd done. 'Look at the shtetl girl,' the backs of fashion magazines would taunt me, the flawless pearls and smiles calling me to judgment.*

*I was dating my husband at the time, at first to appease my mother, but eventually because he was kind, and generous, and his kindness and generosity reminded me of my father, who'd smile at me when I came home from dates with Morty in a way he'd never smiled beforehand. I let them think this man was wooing me, but truth be told I wasn't serious about him. I didn't want a husband, not yet.*

*And I slept with him. It was no big deal, I had slept with others before him. It was the Seventies after all, even if my mother still thought it was the Forties. But being cavalier about sex doesn't mean you know the ways of the world. When my period was a week late, I panicked. Naïve girl that I was, I thought if we planned well enough, it couldn't happen.*

*I tried to stay calm, but my mother, with her uncanny ability to sniff out fear, knew something was wrong. She hounded me with questions, wore me down until I broke down and confessed. God Forbid you go to* a local doctor, she told me. So she made arrangements through a reliable source with a physician in the Upper East Side, whose office we'd slip into unnoticed, invisible, anonymous as shadows.

The doctor sat me down and said: the results have come back positive. Such a short, sharp sentence, slashing through my skin and carving out my soul. I felt empty, more helpless than I'd ever felt. I could see, plainly, all the things that would be taken from me now, all the choices that would be stripped away so that I could preserve my dignity, that final, essential layer of skin that all women must hold on to.

"I'll handle everything," Mother said, knowing that in my wounded state I couldn't be trusted. I know little about her conversation with Morty except that it clearly had its intended effect: three days later, looking at me with great conviction, using a voice he had no doubt used in front of a mirror to convince himself it was the right thing to do, Mordechai Samuel Levy asked me to marry him.

I didn't hesitate. Mother greeted the news with incalculable glee; even my father, who despised the circumstances, learned to embrace the outcome. They decreed a ceremony in six weeks. This was not unusual in our community. What was the point in delaying a couple's happiness? But when I saw no changes in my body in another three, nor felt any of the sicknesses or mood swings I knew to associate with pregnancy, I began to wonder.

Two weeks before our wedding I received an unexpected present. Stunned, I went to a doctor – another outsider – to confirm what I already knew: my period had returned. I ran to my mother, swollen with tears. "You've miscarried, darling. It happens all the time." She explained my sadness to me, gave my confusion a name so I could mourn for it. I wept, silently, as Mother commanded me to do. "Your most joyous moment awaits," she said. "In two weeks you'll have infinite opportunity."

But I didn't want Morty to marry me out of fear or dubious notions of honor. I told my mother it was wrong; he had to know. She looked at me for twenty silent seconds, boring into me with her eyes. "You can speak to him," she said, finally. "But if you do, know this: I'll make you speak to the caterer. I'll make you speak to the florist, the photographer. You'll explain it to the rabbi. You'll call your aunts and uncles, your first and fourth cousins – even the ones in far-off places, and you'll tell them to cancel their trips. You can burden your fiancé with your cruel truth, cloud up his mind and steal away his chance at bliss. You can do this, my dear. Or you can keep quiet, and let the gift of your silence allow for a different truth, one every bit as valid."

I couldn't speak. Her brutality froze me, an ice pick through the heart, robbing me of my last breath. I began to wonder if I'd been pregnant at all. Her words seemed premeditated, like she'd anticipated this wrench in her plan. Would it take much for this woman to convince a doctor to lie? She had convinced me in a matter of seconds.

I hated her, but I knew I wouldn't defy her. I was weaker than I thought. For years I'd flirted with rebellion. But now that I stood before true uncertainty, I cowed. I ran back to the womb of shelter, to the opening lines of the fairy tale.

But do not weep for me. I've led a happy life. Stash away the violins. I've led a happy life. A bubble bath of a life, a catered smorgasbord of tea cakes and strawberries dipped in chocolate.

I have no right to say anything. Look at my daughter! Arianna is brilliant. Self-actualized. Everything I want her to be. Everything any mother could ask for! She is everything.

I have no right. No right.

*

But nothing was confessed, not then and not now. Like the groundskeeper to a chamber of horrors, Gabrielle's guilt offered her a glimpse past the door into the terrors within, only to quickly shut it. She offered Mandela vague non-answers instead, supplied her own questions to pass the time.

The day had given way to a chilly night. Bodies whisked by her with tremendous energy, larvae just emerging from the shell. They crossed Houston Street. She felt unsettled and strangely self-possessed at the same time, like a brash drunk demanding yet another round at a bar. In half an hour Morty would enter their apartment and find his daughter upstairs. *Your Mother?* he'll ask. *Not a clue,* she'll respond. And a quivering spark of insecurity would travel between them. She had kept her cell off the whole time.

"I never walk anymore," she said. "I've forgotten how much fun it is."

"Especially here," Mandela replied. "Lots of eye candy."

"Do you want to get a bite?" The words hurried out of her mouth. "I remember this great café on Second. Terrific blintzes. You like blintzes?"

"I'm no expert," he said. "But sure."

So they found themselves seated by a window at Kiev. Gabrielle noted with glee that the waitresses were still rude, the place still passionately dumpy. They ordered cheese and cherry and some coffee.

"Am I keeping you?" she asked. "I'd feel weird if I am."

"Stop worrying." He smiled without a trace of malice. "I'm fine. This is cool."

"It is cool, isn't it?" she said, savoring the sound of the word coming from her mouth. "I mean, a *little* weird. But..."

"Yeah." He nodded his head. Elaboration was unnecessary.

He reached into his coat pocket and took out a small case. "I was thinking," he said. "Would you mind if I took some photos?"

"Had I known I would've gotten my hair done," she said. But inside, she was singing. She was touched.

He removed a Pentax manual from the case, the kind used in beginner's photography classes, and began composing his first shot.

"Is there a purpose to this? Something I should know about?"

"Just look natural," he said, snapping the first. Then another. After the third, she stuck her tongue out at him and started putting on extravagant poses.

"Who knew you could be silly," he said.

"*I* knew," she said. "I just never told anyone."

Outside the window, a crowd had gathered. Four men, wearing tweed suits and polka dot bow ties, looked ready to perform. One of the men, gangly tall, had an accordion strapped to his back while another, bald, short, with a mustache that swallowed his upper lip, was mouthing a harmonica. The other two, one black, one white, were hunched over, faces cheek to cheek, snapping their fingers and swaying back and forth.

"Ladies and Gentlemen." The black man straightened his back and offered his voice to the world. "We present to you, the greatest hits of the Eighties."

Gabrielle turned to Mandela, who passed her a puzzled look. The men snapped their fingers again in unison. The harmonica hummed. The accordion snapped. Then, in a whisper building to a howl, the men kept repeating "Hungry Like the Wolf," followed by a glorious acapella version of the Duran Duran song, doo-doo-doo's and all.

Duran Duran! She even remembered the name of the group. And then, another memory: Pregnant with Arianna, in a shopping mall in Jersey with her mother, searching for a layette, dancing to the same song as it played in the background. Selma scolded her to stop bouncing: *You're not alone anymore, Gaby.*

Duran Duran was followed by Lionel Richie's "All Night Long", Wham's "Wake Me Up Before You Go Go", Cyndi Lauper's "Time After Time."

Gabrielle looked to Mandela who was laughing, mouth wide

open, his eyes fixated on the quartet. She looked at him and realized that his laugh was hers and hers alone, that this blistering instant would never be repeated or taken away from them. She was building memories with Mandela Robinson. It was astonishing.

"Do you even know these songs?" she asked him.

"Of course. Do you?"

"I'm not as old as you think." To prove her point, she began to sing along: *You said, Go slow, I fall behind. The second hand unwinds...*

Mandela began to clap. "What did they put in those blintzes?"

She laughed, feeling her insides vibrate. She looked out the window. A homeless man—judging from his muck of clothes and the pink scarf wrapped around his neck—had taken center stage, dancing circles to the music. The crowd cheerfully egged him on. She examined the sea of smiling faces, embracing the moment without embarrassment, without judgment. It took her several seconds before she realized that one face in particular seemed to be looking back at her.

But no, it couldn't be.

*Oh yes, my dear, it is.*

Gabrielle closed her eyes. She felt a sharp pain in the back of her neck, crushing her. She couldn't open her eyes. She knew what she'd see if she did. Cautiously, one hand over her forehead, she cracked them open. *Oh God.* Reaching over, she fumbled for her purse, took out two twenties and threw them onto the table.

"Whoa. You OK?" Mandela's voice only made it worse.

"I have to go," she said. "Keep the change."

"What the hell?"

Maybe he didn't see me, she thought.

*Of course he saw you. We all see you.*

Leave me alone, she thought. Down, down. She had to cast her eyes down, always. She reached for her coat. Her pills were in her purse, she knew that.

*They won't help, Gaby.*

"Why are you covering your face?" Mandela asked. "Is there someone...?"

*You thought you could just come down here for a snack with your new friend?*

"We shouldn't have come," Gabrielle said.

Mandela looked outside the window. "Shit. That's weird," she heard him say.

She got up. She had to find her way to the door. She could see people's feet, coffee stains on the linoleum floor.

"Wait a second!" Mandela was following her.

She pushed her way towards the front. A throng of people were idling by the cash register. She saw trouser legs, a man's rotund belly, an octogenarian in a wheelchair.

She pleaded with their lower bodies. "Excuse me please excuse me."

"Hey!" someone shouted. "You have to pay first."

"The money's on the table," she said.

*Why are you doing this, Gabrielle?*

"Hey!" Someone had grabbed her arm. Was it the boy? The waitress? Some other demon sent to destroy her?

*Proud of yourself, Ms. Lowenstein?*

"I'm going home!" she shouted, tugging free from the hand that grabbed her. Randall was probably still there, but she didn't care. She had to get out. She'd lose herself in the crowds, pray for the best. She flung open the door.

Outside, a bitter wind chewed at her skin. The men were still singing, the hobo dancing, everything louder now, more real, more frightening. She looked around. She felt dizzy. She couldn't make out the direction. Which way was north? Which way home?

*If you head north, you must first go west. Only when you reach Broadway may you change direction.*

"Leave me alone! You have no right!"

Gabrielle ran into the street. She stuck two fingers in the air like a frantic broker on the exchange floor. Blessedly, her salvation came quick. She got inside the cab and shouted her address. When she felt the vehicle move, she sighed, opening her eyes for the first time in minutes. The cabbie would know where to take her. He'd know how to get her home, even if she didn't.

# 9. EXCERPTS FROM ARIANNA LEVY'S JOURNALS

March 12th

It's *not* my imagination. Mandela Dorkinson is sitting in class gawking at me. It's like his new purpose in life. How long can one person hold a grudge?

But I can't make out his intentions. The looks he passes—not exactly malicious, not quite fear, certainly not lust. No, if I were to pick a word to describe them it would be *flummoxed,* like I'm a bullet in one of Gluckman's calculus problems and he can't figure out how to graph the arc of my trajectory.

Either that or he's just rubbernecking the latest zit that took my face hostage two nights ago. Like I don't have enough to worry about. Three craters in the past two weeks, and it all boils down to one thing: stress! I mean, not only am I expected to excel, I also have to look good while doing so. I have to live up to the covers of fashion magazines and the willowy ladies of *Ally McBeal.* Meanwhile, I can't stand my haircut, my thighs are getting jiggly and I absolutely detest my chin. It *protrudes.* I'd like to think I'm above this superficial nonsense, but honestly if you heard the way Penelope, Sharon and I pick apart every single girl in the lunchroom then you'd know just how vicious girls can be.

Anyway, the real reason the zit's haunting me is because Douglas Meisel asked me out yesterday and I didn't exactly say no. Douglas Meisel: Not Ben Affleck cool, more like Ben's younger brother, Casey. I won't win popularity points by dating him, but I won't lose any either. Here's the lowdown: Persian, a smidge on the thin side, but not in a Screech way. He has the most enviable cheekbones and he dresses like an Italian architect. He's also terrifically chatty—the kind of guy girls spend half a night with at a party just to avoid the salivating troll that's asked them to dance. But that's the problem: Douglas Meisel is almost *too* harmless. He's barely an inch taller than me. How funny would we look in photos? Plus, his track record's a mystery, which means he'll probably either respect me too much or run his hands up my thigh by the end of date one.

So I told him, maybe, I have a lot to focus on right now. The thing is, I'm going to have to say yes eventually. If I keep saying no that will somehow confirm for all the guys in my school that I'm a frigid bitch. Boys my age aren't exactly independent thinkers. I'll be branded for life. Besides, I *want* to go on a date. It's been way too long. I want to get all dressed up. I want to see him try to impress me with his wit and well-chosen itinerary. I want to talk about stupid things and laugh so hard it hurts. I just know Douglas will be good that way.

I wonder what Mother will say. Normally she'd sit Douglas down for an interview, but honestly it's gone from bad to worse lately. I just don't get her at all. She's been *forgetting* things lately. My mother, the woman who can list the names of all my third grade substitute teachers, has suddenly become absent-minded. She forgot to pick up my costume the other day, which totally almost cost me the part. And get this, three times last week, I've come home to an empty house—no note, no voicemail, nada. I'd be here for *hours* before she'd prance in, all nonchalant, like it was perfectly normal for her to be out until seven. I asked her once where she was and she said, oh you know, out, groaning her hazy replies like I was the nagging mom and she was the frustrated teen. Once she graced me with some talk about an art exhibit, but it was strange how vague she was.

Could my mother be having an affair?? It makes me gag to think about it. Still, it's not like I haven't lain awake a few nights wondering if my parents are compatible. They get along, I guess, as parents do. They certainly bicker gamely enough. But I've always found their skirmishes comforting, sort of cuddly and familiar. And that's the problem—she and Daddy have been unfailingly civil lately. Mother's not the suffer-in-silence type; she tends to growl openly and with gusto. This silence is bizarre. You'd think we turned WASP and moved to Greenwich the way they carried on at the last Shabbat dinner.

I wonder if it's a sex thing. God bless Daddy, but he's ten years older and well, he's got to be *tired*. I just know they haven't had sex in years. Most people think that about their parents, but my parents *really* haven't. No way. That fountain has dried up and the birds have flown away. Which isn't healthy. I mean, Mother's only forty. She's got at least a *few* good years left.

God, I'm being ridiculous. There's no way she's having an affair! She's not brave enough to pull it off. She'd worry herself sick about it before it even began. Still, something's up and I need to know what.


March 21st

First the good news: just got back the results of my 2nd diagnostic. 1470. Hello! I *so* rock! And Randall assures me these supervised tests he's been organizing are far more reliable indicators than, let's say, a test I took on my own curled up in bed with some Cheetos. I guess the group dynamic brings out my competitive side. I wonder why I never see Legion Cartwright at any of these shindigs. I asked Randall about it last week, but he just shrugged like there was way more to that story, but he wasn't going to get into it. No doubt Legion's a bitch to tutor.

More good news: Douglas and I went out last night. Asia de Cuba, hello! It was such a *scene* — we sat at the communal table next to these wafer-thin model types who kept buying mojitos for us on the sly. And Douglas was Mr. Charming all night. I think he may even *like* me.

Ok, now the bad news. Get ready for this. Yesterday, out of the blue, Randall asked me if something was up with Mother. I almost gasped out loud. Because if Randall could notice — he spends a few hours *a week* here — then surely I'm not imagining things.

So I asked him why he was asking and he told me Mother hadn't asked him for a progress report in three weeks. I told him I wasn't surprised, that she'd been acting weird lately, and then he said funny enough, he thought he saw her the other day in the East Village.

If I had rabbit ears, they would have shot up straight in the air. It was like that moment in a psychological thriller where the hero stumbles upon that piece of information that turns everything he knew so far on its head.

"Really," I said. "The East Village. Where?"

"Second Avenue. In a café. But I could be mistaken."

"Was she alone?" I asked, trying to sound only mildly curious.

"I don't think so. She was with someone…African American."

I literally could feel the blood rushing to my head at this point.

"Intriguing. An African American man?"

"Not exactly. More like a…teenager," he said, his voice more tentative. My poker face must have broken. "Have I just ratted her out or something?"

"Don't be ridiculous," I said. "Chill out, Randall. My mother's a grown woman. It's not my business anyway."

To emphasize my point, I rolled my eyes, let out a deep yawn and plunged back into the lesson. Inside, though, the detonator was counting down the seconds. But I can't explode. Not yet. I don't have the facts. I don't know the motives. I have little to go on, just enough to confirm my fears: Mother *is* up to no good, and that something involves Mandela Robinson. Oh sure, it could be another black teenager. *Sure.*

The whole thing makes sense now. Mandela's glances. The Robinson's invitation to dinner that night. Mother's sudden disappearances. Her erratic behavior—she hasn't brought Mandela up in conversation in weeks! She's scheming. She's withholding. But she won't keep up this façade much longer. I'll get to the bottom of this, so help me. I'll unlock the truth and make her explain how she could be doing these things behind my back for months. Months!


March 28th

Snaring the unsuspecting *prevaricator* ain't easy. Case in point: three days ago, I came home early from school and caught Mother whispering in the den. Before she noticed me I tiptoed away. Finally I had a lead: she was making mysterious calls. All I had to do now was fill in the details. This required a bit of craftiness, but hey, I am my mother's daughter. I had to create a diversion and check her call history, so I cunningly hid my psychology textbook the day before the midterm and pleaded with her to help me find it. Which gave me just enough time to go upstairs and rifle with her cell and, lo and behold, what should pop up right between Dr.

Carl and Frederic Fekkai's numbers but the digits of one Mandela Robinson. (I had purposely fawned over Legion Cartwright's phone at lunch yesterday, the one person I knew would have Mandela's number)

My Mother is mingling with the enemy! She's having *conversations* with Mandela. She's meeting with him in the East Village. WHAT THE HELL??

OK, don't panic, Arianna. Maybe she just met him that one time. To try to convince him not to apply. Maybe she worked out some sort of deal. But why should there be a deal?? She's gone psycho! That crazy aunt in Lithuania that Grandma always talks about? The gene has passed on. This is taking things way too far. I want to go to Princeton, but not like this. Not because my whack-job mother pulled off some scheme.

Imagine if people found out! How could she trust Mandela not to talk? Oh, he is biding his time to unleash this one on me. I'm going to be the laughingstock of the school. What am I saying? The laughingstock of the world! Mandela will go to the media, and turn this into one of those racially motivated incidents. He'll become the poster child of discrimination and get full scholarship at Princeton while I become a joke, a walking corpse, a Trivial Pursuit question. No one will take me seriously again.

I just don't get it. I've done everything right. I've followed every dictate she's laid before me since freshman year—every course, every summer program, every extra-curric. I fucking made sure I was the best, and now she's gone and ruined everything. How can she do this to me??

I'm telling her tomorrow that I'm not applying to Princeton anymore. And then I'm going to let her seethe. I want to see how long she can keep up this game. To think, she's kept this to herself for weeks, months maybe.

FUUUUUUUUUUUCK!

And I've kept this diary in my drawer *this whole time*…she's read it all! She knows *everything*. Double-crossing witch! I trusted her more than I've ever trusted anyone. I HATE her. I wish leeches would rise up from the murky swamp and suck the marrow from her bones as surely as she has sucked every last fiber of my freedom.

But do not think I will tell her. Oh no. Not yet. Let her think I'm still her naïve daughter. From now on, if she wants some sweet secrets to feast upon, I will provide an extravagance of freshly-baked intimacies. She will get her own Arianna. As for the real thing, she will never, ever know me again.

## 10. MANDELA

Four thousand dollars. Shit, it looked like a lot of money. It *smelled* like a lot of money. Nothing quite like the blunt aroma of a stack of Benjamins.

The wad was getting unwieldy. There was reason to be wary, with every new injection. His parents he wasn't concerned about. Tyrese, though, was a termite, burrowing through the walls with his boundless appetite. His brother was at an age where the fog of childhood was just beginning to clear. Threats wouldn't stop the little mole. They'd only give him more reason to search.

The best spot then was somewhere so devoid of mystery that Tyrese wouldn't even want to snoop around there. Easy: Aunt Mozelle's linen cabinet. There was nothing exotic about musty tablecloths and doilies. Tyrese would be afraid the moss growing over these decaying collectibles would somehow spread to his fingers.

Deidre and Joe were busy packing lunches in the kitchen. Mandela took his treasure along with his knapsack to the bathroom. He'd add something else to the collection that day.

He had developed them himself at school, after hours when the darkroom was empty. He had not expected much and was surprised by the outcome. They were *strange*. Somehow, reflected in Gabrielle's facial expressions, in the disquiet in her eyes, was a summation of all that was special about that afternoon. It weighed on his mind like a fresh dream, an itch of inspiration wriggling about his thoughts. Ideas came and built on one another. He needed to do something with these.

He would paint her portrait. Yes. He never felt so sure about something before. More than that: He would go to Europe that summer. Fuck it. She was right. He had the money. He had the will. His parents would just have to understand. He could find a way.

The knocking on the door was furious. "Boy, it's a bathroom, not a day spa. Do your business and get out," Joe shouted.

"Alright! Jeez!" Mandela zipped the bag and hastily flushed the toilet for effect. He opened the door to his father's smoldering grimace.

"Son, you're a Robinson. No need for all this primping. Your genes have done the work for you."

"Whatever, Dad," Mandela mumbled, sliding past his father.

"Wait." Joe searched the medicine cabinet for his cologne. "What's today, Mandela?"

*Not again,* Mandela thought. "Tuesday."

Joe slapped the back of his neck with the musk. "Your ass is here at 3:30pm. This guy doesn't come cheap, do you understand?"

"I didn't *ask* you to get me a tutor."

Joe lifted his toothbrush hand into the air. "3:30, Mandela. Just be here." He stuck the toothbrush in his mouth. Case closed.

Mandela nodded his head. Five days of school, twice a week sessions with the SAT guy, afternoons babysitting, endless homework—he had no life. The relief of summer would arrive only to be appropriated by his parents arranging interviews and overnight trips for weekend college visits based on region. This would be his vacation: stuck in the back of the Volvo with his squealing siblings, swimming in the dingy pools of roadside Hampton Inns and tramping to IHOP for half-price kid's breakfast deals.

Well, he hopes they have a jolly good time. He was going to paint a portrait of Gabrielle Levy. Then he was off to Barcelona, goddammit.

He would find a way.

\*

Valhalla: not just a private school, an institution. A converted neo-Baroque mansion once owned by the descendants of Andrew Carnegie. The musty scent of history emanating from its walls. Glossy pictures of the famous and powerful—some visitors, others former students—adorning the walls in a patchwork quilt of self-congratulation. Letters laminated in mahogany frames highlighting alumni accomplishments, magazine covers referring to "one of the finest institutions of learning in the world." Teachers with PhDs from the same universities their students were being farmed to attend. The soothing gurgles of Principal McKinley wafting from a loudspeaker, his tone relentlessly satisfied, almost always pointing out another milestone or an opportunity for one.

Through the halls he drifts, like a dead log in a river, past the high-fiving aristocrats, the vacant glances of fashionistas, the exclusive conversations to which he is only a spectator. His clothes aren't trendy enough. He doesn't have a bitchin' haircut. He doesn't *scare* anybody—people think he's weird, not intimidating. The tides move swiftly and suddenly. If he did something memorable at a party, he might get instant fame for a week. And if he knew how to ride the moment, perhaps he'd maintain his status. Otherwise things were soon forgotten, and popularity left best to those who were born into it or acquired it by trade—kids with famous parents, the super wealthy, drug dealers, the occasional jock or cheerleader, especially if they were eye candy.

Mandela had no idea who he was in that building. He was unclassifiable, the final box marked "other" on the questionnaire. He knew it shouldn't bother him. He didn't *want* to be one of them. He was an independent thinker, happily so. But it would be nice to be recognized as such, and not just by white teachers eager to connect. It would be nice to have friends who'd laugh at his jokes, engage in conversations that didn't revolve around classes or frivolous gossip about what the hip kids were up to. Not that he didn't have friends, just the few he had were desultory souls themselves, a group assembled not by choice but by fate, like patients in a doctor's waiting room.

Except for Legion. Legion was his one cool friend. Nobody had much shit to say about Legion except maybe that he was aloof. Legion had model good looks, and good looking, rich white boys never get shat on. When Mandela came to Valhalla the year before, the cliques had already been established. His outsider status seemed destined to stick forever until one day he and Legion got to talking and the next they were hanging out. He knew it was a choice Legion had made. He just didn't get why. Still, the kid *was* aloof. There were so many things he'd like to tell Legion, but it wasn't that easy. He was never sure where the line he wasn't supposed to cross was.

Seeing him downtown the other night only added to Mandela's confusion. From the way Gabrielle had run off, Mandela figured the guy Legion had been with was his tutor. Legion had mentioned he and Arianna shared the same tutor. So what the hell was he doing on Second Avenue with his *tutor?* They looked like they were *hanging out.* The whole thing was fucked up. He wanted to ask, but didn't want to piss Legion off.

First period bell rang and the masses began shuffling towards their home rooms. Mandela found Legion loitering by his locker, staring vacantly inside it. He slouched against an adjacent locker.

"Hey." Legion looked up. "A black hole has sucked up my psych book."

"Use mine if you want," Mandela said. "Just give it back before third."

Legion shook his head. "If I have the book, then what's my excuse for not reading Chapter Eight?"

Mandela smiled. "So how's the market?"

"Sucks donkey dick, dude."

"Shit. Guess it's community college then."

"Bite me, affirmative action maggot. See you in Cambridge."

"Bitch, I get white boy grades," Mandela said, laughing. "I'd get in anyway."

"I know. That's why I hate you."

"Don't. I don't plan on going. I'm taking a year off."

Legion smirked. "Uh, *sure.* After four years at Harvard, you mean?"

"Just because my parents think they know what I want doesn't mean I do."

"I know what you want." Legion's eyes beaded. "You want to cut first period with me and get stoopid on the roof."

"You, my friend," Mandela said, "are fucking psychic."

Doing the roof properly was an art form. Legion wasn't one for hiding; instead he preferred to get to know the security guards. He introduced himself to these men in the first few days of the school year, usually young guys living in Queens or the Bronx, and he'd ask them their names and about their families. A little respect went a long way. Probably he brokered a deal with them, because other people seemed to get caught on the roof way more often than he did. Smoking with him, Mandela never felt any real danger. It was like they were on *Star Trek,* in one of those force field bubbles, immune to the consequences that more vulnerable kids had to deal with. And Legion's shit was always the real deal. He had to be careful not to smoke too much; he just wanted to get a buzz going, something to make him forget the suffocating monotony of school.

After three hits he could feel the blood flowing through his veins like seltzer. Once the initial paranoia faded, he settled into the moment. The evening in the Village kept weighing down in his mind, and the marijuana was making him feel brave.

"So how's the tutoring going?" he asked.

"All good." Legion was studying the joint. "I think I may surprise everybody."

"Yeah? That guy teaching you some shit?"

"Yeah." Legion shifted his legs. "He's cool. I mean, you know, for a tutor."

"Really? The guy my parents got me has all the personality of a textbook. I couldn't imagine hanging out with him. I guess your guy is cooler."

Legion shrugged. "I guess."

"Were you down in the Village two nights ago?"

"Maybe. Why?"

"I thought I saw you," Mandela said. "With that guy. Your tutor."

"Ah. I see." Legion nodded his head. He took an extra long toke off the joint. His eyes were dilated and runny. "Shoulda said hi, dude," he said, his lungs still filled with junk. He exhaled deeply. "You know what's funny? I did see someone that night. You'd never guess who. Arianna Levy's *mom*."

"Really." Mandela made sure to sound like he was bored. "You know her?"

"Randall pointed her out to me. I wonder what she was doing down there."

"Who the fuck cares, dude," Mandela said.

"Of course. It's just…small world, man. You still applying to Princeton?"

Mandela knew it was time to change the subject. "Doubt it. You think things will be different in college?"

"Fuck yeah, dude. *Everything* about college will be better. Being on your own is like getting to be someone new."

Mandela laughed. "You want to be someone new?"

"Sometimes. I always wonder what it would be like to shut everything down. Forget everything that's ever happened to me and just start from scratch."

"Shit, dude," Mandela said. "I'd take your life any day."

Legion shook his head. "You think being rich is the answer to everything."

"Not just rich. Rich and white."

"Listen, don't get all Malcolm X on my ass when I'm fucked up. We can talk about the Man keeping you down later. But trust me: Mo money mo problems, dog."

"Oh yeah? So tell me about your problems. Spill some secrets."

"You think I'm keeping secrets?"

"Dude, we all have secrets."

"Yeah." Legion looked away. He nodded his head and took another drag.

"What's the matter, you don't trust me?" Mandela asked.

A rumble from the stairway interrupted them. In three seconds Legion managed to put out the joint, stick it in his sneaker, whip out a pack of cigarettes, light two of them up and hand one to Mandela. The door made a heavy creek when it opened, followed by the shrill voice of Sharon Palmer asking if anyone was there.

"Nobody," Legion said, putting out his cigarette.

Sharon came around to the other side. Lauren Lipton was with her. Sharon was such a pretentious bitch, Mandela wondered why Lauren would hang out with her. Lauren was pretty, edgy, and way less shallow than most. Still, she was in with the popular girls, probably because guys liked to hang out with Lauren. No doubt that impressed Sharon.

"Hey." Lauren dropped down right next to them. "So who do you have now?"

"Psych," Legion said. "Del has French, right, Del? Madame Suckass."

"I have her," Lauren said. "She wears a wig, you know. She had chemo last year."

"So what are you two up to?" Sharon asked, making it sound like a threat.

"Slowly committing suicide." Legion removed the joint from his sneaker. "Wanna join us?"

"Sure," Lauren said, giggling.

"No thanks." Sharon kept her hands folded under her chest.

Legion lit the joint again and passed it around. Sharon stood there stoically, probably upset that someone else had stolen her idea of spending first period on the roof.

"So you're going to just pout then," Legion said.

Sharon turned to him and smirked. "I don't want to get in the way of the special bond you guys have," she said.

"You mean friendship?" Mandela replied. "Yeah, I guess that's weird for you."

Legion laughed.

"You know if you guys are gay," Sharon said, "it's totally no big deal. You can be open about it."

"Oh Shar," Lauren said, coughing up her last toke. "That's so harsh."

"Fuck you, Sharon," Mandela said.

"Shite." Sharon said. "Have I hit a nerve? Sorry."

Legion cracked a crooked smile. Mandela wasn't certain what the smile was hiding. Anger? Fear? Indifference?

"Jealous, Sharon?" Legion finally said. "Is there something you want?"

"Hey now," Lauren said.

"Don't flatter yourself, Legion," Sharon replied.

Mandela decided not to hold back. "Listen, Sharon, if you're hot for some boy-on-boy action, why don't you ask your dad to lend you one of his videos?"

"Oh my God." Lauren cheeks turned pink. She covered her mouth to stop herself from laughing too hard. "Ouch."

Sharon rolled her eyes. "Such a swift mouth you have, Mandela. No wonder so many people like you. Catch you later, Lauren. Adios, ladies."

"Hasta la vista!" Mandela shouted after her.

"Don't mind her," Lauren said, once the door slammed. She grabbed for another go with the joint. "She's in a mood."

"Heavy flow day?" Mandela asked.

Lauren laughed. "Maybe."

"You guys enjoy." Legion handed Mandela the roach. "I gotta jet."

"There's a lot left, dude," Mandela said.

"I gotta knock back some Bacardi before second period. Get the smell of weed off my breath."

"Second period's not for another fifteen minutes," Mandela said.

"Chill out, Del. Lauren won't bite, will you Lauren?"

Lauren laughed. Mandela blushed. He watched his friend walk away and wondered if Legion was doing it on purpose, allowing him some quality time with Lauren Lipton on the roof. Or was he just trying to get out of their earlier conversation? Why had Sharon said what she did? Did people really think he and Legion were gay?

"Don't mind Shar," Lauren said. "She just did that to dig at him."

"Already forgotten," Mandela said. He smiled, looked over at Lauren's lips. He wanted to keep watching those lips move. He wanted to taste them.

"So," Lauren said, before taking a long drag. "Tell me about yourself. I don't usually party with guys I barely know."

"What do you want to know?" he asked.

"Why everything, of course," she said.

## 11. RANDALL

Voyaging into Manhattan to get your hair cut at Astor Place was just about the coolest thing you could do in 1987 when you're a fifteen year old from Fairlawn, New Jersey. The R train dropped you off at Eighth street, and you and your friends would scamper around the block to the sloppy storefront between Broadway and Lafayette, the one with all the autographed pictures in the window, mostly faces you didn't know scattered among a few big names *(Look, there's Sylvester Stallone!).*

You didn't get to choose your barber. Sometimes they sent you to the veterans upstairs, even less often to the hot shots on the first floor. Most of the time, you were sent downstairs. And downstairs was where all the action was: a cavernous Mecca, the Lost City of Barbers, an assembly line of old Italian men in brown polyester pants, most balding with hairy forearms, their nimble fingers snipping, clipping, shaving with straight blades, the free ones lazing about in their old-fashioned barber's chairs, one eye in *La Strada,* the other checking the stairs for their next customer. Astor was not your mother's salon; this was a guy's place. Your basic cut, fifteen minutes tops, eight dollars a pop. Which isn't to say they only did basic cuts; on the contrary, Astor was famous for its Sigue Sigue Sputnik Mohawks, the Tantric mandalas carved into scalps, the hairs dyed to every color of the rainbow. Just don't expect frills. Astor was all about economies of scale: keep the prices low, your mouth shut, and cut as many heads as you can.

Not much had changed in thirteen years. The syrupy stench of fried hair still hung heavily in the air. The Italians had been mostly replaced by men from more Eastern frontiers, Slavs and Croats with gruffer dispositions and even less facility with English.

Randall stared at himself in the mirror. Finally, after so many years, he was going to get the haircut he never had the balls to get in high school. Cabbage-faced Natalya, head surgeon of bleach, finished brushing a viscous white paste through his follicles and wrapped the concoction with strips of aluminum foil. Miklosh, the barber, sporting the kind of bushy mustache you can only grow in eastern Hungary, checked his watch and whistled to himself. Behind them, Legion sat, flipping through pages of *Maxim*.

Two nights ago, Legion had asked him where he wanted to go for the "big change." Almost by reflex, he said *Astor Place*. Legion smiled and said he'd heard of the place. But it was clear the Astor name held none of the magic it did back in his day.

"It's gonna be wicked, dude," the boy had said. They'd ordered take out Thai and Legion was scarfing down a piece of chicken satay. "Being blonde is a total head rush."

Randall nodded along with this assessment. Never mind that blonde hair would look ridiculous with his skin complexion. Never mind what his friends would think. What friends? He'd been out of commission for so long he barely remembered what they looked like. Never mind what his parents would think. He pictured his mother's furious scowl. *I don't understand,* Sylvie Miller would whine. *Why ruin such a beautiful head of hair? It's what they do, Sylvie,* his father would say. Then, continuing in a whisper: *You know, the gays. We gave him that hair,* Sylvie would protest. *Couldn't he just buy himself a new hat?*

Never mind what his clients would think—the few that remained. He imagined Arianna Levy's analysis: *Getting in touch with yourself, Randall?* The girl had been making comments for weeks which he'd chosen to ignore, mostly because she was his only cash cow and his prize student, the kind that would prove to be an invaluable reference. That is, if he didn't piss off Mommy Levy. When he saw her down at Kiev that time, she'd ran away from him like he was an airborne disease.

Never mind what Cha-Cha and Wheezy would think. Three days before, he had received an unsettling letter in the mail, a "general release" sent to all employees reiterating the company's explicit decree against non-contractual third party tutoring: *failure to adhere to this policy will result in immediate dismissal and possible legal action.* Was this letter meant for him? The brutal irony was that he hadn't taken on a new client in months. Of course, now that he didn't have so many of his own, now that he'd been scared into relying on CATPEE classes for his paycheck—*now* he was going to get found out, taken down, sent packing.

Never mind all of it. Because Legion was smiling again. His Dolphin had returned to the cove, rediscovered his Pop Tarts in the cabinet, resuming his place in Randall's life as if the past two months had never happened. All Randall had to do was say yes.

"You will feel burning sensation," Natalya said to him. She lowered the seat so his head would reach the sink. "This feeling will pass." She immersed his head into the bowl. The water was fucking hot. The bleach was eating his scalp alive. From the corner of his eye he noticed Legion, hanging over him like an anxious parent.

Acquiescing. It was easier than he thought. If he strictly focused on the present, then what he was doing didn't seem that ridiculous. He was bleaching his hair. Big deal. People bleached their hair because they had a bad day at work. Later, they'd take pictures for fake IDs. So what. Fake IDs were harmless. He had a fake ID when he was seventeen, too. Everything in steps. Everything broken down into bite-sized pieces so when the fateful day came, it would already be too late, a foregone conclusion. *You can't stop now, Randall.*

No, he couldn't stop. He had corrupted the boy. A lesson in sacrifice was in order. He had to set a new example. Besides, he was writing furiously—forty pages just last week. He couldn't stop now. Every day forward was potential material. He had to study the room, absorb its details. Process them for future creative recycling.

Miklosh removed the towel from around his head. Together Randall and the Hungarian stared into the mirror.

"What you think?" The man rubbed his fingers through Randall's scalp.

What did he think? His hair was cheddar cheese. Saffron-infused carrot soup.

Legion stood behind him, an ear-to-ear grin lighting up his face. "Dude, it's *tremendous*."

"We can make more blond," Miklosh offered as consolation.

"Don't bother," Legion said. "It's kickass. The color will fade anyway."

"It's kickass," Randall repeated, to the indifferent Hungarian.

"How you want cut?" the man demanded, spinning the scissors in his hand.

"Short," Legion said. "Spike the front and buzz the back."

Miklosh laughed. "You friend knows better than you, eh?"

"Tell me something, Miklosh," Legion asked. "How old you think my buddy is?"

Miklosh pushed out his bottom lip. "I donno. You both eighteen, nineteen."

"That's right," Legion said. "Just about eighteen."

So he was eighteen again. Maybe he could go back to high school now and show off his haircut. Fairlawn. Fucking cesspool. Here's your second chance, Randall. Go back and show them your kickass haircut. You don't have to be afraid anymore. You weren't *that* big a loser. You had your share of friends—playing the hetero-chameleon game well, camouflaging your brighter colors to blend in with the khakis and grays of the straight boys. Go back now, show off your oranges and pinks.

So what if some people snickered behind your back, called you a flamethrower, a fairy, a poof? The charges didn't really stick then. You were dating girls. You even fucked a few, remember? Popping your cherry with Sheila Lovitz. Closing your eyes as you pressed yourself inside her—you just had to *do it*, get this virginity business over with, *become a man*. So you imagined Danny Gador from summer camp, best friend Danny reaching for your hand on a moon-soaked night in the gazebo beside the baseball field. You and Danny were cutting the talent show and no one knew where you were. Danny was sitting close to you, close enough for you to see the lust dewing his eyes, close enough for him to reach for your hand, grab it in his sweaty palm and place it onto his swollen crotch, close enough for you to realize that you wanted nothing more in the world, that all your desires up until then were meaningless compared to this moment, this second, and yet—you pulled your hand away. Pulled it out of fear. Of what? Being caught? Finally getting what you want? Confirming for all those tittering voices in the halls of Fairlawn High that you were the full-on faggot they suspected you were?

Because it was 1987, and in 1987 you were not gay. Gay men were Boy George. Gay men were dying of AIDS, protesting the lack of government funding for the disease with shaved heads and pink triangles. Axl Rose was sick of homos, and Sebastian Bach wore an "AIDS Kills Fags Dead" T-shirt, and though some people cried foul, many more laughed. Gay men made supporting guest-star roles in Hollywood movies as swishy interior-decorator next-door-neighbors with Persian cats and sassy lines and cashmere-lined shoulders for their straight sisters to cry on, *see we're just harmless and laughable, not dangerous and sick.*

No, you weren't gay then. But now you are. Now you can be. So go back, Randall. Go back you sad, repressed fuck, and show them your flaming haircut, find Danny Gador and let him fuck you in that gazebo, locate those sniggering bozos in the hall and stand up for yourself now—the years have given you some great comeback lines. Go back and reclaim what was stolen from you. Go back and squash that fear, that cruel fear you swallowed into your stomach at eleven years old, that indigestible lump that has grown inside you like a cyst, seizing you, disabling you, mocking you.

You are eighteen again, Randall. Go back. Go back.

"Dude, you should fucking thank me." Legion's words knocked him out of his daydream. Miklosh's bushy hands were wiping stray hairs off his neck. He looked up. The mirror had to be lying. Who was this boy staring back at him, with the orange swizzle sticks on his head?

"Totally kickass, right?" Legion asked the Hungarian.

"You want, I do same for you," Miklosh responded. He removed the barber's smock, handed Randall a slip of paper with "$24" written on it.

Randall's eyes studied the mirror. He looked over at Legion, beaming with something like fatherly pride, and the scary thought that occurred to him was *now I'm more like him so maybe he'll stay with me.*

"I can't believe you've never dyed your hair before." Legion ran his hand through the back of Randall's head. "Look how killer you look."

"I look fucking killer," Randall said. And then he laughed. The words tasted good coming out of his mouth.

Randall paid and out they went, into the chill of an early Saturday in April, past the harried shoppers rushing in and out of Barnes and Noble.

"So. Passport photos," Legion said, clapping his hands together.

"You know where to go?" he asked.

Legion shot him a knowing smirk. "Just follow me, kiddo."

Randall smiled. "Sure thing, Mr. Cartwright."

They made a right on Broadway and headed down Eighth,

past the garishly painted storefronts hawking kitschy rock-n-roll prints, pizza joints, and the occasional tattoo parlor. Shoe stores, same as back in '87, the shoes not nearly as shocking. No more gold lamé thigh-high boots or six inch platform sneakers. Eighth Street had lost its edge. The Goths had lost their Antique Boutiques, the stoners pushing past Minnesotans to buy their skull-shaped bongs. Black nail polish was an accessory for guys. Vinyl was dead.

"Listen, aim for a 1500. More than that would be pushing it," the boy advised. "But not much less either."

"I'll do my best, Mr. Cartwright. Anything else?"

"Yeah. You might wanna get used to responding to my name, OK, Legion?"

Randall took this in. The ultimate wish fulfillment: complete custody of the object of his desire. Soon, an identity card would be issued with his new name next to a picture of his new, younger self: Legion Cartwright, age seventeen. His throat got dry and his cock shifted in his pants. "So, if I'm Legion," he asked. "Then who are you?"

A puckish grin took over the boy's face. Suddenly his back stiffened and his eyes darted around anxiously. "Dolphin, if you just focused on your homework once every mil*lenn*ia then *maybe* you'd get that 1400," the boy blurted out, in a neurotic high-pitched quiver. "And don't think you can grab my crotch to get out of this one, Mister. No way. Okay maybe. Just this once."

Randall tapped his index fingers against each other. "Bravo. Your Oscar is being engraved. I'm glad you see me that way."

"You're such a dork, Randall." The boy chuckled. He reached over and planted a sloppy kiss on Randall's cheek. Randall recoiled. He could feel his body stiffen much the same way Legion's caricature of him stiffened.

"You're OK with that," he said. "Kissing me on the street."

"Who the fuck's gonna see us?"

"I don't know. Your friends? Ken maybe?"

The boy smirked. "Ken is in an office getting head from his secretary. And boy would that be rich. *Him* passing judgment on who *I* mess around with."

Randall shook his head. "Listen, what's going on with your dad...it's OK to be mad."

Legion released a drawn out sigh. "I don't want to talk about Ken."

"It's not normal," Randall said. How could he phrase it? He just wanted the boy to understand that someone cared. "It's not love."

"Oh, right. Love." The boy laughed nervously. He repeated "love" several times. "You know you're the only person who uses that word with me? Well, aside from my mother, who uses it a bit too much, I'd say. Kinda like instead of hello."

Randall sighed. "I don't know what to say to that."

Legion smiled. "Say nothing, dude. It's all good."

"Does your mom know about the stock money?"

Legion laughed. "I appreciate the concern. But you're analyzing this way too much."

"I'm sorry," he replied. "I don't want to fight."

"We're not fighting. We're getting passport photos. Right over here."

Legion grabbed his hand and guided him into a one-hour photo lab. How strange it felt, this soft hand grabbing his with so much confidence, how weird for Randall to accept and give in to this moment, to feel safe in it even though it provided no safety.

Look how the boy takes control! See him ask the Chinese grandmother behind the counter for assistance, opening his wallet and paying for the photos himself. Look how he guides you to the black stool in front of the screen, how he musses with your spiky hair to get it just right, how he repeats the woman's dictum to lift your chin and tilt your head to the right, her choppy commands to *relax, young man, relax.*

"Relax," the woman insisted, holding a camera bigger than her head up to her eye. "*Big* smile. If you don't like passport photo you have to wait ten years for change."

*Ten years,* Randall thought. *Gosh, I'll be twenty-eight then.*

"Say cheese," Legion said, giving him two thumbs up.

"Cheese," Randall said.

## 12. GABRIELLE

The doctor's examination table pressed against her bare ass. A mirror on the door left nothing to the imagination: dressed in a flimsy patient's gown, her naked back to the wall, her tumid breasts pulping against her swollen stomach. What was she doing in this wicked white room, with its assortment of Mengele-style utensils housed in formaldehyde jars, a spotlight glaring down on her like a magnifying glass scorching an ant on a blistering July day?

The doctor entered, along with her husband. The doctor gift-wrapped in surgeon green, a mask snug over his mouth. Morty looked lean, tan, sprightly. She was mortified to be seen this way.

"Shouldn't he be outside?" she asked the doctor.

"Are you kidding?" Morty said. "This is important."

"They're just cramps," she snapped. "My therapist says it's stress."

The doctor's laugh echoed in her ears. "I think we both know better, Gaby."

She studied his eyes more carefully. It was Dr. Carl.

"Carl!" she screamed. "But you're not a doctor."

"Relax," Morty said, taking her jaundiced hand in his.

"He's a shrink!" she yelled at her husband.

"Settle down." Carl was smearing a lubricant over his latexed hands. "I'm going to massage your belly first." He looked over at Morty,

*who edged closer to her, holding her hands gently but forcefully.*
*"I don't understand!" she protested, trying to break free.*
*Morty was beaming. "Don't you want to know the sex of our baby?"*

Someone was touching her. Gabrielle swatted the trespasser away and yanked the sheets over her head. "Get off me!" she shouted.

"Gabrielle. It's 7:45. I just thought you'd want to know."

7:45? How was that possible? She flung the sheets off her body and jerked her head towards the nightstand clock. "This is insane. Why didn't you wake me?"

"The way you tossed all night?" Morty said. "Besides, you've been so edgy lately."

"And throwing my whole day off will take away the edge? Is Arianna up?"

"I knocked on her door at 7:15 and again at 7:30..."

"Very *nice*, Morty. Arianna!" she screamed. And then again, even louder.

"Down. Stairs," came the withering reply.

Morty chuckled. Gabrielle jumped out of bed and rushed to her closet.

"It's not funny," she told him.

"Sure it is," he said. "Want to tell me about your dream?"

"What dream?"

"The one I knocked you out of."

"I don't remember," she lied.

He sighed. "You seemed quite upset by it."

He was being kind, as always. But what was she going to tell him? "Morty." She threw her clothes on the bed. "Back when we were dating? Was I much different then?"

"In what sense?" he asked.

"I was more interesting, wasn't I? I had more...dimensions."

He came over and kissed her on the cheek. "You've always been the most interesting woman I've ever known. Still are," he said.

But this was what she expected him to say. Even if it was true, it was unexamined truth. It was superficial, patronizing. Morty didn't want to delve. She wasn't sure if she wanted to either. Sometimes you go searching for gold, and you find nothing but the blackest coal, and even if you expected coal all along, it shocks you. It disheartens you.

"So you love me," she said. "Even if I've disappointed you."

"Where is this coming from, Gaby?" Morty reached clumsily

for her shoulders. "The dream? Has Carl said something? Do you want me to come next time?"

Gabrielle observed her husband's pained features. How she hated this panicky refrain. It made her feel like a child. If only she were Catholic. She could run to a priest and confess everything. Instead she kept treading water, over and over. How tired her arms were. How she wished to jump out of that ocean, feel the firmness of land underneath her feet.

There was no time for this. Her day was speeding away. "Go to work, Morty." She pecked her husband on the cheek. "I'm just playing the over-emotional wife today."

"Gaby, if there's something you want to say..." He began to plea. Why had she opened her mouth? She headed to the bathroom. "We haven't talked in so long." The line trailed behind her like a puppy chasing fruitlessly after a speeding bus.

"Nonsense. We speak every day." She closed the bathroom door behind her. "I have to shower. And you'll be late for work."

"Gaby," he said.

"Morty. I'm turning on the water."

"Alright," he said. "I still love you, Gaby."

She twisted the shower knobs. Let the water drown out his awful words. He *still* loved her. *Still,* as in until this day. *Still,* despite her caprices. *Still* — just like the still he'd given her after their wedding, when she'd told him about her miscarriage — that split-second of buyer's remorse before the hug and the oh my poor darling and the *still* — we're married now, *still* — water under the bridge, *still* — we would've gotten married anyway. Eventually.

*Still* as they began the infancy of their marriage, both of them learning to crawl through the obstacles of newfound intimacy, so new, so strange. And even if she had some time to dwell on alternate realities, suddenly there was Arianna. Precious Arianna. Their treasure. Their lioness. Their strength.

She remembered her father's face when he'd first laid eyes upon his granddaughter: this look of triumph that said every sacrifice made was worth bearing witness to this moment. How true this feeling was. She felt it deeply herself. Her child erased everything: all the vagaries of pregnancy, all the misgivings of her rush to the altar, all her unanswered questions about identity. She had found her role, and took to it.

And she had loved herself then. She had loved her busy life and her new family and her successful husband. Didn't she? Then, and even now — still? Was this love she felt, or was it habit? Because there's a difference between convention and passion.

She could sense it, now that something resembling true passion had reentered her life. But what if passion was a temporary guest, someone who'd take off again without warning? What were you left with then, aside from the festering scars of your memories, scabbing over your heart?

Gabrielle toweled herself off briskly and returned to the bedroom. The clock read 8:03.

"Arianna!" she screamed, pulling on her pants. There was no reply.

Once dressed, she checked her voicemail. Mandela Robinson's voice entered her conscious like a migraine: *Hi...just checking, you know, to see if everything was cool and you know, just wondering if we're still meeting later this week...*

Gabrielle threw the phone onto the bed. Only a simpering idiot could have dug herself into a hole so deep. To think she'd almost been caught red-handed by Randall. He might have even seen her. There could be no more foolishness. She had lost herself in the fog of these rendezvous, forgotten that they had a purpose. Soon it would be over. Two more meetings and he'd have half the twenty thousand; the other half would wait until after the application deadlines. *This* was the purpose.

After all, if she wasn't going to make sacrifices for Arianna, then for whom else? Her mother never ceased to remind her of the sacrifices she and her father had made for her. *The scarves I sewed: for you.* Selma's blustering nostalgias drilled into her head like a jackhammer. *The shoes I wore – cracked to the bone and still we'd buy you a new pair every three months. Your father would stay open seventy hours a week so we could send you to your art classes and feed you steak twice a week. But don't think I'm complaining. Look at where you are. Look at who you are now.*

Gabrielle examined herself in the full length mirror: Fekkai perm. Mani/pedi at Oscar Bondi, facial by Mario Badescu. Chanel lipstick. La Mer skin cream. Jo Malone perfume. Cartier Pasha watch. Asprey earrings, Bulgari around the neck. Hermes Birken bag. Blouse by Michael Kors, pants by Ralph Lauren, shoes by Tod's. How dare she feel confined. How small her sacrifices were compared to her parents', how selfish of her to expect more. *Look at you,* the mirror whispered to her. *You're outstanding.*

She walked across the hallway towards the stairs, looking down at the quiet efficiency of her home: Marjorie fluffing pillows on the couch, Tatiana dusting the fireplace, a cascade of morning sunlight washing over her capacious palace. Perfect. Suffocatingly perfect.

She descended briskly. Tatiana suspended her dusting and approached her.

"Good morning, Madam. Should I prepare breakfast for you?"

"I'll manage on my own, Tatiana. How long ago did my daughter leave?"

"She's in the kitchen, Missus," Tatiana said.

"Really?" Gabrielle checked her watch and bee-lined directly to the kitchen.

Her daughter sat on a stool by the center island, a plate of half-eaten French toast resting beside her. She took a second to look up from the magazine she was paging through, and then resumed browsing, scooping a large piece of the toast into her mouth.

Gabrielle decided to reserve judgment. "Good morning," she said, cheerfully.

Arianna's eyes never left the magazine. "Morning."

"Doesn't first period start at 8:15, dear?" Gabrielle asked.

Arianna put down the magazine. "I guess someone's running late then." She stuck another slab of the toast in her mouth. Gabrielle tried to grab the plate away but Arianna quickly snatched it back.

"Darling, just because I wake up late one day does not give you the right to behave erratically."

Arianna tossed her fork down onto the plate. "Erratically? Oh that's rich. Define erratic for me, Mother. Seems to me you've become very familiar with that word."

"So I've had a few things on my mind. You could try to be understanding."

"Tell me what it is you want me to *understand*." Gabrielle did not like the look her daughter was giving her. "Make me understand why it matters that I show up for school on time every day. Why I get good grades and join every idiotic club—"

"Hold it right there, young lady. What the hell's gotten into you?"

"What the hell's gotten into *me*? Do you even have any idea what's been going on in my life lately?"

"Sweetie, I'm sorry," Gabrielle said, meekly. She hadn't prepared for this. "I hear what you're saying. I've been distracted."

"What's been distracting you, Mother?"

"Darling, please calm down."

"Tell me. I tell you *everything*. Where have you been every other afternoon for the past few weeks? And last Tuesday, when you came home after nine?"

Gabrielle turned away. Wherever this was heading, it was trouble. "I don't know. Does it matter?"

"Let me help you then. The East Village, maybe? A café on Second Avenue?"

The accusation throttled inside her ears. "Where are you coming up with this?"

"You're meeting with Mandela Robinson!" Arianna screamed.

"I am most certainly *not*..."

"Liar! I saw his number on your cell phone. You're a fucking liar! Tell me, are you two having a fun time together?"

"Wait, Arianna..." Gabrielle attempted, but her mouth went limp. She closed her eyes. Arianna's words had sucked the air out of her head, making her dizzy. If she kept listening, she'd fall down. Collapse. She couldn't respond; yet *how* could she not respond?

"Is he the son you never had but wished you did?"

"Arianna. *Enough!*" Gabrielle wailed. A monstrous bellow from deep within, a sound she didn't know she was capable of. "*Enough.* Yes. I met with him. Please. Enough!" Her eyes were still closed. Only the soft whimpers of her daughter remained. She needed to get out of the room. But she could not. She had to stay and fix things.

"Why didn't you tell me? Why are you hiding everything from me?"

Gabrielle winced. Yes, she'd been hiding. She had her reasons. *Valid* reasons. She took a deep breath and cleared her mind. She would salvage this situation. She had to. "If I had said anything you would have told me not to do it."

"Are you crazy?" Arianna bawled. "Are you *completely* out of your mind?"

"Darling, you don't understand. He's agreed not to apply to Princeton."

"*Why* would he agree?" Arianna was spitting out her arguments. "Have you paid him off? Do you have any idea what would happen if people found out?"

Arianna threw her hands in the air, her voice full of rage and pain. But rage and pain were like bottles of soda shaken too hard—open them and the gas escapes in a furious flurry, but quickly dissipates. If she just kept a cool head, soon this would be over.

"Arianna," Gabrielle's voice turned softer. "I'm not crazy. I've convinced him not to apply. I kept this from you because I didn't want you to get all hysterical. Obviously, that was a mistake. But darling, Mandela won't say anything. You have to believe me."

"*Believe* you?" Arianna's lips were trembling. "I don't want to go to Princeton. Not like this. You're not *normal*, Mother. This isn't normal."

Gabrielle grabbed her daughter's hands. Arianna tried to pull away but Gabrielle knew enough to insist. Through those first few seconds of struggle she held on tight, until Arianna collapsed, the tears flowing harder. "Sweetheart." Gabrielle caressed her daughter's head. "Would I do anything to harm you? I know how much Princeton means to you, honey. So I did this for you."

Arianna kept sobbing. Gabrielle kept talking, hoping the flood of her words would numb her daughter's pain. She had to sponge up the tears and the anger, suck them into her pores and dispose of them later.

"I know you're mad. But I just wanted you to be assured of your chances. And now you will be. We'll never have to worry about this again."

"But why did you meet him downtown?"

Gaby could sense her daughter's anger turning to curiosity. "We've talked a few times, darling. He's an artist. We discussed painters. Remember how I told you that I used to paint? We spoke about that. It's *nothing*." The white lies flowed out of her so readily, smoother than truth and gentler on the tongue. "Hate me if you have to but keep this in mind: all these distractions were all about you. You are my *life*. You're *everything* to me. You know that, sweetheart. Who has been there for you, through everything?"

Arianna unlocked herself from her mother's embrace. "I'm going upstairs," she said, her face hard and unreadable.

"Of course. Stay home and relax. Don't worry about this. You've worked so hard and I'm so proud of you..." The words continued to pour out of her, even as the kitchen door swung shut. She continued to talk out loud for a few more seconds, hoping, like a mantra, that the words would convince her of their truth, until she realized the maids could be listening. And so she stopped. The room was silent. Her mouth was dry and her legs were Jello. She steadied herself against the counter and tried to level her breathing.

Arianna's unfinished French toast stared back at her. She grabbed the fork, scooped up the remains and stuffed it into her mouth. She eyed the traces of syrup on the plate, wondering if she should sop them up with her tongue. What the hell had just happened? Everything was collapsing, and she was gorging on

French toast. She was a lousy mother. She should run after Arianna. No, she should wait. Let the dust settle.

She raided the kitchen cabinets. She had hidden a stash of Valium somewhere. The word *disaster* kept popping up in her mind. She tried to zap it away. It was not a disaster. She had handled the situation as well as she could.

*Better than you imagine.*

Gabrielle twisted around frantically, half-expecting the voice in her head to have taken form.

*Relax, you've done nothing wrong.*

Gabrielle looked up, defiantly. "I'm a monster! I've traumatized my daughter."

*Fool. There's nothing wrong with wanting the best for her. Change the plan now and you'll only make things worse.*

Gabrielle closed her eyes. What if the voice was right? Wasn't it too late to turn back? She could feel tears gathering in her eyes, but she wasn't going to allow herself to cry. She wasn't going to let these voices control her, so instead she began to chuckle. There was no time to dabble in self-pity. Her day was waiting.

She left the kitchen. She was going to grab her coat and leave. She had appointments: with the bank, Dr. Carl, the Pilates instructor. Perhaps she'd stop by Bliss and make an appointment for her and Arianna over the weekend. Yes. She'd come home with this surprise treat for Arianna, along with more words of comfort, words that would gradually erase the pain of their earlier conversation.

She had gotten as far as the closet when the phone rang. Seconds later, Tatiana, came in from the den, with the cordless in hand.

"Your mother, Missus," the woman said, extending the phone.

Gabrielle stared at it coldly. "Tell her you can't find me. And if she calls again, tell her I've disappeared."

# 13. EXCERPTS FROM ARIANNA LEVY'S JOURNALS

April 3rd

I feel like I'm going to explode. My life has been stolen. My future is limping like a wounded goat in the desert, and the vultures are hovering overhead, ready for the kill. Very soon I'll be ruined. Obviously someone knows. They all know what my screwy mother has been up to. I can't even look at Mandela anymore. I see him and run in the opposite direction. The whole thing's obviously one big joke to him. He's playing my mother for a fool. He's keeping quiet now, but one day he'll blow the whole thing up in my face.

All this time I thought Mother was right. Like a docile puppy, I rolled over and did my tricks, even when I wanted to say fuck this, I just want to *breathe*. Because there was a point. What's the point now? This whole behind my back thing is sickening. Of course, Mommy's fragile baby girl can't be exposed to the truth. It's like she thinks I'm a roll of film; the only way I get to develop is to keep me in the dark. Worse than that, what does it say about her faith in my abilities? If anything is getting me into Princeton, it's going to be *my* grades, *my* SAT score and *my* resumé. How does she know Princeton won't just take us both? How does she know they even want *him*, anyway? It's all speculation. She's fucked with my chances based on a guess she's making.

She's been trying to talk to me for the past four days. She even slipped a letter under my door but I ripped it up without reading it. Let her stew for a while. Let her be fucking miserable because you know what she *deserves* to be miserable. I guess I shouldn't be so shocked. The woman's always been one seriously crafty bitch. She's convinced herself she's done nothing wrong. Told me I'd *thank her* someday. Ha. I thought about saying something to Daddy — God knows I'm desperate to tell *someone* — but I know that will only make things worse. The two of them will start to fight and next thing you know it's all out war.

Well, let's see what she thinks of her precious daughter now. Because Arianna Levy's taking a holiday. I don't care what the pluperfect tense for *debrouiller* is. The *Canterbury Tales* are not relevant to my life. This morning, before fourth period, I shuttled Penelope into the bathroom and told her we were hitting Serendipity and Bloomingdale's come lunchtime. She looked at me like I was possessed, but I told her not to protest. I cut the whole fucking day. Who knows, maybe I'll do it again tomorrow. Then Mother can field phone calls from concerned teachers, and she can make up some more terrific excuses. God knows she's good at that.

I've been living in Mommie Dearest's box for too long now, and it's high time I see what's on the outside. I guess she might have to settle for a real daughter instead of her made up one.

April 7th

Douglas invited me over Saturday night. His parents were at some function so we had the place to ourselves. We've been seeing each other for about a month now, and he probably was hoping to use this opportunity to take our relationship to the next level. Boy was he in for a surprise.

He got some Mike's Hard Lemonades from the fridge, so I let out this chuckle and asked him where the liquor cabinet was. He was surprised, but he pointed me in the right direction. *I like this side of you, Arianna,* he said. I started sifting through the bottles like I knew what I was doing. We experimented with different concoctions: Ketel One and Kahlua. Bacardi O and Cointreau. I wanted to get smashed.

After four drinks we were going at it on the floor all sloppy. We had made out a few times before and it had always been sweet and nice. But I didn't want it to be nice anymore. I wanted it to be angry.

I never thought I'd end up doing it with Douglas Meisel. He just wasn't the one I pictured my first time with. But it dawned on me that was *exactly* my problem: I'm constantly living in a world of expectations. Then I thought, why *not* Douglas? He's cute enough. He's not an asshole. He wouldn't be that bad memory scarring me for life.

He started to rub the crotch area of my jeans. I opened my fly and guided his hand inside. His eyes got sweaty and wide. He was very respectful with his newfound freedom at first, like he wasn't sure what I was allowing him. But then I started biting him on the neck, and his fingers explored deeper.

I can't perfectly get at the next few moments. My eyes were closed and I felt both detached and there at the same time, like there were two Mes, the one on the floor getting nasty, and the other watching it all from a chair. I think I started moaning. I might have pulled down his pants, or maybe he did. He positioned himself on top of me and I could feel how hard he was. I heard him whispering my name over and over, between his kisses on my neck. He said something about a condom and I nodded my head. I could sense him fumbling to get up. I heard some stuff being knocked over, and then the sounds grew distant. I lay there silent and dizzy.

My eyes felt heavy. I had to struggle to keep them open. I looked down at the mess my body was making on the floor: naked from the waist up, my underwear rolled down almost to my knees. Suddenly the lights dimmed. Douglas walked past me. I looked up at his lanky frame. He was still wearing socks, and his dick head was poking through the fly of his boxers. He went over to the stereo and I watched him anxiously thumb through a CD collection. I started to chuckle, but he ignored me. Next thing I knew Barry White was setting the mood. Maybe he thought I wanted it to be more special.

He set himself down beside me. He was looking at me, searching for signs I didn't want to give. Then he caressed my face and asked me if I was sure. What a horrible question. I just nodded my head. I could hear the rustle of a wrapper being torn open, and Douglas fumbling to put it on. I tried to put on a willing smile as he kissed my neck. He maneuvered himself upon me and I braced myself as he pushed once, and I think he grunted, and then he pushed again. That's when I felt it. My hands gripped the back of his arms and I sucked in my chest and he pushed again and then came a quick sharp pain, followed by a longer, blurry kind of pain and then I knew he was inside me. I knew how much he wanted this to happen. I could tell it was his first time too.

He moved tenuously at first, until he found his rhythm. For a few seconds I allowed myself to study the concentration in his face, his eyes scrunched tight under the folds of his eyebrows, and then he opened them, and he looked at me with *awe*, looked at me like I was *his savior*, this angel coming down to unburden him of the yoke of his childhood. And then he pushed faster and his mouth flopped open and he was so lost in the moment I wanted to lose myself too, so I closed my eyes and let the process take over. I wanted to believe in this as much as he did. I smiled as he let himself go inside of me; I really thought I did. He collapsed on top of my body and I sat there and thought, *it's over, it's over, it's over*. And when I opened my eyes I saw Douglas hovering over me with sober compassion and he said *Arianna you're crying* and I denied it, so he put his fingers on my face to catch the tears, but I told him not to worry, that it didn't hurt, that I wanted to do it. He kissed me and told me not to cry because he really liked me and then I *really* started crying, bawling like a sad little freak baby because I didn't know who that girl on the floor was, I don't know if I can be her no matter how much I want to be.

I'm so fucking hopeless I can't even fuck up right. It's days later and I should be savoring my womanhood and instead everything is worse now. Douglas's calls and his letters and his calling me his *girlfriend*—it means nothing, because I still feel dead inside. I feel nothing but creepy numbness suffocating me because I know this too will be revealed, this too just another mark against me—like Mother says, tigers piss on the ground to mark their territory and high school boys talk about scoring. And even if he keeps quiet, I don't know *what I'm doing*. I don't want to be Douglas's girlfriend because he's going to find out things too, and then he'll hate me and I'll be a pariah, a nobody, I'll have to become the black-nail-polish, chain-smoking, class-cutting, flask-drinking girl with a reputation. There's no turning back now. Who can I turn back to? The old me doesn't exist anymore; she was just a sad mirage, a sick joke Mother was playing on me.

I have to find a new me and I don't even know where to look. Where is she? *Who* is she? Do people care about her? Does she have friends and goals and a normal family? Does she care about

homework and grades and volleyball and drama club? Is she going to ace her SAT or does she even give a shit?
   Is there any point to giving a shit anymore?

## 14. MANDELA

There were artists famous for their self-portraits—Rembrandt, Picasso, Egon Schiele. There were even paintings of artists painting portraits—a Vermeer comes to mind. As far as he could tell, though, his idea was a fairly original one. Still, most portrait painters had the benefit of having their subjects sit for them. What was he going to do, have Gabrielle come over for tea and ask her to pose on the sofa?

So he was left with his photographs, and his memories. His first attempts bored him. There was a reason portraiture was so outdated; it was hard to say anything new with the form. Still, he knew it *had* to be a portrait. He'd seen something in her that he wasn't used to seeing on the faces of the adults in his life: confusion and vulnerability duking it out with decorum and reserve. Hers was the face of someone seeing her own defeat, recognizing, for the first time, that something had been lost, and facing up to it.

But a picture of a face wouldn't be enough. He had to paint her as an artist. Not just any artist, but an artist painting herself. *Realizing* herself. He'd do what she was afraid to do, lay out her inner being on the canvas, a picture of a Gabrielle long forgotten, oxidized by time and neglect. This was how it started. Then more ideas came, building upon each other. The current version had

Gabrielle holding a mirror in one hand, a paintbrush in the other. The hand holding the mirror was clean, with a diamond on the ring finger and a bracelet around its wrist—but this hand looked old. The hand holding the brush was dirty—dried paint dappled its knuckles—but it seemed to belong to a much younger woman.

The artist's face was indistinct. At first he'd painted a young woman, then an older woman, until he realized it had to be neither. But the face in the mirror was unmistakable; a face he imagined she had at one time, a face of hope and possibility. The artist was trying to recreate this face on the canvas. Her work looked promising, but there was much left to be done. In the background were old portraits the artist had previously made of herself—precise, overly formal works. The details were outstanding and yet seemed lifeless. More than that, the pictures were cracking. Time had exposed some defects, and these faces were no longer holding up.

This would be his gift to her. The irony wasn't lost on him. She had been the one originally offering dubious gifts, and yet here he was, offering something in return. It was alright; she had inspired him. She had offered him the idea of Europe. She had given this idea a shape, a specificity that his other dreams were incapable of acquiring.

The past few weeks Europe had weighed upon him. He'd taken out books from the library, went online to travel sites. He'd discovered STA travel for cheap student fares, looked into Eurorail passes. Perhaps he'd hitchhike; it seemed common there. He thought about foreign languages and customs, and the institutional whiteness of Europeans. How strange it would be for him and yet how blasé, surrounded as he was by white people most of his life.

An International Student Identity Card would provide him access to thousands of youth hostels and campgrounds. He'd meet leggy Latvian linguists in Lourdes, Proust-espousing Parisians in Prague, Danish Dali disciples in Düsseldorf. He'd go to the Biennale in Venice, tour the famous museums, visit the birthplaces of Ernst and Dubuffet, pick up free rags on street corners about the local artists, hang out with them, learn from them, share with them some zany tidbits of America, buy falafels from late night kiosks, smoke hash from Turkish bongs. And everyone would be *cool*—crazy cool—and they'd all speak *English*. Fucking English.

If he packaged it successfully—as fodder for his personal essay, say—then maybe, just maybe, he could get away with it. Sure, his parents would have suspicions. They'd bring up the cost, and he'd have to come up with an airtight scheme. He'd get Gabrielle in on it, convince her to get one of her socialite friends to play a director of an art school in Milan that offers scholarships to emerging artists. Something like that. Gabrielle would figure it out. She could pull a scam like that; she was the *queen* of scams.

Sarafina's screams from the kitchen, followed by his mother's protests, jolted him out of his reverie. He lay his brush down on the easel and wiped his hands against his smock. He stared at his work-in-progress. He was arriving at something, even if that something was still nebulous. His mother was putting on the voice she used whenever things reached *that point*, when she'd *had it up to here*. She had come home early that day, after what apparently had been a tense mother/daughter day at school. The good news was now he had the afternoon off. The bad news was that despite her promises, she really wasn't going to leave him alone for more than an hour; the SAT was ten days away and everything else *would have to wait*.

The phone rang. His instincts told him it might be Gabrielle, so he ran over to the nightstand. This time they were right.

"Is this a bad time?" The words tumbled out of her mouth, like she already knew it was and just wanted confirmation.

"Kinda," he said.

"I can call back," she said.

"No. Go ahead."

She sighed. "My daughter has found out certain things."

*Her daughter*? This was bad. All he could say was "Oh."

"I don't know how to proceed. I'm a bit confused."

"I haven't mentioned anything." He had no idea how this could have happened. He wasn't going to take the blame.

"I know that. Don't worry. I just need to think of a plan."

"Don't sweat it." He thought it was the right thing to say, given the circumstances.

"I'm not trying to cheat you. It's just...she's talking about *dropping Princeton*." She punctuated the last words with a whisper. "She's in such a *state*."

What was he supposed to say to that? That he was sorry? It wasn't his fault.

"I'm sorry," Gabrielle said. "I should let you go."

"No, it' just...my mom's home."

"Good God. Say no more. I'm hanging up now."

"Wait!" He couldn't let it end. Not like this. "I need to see you about something."

She paused. "That is inconceivable," she said.

"Not now. In a few weeks, maybe. I need to show something to you."

"Mandela, she's not *speaking* to me."

Her voice was tremulous and uncertain. She wasn't the kind of woman used to feeling lost, he knew that. "If we meet this one time, it can be over," he said, surprised by his own words. "We can settle everything."

"I can't agree," she mumbled. She was agreeing, though.

"I'll call you. When I'm ready."

"I'm *horrible*. A horrible person."

"You're not horrible…"

"I have to go," she said. "*You* have to go."

"Think about it. Please."

She hung up the phone. Mandela paced around the room. Shit. This wasn't good.

How the fuck did this happen? Had Legion said something? He wasn't the type. And what the hell did he know, anyway? Maybe Gabrielle had been sloppy. But she had the most to lose by being sloppy. This was fucked up. Arianna *had* been acting kind of strange in school the past week. Poor Arianna. He could even feel bad for her now.

He picked up his paintbrush and began curling long strokes of black into Gabrielle's hair when there was a knock on the door. Deidre Robinson swooped into her bedroom, sealing the door and clutching the knob behind her back like she'd found sanctuary from a pack of wolves. Her face was full of dispatch. She walked over and stood beside him, folding her arms emphatically.

"Your sister has become a gourmand," she said. "Turns out Edy's vanilla isn't good enough, and she can only have Häagen Dazs."

"That's what happens when you move to Manhattan," he said. He lifted the tarp to cover his painting but she moved closer to stop him.

"Hold up," she said. "Let me see what you've been doing."

He hesitated. He could tell her it wasn't ready, which wouldn't be a lie. But he knew, he *knew,* this was his best work; he knew she wouldn't deny it. He knew she'd be surprised by it. So instead he just moved out of her way. He stood and watched her eyes as she took it all in, watched them dilate with—what? Wonder? Confusion? Fear? She looked upset, almost intimidated. It took her a minute to say anything at all.

"This is intense, Mandela," she said. "Very intense."

"Yeah. I guess it is."

"It's really good, baby. A big step forward."

"Thanks." He smiled. It made his skin quiver, how moved she was.

"This woman. Is she white?"

He hesitated. "I can't tell you what to see, Mom."

"Of course not, honey, I'm sorry. The artist creates and the viewer interprets. I know. It's just...interesting."

He wasn't sure where her thoughts were heading. He was pretty sure his mother wouldn't make the connection to Gabrielle.

"You know, you're not the only creative one in the family," she said.

Mandela laughed. Why did parents always have to somehow take credit for everything? "Right. When Dad gets home you guys can argue again about who's more responsible for my genius."

"No argument where that's concerned. Your father's family is full of accountants and insurance salesmen."

Mandela laughed.

"I used to make dresses. In high school. Did I ever tell you that?"

"I think you may have mentioned it once in my lifetime."

"Don't get smart. I know you know, but do you *know*? Did I tell you that some of those dresses were entered in competitions? And I won a few? The wife of the mayor of Trenton even bought one at the time."

"So what made you stop?"

"Nothing *made* me stop." She shook her head. "I just stopped. It was a pastime. I enjoyed it, but my heart wasn't into it."

"Maybe yours was, but Grandpa and Grandma's weren't."

Deidre frowned. "Lord, Mandela. Not at all. My mother adored my dresses. I think she would have preferred I stayed home after high school and set up shop downtown instead of going 'halfway round the world' as she put it, to Cambridge. Not that she said anything. Or your granddaddy, for that matter. They were *ecstatic* when I made Harvard. And you know what? The dressmaking probably helped me get in. I sent pictures of the gowns I'd made along with my application. I wrote about it in my essay."

"Sounds a bit more than just a pastime then."

"Honey, when you're a young black girl in Edison and Harvard sends a letter, you don't turn them down. You thank your lucky stars. Anyway, I found other interests."

"Maybe that's just creative hindsight," he said. "Maybe that's just the way you'd like to see it now."

His mother looked down at the ground. A painfully phony smile crept onto her face as she bit her lip. "You think I have regrets? Well, I don't. Which doesn't mean there aren't moments when I look back and say, what if. But they're fleeting moments, Del. They're not the measure of a life. They don't take away anything from me, because I know that I'm happy."

She stared coldly at the painting. Something was making her uncomfortable. Not just his words, but the painting; something about it irritated her, put her on the defensive.

"I wasn't saying you're unhappy, Ma."

"The thing about being seventeen, Mandela," she said, "is that the arc of your life can often seem so certain. But the reality is that as you mature you'll look back at yourself and say, oh how stubborn, how willfully stupid I was when I was younger. And if you're smart you'll do this every few years for the rest of your life because this is how you teach yourself humility. Honey, your father and I are not your enemies."

"What? I never said anything like that, Mom."

"The world is huge, Mandela. We just want you to see past the immediate."

"You're being unfair." He was shouting. "You're taking your day out on me now."

She sighed a long, heavy sigh. "You know what? I'm going to make dinner. Please hit the books, Mandela. Your hour is up. I'm not going to say it again. OK?"

He nodded his head. She reached over to peck him on the cheek but it was a lifeless kiss, a formality. He had pained her, and this kiss meant she was going to overlook his foolishness, his immaturity. But he was not foolish or immature. Even if he didn't have all the answers at least he kept asking questions. At least he wasn't holding up ideals only to compromise them when it suited him.

She left the room without another word. Later, she'd rehash this conversation with his dad. No matter, he was even more resolved. He was going to paint, goddammit. He was going to Europe this summer. Gabrielle was going to help him.

He wondered what his parents would do if they found out about him and Gabrielle. The demon from Central Park West, a woman who had everything handed to her on a solid gold platter. She had earned their venom by living up to every expectation they had of upper-class white *noblesse oblige*. No matter that it was her life they were aspiring to, because somehow *they* would do it right, without her ignorance or recklessness. No matter that the destiny they'd set out for him seemed to uncannily resemble the plan laid out by Gabrielle for Arianna. No matter that this crushing homogeny of expectations allowed for little personal liberty.

Cogs in the machine. Was that all we were in life? Then it occurred to him. This was his painting—Gabrielle's awakening to this fact. She was seeing herself in the machine, the part she was playing in the hopeless pursuit of the perfect life plan, and it was beginning to unhinge her, forcing her to ask questions she didn't have answers for. He had helped open her eyes. Soon he'd do the same for his parents, whether they liked it or not.

## 15. RANDALL

His feet shuffle up the stairs of the desolate N train station. The air smells faintly of stale peanuts and despair. Above ground, his eyes squint, unaccustomed as they are to early morning sunlight. He opens them and sees: a pale sky, the bloom of May leaves on elm trees, an old woman walking her scabby dog, pigeons pecking at sidewalk debris.

Dear God, he was in Brooklyn. On a Saturday. *At 7:45 in the morning.*

And not trendy Brooklyn. Not Williamsburg or the Heights, the Slope or one of the Hills; anonymous Brooklyn. People with accents lived here. People who ended their sentences with "but." Salt-of-the-earth types paraded in wacky sitcoms for the humorous titillation of Middle America.

*My name is Legion Cartwright and I am here to take the SAT.*

Today's Legion Cartwright is sporting cactus-flower red hair, a vintage Ramones T-shirt over a long-sleeve thermal, ragged Dickies pants and a distressingly filthy pair of scuffed-up Vans. Last night Legion himself had brought over the uniform for his doppelganger. Legion-for-a-day tried on the aforementioned outfit, glanced at himself in the mirror, and became outrageously hard. Whether it was the clothes, or the resemblance to his object of lust, or a combination of both, Randall wasn't able to tell.

The sight had intoxicated the real Legion as well. The boy had dropped to his knees, opened up the fly of his own pants and proceeded to give Randall the rarest of blowjobs. Then he shucked the Dickies down, stood up and spun Randall around so they both pressed against the full-length mirror. One of his hands pinned Randall's body to the mirror while he spat into the other. He plunged two fingers inside Randall, unzipped his own fly and savagely entered in one thrust. Randall was too shocked to scream. Instead of resisting, his hand found his penis. In little time Legion started to huff ferociously and release himself inside Randall. Only then did Randall find his voice again, a whimpering wheeze heralding the sticky discharge of his own surrender. If there were any doubts about what would happen the following morning, they had been thoroughly eviscerated.

And here he is, obeying tacit orders. He follows his lover's hand-scrawled directions to the gates surrounding Barbra Streisand High School, a rectangular solid with a neo-classical Greek façade. The closer he approaches the more young faces he sees, walking in twos and threes, exiting family-friendly cars, giggling and shouting with the painless grace of their years. The future of America. The gorgeous mosaic, they say, but he notices how they mostly stick to their own kind: Aryan jocks with salon-tanned cheerleaders, dopehounds with Phishheads, Eminem disciples and their abused, frizzy-haired girlfriends. Spit-shined Hindu boys, keeping to themselves. Cocky Asian wannabe gangstas, headbands around their porcupine heads, their girlfriends' bobs pink and red and blonde, their nails polished and studded, their ears hooped. Asians love test day; they own the fucking SAT.

He follows the crowds through the doors. No one notices him. No one cares. High school hallways so depressing. Are they depressing or is it just his memories that are depressing? Meek lighting. Sickly beiges and light blues, the colors of nursing home lunchrooms. Clocks everywhere: *gotta be on time. Gotta keep moving.* Lockers lined up somberly. An indescribable odor wilting the air. He breathes it in like a wine aficionado, attempting to sort out the palettes: chlorine, mildew, industrial disinfectant, lunch meat?

A portly security guard decrees: Down to the auditorium, guys. He will listen and follow and obey. *My name is Legion Cartwright and I am here to take the SAT.*

The auditorium: home of the talentless talent shows, drama club destructions of *Oklahoma*, sobering reminders by guest-speaking former addicts reminding everyone to stay in school and Just Say No. No to drugs, alcohol, sex, bad hygiene. Yes to life?

They are gathered here, for what he's not sure. Ritual execution by firing squad? No one else seems to question it. They seem less tired than he is. They're young; they've probably slept well. Cliques assemble in clusters, but he has no friends (déjà vu?) so he skulks at the far end of an empty row, so as not to dilute anyone's coolness.

He observes them silently. So this is the slaughter he sends his lambs to. He can make out the pockets of anxiety bubbling among the disaffected faces. Nervous Nellies acting out their fears with last minute jokes, incurable dorks with forty-seven sharpened pencils, each individually inspected for #2 status, frustrated math divas punching quadratic formulas into their back-up calculators. He feels somewhat responsible for this collective paranoia. His instincts urge him to dole out last-minute pointers, then he remembers he is seventeen and just another dork himself. Should he act nervous? He tries to conjure up memories from his own SAT, but nothing comes to him, aside from his disappointing first score. No doubt he had been careless.

After several minutes, a camel-faced woman steps up to the front and makes an announcement: *Ladies and gentlemen, please exit slowly to the hallway where you'll find sheets with your names printed in alphabetical...*Everyone gets up before she even finishes the cattle call. Shuffling and elbowing, Randall finds the C's. 207. He heads to the stairs.

Just outside room 207 he joins the line that has formed. He takes out his ticket and IDs, and then, realizing eagerness is a sign of guilt, puts them back into his pocket. He rubs his hands to stop them from shaking, tries to affect a look of vacuous indifference. He peeks in to assess the proctor. A woman in her early sixties. She greets everyone with a thin smile, but he can tell she's all business. Some hooligan three persons ahead of him apparently doesn't have proper ID. *I'm sorry, it must have a picture.* He protests but she doesn't budge.

*Downstairs,* she snaps. *Find the ETS agent. I can't help you.* The boy lumbers out of the room. Randall is nervous—the boy might go postal and return with a shotgun, pop them off one by one.

Approaching the woman, he sees his fears are unfounded. The surface stringency is there, but underneath she's positively grandmotherly. A mole sprouts northwest of her chin. No doubt she has a college-bound grandson herself, for whom she'll knit a scarf this afternoon.

"You are?" she asks.

"Legion Cartwright." He shows her the ticket.

"Identification," she says.

He takes out the best of the bunch and hands it to her.

"You're a long way from home, Mr. Cartwright," she says, eyeing his address.

"My mom lives in the neighborhood." He was ready for that one.

"I see," she says. "The desks are numbered. Please sit in seat fifteen."

Seat fifteen is in the back of the room, where class clowns prefer to sit. Randall opens his backpack and takes out a regulation calculator and three pencils. A ripple of calmness drifts over him. He has cleared the first hurdle.

Quickly the other chairs fill up. Helga (she looks Austrian) is still allowing chatter at this point. Someone makes the usual don't-forget-to-sign-your-name-to-get-a-400 joke, another chimes in with the whaddayu-care-you're-going-to-community-college joke, then the let-me-sit-next-to-her-she's-a-genius joke. The worry wart to his left laughs at everything, openly proclaiming he's going to fail miserably, even though Randall can tell the kid will easily break 1300 and just wants to fit in with his stupendously mediocre friends. Some Long Island refugee whines about how "friggin early" it is, and how she had no sleep the night before because Sal's party was "da-bomb-diggity."

Mole Helga stands up to silence the crowd. Grids are handed out, followed by booklets. She explains the procedure: All responses must be bubbled in. The center and test IDs are on the board. The final paragraph—the "no cheating clause" she calls it—must be reprinted by hand, signed and dated. The procession is endless and Randall finds himself tuning out. His eyes survey the room. A history of the civil rights movement banner rests proudly above the blackboard. Prosaic plants line the window sill, waiting to die. Generic motivators in poster frames cloyingly adorn the opposite walls. He knows them well—similar to the ones at CATPEE—sappy attempts at positivity that teenagers readily dismiss as bullshit: *The world is yours if you seize it. I am the future of America.*

Helga is answering questions before they are asked. No scrap paper. No food of any kind. Bathroom visits allowed only during the breaks. At 9:15, she finally begins section one. Randall attacks the questions. Math. This is the easy part. The fun part. It thrills him that they see him as just another student, electrifies him that no one knows.

*OK, Randall. Focus. Grid in one page at a time. No careless mistakes.* Shit. How simple it was to shell out the advice, not nearly as easy to follow it with the pressure on. Helga eyeballs him suspiciously from her desk. She looks like the checkout lady at his local Whole Foods; that one has a mole too. What if it's her and she remembers seeing him fill up his basket with arugula and flaxseed oil? Teenagers don't buy such precious things. She's going to rat him out. *Stop being paranoid. Focus. Focus.*

The average of consecutive numbers is always equal to their median. When variables are on the same side of the equal side in a system of equations, combine the equations by adding or subtracting; otherwise, solve for one in terms of the other and substitute. The measure of each interior angle of a regular polygon is found using the formula *180 (n-2) /n* where *n* equals the number of sides in the polygon.

Fuck, what's the square root of 289? Use the calculator. You don't have to know everything. You *don't* know everything. You think you can get a 1600? You can't. You'll fuck up somehow.

Section 2, Verbal: God speaks to him through the sentence completions and analogies: Libido. Wheedle. Wanton. Embroil. Lackey: Obsequious as Randall: Both

His crimes were _____; the aftereffects were felt for many years to come. (Answer: Insidious.)

The supposed specialist was nothing but a _____; his false claims of expertise were thoroughly _____ by his critics. (Answers: charlatan; debunked.)

*Repent, Randall, repent!*

Contrite. Indenture. Sudorific. Sudorific? What the fuck was sudorific? *Jesus, you don't know shit. Has it really come down to this, Randall? I'm doing research! For my novel! Tsk, tsk. Do you research, then. Do your dirty deeds, your dastardly and diabolical disservice to society. Or maybe you can do yourself a favor and grow up.*

No. No time for guilt now. A passage about parasitic plants and their hosts. Who was the parasite, him or Legion? Irrelevant. *Focus.* Answer the questions.

Section 3: Back-to-back verbal means one of them doesn't count. You're not supposed to be able to tell which the "equating" section is, but this one's obvious.

Prevaricate. Misanthrope. The misanthrope prevaricated to avoid facing up to the pathetic realities of his life.

A passage about art forgeries. *Repent! Repent!*

Helga announces pencils down; there will be a seven minute

break. The kids moan sighs of relief and *jeez this bitch is long* and *OMG, that passage was mad hard.* He will not stray from his desk. He will not engage in witty banter, no matter how much he wants to know if he can really pass and if some of the girls (and boys) think he's cute and wonder why they've never seen him around. He stretches his legs, circles the desk within a courteous radius and sits down.

He feels a tap on his shoulder and turns around. It's the black girl with the canary eyes from two seats over. She's chewing gum, in blatant defiance of Helga's decree.

"So what's your name?" She tilts her chin forward.

"Legion," he says, trying to sound like the most reasonable person in the world.

"Uh-hunh." She grimaces. "You look kinda old."

"I get that," he says.

"Don't worry, I won't tell." She smirks. "We all do what we gotta do."

He laughs like a retarded mule. "And your name?"

"Wouldn't you like to know," she says, bobbing an eyebrow. "Later, Legion."

She sails away. He's been spotted. The guillotine will be prepared. His head will roll. But no. Helga rushes everyone back to their seats and begins Section 4.

**Quantitative Comparisons**: Choose A if the quantity in column A is greater; B if the quantity in column B is greater; C if the quantities are equal; D, if the relationship between the columns cannot be determined from the information given.

| Column A | Column B |
| --- | --- |
| 1) My lust for Legion | My capacity for self-destruction |

    Answer: C

| | |
| --- | --- |
| 2) The probability that Legion will stop speaking to me once the results are in. | The probability that I will find a suitable boyfriend in the near future. |

    Answer: A

Section 5, Verbal: Verisimilitude. Sophistry. Debacle. *What is the end game, Randall? I'm making sacrifices. Isn't that what love's* all about? *Love? Did you say love?*

Poor, poor Wilder. He can't even bring himself to think his name any more. And Life? He's been panhandling on subway platforms ever since the bistro was boarded up, wholesaling Metrocard swipes and glow-in-the-dark pens.

This is pointless. I'm going to fuck up. *Too late, Randall. Too late.*

Section 6, Short Math. It's almost over. He feels sick. His stomach is speaking in tongues. Not now. Now is the time for the surface area of rectangular solids. He wills the nausea out of his mind.

Section 7, Final Section. Mole Helga barks: *Fifteen minutes.* More reading. Paired passages on the duality of Aztec Civilization. Are the architectural accomplishments of the Aztecs overshadowed by their barbaric devotion to human sacrifice, or must these sacrifices be placed in the greater context of Mesoamerican history? Within three minutes the intellectually challenged turn in their grids and break for the door. No point in being pretentious when Devry was your future. Jesus, how can he be so cynical? He's a tutor, for heaven's sake. He tries to tune out the looming crisis brewing in his belly, spreading to his intestines. *It's over, it's over. A few more questions.* He can go home, and be himself again. Was this preferable?

Helga stands up and whispers *thirty seconds,* a wicked gleam in her eye. Slavs and their stopwatch fetishes. No doubt she's thrilled to snatch the test booklets from the last minute poindexters. He gets up and gathers his things. He doesn't know how he's done. He has played Lotto with Legion's future. It sickens him. It expedites his bowels. He leaves the grid on Helga's desk. She offers a sympathetic *Have a good afternoon.* See you in Whole Foods, he wants to say. He doesn't.

He's done it. He can leave. So why is he ready to hurl? His stomach burbles like a rabid Jesus freak on the subway: *Repent. Repent.* He's going to blow chunks, right then and there. On Helga's lap. On the test grids. He'll ruin them and be forced to do it all over again. *No. No.* He pushes past the door in search of the nearest boy's room. Christ, he is going to have IBS in a high school bathroom. There's no way he'll make it home.

The hallway is teeming with students. *That was impossible. Nah, I aced the muthafucka. I need some sleep, yo.* They are comfortable here; they spend most of their waking hours in this cesspool. He thought he'd be comfortable, too. At the very least, he's absorbed some details for his novel. Finally, the door marked

"MEN." He lurches, thrusts himself inside. Fluorescent overhead bulbs twitching. A damp claustrophobia. Two lanky boys loiter inside. A lingering fear resurfaces. He has not made out well in high school bathrooms. He's always looked scrawny for his age, and when frightened (easily), it was as if a pink triangle suddenly materialized on his forehead.

But the boys don't cast a single eye his way. They are engrossed in conversation, scrutinizing their acne-full chins in bleary, oxidized mirrors. He finds a stall and yanks down his Dickies. A deluge. The seal, broken. *Let it all out, Randall: Toxins, fears, frustrations, any remaining vestiges of dignity.* Scratchiti and graffiti bedeck the stall walls, illustrating the tales of the natives like prehistoric cave paintings. Apparently Streisand High was rife with cocksuckers, many of whom were willing to post their phone numbers. He thinks about adding his name to the list. *For expert service, call Randall. Tutoring also available.*

When he's sure he's done, he flushes. His neck is wet with sweat. There is relief, but also a lingering disgust; the smell is overpowering. He exits the stall and washes his hands. A bewildered reflection stares back at him in the mirror. His eyes glaze over with confusion. He cannot see the person underneath the disguise anymore. Was there anyone left? *Who are you?* I am Randall Miller. Randall Miller. Right? Right??

He had to leave now, rejoin Randall Miller in medias res. The hallway stretches endlessly. Up ahead, the front doors beckon like a lighthouse in the fog. He recalls, vaguely, all those news stories of little girls trapped in wells. He wonders: how does it feel down there without context, every sound another variable, the light above so remote it's almost an abstraction? The dampness is what's real. The cold and the dark. Hearing the voices from above was probably the only thing those girls could hold on to. Knowing that someone was out there was the only way to drown out the reality of the well.

He swings open the front doors and sucks in a long overdue breath of fresh air. He has a promising chapter ahead of him.

# 16. EXCERPTS FROM ARIANNA LEVY'S JOURNALS

April 21st

Last night, after ten days of ignoring her pleas, I finally allowed Mother some face time with me in my room. Not because my anger is dissipating, but more because the fucking up I've been doing lately has reached a tipping point—Carlotta Piper actually asked Mother for her, Daddy, and me to come in for a "chat."

But I don't want to get Daddy involved. So far Mother and I have managed to keep him out of this. I just know the truth will destroy him. So when I came home from school yesterday I told Mother she'd have fifteen minutes after dinner to plead her case. She'd obviously been preparing her spiel for a while now. She told me she was sorrier than I could imagine, that she held herself unconditionally responsible for everything and that it was perfectly normal of me to be acting the way I was. Then she switched gears. She said no matter how I felt about her, I couldn't continue down this road. For my own sake I just needed to be who I am. And who I am, she said, is the future valedictorian of Valhalla. Everyone knows it. That's why there were so many calls, so many concerned people. Because they *knew*.

I sat patiently, and what I finally understood, filtering through the subtext of her seemingly rational arguments, was that my mother is a desperate woman. A sad and desperate woman. She's a mess. A mess I no longer recognize, not quite a totally different person but on her way there, in a pupa stage. The ground beneath her feet is shifting, and while I'm part of this shift it's *more* than me; it's bigger than me.

There are other secrets. I can tell. You just can't ever really know a person — we really are all alone in the world. We're all our own little messes that most of the time we manage to hide from others and even ourselves. But sometimes something happens and the mess is exposed. This is where my mother is now. She sat on my bed trying so hard to sweep up her mess, but I could tell it was all desperation. There were too many shards, too much muck piling up.

And so for the first time in my life I looked at my mother and saw something unbelievable: I saw my father. My father and his simple eyes and transparent smile, the way he wears his love for me on his sleeve. I saw this on my mother's face, I saw what must have been there long ago, something my father must have seen too, something he recognized and loved and married. Your parents tell you that one day you'll grow up and see them as real human beings. My mother's mask is falling off, and I'm afraid of what will emerge. But I have to allow for it.

And even though I yelled and bitched at her about how sick she's made me feel, even though it felt good letting it all out, I knew that the next day — today — I'd get up, go to school, do my homework, and go back to studying because we both can't be messes now; one of us has to be strong and sweep things away. Hers has grown too large and I don't know how she'll deal with it, but I will not add to it any longer.

I'm going to apply myself again. Even if I can't much believe in anything right now, at least I'll try. I don't want to face my father's sad eyes any more. I don't want to see my mother continue to fall apart.

May 1st

The SAT is two days away. A few hours ago, I had what I know will be my last session with Randall. It was bittersweet saying goodbye to him. He kept mentioning the fall and SAT IIs and I kept nodding along. Even if I do take them, Mother will hire someone else. She'll want to start fresh, put poor clueless Randall out to pasture, not a bad tutor really, but perhaps the only person I know who seems more confused with life than Mother. I hope he figures out what to do with his hair. Talk about early mid-life crisis.

It was a strange session. We just talked. We've sorta been coasting in neutral since the Mandela fiasco, but even before that, Randall's magical powers had been slipping. He seemed perpetually distracted, like his life was a series of math problems, all without solutions. (Isn't everyone's?) It's funny: I guess because I knew I wouldn't see him again I decided to really open up. It's so fucked up, but I have no one else to turn to at this point. So I just went ahead and spilled it. Every last iota. I told him about Mother and Mandela and the whole Princeton thing, how I wasn't sure if I wanted to go anymore. I wasn't sure if I cared about the SAT at all, but I was going to try to care anyway. I was going to do my best because I had worked so hard and I might as well give my future a fighting chance.

I expected him to shoot me this pained look of TMI, but instead his face turned soft and sober. He even took my hand, which normally would be so wrong, but at the moment just wasn't. He rubbed it gently and said that he was sorry, that it was a terrible thing to find out about your mother of all people, but that I was smart for trying to move on. I was a bit shaken by this sudden act of compassion, but also moved. I turned away for a second because I felt I might cry, right there in front of my SAT tutor, who wasn't really a friend. But then I changed my mind and I did cry, soft, tiny whimpers, nothing major, but there they were. It was such a relief.

And I wondered if Randall was touched by my tears, if somehow he needed to see someone else's pain to alleviate his own. Suddenly I got ballsy and told him that he looked dazed and overwhelmed and had been looking that way for like, ever. I told him he owed it to me to share, and how good it felt, and so he sighed the longest, cruelest sigh and I said *You must be in love with someone causing you grief,* and he closed his eyes and squirmed and said, *Yes, I'm in love with the wrong person, I'm in love with a shadow that will disappear in the night and leave me stranded and miserable.*

I laughed at how dramatic his choice of words were, so much like ones I'd use myself. I told him he should write things down and how much better it made me feel. He told me he was writing a novel and it was fast becoming his therapist and best friend all in one. I smiled because I knew the feeling—I know how much just putting words down on paper can help you get through another day.

And it worked. It worked because seeing Randall finally crack his shell, hearing him admit things out loud, made me feel less alone, made me understand that I don't have to be perfect or pretend to be. No one is. We're nothing but scattered particles loosely held together by a nucleus. We're all acrobats on unicycles stranded on high wires with plates spinning from our mouths, desperately trying to maintain our balance, always one step away from everything falling apart. We want to let go, but we're afraid of being thought of as failures. So we keep up the dance even when it makes us miserable.

Randall gave me a short hug by the door before he left. A sweet, perfect ending. Because we can't go back now. We crossed a line and any future sessions would embarrass us. Like strangers stuck for hours on an elevator, a moment of intimacy had seized us. But now the doors have opened and we have to go back to our previous lives.

## 17. LEGION

700 verbal. 760 Math. *To hear your scores again, press three.* He pressed three. He heard them again: 700 Verbal, 760 Math. 1460. He got a 1460. Shit. Not a 1500, but shit. He had his score now. He *owned* that score. *How'd you do, Legion?* I got a 1460. *Shit, dude, really?* Really.

He hung up the phone and paced around his room. The scheme had worked. It fucking worked. It wasn't a dream anymore. The score was fucking tremendous.

He had to tell Veronica.

Veronica had been holed up in the apartment all day with the men who were redoing the bathrooms. A few weeks ago she'd decided that the apartment was "sterile," that it lacked "character." *This apartment is bored with its own beauty,* she said. He had no idea what the fuck that meant.

He found her in the living room, hands grabbing at her hair. A hefty assortment of brochures covered every nook of the coffee table. She looked overwhelmed and harried, like there was going to be a final exam in an hour and there was no way she'd be able to memorize everything. A large martini glass rested in her right hand. Almost empty.

"They don't have my faucets," she said. "They've stopped

making my model, and to custom make one piece will take ten weeks. I may just as well start from scratch."

"Then what are they doing in the bathroom then?"

"Installing the tub. Everything else can be replaced, but we are keeping that tub."

She was ferociously beautiful when frustrated. No doubt she was a tigress in bed. She had certainly cast a spell on Ken if he allowed her to make decisions in his house.

"I just got my SAT score," he said.

She looked up at him. "Really. And?"

"1460," he said, cocking his head and fluttering his eyes.

"Wow. Are you serious? I'm shocked. I mean, not *shocked* but. Wow. That's better than I did."

"And you're a fucking genius. You went to Smith."

"Ken's going to be blitzed," she said, tossing back the rest of her drink. "Congrats." She reached over to hug him. He embraced her back, awkwardly. "We should celebrate. Let's go down to Ken's office and surprise him."

"What?" He was confused by this suggestion. She moved over to the bar to fix herself another drink, pouring the remains of the shaker into another glass.

"It'll be great," she continued. "We'll pop open a bottle of Dom, go out to dinner. Go throw on a shirt. Here." She handed him the martini.

"How do you even know Ken's there?"

"Where else would he be?" she said, shrugging her shoulders.

In the back of the town car, Veronica found the Johnny Walker Blue and took out two glasses. Legion stared out the window, at the City of all Cities in the midst of rush hour panic. Approaching the Queensboro Bridge was pandemonium, a cacophony of frustrated drivers leaning into their horns.

Veronica put down the booze and knocked briskly on the dividing glass. "Shouldn't we take the FDR?" she asked the driver, once he had lowered the window.

"Radio says forty-five minute delays, miss," the driver said. "It might be worse."

"OK. Thanks." Veronica sighed once the divider snapped back up.

"He's not going to believe me," Legion said. "About the score."

"He won't have much of a choice. Scotch?"

"Sure. I guess he may actually have to realize I'm not the fuck up he thinks I am."

She reclaimed the bottle and poured two shots. "Your dad doesn't think you're a fuck-up, Legion."

"Oh no. Not at all."

"Seriously. You guys misinterpret each other sometimes. He'll be very proud."

"Like you said, he won't have a choice now."

"I did say that," she said. "I didn't mean it that way."

He took the glass from her hand. "Prost," he said. "To thirty year old scotch. And Harvard."

"Sláinte." She raised her glass. "To your future."

He took in a mouthful of the scotch and sloshed it around before letting it incinerate his insides. Fuck was it strong. But the burn felt good. He closed his eyes and quickly downed the remains of the glass.

"Rookie." Veronica smiled at him. "Seriously. Congratulations. You did it."

"Thanks," he said.

They sat silently for the rest of the trip. Restless and giddy, he thought about calling his mom. She was in—Guatemala, was it? With that Hopi guy. She'd be back in town by the weekend or—what had her last message said? He'd have to check his voicemail. She'd left a number. Or he could always leave a message on her machine. He wanted to tell her so she could call Ken. Then the fucker would get it from every side.

The offices of Cartwright/McKinley Development took up the Sixtieth and Sixty-first floors of a slick modern high-rise in the financial district. A stench of self-congratulation roamed the halls—a syrupy smell, the smell of refined oxygen mingling with the tangy possibility of money. He looked around and saw sharp lines, crisp suits, Zegna ties, horn-rimmed frames, pantsuits. A concerto of unfailingly polite smiles and good-afternoons welcomed him. He tried to greet everyone by name—he didn't want to come across as the asshole son of the asshole boss—but he didn't recognize a lot of people. After all, it was their job to know who he was, not the reverse. He detected fear in some of the faces, sucking away the color from their cheeks; he could send any one of these guys out to get him a sandwich and not a single one would refuse. People were assholes because it was so goddamn easy.

Ken's office was at the end of the hallway. No doubt the king fueled his ego every morning with this same walk of coronation. The first set of imposing doors opened up to a plush seating area which served as the romping grounds of Ken's personal secretary, Chastity. Chastity was a porn-star blond with pillowy lips. She was a prize concubine, a walking cliché, really—except she was sharper than a factory-fresh Ginzu knife and easily the most efficient, ruthlessly cheerful employee Ken had. She greeted Veronica like a long-lost sorority sister and kissed both his cheeks with gusto, wiping the lipstick off with her fingers.

"My gosh, look at you," she said to him. "If I were only seventeen again!"

"I like that you're older," he replied. "Besides, I won't tell your boyfriend."

"You just *hush* now!" Chastity squealed. "Let me get a hold of Ken. He'll be so excited to see you both."

"Oh? Is he in a meeting?" Veronica asked.

Chastity was already on the phone. She lifted her right index finger. "Just give me one sec."

Legion wondered if Veronica despised Chastity's Cheshire cat smile and the chipper resolve she applied to her job, which clearly was to have Ken's back, no matter who was doing the asking.

"Don't bother trying his cell phone. He never turns it on," Veronica said.

"Oh honey, don't I know it," Chastity said. "He's *impossible* sometimes. I'm just calling downstairs. He was just with his lawyers so Brian should know where he is now." Veronica was about to interrupt, but Chastity raised her finger again. "Brian? Chastity. I have Veronica and Legion Cartwright here. Any idea where the big man has run off to?"

"I'm going in," Legion told Chastity, nodding in the direction of Ken's office. Chastity mouthed the word *okay* and winked at him.

Ken's office faced north and east; Legion saw Manhattan and the better neighborhoods of Brooklyn stretching out before him through the floor-to-ceiling windows. Everything about the office said: *I fucking rock*. A schmooze area with two leather couches facing a fake fireplace and a 30" plasma TV. A desk and executive chair fit for the Oval Office. Pictures of Ken kissing the asses of rich and famous schmucks on the wall, the usual suspects, Trump and Tisch and Giuliani, but also one of Ken and David Hasselhoff on the greens of some golf club in Palm Beach. Ken and Hasselhoff were "old buddies"; Hasselhoff had invited Ken to the premiere of *Jekyll and Hyde*.

Legion headed over to the bar, hoping to keep his buzz going. Above it was a painting by some Rauschenberg guy; Ken liked to announce its current market value every time Legion visited the office (*two million easy*). He poured himself another scotch and sat behind Ken's desk. Ken's father-in-law had started the enterprise back in the Seventies. It hadn't been much of anything when Ken came along—just a small venture involving a few ratty buildings in the Bronx. But Ken was a quick study, and Grandpa McKinley taught his son-in-law early on to buy cheap buildings in rundown areas. By 1981, NYC real estate was a disaster, especially with interest rates so high. As rates fell, and Reagan took over from Carter, things got brighter. A few buildings became several, and Ken soon expanded into commercial properties. Ken's greatest act of foresight came in the mid-Eighties, when he started buying up buildings in the west Forties where the porn shops and titty bars were. Giuliani arrived with his Clean Up New York campaign in the Nineties, and suddenly Times Square was the new Disneyland. That's when Ken cashed in big. The city claimed eminent domain, but Ken sued their asses hard and won. The city was forced to buy his properties at twelve times what he paid for them only seven years earlier.

He turned on his father's computer and navigated to his brokerage account. Outside the office, he could hear Veronica and Chastity straining to make small talk. He scanned the closing prices and looked at some weekly moving averages. It felt strange, entering Lucinda's lair again. For months he had avoided her entirely. You had to have balls to play Lucinda's game, be willing to take chances. It paid to take chances. He took a chance with the SAT, and that paid off spectacularly. What was Ken going to do, *not* send him to college with a 1460? No fucking way. Ken would pay for whatever school Legion got into. He'd brag about it now, pull whatever strings necessary.

As he was making his picks his phone rang.

"Hey," Randall said. "So are we pleased?"

"You tell me. I know you called up yourself."

Randall laughed. "Touché. Well I know it's not exactly what you wanted."

"Fuck that, Randall. I'm ecstatic. And I owe it all to you."

"You're happy, what a relief. But don't give me all the credit. You planned everything. I just showed up."

"Exactly. You showed up. That was awesome. I'm eternally grateful." He was going to lay it on thick now. Despite the modesty routine, he knew what Randall really wanted was a rich display of gratitude on his part. Today he was all too willing.

"So do you plan on studying for SAT IIs now, or am I gonna be Legion Cartwright one more time?"

Legion laughed. "All in due time. For now let us savor our victory."

"And when do *I* get to savor our victory?"

Legion stared at the screen. Futures orders were all about timing. You had to anticipate people's reactions and always stay one step ahead of them. "Soon," he said.

"When soon?"

"I don't know. The downside of getting this score is I'm actually going to have to study to pull off the grades this semester."

Randall laughed. "Lucky for us it's almost over. We'll have all summer to celebrate."

"Yeah." He knew he'd have to say something eventually. He'd be away most of the summer. Even when he was around, he wasn't going to bog down his time with Randall. But there was no reason to mention that yet. "The summer's going to be great, Randall."

"Excellent. Go hit the books, Dolphin."

"Already there. Go jerk off thinking about me."

"Already have. But I can go again in an hour."

"That long? Take care, old man."

Legion hung up the phone. If only Lucinda was as easy to manipulate as Randall, he'd be a fucking millionaire. Sooner or later, he knew his fortunes would change. The market would bounce back while the energy fueling Randall's delusions would suddenly grow thin. At least for now, the fog of lust was thick. He hoped to never want anyone, never need anyone, as much as Randall needed him. It was sickening.

Some scuffling on the other side of the door told him Ken was back. Legion could practically smell the musk of the jungle beast returning to his territory. Veronica was probably questioning his whereabouts, and Ken was equivocating, with Chastity corroborating. Soon Veronica would point to the office and tell Ken the score. Soon he'd get to see his father's reaction.

When Ken entered the office a few minutes later, he was on his cell phone. The one he never turned on, apparently. He was talking up Brooklyn, his next target.

"Jerry, there's no room in Manhattan anymore," Ken said. "The white people are coming, Jerry! To Fort Greene. To Clinton Hill. To Bed-Stuy. That's right, Bed-Stuy, the most dangerous fucking neighborhood outside of East Beirut, Bed-Stuy, is going to be *the* neighborhood. The kids today working on Wall Street and Madison Ave—they don't mind black people. They *love* black people. They think they add 'flava' to the hood. Trust me, Jer. In ten years the John and Wendy Wassermans of the world are going to be shelling out half a mil for a 700 square one bedroom in Bed-Stuy. They're going to graduate, pile up their Saabs, wave goodbye to their pussy college friends in Boston and they're going to head to New York for their media jobs and stare out their fucking windows in awe at how goddamn lucky they are, and then, *then*, they're going to try to rent in *Manhattan*. And oh, how fast the mighty will fall. Because not only will below Ninety-sixth be completely out of reach, not only will Harlem be crazy expensive, they'll have student loans to pay, and cocktails are nine dollars a piece and dinner sets you back fifty a night, and even though Mommy and Daddy are helping out, how long's that gonna last? So off to the frontiers they will trot. Manifest Fucking Destiny. First the fags will open cafes and boutiques, and then that fly restaurant the *Times* will adore, and then the bars and clubs, and next thing you know, here comes the entire class of Bennington 2006. Here comes every JAP from the eastern seaboard looking for a Viking Stove and a sub-zero fridge and a cute Croatian doorman who'll carry her bags from the food co-op for her. And of course, *we'll be there already*. We'll be waiting and—hold on, Jerry."

Ken Cartwright approached his son and scuffed up his hair. "You're digging the chair, right? Custom made. Estonia of all places. Cost a fortune." His eyes momentarily canvassed the computer screen. "Jerry, Jerry, Midtown is *over*. I'm talking 100% returns in three years, Jerry. I'm talking cutting the bureaucratic bullshit in half, and not having to pay off every fucking zoning and ordinance dyke with an organic cow chip on her shoulder and OK, listen, more later, my son's in the office. With terrific news I might add. The DNA tests came back on the maid. It's not his baby."

Legion could hear Jerry's bellowing on the other end.

"The SAT, Jerry, remember that fucking thing? Looks like the kid struck gold. I'll call you later."

Ken hung up the phone. "Mr. Big Shot!" He clapped his hands together. "I heard the news. Congrats, kiddo. Guess you copied off the right guy."

Legion didn't budge. "You taught me well," he said.

"So Chastity called Nobu and scammed us a table. You need real clothes, though. You wanna pick up something underneath World Trade? Go to Banana Republic."

"Do I have a say in this?"

"What, you don't like Nobu all of a sudden?"

"No, Dad. It rocks, Dad."

"Then why the pouty puss?" Ken glanced down at the screen.

"Putting in some futures, I see. Global Crossing! Christ, kid, that takes balls nowadays."

Legion looked right into his father's eyes. "I'm feeling lucky all of a sudden."

"Oh yeah? Everything going peachy?"

This was it. He'd tell the fucker everything now. "You really want to know?"

Ken laughed. "You think I don't already?"

It took several seconds for the words to register. He imagined them traveling through the canals of his ear, up to the velvet ropes of his brain only to be turned away by the truth bouncer cell, the one that could sniff out bullshit. But then they returned again, persistent fuckers. And they got in somehow. And then he *understood*. He kept his eyes squarely on the screen. He typed in another order, then erased it. It was important not to panic. No way. The asshole was bluffing. He had to play it cool. "What do you mean?"

"Christ. How stupid do you think I am? Last I heard you were down to eleven thousand. And now you're betting the farm on Global Crossing? Sheesh."

"Last you heard?" He couldn't believe his ears. He had been careful. Promises had been made. "So Roger told you my balance? Isn't that like, against the law or something?"

"Kid, he's my broker. He's bought houses in Hawaii with the money he's made off of me. He can either tell me the truth when I ask, or he can lie and piss me off and I take my money elsewhere. Come on, quit the drama routine. You seriously thought I didn't know?"

"And all this time you said nothing." He was dumbfounded. Ken, big mouth Ken, had said nothing. The fucker who rubbed your face into every small failure you made. The man who couldn't keep a secret to save his life. Ken. His father. Knew. *For months.*

"Kid, once I gave you the money, it was yours." Ken had grabbed a cigar from the box on the brass table. "I wasn't going to sit over your shoulder. I gave up trying to control people with your mother. The harder you hold on, the faster they slip away."

"Maybe your grip's a little too loose, ever think of that?" He didn't know what else to say. "Maybe it's like you're not holding on at all." The walls were closing in on him. He felt like he was upside down, the blood flooding his head. Soon, if he was lucky, he'd pass out.

"Listen, I know you think I'm an asshole."

"You *are* an asshole." Christ, how good it felt to say it.

Ken looked taken aback. He lit the cigar, looked at it from a few angles, as if he were considering it for the first time, considering it along with his assholeness. "Maybe. Yeah. Sometimes I am." He looked out the window. "Maybe I don't know how to do the daddy stuff. Looks like you're turning out just fine anyway. If my being an asshole has taught you to trust yourself, to rely on yourself to get ahead, then fuck if I haven't done a good job."

"So you're *taking credit* now? You're such an *asshole*. To me. To Mom. You're even an asshole to Veronica."

"Well, I'm an equal opportunity asshole then."

"You don't have to be such a fucking asshole, Ken. You can try being nice. Say a few kind words sometimes."

Ken sighed, shook his head. "You want the sweet talk, is that it? Go to your mother for that. She's very sweet, if you can find her. But fuck, I just raised you, I guess that doesn't mean much." Ken waltzed around the room. "Listen, let's go to dinner. I'll try to be nicer, alright? Can I get a little credit for trying?"

Legion was too thunderstruck to talk.

"I need a drink." Ken sidled over to the bar. "Care for another?" He poured some scotch into Legion's glass and handed it to him. A peace offering. Legion pushed it away. He got up from the desk and barreled towards the door, but Ken grabbed his arm before he got away.

"Jesus, son, calm down. Don't you get it? One day, all of this will all be yours."

Ken pulled him closer and spun him around. It seemed his father wanted him to take in not only the office, but also what lay beyond, outside the windows. All of Manhattan was his. "Listen...we made a lot of mistakes, your mother and me. But you weren't one of them. An *accident*, maybe, but not a mistake."

Ken was laughing. It was a disease. What was the point in hating this man, who thought these things were funny, who couldn't see the cruelty in his comments? Some people just can't be parents. This really was the best Ken could do; he didn't know how to be a dad. He should pity the fucker instead. And what Ken would do if he knew the truth? About Randall. About the test. About the fact that he'd slept with guys and girls and wasn't sure where on the chart he'd end up. Would his father finally wake up then?

"Listen." Ken grabbed his son tenderly around the shoulders. He guided Legion back to the CEO chair and sat him down in it. "I have to tend to Veronica. Turns out you're not the only one with issues at the moment. So take a few deep breaths, watch some TV, and help yourself to the bar. Soon we'll head over to Nobu, one big happy family, say *omakase* to the chef and eat the best fucking food in the world and forget all our worries. We'll celebrate your score and be as happy as sunshine. You'll be fine, kid. Just fine. Trust me."

Legion spun the chair around to look out the window. He could not face the man. Outside, far below, the insects of Manhattan crawled, Matchbox cars maneuvering through traffic. So many stories separated him from the world. It was too much. Too much. He wasn't a fighter, like Ken. He was weak. He had others do his work for him, and he had grown comfortable with it.

"So whaddya say, kid?" Ken took a long puff on his cigar, his smile genuine. Always genuine.

"Sure," he replied. "Ok, Dad."

## 18. MANDELA

The reward for his score: dinner at a fancy midtown restaurant. The ceiling soared twenty feet above them. Bouquets of fresh seafood poked out of a centerpiece of elaborately carved iced sculptures. Blue and green tones everywhere, all very congruous; Renoir would be proud.

Waiters zipped by in crisp uniforms. The place was titanic, bustling, buzzing. Supposedly chi-chi, but tell that to the tourists from Iowa in their Hawaiian shirts and cargo shorts. Meanwhile, his father, Tyrese and he were sporting blazers, and Sarafina and his mother were in silky dresses. His parents wanted ostentation — leatherback menus, ten piece place settings — but somewhere safe enough to bring the under-ten crowd. Upscale, yet family friendly. Fish sticks at caviar prices.

"Order whatever you want, children," his father decreed, just as the waiter placed a basket of garlic bread onto the table.

"I'm having lobster!" Sarafina called out.

Deidre cleared her throat. Joe addressed the waiter: "That handsome gentleman across from me just received a 1500 on his SAT, and we're here to celebrate."

"Fourteen-*ninety*, Dad," Mandela quickly corrected.

"Wow, that's quite a score." The waiter played along enthusiastically. "I bet all the colleges will be chasing after you."

"He's weighing his options," Deidre said. "We're very proud."

"Congratulations." The waiter offered a handshake which Mandela accepted, more than a little embarrassed. Why did his parents have to be so naïve? There were thousands of 1490s, an army of them in NYC alone. All these pretensions of sophistication and politesse. What a turn off. His parents had cautioned all of them before they arrived: No slumping at the table; shoulders back, chins up. Words were to be enunciated with the precision of phrases repeated on language-learning videos. Joe and Deidre liked to act as if they were emissaries from the Planet Negro whose mission it was to make the proper impression upon the Caucasians. What ever happened to being real?

"So tell me again." Joe was generously dabbing butter onto his bread. "By how much did you beat that Levy girl?"

Mandela sighed. "She got a 1450."

"Let me get this straight. That vulture spent five thousand dollars—"

"More likely ten," Deidre said.

"She spent ten thousand dollars to tutor that hotshot daughter of hers and you *still* beat her by fifty points."

"Forty, Dad. I got a 1490, Dad."

"She must have thrown a fit," his mother said. "Can you imagine? The Princess of Princeton might not make the Ivy League!"

Joe chuckled. "Bite your tongue. Of course she will. Her father can always buy a new wing somewhere."

"Speaking of Princeton…" Deidre cupped her hands and tilted her head towards Mandela. "I've been snooping around and there are certain scholarships only Jersey residents can apply for."

"Jersey residents?" he said. "We're moving back?"

"Of course not. Grandma Lucille lives in Toms River," Joe said. "Plus, you grew up there. Spent ten years of your life in Jersey public schools."

"And the fact that I have *no desire* to go there?"

"Son, we're not asking you to *go*," Joe said. "Just visit. Maybe you'll like it."

"Maybe I *won't*," Mandela said.

"Yeah, maybe he won't," Tyrese repeated, laughing. Then Sarafina started laughing.

"Keep it up, you two," Deidre said. "And Daddy and I will sell the *AIDA* tickets."

Mandela closed his eyes. Tonight was supposed to be a celebration of his score. Tonight, he thought, would be the perfect time to propose his summer plans. But everything was already off. They were bullying him, making him angry. He'd have to summon up some patience.

"Mom, Dad," he said, softly but with gravity. Both of them looked up. "I know you're happy about my score. Plus I've raised my average this semester."

Joe shot Deidre a suspicious look. "Go on."

"So let's talk about summer," Mandela said. "I want to go to Europe."

He might as well have said outer Mongolia, judging from the way Deidre's eyes widened. Joe, however, kept sipping his beer without the slightest pause.

"There's this art program in Barcelona..." He had prepared his plea well. So what if it wasn't all true? Some of it was. "It's open to high school students from all over the world. I'm pretty sure I've been accepted."

"You're pretty sure you've been *accepted*?" Deidre's mouth tightened. "When did you even apply?"

"A few months ago. It's a four week program. They have really cool classes in non-linear representation and mixed media. Plus in the end we travel around Spain..."

Joe Robinson fixed his tie and cleared his throat. "Is this a joke?" he asked.

"Am I laughing?" Mandela replied.

Sarafina looked up. "Are you guys gonna fight now?"

"Sit still, Sarafina," Joe said.

Sarafina sighed. Tyrese smiled with perverse glee. Deidre took out the Game Boys from her pocket and handed them to her children. *Don't talk,* she said. *Don't look up. Play.* Tyrese and Sarafina nodded their heads: they understood just fine.

The most appalling smirk occupied his mother's face. "Under whose guidance did you apply to this program?"

"Ms. Clover sponsored me. She sent them slides of my work."

His mother was unimpressed. "You think she might want to call us first."

"I told her not to. Not until I heard."

"You told her not to call." Joe repeated things when he was angry.

"You've kept this a *secret* all this time." The scorn in Deidre's voice was thick, tiny needles of rage that propelled through the air and stung him in the neck.

"You would've discouraged me," he said. "And then I wouldn't even know if I could get in. Well, I did."

"So since you know us so well, Mandela, why are you telling us now?" his father asked. "Don't you already know our answer?"

"Listen," he said. He hoped to appeal to their logic. But they looked frustrated, pissed to be discussing this in public. "This is an amazing opportunity. Even you have to admit that. And I've kept up my end of the bargain."

"Your end of the bargain!" A wet grunt escaped Joe Robinson's mouth, followed by a throaty cackle. "Hear that, Deidre? Our son has kept up *his end of the bargain*." He stared at his wife as he wiped the bread crumbs that had gathered around his plate, then looked Mandela squarely in the eye: "So you think you can drop everything and run off to Europe? You already have summer plans, son. They aren't arbitrary. They're *deliberate*. Necessary."

Deidre reached over to grip her husband's arm. Soon people would start staring, the grip said. But Joe gingerly removed her hand and placed it back onto the table.

"The program offers college credit," Mandela said. "It will look great on my applications. I can write about—"

"What will look great on your application, son, is the internship down at Morgan Stanley that your mother busted her ass to get you, not you running around the streets of Barcelona like a hobo doing sidewalk face-paintings and braiding people's hair. You wanna talk about holding up your end of the bargain? Well let me spell out how *we've* held up our end, junior. We moved to New York. To send you to Valhalla—"

"I *never* asked you to move. I wanted to stay in Montclair—"

"We bust our ass sixty hours a week so that we can afford every last life-enriching, self-discovering activity that you kids need to engage in to make it in the 21st century. We've done this day after day, week after week, year after goddamn year and you know why? Because your great grandmother had to sit at the back of a bus."

"This is insane," he said.

"Joe, keep it down," Deidre pleaded.

"Insane. You got that right," Joe continued. "Your *request* is insane. Your whims are *insane*."

"So let me get this straight: you struggle every day so I get to make choices and now you want to *deny* me that right? You just said you made compromises so that I don't have to. So what if I don't want to compromise?"

Joe's cheeks were bloating and his lower lip began to tremble. He grabbed the handkerchief from his lap and ran it across his sweaty head. Sarafina looked up, slightly scared. Tyrese, too. It was left to his mother to keep things under control. She raised two fingers in the air, oscillating them between husband and son. "You think your father and I don't understand. That we're jaded to your dreams. But that's not it, baby. *Nothing* is being taken from you. We just want you to allow yourself more options. You can paint *anywhere*. Honey, on your Aunt Mozelle's grave, I swear we *want* you to keep painting. We want you to get better and be *the best*. But if your dreams are real, they'll survive anything. Including four years of the Ivy League. Because just in case you change your mind, well then at least you allowed yourself that option. Why close yourself off to possibility?"

She sounded so reasonable. It only made him angrier. "Mom, we're talking about a one month supervised trip! I'm not asking for a year off. Just four weeks. And still you're giving me a hard time."

"This is pointless," Joe said. "You can't go to Europe, Mandela. I can give you a thousand reasons why and you'll try to find your way around every one. So here's the final word: you can't go because you're seventeen and you're living under my roof. Until you turn eighteen you'll abide by my rules. Look, we're proud of you. You have *no idea* how proud. But your mother and I would like to think that we had some hand in how you turned out. And right now, we think Europe is a bad idea. Perhaps next summer we'll consider it. If you can afford it, and you really want to, you can go then."

"This is slavery, that's what this is."

"Slavery?" Tender veins danced along the surface of Deidre's neck. "Mandela, you did *not* just say that."

"What is it, then?" Mandela got up from his chair. "I've done everything right. I'm not a slacker. I've followed your guidance. I've thought this through and I really want to go. Next summer you'll just find another excuse."

"Sit down, Mandela," Deidre said. "*Now.*"

"Why? Am I embarrassing you? I'm sorry, let me not embarrass you anymore. I'll go." He took off his tie and left it on his seat. "This whole thing is a joke."

"Watch yourself, boy," Joe said. But his father wouldn't get up. People were already beginning to stare, and Joe and Deidre were not going to give them reason.

"I'm tired. Have fun at *AIDA*. That's a laugh, this was supposed to be about celebrating my SAT score and you get tickets to a fucking Disney show. Thanks."

"You are so *ungrateful*," Deidre whispered. It made him want to laugh.

"Keep it up, Mandela," Joe said. "Don't worry about preserving any dignity."

"Like I have any dignity left? Oh, and don't worry about punishing me. I'm going straight home now anyway. Bury my head in some books and not go out for the next month. What's the difference? My life is preordained anyway."

He looked over at his brother and sister. They looked genuinely afraid. He felt bad, but he was determined nonetheless. Maybe he could set an example that they'd follow one day. He saluted them goodbye, turned around and walked right out.

Outside the air was more humid than death. Hot air sprayed against his face. Fuck did it feel good. The chaos. The release. The truth, the *fucking* truth, for once. He felt so alive. He had tasted power, for a few seconds. It tasted sweet and fleshy. About time he stood up. He wasn't their puppet. Just wait. He'd show them. Maybe he wouldn't even wait. Who needed to find some program? Maybe he'd just run the fuck away to Europe. Did he have the balls to do it? He didn't know. It was time he found out.

The whole thing was such a mess. Fucking Gabrielle Levy. Why'd she have to plant seeds in him? Why'd she have to give him so much money? She'd *have* to help him, somehow. She'd have to save him. He had to get out. Get away. Christ! It'll never happen now. Not after his little speech. How stupid he was to think they'd consider it. Fucking robots. They had no imagination. What's the point of being free if you have no imagination?

He wasn't going anywhere. He couldn't. He thought he could. Thought he'd lay down the law, take a stand and live free like a condor. But he couldn't. He thought there was a way around the obstacles. But there wasn't. He couldn't go. All because of one truth he'd been avoiding for so long, one that continuously gnawed at him no matter how he tried to ignore it: he wouldn't go because in the end, he'd have to spend *that money* to do it, make use of the bills gathering dust in his dead aunt's closet. Sure, Gabrielle had given it to him. But he knew he'd never use that money. He *always* knew. The bills would leave blood stains on his hands.

How simple things had been five months ago. Sure, his world had been smaller, lonelier, but it made some sort of sense. Nothing did anymore. He had to give Gabrielle back her money. He had to forget what happened between them. He had to stop being a fool. A starry-eyed fool. He didn't live on Central Park West. He wasn't her long-lost son and she wasn't his fairy Godmother.

It was over. The foundation was crumbling because it was based on lies. The lie about a school he never planned on applying to. The lie that he could escape the tide of history, that he was more than just a checklist of his parents' accomplishments. The lie that he was in control of his destiny, that passion and resolve were all that mattered. Lies. All lies.

He sauntered down Fifty-seventh Street in a daze. Midtown Manhattan was a Kandinsky canvas, an assault of chaotic colors. Fuck it. Maybe he wasn't going to Europe, but Goddamn if he was going to waste his summer on a fucking Internship. He had New York, and even if she was a tease sometimes, even if she tempted him with dreams beyond his reach, she also set a place for everyone at her cluttered table. The city was a jamboree. Around every corner, an accident waiting to happen, a spark causing another spark causing a fire. He would burn the summer away.

There was no one looking out for him. *No one.* Adults were phonies. Complicators. They'd all lost their vision. He had to stop himself before he lost his too, before they stole whatever was left of his soul. He reached Columbus Circle. Dusk was closing in. In New York, the sun, much like the residents of the city, never went down without a fight; her pinks and purples shadow-boxed in the mirrored windows of the tall towers stretching up Broadway towards the Upper West Side.

Central Park spread like a promised land before him. He had no money and would have to walk home. It was a long way, but no matter. He'd breathe in Manhattan, making plans.

## 19. EXCERPTS FROM ARIANNA LEVY'S JOURNALS

May 23rd

Earlier this afternoon, at brunch at Café des Artistes, Daddy proposed a toast to my future. He made a short speech about how proud he was of me, and then we lifted our champagne flutes in unison—Mother, Daddy, Douglas and me—and clinked glasses. Mother insisted I invite Douglas, so the conversation galloped along oh-so-pleasantly; this way she could continue to labor under the illusion of her picture perfect family.

Right in the middle of the meal, she reached into her purse and took out an exquisitely wrapped box and handed it to me. I opened it to find the Ebel I'd been salivating over for several months. I was genuinely shocked, so I let out a little scream. I reached over and hugged Daddy and kissed his cheeks. And even though she was buying my affections, I blew kisses at Mother too. But I did not go over to her.

*You can take it with you to England*, Mother said, continuing the show for Douglas's sake. She reiterated my plans for the summer, six weeks of glorious classes at the Royal Dramatic Theatre of Cambridge. No matter that three months earlier she had ruled this idea "out of the question." No matter that Daddy had to engage in who-knows-what kind of finagling to get me such a late acceptance into the program. No matter to all that—because I got a 1450 on my SAT.

All this bullshit pageantry, as if suddenly a 1450 was a great score, when everyone knew I was aiming for a 1550. Who was it that said that lies repeated long enough start to take on the semblance of truth? I guess it's easier to keep feeding your illusions after a while. Whatever I said, Mother found a way to spin it to the positive. Even when I mentioned that half my grade seemed to have broken 1400, nothing would break her stride. I gave up arguing once the waiter spilled water onto the table and Mother told him "it was quite alright" without flinching. Normally, she'd have his head on a platter.

After brunch we walked down CPW and Daddy suggested a carriage ride through the park. I didn't know how much more of this I wanted to subject Douglas to, but he seemed game, eager even. Daddy talked about Frederick Law Olmsted and what a farfetched scheme it seemed at the time, to build a park to rival the grand parks of Paris and London on the bleak swampy morass that stretched between Fifth and Eighth avenues. He told us that back in the early Eighties when we were born, few people wanted to enter the park, and how lucky we were to experience it now as a splendid sanctuary, a real cross-section of New York. Douglas soaked it in and asked polite questions, and I love him a little for that, how he always makes things easy for me.

In the carriage I looked across at my parents. They seemed faintly ridiculous sitting there, the way goats do in petting zoos, frail and aloof and unknowable. I saw Daddy fumble for Mother's hand, and she seemed uneasy giving it to him at first, but her hand soon forgot to resist. I wondered if this was how I'd end up one day, uneasy about holding my husband's hand but giving in anyway. I don't know if they're happy or just pretending for my sake. I don't want to have to pretend. But just as I was dwelling on this depressing thought I felt Douglas reach for *my* hand, right there in front of my parents, and he looked at me with a glint in his eyes and told me that his parents were planning a trip to London in August, so we'd be able to see each other overseas.

And just like that I embraced Douglas. I hugged him like his was the greatest idea in the world. Because when I look at Douglas I want to believe in us, in never having to pretend. And sitting there, in his arms, I did believe it. I looked out at all the people passing by, enjoying the perfect summer day, the rollerbladers, the old ladies walking their Shih Tzus, the mothers jogging with strollers, the sunbathers, the hippies hackey-sacking, the Rastas laughing on top of benches, the children running and screaming and spilling ice cream — all of it, happening at once, with the skyscrapers on all sides, bearing witness, and I thought, how impossible it is to be sad in New York in the summertime. And I could smell it, in the air. I could taste it: Hope. It sounds ridiculous, but there you go. I let go of everything for a few seconds and felt weightless.

Even now, the feeling remains. Mother came into my room an hour ago and told me what a terrific day we had, and I knew how much she wanted to believe it — how much she wanted me to believe it. She sat down on my bed and I allowed her to take my hands. *You're going to adore England,* she said. She looked me in the eye, and I even looked back, because I knew what she was telling me, that distance and time blur memories, make the pain less specific. She and I would find our way somehow.

I asked her about summer plans and she gave me the usual laundry list, and even though I was uneasy with these pleasantries, even though I wanted assurances that she wouldn't spend the summer crafting deals with Mandela Robinson, I said nothing, because she was trying, and I was going to let her try to be my mother again.

Before she left I noticed her surveying my room. She scanned across the stuffed animals crowding my bed and she called out their names, remembering everyone. One of the dolls caught her eye, Rafiki the monkey from the *Lion King*. I had attached a charm bracelet around his arm, one my mother had given me when I was five. She loved to tell me the story behind the bracelet and she recited it again just then, how someone had thrown a block at my head in nursery school and how I had cried and cried, screaming for no one but her. It took her almost an hour to arrive, and because of that I wouldn't talk to her for days afterward. Later that week she gave me the charm bracelet and told me it had magical powers. Whenever I wore it, she said, she could see me even when she wasn't there. All I had to do was hold it tight and she'd come, but I couldn't cry, because my tears would cloud up the magical lenses that allowed her to see me.

We always laughed at that part because it was a little devious, but of course it worked; I wasn't much of a crier after that. Mother jokingly asked if I was going to take the bracelet with me to London, wondering aloud if it still fit me, and I told her of course not, it fit when I was five. She insisted she'd had the bracelet made big so I could grow into it, so then I took it off Rafiki's wrist just to prove to her that it wouldn't, and of course I was right, it didn't, but surprisingly enough it *almost* did, like half an inch more and it would have, like I had only recently grown out of it.

So I told Mother that the new watch could be my charm bracelet now. But then she did a strange thing. She took the bracelet from my hand and put it back on Rafiki's arm. She got off the bed and looked away from me and said, *You don't need charm bracelets anymore.* I think that's what she said, but her voice was almost a whisper and I couldn't tell. Instead, we hugged each other and I didn't ask questions.

I'm not going to ask questions. I'm going away for six weeks and when I get back, we can start over. I want nothing more than to start over.

## 20. GABRIELLE

Sitting in the back of a cab that was zigzagging through Central Park, Gabrielle looked out the window. The stifling humidity of June had seized control of New York. Cantankerous clouds hijacked the sky, ready to engage in battle. She couldn't stop glancing at her watch. Her eyelids felt heavy and her stomach was Morse-coding signals of distress up to her mouth, refluxes of acid reminding her that she was lying once again, engaging in covert meetings she'd promised herself were over. But Mandela Robinson was not taking no for an answer. He had something to give her, he said, and then it would be over.

*It would be over.* The words flashed through her mind. Closure at that point seemed so impossible that the mere suggestion of it made her shiver. She'd entertain any opportunity for its arrival, despite her doubts about Mandela's intentions.

On Madison and Seventy-fourth, traffic slowed to a crawl. Gabrielle clutched her forehead and sighed. The din of honking horns, compounded by the off-key renditions of her Pakistani driver singing along to Islamabad's greatest hits, made her skin crawl. She commanded the man to stop on the next corner and slid a ten into the money slot. The man chirped a thank you in between his singing. How she loathed relentlessly cheerful people.

The heat was unbearable, but even this she'd tolerate today. So much hell she'd been through the past few weeks. Arianna had been a ticking time bomb that only the most careful words and vast amounts of patience were able to defuse. When she thought about what could have happened—Arianna could have told Morty *everything*, for Heaven's sake—she realized how lucky she was. A painful lesson that hadn't come without great cost. In the end, though, the fog of war was clearing. Last Saturday's brunch had been the turning point. Never mind the naysayers, money *can* buy happiness sometimes. Arianna was euphoric about the Ebel. And asking that boy to join them was brilliant. The frisky pup had shamelessly kissed Arianna right in front of her and Morty. Six months ago she'd have had his head; right then she wanted to hug him. She looked over at her husband and for a few minutes, feelings of tenderness welled up inside her. She'd once felt similar passion for this gentle man years ago, had she not? And if it wasn't exactly love, surely it was a most effective placebo, one that carried them along for so long. She could almost forget the torrent of doubts that had been plaguing her, almost deny the disease in her heart.

Perhaps when Arianna went away to college she'd say something. He deserved better. Morty wasn't a bad man. He tried to reach out to her but she avoided his advances, fearing that in her pity for him some unexpected insight might lava out of her mouth and ruin things forever. For now, at least, she'd keep silent.

She pulled out some Tums from her purse and chewed the pills briskly before taking a second to inspect her teeth in the facade of a swanky dog-grooming parlor. Madison Avenue never ceased to amuse her. Easily the most *goyishe* avenue in Manhattan. A procession of svelte blonde *uberfraulein* with alabaster necks choked by teardrop pearls and button noses inculcated to sniff out the Jews, whose chicken broth and goulash perfumes had been genetically encoded into their sweat glands. The ladies of Madison far preferred the comforting aromas of tea cakes and Episcopalians.

Heading west on Seventy-ninth, she went over the bullet points in her mind. Surely Mandela understood it was over. She wouldn't ask for anything back, but neither would she make any more payments. Her only request was that he say nothing, ever, about what conspired between them. Still, she'd have to be careful. She couldn't afford to offend him.

Turning right onto Fifth Avenue, the Baroness loomed regally before her. How so very Upper East she was, this Metropolitan

Museum of Art. How effortlessly she commanded attention, how aware of her own fabulousness, Central Park serving as backdrop to her larger-than-life performance. Three story banners heralding current and upcoming exhibits draped down her facade. Tourists and natives alike pockmarked the stairs leading up to her entrance like woozy paparazzi.

Gabrielle shivered. No matter how many visits she made, its marvel never diminished. The dreams of her adolescence roamed its hallways, visions that transported an Essex street stoop-sitter to a world of cosmic colors and forms. In her early teens she'd sit trance-like in the Impressionist rooms for hours at a time, allowing the elastic pulp of inspiration to sponge through her mind. Her soul felt lighter there, inflated with so much possibility.

She approached the base of the stairs and canvassed the area. Mandela Robinson stood above on the second landing, gripping a package against his body large enough to obscure his legs. Its size and shape suggested a canvas. Gabrielle ascended to him. She swallowed hard, trying to will the anxiety out of her mind. Mandela looked flush with worry. Confusion filled his eyes, and he appeared ready to surrender to it. She did not like his face. She had not prepared for it.

"A bit overcast for sunglasses, don't you think?" he said.

Her eyes scoped the area. She could run away if she needed to. "Don't get smart," she said. "What's with the package?"

"I'll get to that." He sighed. "Listen, it's good to see you."

"There are things I need to say, Mandela."

"Me first, Gaby. Please."

*Gaby*, she thought. He so rarely called her Gaby. She watched as he took off his knapsack and unzipped it, removing a brown paper bag from the inside.

"This is yours," he said, handing it to her.

She grabbed the bag and stuffed it under her arm. She didn't need to open it to know what was inside. "You're overreacting," she said.

"Don't misunderstand," he said. "I'm not trying to embarrass you. I never should have taken it. Any of it. So now I'm just giving it back."

"I didn't come to ask for it back."

"I know that. Please, let me continue. I never...damn, how do I say this...I never planned on applying to Princeton."

"I'm sorry?"

"Just *listen*. I made a comment to Arianna one day. I wasn't serious, but the two of you believed what you wanted to believe.

You took me for a spin in your car and made your assumptions, and at first I was insulted, so I thought I'd teach you a lesson. But then I was intrigued. I decided to entertain myself for a while. I was curious to see how far you'd go, see just how much you'd be willing to embarrass yourself. But then we met at the Guggenheim. And spoke about Richter. We kept meeting and discussing Schiele and DeKooning and then, well, it became something else. I was tricking you, and it started to eat at me. Sure, you're presumptuous and privileged, but you also convinced me that Rothko is worthwhile. So even if what you were doing was wrong, it didn't make me right. I'm not on this earth to teach people lessons. So just take back your money. It's not the magic potion I thought it was. More like snake oil. Stupid me, I thought I'd go to Europe. I believed you because you were the only one telling me what I wanted to hear. But life doesn't work that way. My parents own me until I'm eighteen. But that's OK. That which doesn't kill you, right? Anyway, that's it. End of story."

Gabrielle kept nodding her head. She felt that if she focused on keeping that one action constant, then maybe she wouldn't scream or faint or cry. The acid inside her was spreading. If only it would reach her brain and burn every remaining thought in her head. Hurricane Gabrielle! Come see the damage left in her wake. What kind of person does the things she had done? The poor child. She wanted to reach out and hug him, root out the cynicism she'd implanted. But how could she? It wasn't feasible. It had to *end*. She had to extract herself, once and for all.

"Your turn," she heard him say.

"Yes. Give me a second," she said. "It's just...you *never* planned on applying to Princeton?" The words cut her tongue like splinters of glass. Six months ago, did it matter how real the rumor was? Six months ago, Mandela Robinson was a tumor that needed to be eradicated. Now after months of chemotherapy, the tumor had turned out to be benign.

"No," he said. "The irony is now my parents want me to. But I wouldn't worry about it. Rest assured, I'm not going to Princeton."

"I see. Well maybe you should." She said it brusquely, without flinching. "You're being too harsh on your parents. Europe can wait a year."

Mandela's face looked like he'd just bitten into a kumquat. "Wow. That's all you have to say?"

"You're young. You should focus on college right now. Princeton is a superb choice."

"You're fucking kidding. If you're mad at me, just tell me."

"I'm not mad. I'm perfectly serious." Of course she *was* mad—everything she had done, for nothing! She was an imbecile.

"Holy Mother of God." He was getting angrier. "Of course, I should just go to Princeton. Me and Arianna both. Put us in the maze, and we'll crawl through like good little mice."

"You're being melodramatic."

He scowled. "Shit, that's right, I'm seventeen. I keep forgetting how naïve I am. How green we children are in the ways of the world. So let me get this straight: I should take advice from you? A woman who tried to buy her daughter's way into college?"

Finally, the venom. Someone had to strike; the poison had to be released. "I'm an idiot," she said. "But your parents just want what's best for you."

"Like you want what's best for Arianna, right? So tell me, how's that working out? Everything dandy back home?"

"I won't do this."

"Do what?" He was staring daggers at her. "Fuck up your daughter's life? But you've become so good at fucking up people's lives."

"I *love* my daughter."

"Are you sure?" Mandela asked. "I think you secretly hate her."

Gabrielle bit down hard. Nothing he could say was worse than what she told herself. "I'm not here to fight. Please. You promised me this would go away."

"Is that all you want? Well, your wish is my command, Mrs. Levy."

He bowed before her and began to walk away, dragging his canvas carelessly along with him. She should have just let him go. It would've been prudent, smart, safe. All of her instincts told her to stay put. All except one, the Mother of all instincts. And like a scorned tiger this one knew when to pounce. *No, not this way,* this instinct told her. *You will try, Gabrielle. The boy has brought a gift, and he is dragging it away like a wounded dream, and you will stop him, because a future you do not know has been drawn onto that canvas, and you have no right to suffocate the future. Not again.*

Her legs revolted against her. They spilled down the steps to catch up with him. "Please! Wait one minute."

He did not disobey. The package was clearly frustrating him.

"You know I like talking with you. Really. I enjoy spending time with you."

"Tragic to admit it, I know. But there's nothing wrong going on here. We had a few conversations. You didn't fuck me, Mrs. Levy."

She couldn't suppress a cackle. "You're being vulgar," she said. But still she laughed. She could only laugh at the irony of his words.

"You're being dishonest. That's more vulgar," he said. "But hey, I get it. That's life."

"Please." She took off her glasses, hoping her eyes would sway him. "Let's not go away mad at each other. Show me what you have there."

"I don't think I want to anymore."

"*Of course* you want to. You want to and you will."

He hesitated, and in his hesitation she saw she was right. He had to show her. It wouldn't be over between them until he did. His hands found the knot as he fumbled to untangle the twine that crisscrossed the wrapping. He threw the rope to the ground and looked up at her, seemingly to register her Before face in order to evaluate the After. He steadied the canvas onto his legs before unmasking it.

"I painted this for you," he said. "When I thought you were my friend."

What shocked her was not that he was talented; she was sure he would be. Nor the fact that he'd chosen her as his subject. No, what was shocking was how fearless the painting was. Savage and true, her nightmare played out on a canvas. He was seeing her, down to the mucky core of her being, and no matter how many layers of complexity she'd thrown on, no matter how much camouflage and steely resolve and imitations of a life she had acquired, still, there it was, the naked acorn of her soul. Not finessed, touched up, made safe for the masses. Messy and sloppy and terribly real.

"There are things I see that you've stopped seeing, Gabrielle. I know it sounds corny but I think people go blind as they get old. Half this fucking world is blind."

Gabrielle's hands began to shiver. What words could she use to reply to him? Only Moses, holiest of all Israelites, could survive seeing the glory of God's naked back. She was going to die from the brightness of his truth. What was she doing, urging Mandela to follow the steady, reasonable path? Parroting her mother, that's what. Kneeling before the expectations of a world she herself had created. Here he was, flirting with bravado, and she was offering him the same tasteless porridge of fear, force-feeding him mushy kernels of caution, gagging him with lowered expectations. Might as well tell the boy to stop breathing.

Gabrielle closed her eyes. She could hear a voice inside her head, singing. Her own voice, the voice of a girl who once sang her dreams into life, dreams long since salted into memories. But voices do not die; they just quiet themselves to accommodate your limitations. Now this voice had seen Mandela's painting and it would be quiet no more. It sang to her of a time when she also believed in herself. The voice was so beautiful she had to stop herself from crying.

"What will you do with it?" she asked, biting her lips.

"I don't know," he said, quietly. "I painted it for you."

"But where could I put it? There will be so many questions."

He sighed. "Then I'll sell it. To the first person who makes me an offer. I'll take anything. I don't care at this point. A banana. An honest smile."

"You can't do that."

"Watch me," he said, beginning to cover up the canvas.

"No." She grabbed his hand. "I'll buy it from you."

He shook her off. "I don't want your money."

She flung the bag he'd returned to her back at him. "Take it. Take it and go to Europe. Forget everything I said. It's all fear. Fear is a cancer. You're an amazing talent. Do what you have to do. Don't settle. Just go."

He looked up, his eyes searching hers, hopeful and cynical at the same time. "Stop lying to me. I can't go."

"There's more than enough there to last you the summer. You can go. You can and you will because…Just go."

She was crying now, the singing in her head so rapturous, so beautiful. It all had to come out, once and for all, here on the steps of the Metropolitan Museum, the lighthouse of her childhood beckoning her back.

Mandela looked lost. Her tears were confusing him. "This is fucked up. You're crying. I don't know what to say."

"Don't say anything. Just go. I'm sorry how things turned out. You're brilliant. An inspiration. Don't ask me to say any more because I can't. I have a family. And no matter what you think I love my daughter more than my last breath. You've earned that money. Take it and go."

She reached over to unravel his hands from the painting. "This is mine," she said, cupping the bag into his palms.

He looked down at the bag incredulously. "You're serious."

"You know I am."

He sighed, and nodded his head. "I won't say anything…"

"Thank you. Who are you again?"

He laughed. "Don't lose that, Gabrielle."

"Are you kidding? I consider it an investment."

"Take care," Mandela said. "I'm going to Europe!" A smile popped up on his face, and she knew, at that moment, that songs had entered his head as well. As he pulled close to her and impulsively kissed her on the cheek, she imagined, as she stood there hugging a boy she'd wanted to strangle not too long ago, their separate songs coming together, a hymn washing over them, carrying away the bile in her stomach, the confusion in his heart. How light she felt in those seconds! She didn't know if he'd really go to Europe, but at least she had put the seed in his mind. Such a delicate seed it was. She had repotted and watered it, and hopefully now it would grow.

And her own seeds, the ones that time's mallet had powdered into a sparse gray dust? Sown into her daughter, went the tale she told herself, she'd experience satisfaction this way. For a long while it seemed to be working. But now too much was riding on Arianna's success. Maybe Mandela was right. Maybe she secretly hated her daughter.

Gabrielle sighed. She followed Mandela's absence with her eyes, his form receding until he became nothing more than just another dot in the landscape. Around her, the other dots continued their histories just as she'd have to continue hers. She looked down at the artist in the painting. It was not over for this woman; she could still paint a different portrait.

She looked around. Cumulonimbi loomed dangerously low in the sky. She could sense, in the thickness of the air, a storm ready to unleash itself. In minutes the city would be drenched, purged of its infernal heat. What would she do with the Gabrielle resting on the ground by her feet? Take it for a walk through the museum? Stash it in storage in the basement of her building? Hide it in the guest bedroom closet?

Then it occurred to her. There was only one thing she could possibly do. She took hold of the heavy canvas and hauled it down the steps to Fifth Avenue, throwing up two taxi-hailing fingers with urgency. As if sensing her resolve, a cab arrived three seconds later.

"550 Park Avenue," Gabrielle told the driver, resting the painting beside her.

There was only one place for this painting. Oh how utterly appropriate it would be. She'd storm into that apartment. She'd find the hammer she'd been searching for twenty years and, on one of her mother's hallowed, gold-trimmed walls, she'd nail that painting, nail it like a stigmata and watch as Selma Lowenstein and her assembly of exquisite antiques bow before it in disgrace. And if the bitch didn't like it, if she'd start grousing and waving her bony index finger in protest, she'd be ready with six final words.

*Take it down,* she'd tell her mother. *I dare you.*

## 21. RANDALL

Out with the Cha-Cha, in with the Chantilly. After sixteen months at CATPEE, Cheryl had decided to go back to hairdressing school. *It's always been my dream,* she declared the day she notified her co-workers, weaving her hand through her fulsome mane as if her audience were the production crew of a shampoo commercial. Chantilly LeFontaine arrived a few days later, and despite her drag-queen-approved name, she seemed far more dreary than diva — the kind of woman who counted out her mid-afternoon-snack carrot sticks as she placed them in a Ziploc bag. Much like her name, there was something whipped cream about her — pale, sugary sweet and insubstantial.

The director's baton quickly passed to Wheezy, who was looking more and more like a pensioner. Randall imagined a retirement dinner in 2035 at a TGI Friday's, where Wheezy would be handed a plaque and a gold-plated #2 pencil. Earlier that afternoon the man had called and asked Randall to come in for a "friendly" chat before class. Randall could practically smell the bullshit on the man's breath through the receiver.

He arrived at CATPEE's office at 5:20, ten minutes earlier than expected. Bottom line, Randall told himself, he'd just smile, pony up a few words of remorse and promise to address whatever the problem was *tout de suite*. Stepping out of the elevator he was greeted by an unusually silent reception area. Co-workers smiled at him demurely. When Miriam said hello without following it with a snide remark, Randall knew: shit was going down.

Seeing no point in delay, he bee-lined to the director's office and entered sans knocking. The dynamic duo was caught off guard. It took them a second to remove the surprise from their faces and don the tight-jawed expressions they had prepared for the occasion. Chantilly looked particularly frazzled.

"Grab a chair, Randal." Wheezy cleared his throat and stepped around his desk. He gestured to Chantilly to pull up a seat alongside him.

"Your roots are showing," Chantilly said, giggling as she plopped into her chair. Her attempt at light-hearted banter.

"So are yours," Randall replied, dryly.

"Guess it's time we see our stylists then!" She let out a stage laugh and smiled. Wheezy stuck a pencil into the electric sharpener and cleared his throat again. Chantilly dropped the smile and placed her hands on her lap.

"Let me get to the point, Randall," Wheezy said, striking a news anchor's tone. "It's come to our attention that you've been behaving, shall we say, *erratically* lately."

Randall nodded his head. "Go on."

"Take, for instance, this new 'act out an analogy' bit in your SAT classes. Explain to me how having students 'become' the word obstreperous in front of the class will help them improve their verbal scores?"

"I was trying to make it more fun for them."

Chantilly looked up from the notepad on her lap and clucked her tongue. "Um, last week did you tell an Eddie Larchmont that it was OK for him not do his homework because he was"—she studied the sheet on her lap—"quote, going to rely on those baby blues to coast through life anyway, end quote."

"I was being facetious, Chantilly. Jocular, even."

Wheezy cleared his throat again. "We thought we were clear last time, Randall. For a while things got better, and then suddenly, they start to pop up again..."

"Kind of like mouth herpes?" he said.

"Funny you mention that." Chantilly sent her index finger skyward. "There have also been reports of inappropriate lip-biting."

*Jesus*, Randall thought. "Elaborate, please. I'm all ears."

"Two girls," Wheezy said. "Sally Schultz and Lavender Lee.

They allege that you stare at them in class and bite your lower lip suggestively. They also say that when you walk around during the in-class drills that you rest your hand on people's shoulders."

Randall tapped his foot and rubbed at an imaginary beard on his face. "And?"

"And when you rest your hand on their shoulders it lingers a bit too long."

"Did one of them take out a stopwatch to time me? I'm not really sure what you're saying here, Wheezy."

Oops. Wheezy was not amused. Throat clear #4, followed by a snarling sigh. "My name," he said, "is *Roger McGee*."

"I'm sorry, Roger. But are you suggesting that I'm making sexual advances on fifteen year old girls?"

"We're saying nothing of the sort. We're simply relaying to you some examples of what I'd earlier described as 'erratic behavior'. We need consistency at CATPEE... Listen, Randall, you've been a super teacher for several years now. My predecessors said your classes were models of efficiency. And don't get me wrong, we love when our teachers bring their personalities to the classroom. But not at the expense of the lesson. We are a *product*. Think of us as a package of Fruity Pebbles. People purchase the box knowing in advance that their choice will be a delicious and nutritious part of their morning. They open the lid expecting to see the same rainbow flakes pouring into their bowls. Sure, sometimes the Post Company makes small changes, but over all, you know what you're getting. You're not going to open the box and find pink marshmallows because *that isn't Fruity Pebbles*. That would confuse people. It would upset you as a customer, and you might start losing faith in the product."

Randall kept rubbing his cheeks. "So you're calling me a misplaced marshmallow then?"

"Your unpredictable behavior is causing our clients to lose faith in our product. And that is unacceptable."

By this point Randall's cheeks were numb. His body tensed. A bell tolled in his mind, followed by a sharp stab in his gut. These scrawny pigeons, these less-than-zeroes were calling *him* out. Who were they kidding? Who was *he* kidding, sitting there, and listening to their trumped up charges? He banged his hand against the table and jumped out of his seat. "You know what's unacceptable, darlings? This meeting is unacceptable. The fact *I'm here* is unacceptable. And do not think I'm blind to the homophobic subtext of your diatribe, Mr. McGee."

Wheezy wheezed and snorted. "Now wait one… "

"*Lavender* Lee. *Rainbow* colored *Fruity* Pebbles. *Pink* Marshmallows. *Queer* behavior."

"Hnnggghhh…"

Chantilly looked over at her boss. The man's tongue had gone slack and his nose was whistling. She grabbed his hand. "Come on, Randall. Roger never said queer. You're completely missing the point."

"Oh I get the point loud and clear, Reverend Falwell! And don't think I'm going to let you get away with this."

Wheezy's breathing turned staccato. He was beginning to sound like a *shofar* on Rosh Hashanah. Frantic, Chantilly grabbed his shoulders and pounded his chest with questions: *What's going on? What do I do?* Wheezy tried to direct her but her persistent blows were disorienting him. She looked up at Randall with panic, opening drawers recklessly. "Can you help me? This is absurd."

"Move, rookie."

Randall shooed her away and reached into a now-familiar location, pulling out Wheezy's inhaler. "You know what's absurd?" he said, holding the inhaler high above his head. "That an overqualified twenty-eight year-old novelist such as yours truly is slumming at a company like this. I have to sit here and listen to you guys tell me I'm not towing the company line when both of you won't even be here in six months? Face it, kids, half your teachers are dope-fried sophomores home for summer vacation and the other half are disgruntled community-college dropouts who can't get a job teaching at a real school. And I've been here *four years*! I must be losing my mind."

"Hnnnggghhhhh"

"Now I know I don't know either of you very well, but I just want to say: fuck you. Fuck you, Wheezy. Fuck you, Chantilly LaFontaine. That's right, FUCK YOU. Fuck you, fuck CATPEE, fuck the fucking SAT. Pucker your lips, lady and gentleman, and kiss my ass goodbye. I quit. And don't tell me I'm fired. I *quit*, got it?"

He tossed the inhaler into Wheezy's lap. The man shoved it between his lips and sucked on it like a coked-up vacuum cleaner. Chantilly held the back of her boss's head. She looked at Randall with unbridled rage. "You're evil," she said. "Get out."

"Hngggn hnggh," Wheezy mumbled.

"What's that?" Randall asked.

"YOU'RE FIRED," Wheezy shouted, his voice finally returning.

"Too late, you *sycophantic* snail-muncher. You know what sycophantic means, don't you, Wheezy? Or should I take out my deck of flashcards?"

"This was supposed to be a two week notice but it's probably best you leave immediately," Chantilly said. The poor thing. Her lower lip was trembling. Randall imagined her on the phone with her mother later that night, weeping.

"Gee, can't I say goodbye to my students first? Boo-hoo. I'll miss them terribly."

"Wow." Chantilly nodded her head. "This is truly a pathetic display."

"You're making thirty thousand a year and you're calling me pathetic?"

"Get out of this office now!" she screamed.

Randall offered up a loud raspberry with his tongue, did a little jig and shimmied out of the room. He walked towards the reception area, singing loudly: *So long. Farewell. Auf wiedersehen. Goodbye*...The bewildered faces of his co-workers stared back at him in silence. Everyone froze: tonight's headliner was on, and they wanted their money's worth. *Shalom. Adieu. To yeu and yeu and yeu*...

He removed the CATPEE lesson book from his messenger bag and threw it in the air. Pressing the down button at the elevators, he turned to face the others. "So long. I'll miss you all terribly. Actually, I'll miss none of you even marginally. This place is a boiling cauldron and you're all oblivious frogs. Escape while you can." When the elevator arrived he waved to the crowd. No one dared to wave back, except Miriam, who clapped vociferously.

"You lucky bastard!" he heard her say.

The elevator took him down. So this was what it was like to go postal. Gosh, it was fun. A clean break. Randall's scorched earth policy: leave no bridge unburned. Sherman's march through Atlanta. Sean Young's career. Motherfuckers. How long overdue was this! Sheila Morningsong, the Plague, Cha-Cha: how long had he wanted to tell somebody at that God-forsaken company where they could shove their job. Finally, he did it. He did it.

And now he was unemployed.

Well, he still had some private clients.

Not really. The season was ending.

No matter. *No way* would he regret this now. They had accused him of making passes at underage girls! They didn't appreciate him. They didn't *deserve* him.

It was time to celebrate. He started walking in the general direction of his apartment when he stopped himself. No! Not today. Today, another path. But where? Anywhere. For now, he'd just walk south. *Swim in the moment.* Downtown spread before him like an Olympic-sized pool of possibility. A delicious June evening awaited. He took it in: the newborn air, the frisky sun free-styling through downy clouds. Was the day mocking him? On the contrary: it was *encouraging* him. Plus all this stuff going down? *Great* material for the book.

He ventured west on Houston towards SoHo. Ah, SoHo. Artists used to call SoHo home. Now tourists did. Still there was no denying its vibrancy. The gods of shopping had perfumed the area with the pheromones of fabulous commerce, and like a twinkle-toed Fred Flintstone rendered weightless by the scent of one of Wilma's pterodactyl stews, the natives floated towards SoHo, salivating, ready to satiate their label addictions. Temptations at every corner. All manner of minutiae to make you look better, feel better, be better. But happiness didn't come cheap. Most writers understood: Work was the problem. It got in the way. Clouded the fucking mind. Drained you of energy. But Randall knew: work provided money. He wanted a brilliant book, but he also wanted a Zegna scarf. Balducci's eleven dollar curried shrimp salad. A gym membership, even if he never went anymore.

Still, if he wasn't ready to make real sacrifices, then he might as well just become an investment banker. The thought of giving up everything scared him, but what exactly would he be giving up? Most of his friends had disappeared into the I'm-too-busy New York black hole. Legion would trot off to an enrichment program for the summer, and even if he didn't, what pretense could he muster up to visit the boy?

Was he in love with Legion? He *had* sacrificed for him. He knew he was being used, and still he did it, so at least his lust wasn't selfish. He thought about the boy's hollow life at home, his callous father. So much emotional deadness. Relationships were never easy. And this was turning out to be his longest one. If he'd found a man his age, would that somehow be more reasonable? Were men his age that much more mature? Gay men certainly weren't. Not in his experience. They just had jobs. They could drink legally. But they were also bitter and jaded.

The mannequins in the Prada store window looked down intimidatingly upon him. *We're not even real and we're better than you,* these mannequins said. So many delicacies, none he could afford. But he had to buy *something* to toast his freedom. A-ha. At the corner of Prince and Broadway, he spotted a man in a guayabera selling hotdogs. Randall pushed through the throng of shopping bags and reached into his pocket for two crumpled bills.

He slapped the dollars onto the man's cart. "What did the Buddhist say to the hot dog vendor?"

"I'm no Buddhist," the man replied.

"Make me one with everything," Randall said, laughing. "Get it?"

The man squirted mustard on top of the dog. "I'm Catholic. And that's $2.50."

"$2.50!" Randall said. "I'm no fucking tourist. But here." He reached into his pocket for another bill. "Keep the change."

The hotdog was deliciously briny. He swirled the meat around his mouth, looking forward to the gassy burps. He kept walking, reaching Spring. Past Spring things got murkier: more ethnic, more street. By the time he hit Grand the icy-cool boutiques had given way to the greasy clutter of Chinatown, the deep-discount dreams and fast-buck haggling, the crush of imitations mocking the luxuries only a few blocks away. On Canal, he could buy himself a Rolex for five dollars, summing up his life now perfectly: he wanted a Rolex, but one for five dollars. He wanted a novel, but one he could finish in a few weeks. He wanted a boyfriend, but...

The thing to do was to stop thinking about it and live in the moment. *Grab life by the balls, Randall.* But where the hell was he going? There was nothing ahead of him but the Financial District, the World Trade Center, Century 21. The Staten Island Ferry...

The Staten Island Ferry! Yes, *that's* where he was going. Staten Island was the most hated of the five boroughs. Staten Island was purgatory, the place where they banished lepers. Staten Island wanted to secede from the rest of New York City and the rest of New York City said, *bitch, please. G'head.*

It made perfect sense. He'd go to Staten Island. The new trajectory of his life: just follow things through to their illogical conclusions. From now on, he was Reckless Randall. Reckless Randall sleeps with underage boys. Reckless Randall takes SATs illegally. Reckless Randall quits his job. What does Reckless Randall do next? Go to Staten Island, of course.

Didn't art thrive on crisis? History teaches that periods of relative peace are eras of creative starvation, while art flourishes in times of war and instability. See: Rococo paintings vs. Picasso's *Demoiselles D'Avignon.* Dylan in the Sixties vs. Backstreet Boys of the Clinton years. Stable careers and loving boyfriends led to creative paralysis. Conversely, depression, insanity and relentless dissatisfaction would give his words the zing and zest of reality. *This* was the logic he was working on now. Yes. His novel was good. Heading towards brilliant. It wallowed in the muck of genuine emotions, stank of the filth of real suffering. He would baptize his readers with a golden shower of truths. He'd read so many worthless novels over the years, arch and clever disposables by transplanted dilettantes, blowjob affirmations by fresh MFA grads eager to cash in on their connections.

Of course, he'd have to make it marketable. But if it was truly brilliant, wouldn't that be enough? Would the gay thing pigeonhole him? He wondered: would Lolita be Lolita if her name had been Lloyd? Stories of teenage boys coming on to their male teachers were fantasies usually limited to the twink shelves of the video stores on Christopher Street. He didn't want to be shoved into the gay writer closet. He wanted to be *successful*. He'd just have to do what he had to do. Wasn't that his problem, in essence? He wasn't committing. Afraid to go all in. But moderation was for losers living half-lives of regret and compromise. Compromise gave you bags under your eyes, grayed your hair, made your dick go limp. So, to the unknown! He'd celebrate his new beginning by taking the ferry less traveled.

Reaching Beaver Street, he hesitated. Battery Park City loomed in the distance. Eventually the island would end and there the ferry would be. Still, he was disoriented. The area was full of anonymous streets clumped together like envelopes in a dead letter office. At Whitehall and South, he made a right and finally, the retro-outfitted Ferry building rose before him like Mecca. He raced inside like a giddy tween on a class trip.

Scores of Staten Islanders sat languidly on plastic chairs, a huddled mass of the tired and blue collar. Except — wait a minute. Could it be? To his right, at the newsstand by the main boarding platform, a man was strumming a mandolin and singing Scritti Politti. Randall gasped. Who was this Archduke of Absurdity, this omen, singing an Eighties obscurity? And who in his right mind chooses the Staten Island Ferry as his point of performance? Only an absolute fucking genius, that's who. The guy came here deliberately, just as he had. Two men, raging against reason, embracing Staten Island. Surely it was a sign.

Randall stood and watched. The poor shmoe was getting no love. Ferry people did not appreciate Scritti Politti. Still, the man sang cheerfully. The longer he was ignored, the sweeter his singing became. Randall became misty-eyed. He approached closer to admire and lo, the man was handsome. About twenty-five. A slacker's goatee with simple eyes. A round face and greasy hair, but he wore his ratty corduroys well. Randall loved him instantly. When the song ended, he clapped raucously and tossed three nickels into the man's mandolin case. "Your courage is slaying me," he told the man.

"Really? I'll have to be more careful."

"Fuck careful. Careful's overrated. Reckless is better. Have you been?"

The man smiled. "Can't say I have."

"Wanna go there sometime, like, let's say now?"

"I'm kind of busy. You know how it is. Gotta get new wheels for the Ferrari."

"Come on. No one's paying attention. And I just quit my job. Let's celebrate."

"Ah." The guy pushed the hair away from his eyes. "The dawn of a new era for you?"

"That, or I'm just losing my mind. Not sure which."

"So what did you do?" The man took out a cigarette from his shirt pocket.

"Sleep with my students. No wait, I still do that. I used to teach," Randall said. "Come with me and I'll tell you all about my seventeen-year-old boyfriend."

The man rolled his eyes, sweetly. "How nice."

"I guess. But we can still sleep together. I mean, he and I aren't going steady or anything."

"What a relief that option's still on the table."

"I don't normally do this." The words tumbled out of Randall's mouth. He couldn't believe he was still speaking. "Normally I'm shy and I over-process and keep to myself. But it's the dawn of a new era. Will you come with me?"

"I'm catching the next ferry."

"Seriously? That's cool. I'm Randall." Randall extended his hand.

"I'm Larry." Larry's hand was moist. It made Randall tingle.

"Larry, you know how sometimes you think your life is spinning out of control but then you just look at it another way and realize that everything is beginning to make sense?"

"Oh yeah." Larry chuckled. "You're making sense."

"Seriously. I'm having an epiphany here. Can you play *Sister Christian*?"

Larry strummed a chord. "Why don't we head over to my place and find out."

"Ouch, is this turning base and sexual? I'm trying to connect the dots and here you are, this new dot and…OK, fine. Let's make out."

Larry smiled. Randall smiled back. A loud horn sounded.

Randall looked out the window. The ferry boat was pulling into the dock. The Staten Islanders rose to their feet and shuffled towards the platform. "Shall we?" Randall asked.

He helped Larry pack up his stuff. Together the two struggling artists boarded the ferry with the rest of the herd. They found two seats on the upper deck, outside, towards the front of the boat. Five minutes later the boat was drifting from shore. Randall reached for Larry's hand and Larry didn't resist. A warm rush of wind slapped against their faces. The sun had lowered considerably by then, and soon its retreat would fill up the sky with toxic pinks and oranges.

Larry poked Randall on the shoulder and pointed to the right. Lovely Lady Liberty was flickering. Sun rays were bouncing off her robe, purpling her green hue.

"She's aging well," Larry said.

"Yes." Randall turned to face Larry, who looked back at him without malice or agenda. He was afraid to keep speaking. "So is this real?"

Larry chuckled. "I have no fucking idea."

"One last question," Randall said. "Is your middle name Wilder?"

# PART THREE
## FALL 2000-SUMMER 2001

# 1. GABRIELLE

The toad was still home, lingering over breakfast like an unemployed Moroccan on the Champs Elysees. Gabrielle lowered the volume. Labor Day was breathing down her neck, and here she was, cursing at the Weather Channel in the den, awaiting the sound of Morty's footsteps as he headed out the door.
  What kind of circus freak hung around New York in August, anyway? Bad enough Morty had left her babysitting their house in East Hampton for three straight weekends. Then, four days before they were supposed to be cruising Europe—gasping at Fjords, sipping ouzo in Mykonos, bartering for caviar in Tallinn—Morty suddenly canceled the trip, to "honor her quest for independence." He'd become crafty, that one.
  Now she was stuck in an abandoned metropolis, caged in her apartment by a toxic heat and an indifferent husband, both of which refused to surrender. If only she had someone to talk to. Someone, of course, besides Dr. Carl, who in the past three months had gone from detached therapist to sudden BFF. She'd visit him later that morning.
  Back in June, she'd strolled into Carl's office, taken her place on his leather ottoman and said, quite seductively, *I have something to confess.* Which she did. Every last detail, all the things

she'd left out for so long. Dr. Carl shifted several times. She imagined the emotions he was experiencing: frustration, confusion, certainly intrigue—a scheming mother plotting a false marriage! A bribery plot involving an underage black boy! She'd never be just another neurotic Jewess from the Upper West again. No, now she had *magnitude*, now she'd snag last minute appointments on a moment's notice.

She quickly became his pet project. *Your problems are crystallizing, Gabrielle,* he said, his face beaming down upon her victoriously. *The fact that you're finally able to face these truths...*From this sprouted his new mantra: facing the truth. She had to stop lying, hiding, justifying. She had to face the truth, accept it, relish it, skip in its unambiguous black and white fields, rub it into her skin like an exfoliant, testify to it like a Baptist in a church choir.

By the first week of July, Dr. Carl had introduced "The Assignment." This involved several phases: 1) Face your truth 2) Help others face their truth 3) Make others understand your truth. He'd handed her a pen and paper, and urged her to write everything down.

Face your truth was easy enough. After all, she had confessed. She just needed the courage to follow through. *You must reconnect with your passion for art,* Carl told her. *Find other people you can bond with. Immerse yourself.* Which she'd done. She allowed a bit of light in, and it felt...good. Strange. Disorienting. But still good. She'd signed up for a portraiture class at the New School, roamed the aisles of Pearl Paints with newfound giddiness, and scrutinized packages of chalks as if they were prescription bottles. She'd sat and listened to Venetia, an orange-lipped woman with three hairs zigzagging off her chin, talk about hatching and chiaroscuro and biomorphic forms. She'd even went out for drinks with some of her classmates: Adrian and Nikolai and Dakota, all several years younger than her. They cursed haphazardly, wore corduroy jackets, drank beer from a pitcher and talked about organic produce. She could have rolled her eyes, but she didn't; she wanted them to like her. And though they weren't prone to judgment she felt judged anyhow. She wore a scarf indoors and her simple sweater was still cashmere. Her timing was off and she didn't know how to be herself yet. Still, they seemed to forgive her. She vowed to keep returning.

Help Others Face the Truth was proving more difficult. Gabrielle had escorted Selma Lowenstein up to her apartment on a rainy afternoon in early July, bribing the woman with chamomile and some biscuits... The speech she'd been preparing for twenty years had taken a week to get down on paper; she had to revise, reword, recalibrate. Selma obliged patiently as Gabrielle trotted through the speech. When it was over, Selma cleared her throat and took a long sip of her tea, her left eyebrow hovering over her eye arrogantly.

"Very interesting," she said. "Let me get this straight: all this wisdom comes from therapy?"

Gabrielle smiled. Carl had taught her to smile, count two seconds before responding, then smile again. "Dr. Carl has helped me get in touch with my truth, Mother."

Selma sighed. "So this is what passes for psychiatry nowadays. No wonder half the world is *meshuggeneh*."

"You're avoiding the topic. A natural impulse when the truth makes us uncomfortable."

"Am I? Sorry, darling. Really, I'm thrilled the good doctor has helped you embrace your victimhood with such zeal. And how lucky you are to have such a first class monster such as myself to project the blame onto."

"Mother." Gabrielle paused before continuing, "I'm not assigning blame. I'm just sharing my reality with you. I've been living a life without meaning for so long."

"Meaning? Forgive me, Princess, if it's difficult for me to discuss *meaning* with you. It's hard to chew over meaning when at five years old your sister is raped in front of you by a lisping Nazi slug while his friends, another two less-than-worms watched and laughed…"

Gabrielle closed her eyes and sucked in air. "This isn't the time…"

"Nuh-nuh-nuh-nuh-nuh." Selma raised a solitary finger into the air. "You had your spotlight. Now me. You know what I ate for sixteen months, Gabrielle? I licked breadcrumbs off the floor of a basement with boarded-up windows. Countless weeks we sat in darkness, whispering, waiting for something, *anything,* to break up the routine. Every once in a while there'd be a knock at the door and suddenly we'd see a hand glowing like the hand of God as it threw a plate of bread down into our hovel. It wasn't the bread that we yearned for. It was the light. Three seconds of light so we could know the sun was still alive…"

Gabrielle cracked her knuckles. She should have hidden a camera. Maybe then Carl would believe her stories about Selma.

"…You think I only wanted one child? Your father *begged* me. God will provide, he told me, and I nodded my head, because I knew…"

*Why not just reason with her,* Carl suggested. What bullshit. Scream and Selma would scream louder. Cry and Selma would accuse her of childish melodrama. She should cut off the woman's allowance. Threaten to stick her in some retirement community in New Jersey. Maybe then...

"...had one daughter. And now this daughter tells me she lacks meaning. So finally I understand how truly blessed I must be, because Sweetheart, if meaning is all you lack, then I've done my job well. You can search the heavens and earth and every village in between, but you won't find meaning because it doesn't *want* to be found. It dodges and ducks and never gets caught or reveals itself to we who are not worthy of it. We are worthy of nothing but faith, my dear."

"This is *grotesque*. Grossly unfair."

"This is the tradeoff for life, Gaby. I didn't ask for meaning and look what I got. A daughter on Central Park South. A granddaughter who'll be valedictorian. I kept my mouth shut and in the end God has lived up to his end of the bargain."

"This is your great wisdom? I should keep my mouth shut? Of course, how easy for you. How happy that would make you."

"Happy? *Tatele*, my days are numbered. I don't reasonably expect many of them to be happy. I don't need happy anymore, just sleep, a little TV and some nice halvah every now and then. If my admitting to something will make you feel better, so be it. Show me the dotted line and I'll sign. But if this involves making me an accomplice to your misery, count me out. I'm too old to cause turbulence to the lives of others."

"Not others, just mine, Mother. Just *me*." Gabrielle stood up. "This conversation is pointless. You think your past gives you license for everything."

"And you don't? What's the reason for this little chitchat if not your rehashing of the past?"

"I'm trying to come to terms with why I've been miserable for so long. But you're right, Mother, you don't owe me anything. Hold on to that. Let me just say this. I'm telling Morty *everything*. That you lied to me about the pregnancy. That you forced me to go through with the wedding. Soon, he'll know. Maybe not tomorrow, but soon."

Selma guffawed. "You're too much, Gaby. Tell him what you want. *Baruch Hashem*, your husband is a million times more forgiving than you. So do what you have to, but please don't pretend it's anything but selfish. I'm sorry you don't have enough meaning in your life. I have what I have and I'm satisfied. You can be, too. But if not, so be it. Like you said, who am I to control you? Your truth and your consequences."

Next stop on the "Truth" train was supposed to be Morty. After the debacle with her mother, Gabrielle had second thoughts about the strategy. So much to say, and still, she dithered. She made a few passing comments to him about "needing space" and wanting to "figure things out." Morty had looked at her, breathless and frustrated. He offered several follow-up questions but she was unwilling to get too specific.

"Give me time," she said, ending these conversations. And so he did. She didn't realize how smooth the transition would be for him. She resented how easily he allowed her to drift, how infrequently the questions came after that first week. Perhaps Morty had done some thinking himself. Maybe he wasn't so happy with the direction his life was taking either. Maybe he'd found someone to talk to, someone young and pouty and unchallenging. Maybe now, almost two months later, Morty looked at his wife and only saw an albatross.

She needed to find out. So before he left, she went to the dining room. Morty had the *Wall Street Journal* folded by his right side, his hands buttering a piece of toast.

"Good morning," she said, taking the seat to his right.

His eyebrows sprung. She imagined a rabbit, its ears sticking straight up, sensing the danger but not quite seeing it yet. "Good morning." He shifted the newspaper to the other side, stuck the bread into his mouth. She took the last piece off his plate and began to butter it. He glanced down at her hands, then shifted his eyes back to the paper. "I'll be home late. Tell Tatiana not to bother with dinner."

"I see." She ripped a chunk of the toast off with her mouth. "I'll probably be out myself."

She had no intention of being out.

"Terrific," Morty said, clearing his throat. "I'm glad you're keeping busy."

"I am," she said. "It's *terrific*."

He smiled. She put the rest of the toast down on his plate.

"Morty. Arianna will be home in three days."

"Yes."

"She's not stupid, Morty."

"Far from it."

"She'll realize something's going on."

"Probably."

"Do we plan on keeping up this charade?"

Morty folded up the newspaper and dropped it on the table. "I think I've been very obliging, Gabrielle. You asked for space."

"I didn't ask to be ignored."

"Neither did I. And yet..."

He sighed. She mimicked him by sighing back.

"Look," he said. "Do you want to discuss this now? I can call in late."

"My. How generous. Are you sure they can manage without you?"

Morty shot out of his chair. "For God's sake. I can't be any more accommodating."

"Of course not." Gabrielle reclaimed the toast. "You've been a doll."

"Don't you ever tire of this sarcasm?"

"Never. I'm a monster. The cross you've been bearing for twenty years, you poor, suffering martyr."

"So this is us resolving things? This is what two months of soul searching has brought you."

"Like you even care! Like you even *ask* me what's going on!"

"I *did* ask. Repeatedly. And every time you seethed and told me to back off. I'm not going to keep asking, Gabrielle. So just tell me now. Tell me *everything*."

Morty extended his face towards her like an ostrich. He was clever, to dare her. But Gabrielle wouldn't oblige. She already had her answer: he was angry, which meant he still cared. Besides, there was no time for the truth now. Instead she lifted her chin and rolled her eyes playfully. "When Arianna comes we should try to get along. She has a lot on her plate."

"Oh, for Pete's sake." Morty picked up his handkerchief, wiped his mouth, and threw it on the floor. "Enjoy your misery. I'm going to work."

"Give me time, Morty. In the meantime can't we just pretend, for her sake...?"

Morty was already out the door.

Dr. Carl's office was on the Seventeenth floor of a flashy high-rise in Tudor City. Normally she'd never step foot in that part of Manhattan. Of course a man with as many clients bordering the Park's perimeters could have found a sensible Fifth Avenue office, but no, that wouldn't do. Carl liked the inconvenience: the journey to one's psyche began with the journey to his office.

Dr. Carl liked to remind his clients how important he was to their lives—how helpless they were without his guidance—not so much with words, but more with gestures, gestures which assumed most of them desired him uncontrollably. The worst part was that he was right. The man looked like he'd stepped out of a Zegna catalog. St. Tropez tan. Lustrous white hair. Manicured but not homosexual fingernails. Viscount tall and dazzling teeth. Blue eyes, remarkable less for their luster than their ability to see through all your flaws and love you anyway. And the man's voice! It played on her spine like a xylophone. It said: *Welcome to my garden, isn't it beautiful? Rest yourself and let's make things better, shall we?* The new age music, the snotty smiles of his wet-lipped Latina secretaries (all Psychology majors; all familiar with his couch), his insistence that everyone be on a first name basis—Gabrielle should have hated the man, dismissed his feeble pretensions and yet—she *adored* Carl.

The cab left her in front of the building seven minutes past the hour. Carmelita, in head-to-ankle Marc Jacobs, smiled a you're-late-but-it's-your-money smile at her and whisked her into the Doctor's office. Carl was kneeling by the side of his desk, gazing up at a house of cards he was studiously constructing. The man was obsessed with the frailty of delicate structures on the verge of collapse; he'd mentioned attending Jenga tournaments in his spare time. Gabrielle shut the door behind her brusquely, causing Carl's three-story tower to topple over. He looked up at her and smiled warmly.

"Foreshadowing," she said. "How appropriate."

"Gabrielle. Lovely to see you."

"As always, Carl." She took her place on the ottoman while he found his way to his chair.

"Please tell me what's on your mind." His standard opener.

"We're barely speaking," she said. "Nine used to be the upper limits of his negligence. Now he comes home after ten. Does he think I'm stupid? He has nothing to keep him past lunchtime in that office. Obviously he's finding *something* to occupy his time."

Carl adjusted the crease line of his right pant leg, which meant he found this angle you were on irrelevant. "What do you think he's doing?"

"I haven't a clue. He wants me to ask him. But I won't give him the satisfaction."

"Do you think that's healthy? Letting those feelings build inside you?"

Gabrielle sighed. So now Carl was asking rhetorical questions.

"You've been out late yourself, Gabrielle, haven't you? With your new friends?"

"Not *every* night, Carl. Besides you told me I should start doing things for myself."

"I also told you it was time for you to communicate your needs better."

"My daughter is coming back in three days. What am I supposed to say, welcome home, Princess, your father and I are separating?"

Dr. Carl tapped his pen against his upper lip: he disapproved of your sentiments. "You seem to believe that shielding your daughter from the truth is healthier than confronting it. But isn't that what caused this tension in the first place?"

"I've *ruined* her life."

"I see." Carl folded up his sleeves: he was about to say something important. "May I suggest your daughter is ready for her mother's honesty."

"May I suggest you're wrong. May I suggest I don't need another member of my family not speaking to me."

"You like the taste of guilt in your mouth, Gabrielle. Like a few shots of whiskey, you can get drunk off it, and there's your excuse for not dealing."

"My, my. Impressive analogy, Doctor. Do you write poetry on the side?"

"Are we going to start deflecting again? I'm not the issue."

"Of course not, Carl. You're a beacon of normalcy. You've flat-lined your highs and lows into a glorious Nebraska cornfield of moderation. How's your ex-wife doing?"

"Instantaneous gratification is fleeting, Gabrielle. Ergo not very gratifying."

"I tried the truth with my mother. Where did that get me?"

"You told me it was liberating."

"No, *you* told *me* it was liberating."

"You know, Gabrielle," Carl stood up. He rarely stood up. Standing up meant a new idea had struck him. "It's fascinating how different cultures forge vastly different attitudes towards the past. For example, your people, the Jews—

"*My* people?"

He paused behind his chair, grabbing the back with his hands. "The Jews cling to their past very firmly, arguably with good reason. They memorialize their losses with rituals and prayers. They latch on to their grief, afraid that if they forget they'll be forced to relive."

"And?"

"Humor me, Gabrielle," Carl said. "But not every culture is so enamored with the past. The Achuar people of Ecuador, for example, try to forget everything. They hate and fear the past. They don't even remember their ancestors' names. Each morning they take feathers to their tonsils and tickle them, making themselves sick in order to purge themselves of their memories."

"You want me to tickle my tonsils, Carl?"

"What I'm saying is, if you allow yourself, you can let go of your past instead of letting it be your crutch. Imagine this: someone calls you and tells you there's a fire in your building. They say, don't panic, it's not a big fire yet. It may go out on its own. Do you stay in the building?"

"For God's sake, Carl, a burning building? You *must* do better."

"Gabrielle." He tilted his head. "Do you stay in the building?"

"No, Carl. And I don't jump out the window either."

"Of course not. There's always the stairs. Only problem is, the phone caller didn't tell you any details about the fire. So which stairs do you take? Is it even safe to take the stairs? You don't know. You think you see smoke. Just the tiniest bit. Could be burnt toast. Does that mean you stay put?"

"I send my maids down each stairwell and the one that comes back with the least burns—"

"You're alone, Gabrielle." Carl enunciated his syllables: *Please don't turn this into a joke.*

"Fine. I look around to see which one seems safest."

"And?"

"And then I get out."

"Even if you don't know what will happen? You might get burned. You might get trapped. You might lose your apartment, your photo albums, your souvenirs."

"If the building is burning, Carl, I'll take my chances."

"Exactly. You take your chances, even though the outcome is unknown. Problem is, most people don't see their lives as a burning building. So they wait until the smoke is at the door, and then they really do have to jump out the window. It's a human tendency to be afraid of the unfamiliar. To carry on with what you know, even when what you know is a burning building. But sometimes it's that leap into the unknown that saves you. Sometimes, Gabrielle, when you let go of everything you think defines you, you become who you really are. You have to be willing to enter the gray area. Are you willing?"

Gabrielle winced; his melody was hard to resist. But she wouldn't let his voice get to her. "I have no idea what you're talking about."

"I think you do. I think you're ready."

"I think our hour is over."

Carl laughed. "You're right."

The two of them got up at the same time. Carl reached for her right hand, cupping it between his own.

"It's already happening," he said, blinding her with his baby blues, his obscenely straight teeth. "I know it. You know it. Don't hesitate. Don't deny yourself."

"May I have my hand back?"

He let go clumsily. "I'm sorry, that was a bit unprofessional."

"It's alright." She winked at him. "I'm used to it."

He wagged his finger and sucked on his bottom lip. "The cleverer ones are always the most fascinating. And dangerous."

"See you next week, Carl."

She left the office in a giddy mood. It was nice to know she could still be thought of as fascinating. Still, visiting Carl was like eating Chinese food—satisfying for ten minutes, leaving you empty and unfulfilled a few hours later. Was he right? Would she have to tell Morty everything? How much could it matter all these years later? He'd dismiss it, laugh it off, and assure her he wouldn't change a thing. He'd say all that, but she wouldn't. She couldn't. Because of course it mattered. Everything about her— everything that defined who she was—had stopped existing at that point. And now she was someone else. Some other woman. This wasn't a crack, this was a canyon. You can't fill canyons. You can only accept that the landscape has changed and deal with it.

To think that this all could be traced back to Mandela Robinson. She'd been sleepwalking and he'd been kind enough to prod her into consciousness. She wondered how he'd spent his summer. Had he been brave enough to follow his dreams to Europe? She hoped he wasn't drowning somewhere. She hoped his hands were getting dirty. It would've been so easy to call him while Arianna was away. But she hadn't. That door needed to remain closed.

And now it was time to move on. She'd have to let go of everything: her past, her viselike grip on Arianna's life, her resentment of her mother, her fear. She'd have to enter the gray areas, like Dr. Carl said. Hold her breath under the murky waters of uncertainty and pray she'd make it out someplace safe.

## 2. RANDALL

Randall paced the uptown #6 platform at Union Square. Better, he told himself, not to think about what he was doing there on a Tuesday afternoon. Better to not dwell on it.

Should the subway be more prominent in his novel? Certainly there was no lack of material down there; the panhandlers alone could fill a few chapters. The way things were going, he'd end up becoming one of them. His last source of steady income had flown back to Iran two weeks ago, a frisky, bulbous-cheeked girl whose expatriate parents packed off to an all-girls boarding school in Isfehan every year. He'd prepped her for the SAT, God only knows why, since as far as Randall could tell her wardrobe and mind were both squarely set on nabbing a husband. The trip required Randall to ride the A train to Far Rockaway and emerge, two hours later, in a frontier of abandoned store fronts where he'd be fetched from the station by the mother, sporting an exquisite silk sari and head wrap, her Lexus SUV inexplicably blasting Wu Tang Clan. This was what he'd been reduced to. Still, at two hundred a pop, he wasn't asking questions.

And the summer hadn't been a total waste, even if Larry from Staten Island hadn't lasted more than a week. 300 pages: not bad for sixty days. He certainly had the time and for once, actually used it. It was all going into the book, he told himself, as the train entered the station. Very soon that book would be finished. Just in time, too. Last week he'd come across a flyer in Tompkins Square Park, one with a recent MFA grad from SMU soliciting "committed writers" to join her for a workshop that promised "constructive feedback at below market rates." At eighty dollars for eight weeks, the price was right but also a warning: anybody with four twenties could join and have two months to shove his "my girlfriend is a whore and this is my revenge fantasy" diatribes onto him. But maybe that was just the kind of unfiltered feedback he needed at this point. Besides, who else could he show his work to? His friends? Yeah, right. The vacuous praise he could handle. But what about the ones who'd demand to know which character was based on them? He had no choice but to go public. Problem was, most of the better classes were pricey, and he and money had been hitting a rough patch lately.

The essentials—rent, utilities, gym membership—were covered by the monthly allowance his parents continued to bestow upon him. Sylvia and Saul Miller had popped by in late July for a surprise visit, and decided to take him to Kin Khao in Soho. In between bites of pad-see-ew his mother pleaded with him to go back to school and brushed aside any talk of his novel while his father silently nodded along, obsessively excavating pieces of basil from his teeth with a toothpick. The catch to these impromptu visits was that the check was always filled out at the end, as if his parents were sizing up the time they'd spent with him and decided upon the amount accordingly. Randall remembered Saul holding a pen in his right hand and the checkbook flat against the table. The first number was key; the next two were always zeroes. He caught a glimpse over his father's shoulder: A six. A six was good. It could be better. But a six would do. If he took the check with less reluctance than usual, neither of them seemed to notice.

At Seventy-seventh he got off the train and began to walk towards Park Avenue. The sun was soft and bright for six o'clock, the summer humidity almost gone. It was eerie returning to Legion's building. After three months he'd pretty much given up on ever seeing the boy again. He thought he had come to terms with it, but then late August rolled around and he called and left a message. The surprise came when Legion called him back. They set up a meeting for a few days later, and he braced himself for it: the insufferably clichéd break-up speech. But then they met, and lo and behold, had primal, mind-bending monkey sex. Nipple biting. Roaming fingers. Multiple orgasms. The last thing he'd expected. Was it a parting gift? He had no idea. And why the need for a parting gift anyway?

It disturbed him. How was he going to bring his saga to a close now? He needed an ending, in more ways than one. Last week's pleasures notwithstanding, there was little left to feast on in their parasitic relationship. Of course he could bring this life lesson into the book and let that be his ending: Gay man swallows bitter pill and finally grows up. But it was such a dull fizzle. How many novels had he read that started off miraculously and then gradually lost steam, only to leave him frustrated and sad? He was enough of a failure; he couldn't allow his book to be. There had to be something else. This, perhaps, was what really brought him uptown that afternoon.

Lost in thought, he almost didn't hear his phone ring.

"Dude, where are you?" Legion's tone was positively giddy.

"Right around the corner."

"Cool. Wait downstairs. We're going to the zoo."

"Oh…I just thought." What was he going to say? *I just thought we're going to fuck?*

"What? Oh, I get it. Dude, *later*. I need to see hippos right now."

"You're high," Randall said, stating the obvious.

Legion laughed. "Ya think?"

"Fine. I'll wait downstairs."

"Don't get pissy, Randall. I'll bring some with. We'll chat with baboons."

Randall hung up the phone. Was he being pissy? Perhaps. Because he was horny? No, it was more than that. Six months ago, when he had a job, he could justify spending an afternoon getting high and staring at hippos. Now it was more of a reminder that he had little else going on.

He turned onto Park. Inside Legion's building, Hector was accepting a package from a stout, bearded UPS delivery man.

"Señor Randall, how are you?"

That the doorman knew his name depressed and elated him equally. "Fine, Hector. Como Estas?"

The man reached for the house phone.

"Don't bother, he's coming down."

"You look sad, Señor Randall. Cheer up."

Hector winked at him. Was it possible he knew something? "I'll try, Hector."

Randall took a seat in the plush sitting area to the right of the elevator bank. He cringed. What was once intimidating had turned exasperating. How many months' rent could the sofa buy him? How many of his credit cards could the coffee table pay off? The left shaft opened and Legion shuffled out and high-fived Hector. Randall watched the two chat effortlessly, reminded once again of Legion's casual charm, his contagious, spontaneous energy. Hector was laughing and it was obvious Legion didn't realize he was there. Crushing, how peripheral he was, how easily he could be subtracted from the boy's equation.

Hector nodded and finally Legion turned around. "Hey. You're here." His eyes were flat and his mouth was fixed in a half-smirk. "Let's mosey. Later, Hector."

Outside, he breathed in hard, sucking on air that seemed to be growing thinner. The Upper East Side hummed with efficiency. Nothing, absolutely nothing extraordinary about the day, and yet he felt somehow it should be, that his angst should manifest itself externally and provide him with a sign, some hint at future meaning.

"You look happy," he managed to say.

"*Sweet* shit, dude. You must partake. We'll find some shaded area. Or the bathroom inside the zoo."

"I'll pass, thanks."

"Fuck, Randall. You want to blow me in the zoo bathroom? That would be hot."

Yes, Randall thought, it would be hot. And then it would be over, and then there would be yearning for the next hot time, and the next, in an endless loop of desire roulette. Which didn't make sense any longer. Things had changed. It was impossible that Legion didn't know that. No, this wasn't naiveté. This was something else, something Randall didn't understand yet. "So how's school?" he said, changing the subject.

"All good. Taking it pretty serious now."

"Where are you applying?"

"Not sure...Ken's got connections at Cornell. So maybe there. I may go out west, though. It's up in the air."

Randall grimaced at the sound of Ken's name, tumbling so effortlessly off of Legion's lips. "So things are better between you and him."

"Yeah." Legion looked down at the ground. "I guess. I mean, the guy's an ass. But whatever."

"Looks like the ass liked your SAT score."

"I guess."

Randall hated these vague non-answers. Too much had happened over the summer. But what could he expect, that time would stand still? He had evolved, and Legion had too.

"So what's the story with SAT IIs," he asked.

"Been looking into those," Legion said, cracking his knuckles. "Even studying a bit."

"So…" Randall paused. They had entered the park, the sun's rays eclipsed by a canopy of trees. The absence of light sent a chill through him. "How are…I mean, do you want my help?"

"Sure," Legion said. "If you want."

Randall snorted, shook his head. He could tolerate anything but this callous passivity. "Listen, what's going on here?"

Not an ounce of guile on the boy's face. "What?"

"Why are we meeting today? If, you know, the while college thing isn't so important anymore."

"I dunno." Legion's eyes searched for cover in the distance. "I thought you wanted to hang out."

"You want to hang out with me."

"Sure," the boy managed. But the word felt mushy, half-hearted.

"And last week?" Randall asked.

"What about it?"

"At my place." He stopped walking and stared at Legion. "It was hot. Really hot."

"Totally. It was."

"You were about to say 'but'."

"Was I?" Legion finally looked up, his voice flickering with frustration.

"You were. So say it."

"OK then. But."

"But what?"

"I don't know, Randall." Legion picked up a pebble from the ground and threw it against a tree. "You tell me."

"But it can't go on like this. It's got to stop."

"Well, I guess…eventually…"

If only he could read the boy's mind at that moment. But his expression wasn't clear: shock? relief? "No need to stutter. It's got to stop. So why are we here today? We could have stopped months ago."

Legion brushed back his hair, his legs shaking, his eyes jumpy. "You called," he said, several seconds later. Harder to lie gracefully when you're high, Randall thought.

"So? You could ignore me. You could have said goodbye. We didn't have to do what we did."

"But I like what we did."

Legion reached for his hand, but Randall swatted him away. "You don't want me."

The boy fumbled through his pocket for a pack of cigarettes, then for a lighter, trying to mask the irritation spreading on his face. "C'mon, Randall. I was looking forward to the monkeys."

"You don't want me. Admit it. End it."

"Listen." Legion lit the cigarette, swallowing hard on his first drag. "Look, I didn't tell you this, but Ken knows about the money. He knows it's gone. So things are, I don't know, better. And you helped with that. I just want to make you happy."

"You want to make me happy or you want to keep me quiet?"

Legion's eyes went dead. "Dude, chill out. Don't get all conspiracy theory on me."

"I just don't know if it's supposed to end this way."

"You keep saying end, not me. It's just..." He looked hard into Randall's eyes. "Randall, I'm seventeen. Cut me some slack."

"You think I don't know?" Randall spat the words through clenched teeth. It was going to be hard, once his voice broke, to hold back the tears. "I know. I *understand*. But let me tell you what you don't know. I got fired months ago. I don't have a job and God knows I don't have a boyfriend. There's not much left for me to lose."

Legion nodded his head. Randall wasn't even sure what he was saying anymore, but the boy seemed to understand something anyway. "Shit. That sucks. I'm sorry. But do you blame me for that?"

"No, I blame myself. But—"

"But what? I mean, what do you want me to do? *Tell* me."

"It just doesn't seem right. Ending it this way."

"*You're* ending it. I thought I was being mature here."

"You are. It's just...I mean, imagine if Ken knew." Randall tensed. He didn't know where these words had come from. Apparently this ending wouldn't satisfy; he had to cut deeper. He was already bleeding to death, what was one more gash? "I bet he wouldn't be so proud then. I bet he'd hate you."

How shameful, the pleasure it brought him. Shameful to watch the pale descend onto Legion's features, relish the terror seizing the boy's mind. He never thought he'd cross that line. The can had refused to open so he smashed it against the wall.

Legion's eyes narrowed. "What are you trying to say, Randall? You want Ken to hate me?"

"No." He couldn't sustain this attack. He didn't have the will for it. Of course, he knew it would end that day. But then the moment came, and his vulnerability cut so deep he couldn't think, he could only hurt and rage and try hard not to just scream. How could he say goodbye? Goodbyes were murder. They were apocalypses.

"Do you want to go back to the apartment?" Legion asked. He reached over, awkwardly adjusting the collar of Randall's shirt. His expression adjusted too, the result of a lifetime of playing chameleon to the thoughtless colors of others. But Randall could no longer accept this pity. He clasped the boy's hands into his own. "You know I want nothing more. But I won't. Not anymore."

"You're sure. I'm not denying you anything."

The evenness of Legion's voice destroyed him. "Oh, you will. Very soon you will."

"Fuck, what do you want from me?" the boy shouted, stepping away from him. Randall turned his head: a lady on a nearby bench looked up from her sandwich. A man and his Great Dane both slowed down. The world was witnessing. He looked back at Legion, the boy's lower lip stuck in an artless half-tremble, and suddenly, his pain lessened. *This*, Randall thought. *That's all I want.*

He breathed hard. "Nothing. It's been nice knowing you. Take care of yourself."

"So it's like that?"

Randall looked away.

"Let's go to the monkeys, Randall." The boy stood too close, his voice quivering, his right hand gripping onto Randall's elbow. "Just look at the monkeys with me for a few minutes. Don't bail on me in the middle of the park."

Randall kept his eyes on the ground.

"Fuck. You're really going." Legion stepped back, digging his fingers into his scalp.

"I am," Randall said. He felt certain, but he'd have to go soon, because his certainty would not last.

"And then? What are you gonna do?"

"I'll figure out something."

Legion reached over and pulled him into a hug. For a few final seconds he would accept. But no more. "Let go of me," Randall whispered. Disentangling himself, he grabbed Legion's face with both of his hands. "Just let go. That's all."

And there it was: a genuine fever in the boy's eyes. The fear of something slipping out of his control. Maybe more than that, maybe something warmer, maybe a feeling closer to love. But if it was love, it had come too late.

He turned around and walked away, passing by the people of the park, lonely people made lonelier by the sun's imminent demise in a sky burning pink and gold. Strange, he thought. He knew if he turned around Legion would still be in the same spot, half-baked but quickly becoming more sober. For a few minutes he'd stand there, half-expecting Randall to come back. At a certain moment he'd become aware of his position, and then, Randall knew, he just *knew*, Legion would simply continue walking to the zoo and find the monkeys. He'd locate the right cage and find one monkey's restless eyes, and together they'd laugh and laugh, a laughter that sounded like crying, until he and the monkey would fall silent.

But this vision Randall would not verify. He walked out of the park, bound downtown, where his computer would be waiting.

# 3. MANDELA

Senior year was proving to be surprising. Hierarchies had shifted, and alliances once considered eternal were quickly becoming more nebulous. How else could Mandela explain how he found himself on a late September Thursday lounging in the coveted red velvet sofas of the student union thirty minutes into fourth period with Lauren, Bridget, Karynne and Markus, a quartet of the highest order, definers of cool if you will, not to work on a project but rather purely voluntarily on their part, discussing Electroclash, the benefits of Red Bull and the eternal question of whether *Pulp Fiction* or *Reservoir Dogs* was in fact Tarantino's greatest achievement?

This wasn't his first meaningful conversation with the deity crowd. That happened two weeks prior, when Karynne had ostensibly needed to borrow a pen and had used the request as a platform from which to jump into an investigation of all things Mandela. Two hours later, sitting at a Starbucks on Sixty-eighth, the remains of several lattes resting between them, Mandela had handed over a wealth of excruciatingly personal information, for which he'd received not much in return. How and why this happened, he could not begin to say. Two years of painting every popular kid at Valhalla into a corner had dissolved in an instant.

The story he told himself—that these clones were uninspired sheep, that they were shallow and unworthy of his friendship—was now nothing more than that, a story. Because Karynne was fucking cool. She was insightful, provocative, razor sharp and pretty damn hilarious. And the rest of them weren't half bad either.

"But that's the problem," Markus said. "It's the moral tone of *Pulp Fiction* that I find so artificial. The non-linear structure which everyone gets off on is really just an excuse for Tarantino to have his cake and eat it too. Feed us the non-stop violence, kill off my man Vincent Vega and then have Sam Jackson spew the Bible and quit the business so the audience can go out feeling good about themselves. That's plain weak."

"You prefer a moral vacuum?" Karynne chimed in. "*Dogs* is great but it's myopic. To not see the obvious evolution dare I say *enlightenment* of Tarantino in *Pulp Fiction* is to fall into that famous-person's-first-work-is-always-the-best trap, which everyone knows is just the biggest sack of bullshit."

"I can name hundreds of bands that never topped their first albums," Markus said. "Even great bands. Stone Roses. Liz Phair. Pearl Jam."

"Yeah. What about *Pablo Honey*?" Karynne asked.

"Underrated."

"Bite me, Markus. *The Bends* is light years better."

"The jury's still out, don't you think?" Mandela was now ready to contribute. "Give Quentin some time. If Picasso was judged strictly on his early works, he'd be considered a mediocre classicist at best. Great artists evolve. They never rest on their laurels."

"Granted, but Picasso's early work was just him paying his dues," Bridget said. "Better to judge his works after 1907, and then ask whether or not his earlier work was still better. I'd say the evidence is inconclusive."

"What about Matisse and Van Gogh?" Lauren asked. "Didn't they almost immediately demonstrate their talent? Wasn't *The Joy of Life* one of Matisse's earliest?"

"Is that his best, or just his most famous?" Markus asked.

Mandela smiled. Were they entertaining this conversation for his benefit?

"So I hear you're applying to Princeton." Bridget, working on a Tootsie Pop, broached the subject without fanfare, but the others still shifted their eyes toward him.

"Am I? That's interesting." He saw no reason to be direct just yet.

"It's been making the rounds," Markus said. "Maybe you and Arianna can dorm together."

Lauren and Karynne giggled.

"She'll have to find another roommate," he said, flatly.

"Does that mean you're not applying or just not interested?" Karynne pursed her lips and raised both eyebrows. He was being teased, which was a good sign.

"Unlikely. But nothing's impossible."

His evasiveness seemed to sit well with this crowd.

"Speaking of…" Markus raised his chin ever so slightly. Mandela turned around. About ten feet away was Ms. Levy herself, searching her purse for something which clearly held great meaning. She looked harried and diminished from his vantage point, free of the shadow of intimidation she normally cast. There was little doubt she saw them. Likely she'd intended to approach, but had spotted Mandela and stopped herself. He wondered if this was as obvious to the others as it was to him.

"Riri!" Karynne called out.

Arianna kept fumbling for a few seconds before reacting. When she did it was a flawless performance: a generous and staggered smile with just a trace of embarrassment. She approached without hesitation.

"I thought I lost my planner. Could you imagine?" she said, to no one in particular.

"Someone should seize that thing and hold it for ransom," Markus said.

"I'd pay any price," she said, looking at Mandela for the thinnest second, just enough time to convey the entire universe. When it melted away, she was Arianna Levy once more. No one had bothered to explain his presence. He could tell Arianna expected an explanation. He wondered if this was a sign that he could turn ordinary among them.

"So Tasti D for lunch today?" Bridget asked.

"Didn't Pen say she was boycotting them?" Karynne said. "Aren't they testing flavors on hamsters or something?"

"Pen's boycotting her own stomach," Arianna said.

Bridget rolled her eyes. "Someone please introduce her to a fat gram. She seriously needs to be locked up in a room with some Ring Dings."

"Make it Krispy Kreme and I am so there with her," Lauren said.

"So Mandela, you coming to Tasti D with us?" Karynne asked.

Without looking up, Mandela could sense the shiver running down Arianna's back. He wanted to collect this shiver in his mind, and paint it. He wanted to will it into existence.

"Sorry, not much of a yogurt guy," he said.

"Good God, what was I thinking?" Arianna blurted out. "I can't lunch today. I have a meeting with the photographers for yearbook. I'll catch up with you guys later. Ciao." She waved and bee-lined for the door.

"Shit that was improvised," Markus said.

"She's a bit edgy lately," Bridget said. "I think her mom's gone Anne Heche on her."

"Her mom's a dyke? That's hot," Markus said.

"Twit," Bridget said. "Post-Ellen Anne Heche. You know, like mid-life crisis shit."

"In that case, she should hang with my mom. They can chant together," Lauren said.

"Your mom is *smoking*, Lauren. She still single?" Markus asked.

"I think she's fucking our Pilates guy who's like twenty two in the shade," Lauren said. "So you never know, Markus, you might have a shot."

"You mean the hottie in your kitchen the other day?" Karynne said. "Good for her."

Nothing was sacred with this crowd, Mandela thought. It was proof of how bored they were with their lives that they could offend so easily without taking offense. He just couldn't bring himself to chime in. What if he got it wrong and crossed an invisible line?

Bridget's eyes dilated golf-ball size mid-sentence. Mandela looked up. Without warning, Legion had found a nook between Markus and Karynne, hooking his arms around each of them. A strange gesture, familiar and somewhat confrontational, Mandela thought—and very much Legion, these sudden bursts of chumminess. Oblivious to hierarchies of cool, Legion followed none of the unwritten laws about whom to hang with, which clearly irritated and fascinated this crowd equally.

"Dude," he said, addressing only Mandela.

"Dude," Mandela said.

"Where've you been, man? Hanging with these clowns?"

Legion reached over and dabbed Karynne's nose gently. Mandela couldn't imagine anyone else getting away with this. Yet he knew Karynne wouldn't take offense.

Karynne turned to face Legion. "Did you show up to Peter's

at 3am? Where the fuck were you until then?"

Legion offered a dubious shoulder shrug in return.

"Probably devirginizing some freshman filly," Bridget said.

Legion laughed. "That's Markus's job."

"I prefer a real challenge," Markus said. "Like Lauren's mom."

"Lauren's mom," Legion said. "Suh-*weet*."

Lauren rolled her eyes and turned to Mandela. "So Del, we have an extra ticket to the Strokes on Friday. Care to join?"

"Are the rest of us invited?" Legion asked.

"Only one ticket." Lauren's smirk was brisk, barely affecting regret.

"Can't we duel for it then?" Legion continued.

"It'll be Penelope, Travis D, me…" Lauren said, ignoring him.

"Sure. I'm down," Mandela replied, trying to pretend this wasn't a very exciting moment for him.

"Sure. I'm down," Legion repeated. "Guess it's settled then."

Mandela's eyes wandered over to his friend. Was Legion being a dick on purpose?

"I hear they suck live. But you kids have a good time," Legion said. "Personally, I prefer Celine Dion." He batted his eyelashes at Markus. "Don't you?"

Everyone laughed. "Shut up," Bridget said.

"Seriously. Her voice is angelic. I'm gonna go listen to her now."

Legion jumped to his feet, tipped an invisible cap to everyone. "Later, man," he said, extending his hand solely to Mandela. As soon as he left the room seemed to expand, like everyone was collectively holding their breath and decided to exhale at once.

"Wow. He's so random," Bridget said.

"You're close with him," Karynne said. "What's his deal?"

"I don't know about close. We didn't hang much over the summer."

"It's an act," Bridget said. "He likes to shroud himself in mystery, but there's probably nothing behind the curtain."

"He's nicer than he comes across," Mandela said.

"Why are we talking about him? Next topic." Lauren reached for Mandela's palm, pulled out a pen and began scrawling. "My digits. Call and we'll set up Friday…"

The rest of the day was like floating. He tried to concentrate on his classes but it was difficult to compete with the delicious play-by-play reconstruction of Lauren asking him out. How crazy, how fucking wild that he'd been chosen. Nothing could get him down today. Even the train ride home became pleasurable, the jostling of New York's commuter class now just a sign of glorious interconnectedness. The world, it turned out, could be wonderful. He looked around the subway car and saw possibility everywhere.

The panels above his head held advertisements for KLM airlines. How long ago that day in July seemed, when he'd gone to the STA travel office downtown and almost bought a round-trip to Amsterdam for less than five hundred dollars. The hot girl behind the counter told him he'd be crazy to pass on such a deal. Despite her flirty smile, he just couldn't hand over the money. That kind of rashness had to have conviction behind it; it was one thing to dream, another to get on a plane. He wondered if this was a flaw in his personality, something that might stop him from becoming a true artist if he didn't address it. Would Basquiat worry about his parents having to shell out for a nanny while he was gone?

There was nothing wrong, he supposed, with giving college a try for a year. At least Deidre and Joe couldn't hold that over him if he tried. In the meantime he had more than eight thousand dollars to ponder. Many times he thought about calling Gabrielle up and demanding she take it back. But he was sure she didn't want to hear from him again. They had their moment; she learned whatever it was about herself that rich white women felt they needed to learn to live with their guilt, and now she had disappeared back into her life of furs and Ferraris, maybe a better person by a smidge, but probably not.

Even if she'd become a different person, what business was it of his? Why couldn't he go more than a few days without thinking about her? Was he in love with her? Sure, he would've slept with her out of curiosity, but it wasn't like he dreamed about it. She was more like an unfinished work that he didn't know how to complete. Gabrielle was best relegated to the past. A girlfriend, or at least someone to hook up with, was the kind of distraction he really needed, and the Strokes concert might just be the ticket. Because he needed to get some. Fast.

These fantasies carried him home: Lauren nibbled on his ear as he got off the subway, she guided him to her bedroom as he walked up Third avenue. When he entered his apartment building, she had taken off her top, beckoning him over to the bed. When he got on the elevator, he could see her breasts in front of him, the same breasts which had brushed against his shoulder earlier that afternoon, breasts he knew would be *perfect*.

He was savoring these thoughts when he put the key into the apartment door, only to realize it was already open. Tyrese and Sarafina had both been warned too many times to lock the door. He entered, in slow motion. Two seconds later he heard his sister's jubilant shouting and exhaled in relief; at least they hadn't been robbed, or worse, weren't being robbed right then.

"Tyrese, you left the Goddamn door open, you stupid runt," he shouted into the empty room. "How many times do I gotta tell you…?"

His mother came out of the kitchen, arresting him mid-sentence. She looked frazzled and pale, her eyes clouded with a ruinous awareness, as if she'd just watched someone get mowed down by a car.

"Mom?" His voice was thick with fear. "Why are you home?"

She motioned him to follow her outside. They stood in the hallway. She closed her eyes and took a heavy breath. "Your grandmother," she said. "She's had an aneurysm."

"Shit," he said. He didn't know what else to say. "Shit."

"I'm getting some things together," she whispered. "Dad's meeting me here and we're driving down to Jersey."

"Is she alright?" he asked.

She shook her head. "I don't know. She might be in a coma."

"Fuck." He could not wrap his mind around that image. Grandma Lucille? In a coma? Jowly, crimson-haired Nana Lucille? She was only sixty something, sleek and strong as a jaguar. A woman he assumed would live past a hundred. How was this possible?

"I need you to stay focused, Mandela." She grabbed his hands and squeezed the panic out of him. He could tell she was trying to find strength inside herself, only it wasn't coming quick enough.

"We should come with you," he said.

"No," she said. "Not yet. Just stay put. We'll call you later."

"What do I tell them?"

"I already told them. Grandma's a little under the weather, so Daddy and I are going to cheer her up. Just talk about other things, OK?"

"OK," he said, even though he knew nothing was okay. This was her mother she was talking about. Grandma Lucille didn't get sick. She had the deepest laugh of anyone he knew. She was fanatic about her garden and walked back and forth from her favorite nursery almost every day, over a mile each way. He could see all this in his mother's eyes, the shock, the denial; he knew she was thinking the same thing.

"Dinner's in the fridge. Just heat it up. If Grandpa calls, tell him we're on our way. Put them both to bed by ten no matter what."

"Mom?" His voice was cracking. He was embarrassed to look at her, to make her show the pain she couldn't show right then.

"I'm fine, honey," she said. And then she shook her head. "You know what, no I'm not. This sucks. It really sucks."

She grabbed her son into a hug and whispered in his ear. "Let's not scare them yet." She looked coldly at him, and he nodded his head, shaking the fear off his face. She grabbed his hand and they reentered the apartment. Once inside, she went to her bedroom.

Tyrese was on the living room couch, watching *TRL* and sucking on a bottle of strawberry Yoo-hoo. Sarafina was on the floor fiddling with a box of crayons. Neither of their faces showed anything but the purest ignorance.

"I didn't leave the door open, dummy," Tyrese shouted, his eyes squarely on the TV set. "So who's the runt now?"

Mandela didn't have to think hard. "I am," he said.

# 4. EXCERPTS FROM ARIANNA LEVY'S JOURNALS

September 3rd

    Something is definitely rotten in the state of Levy-land. Let's face it: unplugged from my life Mother is not. When I go away, she just buys a longer extension cord. But in the weeks before I came home from Cambridge our phone conversations were getting bizarre. She had lost her zest for inquisition and was now asking me the kind of breezy, generic questions I imagine normal mothers ask their daughters when they're away.
    Then I get to the airport and Daddy's there *alone*. We drive home and there she is, waiting downstairs with the doorman. She grabs me like I'm the stuffed animal she lost when she was four. Everything, it seems, is groovy with her. But this obsequious PDA was a bit too affected for me. Mother only gets this way when she's hiding something. I don't want to even think about what it could be.
    I tried a general probe, but the only thing she's mentioned is that she's seeing Dr. Carl more and that things have been "clearing up" for her. When I asked for specifics she quickly changed the subject. And she and Daddy aren't even doing the pretend happy thing; Daddy looks hollow around Mother, like he's tun-

ing into some soundtrack only he can hear. I'm not going to bring it up yet because they'll just lie and say everything's peachy.

As if I have time to worry about this! I'm wayyyy too busy. It's crunch time: SAT IIs, then the SAT again, tweaking my personal essay, Princeton Interview in two weeks, four brutal APs, plus Yearbook, Model UN, and Senior Play which I'm so going to petition for *Proof* because that chick is my life—I will out Mary Louise Parker Mary Louise Parker.

Mother asked me yesterday if I wanted another tutor. Jokingly, I asked about Randall and she rolled her eyes and told me this was no time to get nostalgic. (Poor Randall. I wonder how he's doing.) Anyway I told Mother to just get Helena Rubin's number. She's *the* admissions consultant of the moment. Her connections are insane; it's like she and God could throw the same dinner party. She'll know exactly how to package me right.

I don't even have time to get into details about you-know-who. Ugh. More later.


September 19th

It's weird being back in school. I look around sometimes and think, who are these people? It's strange, now that I've seen outside the box, to realize that Valhalla is not the world. Thank God too because everyone's trying way too hard there. It's such a cliché, but my life really did change over the summer. And I don't mean in that fake *Real World* Southern-jock-learns-to-love-blacks-and-gays kind of way. I'm recognizing different shades now, turning over rocks I once thought couldn't budge. The program really helped me with that. It was transformational. Acting isn't pretending, Professor Broussard would say. Acting is *becoming*. When you start becoming, you start understanding. I'm starting to apply this to my life. Sometimes I'll sit in my room and close my eyes and will myself to become other people. It's trippy, forcing yourself to see things from someone else's perspective. I can even tolerate looking at Mandela now. Apparently he's managed to climb a few rungs on the popularity ladder. Two days ago Karynne actually called Mandela interesting and then Morgan said he might even be cute. I thought they were fucking with me, but no, they were serious. I'm still terrified he'll open his mouth. So far he's been quiet, but who knows.

OH. BTW, Douglas and I are over. If I could go so gaga for Ersin over the summer, there's no point in pretending we have a future. Besides, Douglas is going to Vassar. And not just because the library is named after his grandfather. He belongs there—he's artsy and sensitive in that sleepy trust-fund way, and no doubt he'll pick up a few addictions and be bi for a semester and then find God or Tibet or veganism until senior year when his dad will threaten to cut him off unless he goes to Yale Law. We're giving friendship a try. He's thinking friends with benefits, and I'm thinking not. Like I have time for that.

Anyway, Ersin called yesterday. He invited me to fly out to Turkey over winter break, describing the house they have in Bodrun, twenty-four rooms built into a cliff stretching over the Aegean with tennis courts and lemon trees and wild goats. *I can teach you how to surf, Arianna.* Sigh. We promised each other not to do the whole miss-you-like-crazy thing. And then he up and does it. Repeatedly.

There's really no point. Mother and Daddy may have PhDs in Tolerance, but once I say the word *Turkish* I might as well say *Palestinian*. Muslims are Moslems to them, no matter that Ersin's agnostic, no matter that his mom's a bio-chemist and his dad's one of the world's top ten plastic surgeons. No matter that he grew up in Belgium, studied English at an American School in Bruges and will probably attend Oxford. Why pick that battle, anyway? The whole thing could just be forbidden fruit syndrome. What if we're just each other's pork? God, this sucks. I really like him, but I just can't deal with abstractions right now.


September 23rd

The TRUTH. Mother has found a new best friend: The TRUTH. She's given birth to this new suckling so we're all going to have to make space in our psyches. And to think: this was what I wanted! To know everything. God, was I wrong. Maybe, Mother, some truths aren't worth sharing? Maybe the truth doesn't set you free? Maybe, just maybe, it's not found in a pill or on a therapist's couch?

The layers have gotten so thick. What I thought was just a surface betrayal with Mandela turns out to be an excavation too deep to see bottom. *Eight thousand* dollars my mother gave him, and along with that, a free pass into her soul. She described to me—using several sentences—the smile on some woman's face in one of his paintings. How it *moved* her, this smile. How he's helped awaken a long dormant desire in her. How she's *happier* now.

I listened patiently, trying my best to suppress the puke I was about to hurl onto my bed. Sensing my frustration, she switched gears and insisted it was all over now, that she had no contact with him anymore, even if she "regretted having to end it so abruptly, since they had become friends."

She SAID that. She REGRETTED having to end it. They had become FRIENDS. But wait! She had more things to spew from her truth spout. Her lips quivered and she closed her eyes, and then she began to spittle, feebly, that she and my father weren't happy, that though I had *absolutely nothing* to do with it, it was time for them to stop the charade. That there was the possibility of separation, even divorce, and as awful as it sounded it was for the best because people changed and goodness knows I must know *so many* kids in school with divorced parents and they were just *fine*, weren't they?

There was one surprise she was failing to address: that of my father's absence from this conversation. I wonder if she realizes these things are never done with only one parent. It said *everything*, Daddy's nonattendance—clearly my father did not want to have this conversation.

Dear God, this is too much. I'm trying, *really* trying, to see things from her point of view. I'm trying to sympathize, but I can't get past the Mandela part. I don't think she understands that. I don't think she knows how fucking psychotic it was to sit me down and talk about divorce because of *him*. She approached Mandela to weed *him* out of *my* applicant pool, and now, months later, she's throwing away twenty years of marriage. What kind of person does such a thing? What kind of human being doesn't pull back when she sees the cliff approaching?

But I didn't say any of those things, because none of them came to me at the time. A kaleidoscope of images filled my mind, all of them awful. God help me I saw it—my mother leaning in and kissing Mandela Robinson full on the lips. So then I asked the only questions I knew how to ask: *Did you fuck him, Mother? Is that it? Tell me, is that it?*

She sighed at me with tremendous resignation, like I was severely retarded and would never grasp even the simplest sentence. You know what, Mother: I will *not* understand. Your confession does not entitle you to my understanding, not now, not ever. All of this from a few innocent chats? Maybe they weren't so innocent. In six months Mandela managed to turn my mother into this puddle of mush. Surely he knew what he was doing. Surely he wanted this to happen. It's all just psychological revenge. The bastard has ruined my family.

And I should go to the same college as him?? Four more years with Mandela, I'd rather die. I just won't go. Fuck it—*he* just won't go. I won't let him. Let the asshole think he's making new friends, let him think his stock is on the rise. I may be down, but I'm not out yet. I'll figure out what needs to be done. And when I'm done with him, he'll regret being born.

## 5. LEGION

Look at that.

Your mother, lounging in the Cartwright living room, her frumpy exuberance mocking the clean lines of Ken's stainless spaces. You've seen her once in the previous four months, and then, suddenly, three times this month alone. She and Ken aren't arguing. They're not even silently seething at each other, but laughing, laughing with Veronica, who smiles on cue, one foot tucked behind the other, not even the slightest bit uncomfortable.

This occasion is your doing. You've surprised them all and are in danger of becoming an accomplished young man. You've survived their farcical attempt at child-rearing and somehow managed to turn out normal. So what if you're anything but? They're buying it.

The occasion didn't happen overnight. The ice began melting between you and Ken over the summer. First a Yankee game, then a weekend retreat to the Bellagio in Vegas. Why not let the asshole spend money? And once there, why not enjoy yourself? The guy wasn't that bad to be around. Some of his jokes hit their targets and the perks were pretty fucking cool, like meeting Bono backstage at Caesar's. Why resent it? He's your father, after all.

And when Celine called and Ken told her about your escapades together, and next thing you know they're reminiscing about 1989 over the phone—don't question it, because people have selective memory and being bitter takes so much energy. Remember when they used to enjoy each other? Remember how ordinary it was? 1989: the year of your first memories. You were five and your parents' laughter bounced off every wall in your house. Howling contests featuring Celine's chimpanzee noises. Ken doing slow-motion pantomime. Once, on an elevator in the Bahamas, Ken whispered something into your mother's ear and she cackled so hard champagne milked out of her nostrils. You never thought anything could be that funny.

When the music died between them you can't say; it seems so long ago. Yet here they are. Your mother, a woman always running somewhere, has found a moment to pause, her eyes moist and optimistic like a desert mirage. Finally you've given her a reason to touch the ground with you. If only the moment was real. If only she'd look inside you, witness your chaos and inhabit it, swallow it up with her photographer's eyes and unscramble it, piece you back together. But when she looks at you—when any of them look at you—you know they only see mirrors.

So if it eats you alive to know they're forgiving themselves—she for every second she spent absent from your adolescence, he for every time he laughed at you instead of offering encouragement, say nothing, because your moment has arrived. And if this triumph is built on a foundation of lies, so? What have these two built their foundations on? Your score *was* achieved. It took gumption and ingenuity, skills admired under different circumstances. Cut yourself some slack: you have too much of a problem with self-delusion. No one else seems to worry about it.

You had hope for one player in your life. You thought about the possibility of letting a little light into your dark, of the potential to be truthful with him. Up until your last meeting he had remained faithful to his cause. But then he disappointed you. More than that he *threatened* you, threatened to speak to your father and erase this scene in front of you which has taken so much to achieve. And even if there's something thrilling about exposing the lies and unburdening yourself, at what price this sacrifice? At the cost of not only all this glorious respect, but the next four years of your life, years that will shape you, save you, set you free? *No way.*

If he hadn't made his thinly veiled threat. There was something so spiteful in his words, something that made you think he *would* do it. In his eyes you've ruined him, reduced him to this state where the monster takes over. You know this state well. You understand power plays; you're used to them, maybe even taught him them yourself. If there were something nobler he could have tapped into it and shown it to you. He didn't, and your heart implodes a little to think about it, because you were ready, that afternoon, ready to float in calmer waters, to breathe, to let go.

The lesson learned: Adapt. Survive. Protect yourself from harm above all else. Claim what is your right. Only the consequences matter. Sexual orientation? Irrelevant. Be all things to all people. How does each label get you what you need? Do what you have to, and let that be your truth.

Look at them now, staring at you. See yourself reflected in their eyes and the flutes of Cristal passed around. Time for a celebration! Of your achievements, or perhaps that you too have learned to play the game as well as they have. It makes little difference, the *why*. Just raise your glass in toast to your future. You must keep this momentum going. You cannot—will not—allow anything to be taken away from you. Something must be done, something that will stop Randall from causing unnecessary harm. This is what you know how to do: Save your ass. And if that means Ken will have to get involved, it's a small price to pay, considering. Ken knows how to mop up other people's dignity. He'll clean your mess, preserve the family name and quickly forget it ever happened.

Think about it. Think about what this moment means to you. Devise. Strategize. Adapt. Adapt. Adapt.

\*

In honor of Veronica's birthday, Ken is throwing the soiree to end all soirees. The theme is Arabian Nights and, for two weeks, a swishy party planner with lime-green frames and an affinity for the word fierce took the apartment hostage. You didn't like the way his eyes followed you, the half-smirking hello that watered out of his mouth like secret code: he reminded you of your unfinished business, of the way Ken will look at you when he finds out, of the suffocating accuracy of stereotypes.

You've not only been invited but required to attend. You've been told to ask a few friends over: a couple of discriminating cheerleaders, Ken suggests, because they'll be so blown away by the Tsarist extravagance that they'll certainly tag-team you later that night to show their appreciation. But you've invited no one.

The splendor is undeniable: Uzbek carpets cover every nanometer of the floor. Gold and green satin sheets swing from rods newly affixed to the ceiling, leather and henna sconces house spiced candles on the walls. Pillows in purple and red, embroidered with bronze threads in patterns of improbable complexity, surround hookahs of every imaginable size and shape which are sure to be put to superbly illegal use. The scents—incense, coriander, grilled meats, rosewater—suffuse the entire apartment. Waitresses in shimmery blouses tied at the waist to expose their tan midriffs, the waiters' coifs slicked back, their vests barely covering their hairless, unrestrained chests, their mustaches stretched Dali-style at the ends. The letter V engraved into the napkins, the silverware, and onto each of the hand-painted gift bags commissioned by the fussy planner himself. And the kicker: a gargantuan golden jug with hieroglyphics zigzagging around its base commandeering the center of the living room, from which, at the given hour, Veronica will emerge pupa-like, in full belly-dancer regalia, and let loose her seven veils to the astonishment of the fortunate 150 people in attendance.

What bliss, adulthood. Everything can be bought. Everything smoothed over, laughed at, forgotten. Look around: you don't want in? You do. You fucking do. It looks good. Feels good. Which is as close to being good as it gets, don't you think? Self-loving guffaws. The tinkle of silver spoons against Baccarat plates, the satisfied swish of silken gowns, the crunch of caviar giving way to carnivorous mouths. Fortunes on the wrist, fortunes around the neck: *What, this old thing? It's nothing.*

Imagine all the eyes of the world and what they see. Not this. Imagine what they smell, they hear. Nothing close to this. You have all this, and they: the depressing cruelty of the ordinary. You used to think that's all you were missing: ordinary. But ordinary is an illusion. Ordinary affords nothing, and though it'd be nice if there were more than this, it's not okay for there to be less. This. At least this. If nothing else, this.

Your father not-so-gently silences his jaunty flock:

"Ladies and Gents, the time has come for us to raise our glasses to the light of my life and the finest woman I've been lucky enough to know...but my mother couldn't make it tonight, so I guess Veronica will have to do." (laughter) "Seriously, folks, it's not easy for me to describe in words how much this woman means to me—so I've let my money do the talking instead." (more laughter) "Birthdays come but once a year—thank God for that— but Veronica, you bring me joy every minute of every day. You're my treasure, my strength, the light that guides me back to shore.

You're gorgeous, patient, kind—did I mention gorgeous? Because if I don't talk up her thighs, I think her trainer—he's around here somewhere—is gonna have my hide." (the laughs keep coming) "It's more than that, folks. Some might say I'm not particularly known for my compassion. But this woman you see before you has promised to stick around and change my diapers in oh, about fifty years when I turn eighty. To quote Jack Nicholson, my dear, you've made me want to become a better man. And who knows, maybe I have." (sporadic awwws) "I could end it there, but a few days ago I found out something that puts all of this extravagance in perspective. My darling Veronica is about to become a mom." (a few oohs and aahs) "As for you skeptics, yes, the baby is mine. The old man's a dad once more. Maybe this time I'll get it right. So Darling, here's to you. I can only dream of giving you half the gifts that you've brought me. Cheers. To Veronica!" ("To Veronica" all around)

Roars of applause fill the room. Flutes raised, atta-boy pats on the back. What inspires more good will than the announcement of new life? The cabal is satisfied: they're adding to their ranks.

And among this carnival, the carnival of your own emotions. You didn't see this coming. How strange it is to feel genuine surprise. What else? Jealousy? Relief? Pity? But also: opportunity. Maybe it's time to say something. To save yourself.

Strike later, when the guests are mostly gone. Sit your father down in his groggy state and offer up a congratulatory hug for the new arrival. All the more reason to avoid scandal, don't you think? Best to say as little as possible. He'll be too drunk on his own news for yours to fully register. Feel him out; impart seriousness with your tone, suggesting that only fatherly wisdom could solve this problem. Summarize the back-story and quickly get to the point. This won't be easy. You'll have to allow for confusion, anger. You have to be ready for it. Still, never say it: I'm gay. If he asks, stay quiet. If he insists, say *I don't know* and then quiet. If he screams or shouts, quiet.

Don't blame Randall, exactly. Couch things well. Use terms like *confused* and *one thing lead to another*. Tell him how much you want to be the success he expects you to be, tell him it's hard living up to a story as great as his. *I'm just a kid. Kids can be reckless and stupid sometimes, right Dad?* You don't want anybody hurt. Randall just needs to be reminded that there are options. Conversation can be very persuasive. Perspective is key. Tell your dad: *Come to think of it, I was only sixteen when he first started tutoring me*...Ken will get the drift.

Don't overanalyze. Analysis can come later. This is a chance at happiness you're offering him. A bonding moment where the two of you can problem-solve together. Should things go less well than planned, bring up a more innocent time. *Remember that day when we…?* Rack your brain if you have to, spin insignificant moments into life-affirming ones, and baste everything with the warm juices of nostalgia. Then remind him of where things stand: your grades rock. Your SAT score rocks. Remind him; it will reinforce what could be. If things look truly bleak, break out old reliable: the D word. You've never really gotten over the divorce, have you? Don't say it, just hint at it. Mention how weird it was to see your mom and him together lately, how much it hurt you inside to know the pain you were going to cause them.

The shock of all this is that somewhere inside these blueprints, somewhere not so deep, is the truth. Sometimes it takes the most devious lies to get to it. You understand that: manipulation is part of the natural order. Some people say the truth shall set you free, but not always, sometimes the truth will fuck you up in ways that small lies never can. Besides, you're not really lying. You're just adapting. You have a right to survive.

Are you scared? Don't be. It's not your fault. Later, get outrageously high. Leprechauns and talking unicorns high. The only state worth being in, when you can tune out the negative noise, hand pick the colors that define the palette of your being. Go online and troll the chat rooms. Watch the thirsty chicken hawks offer you their souls for a chance to drink your semen. Choose a lucky winner, and as it unfolds, allow the current of abandon to wash over you. It's all about sensations replacing other sensations. There's always room for better sensations. Better than crying. Better than anger or loneliness or feelings you can't even begin to describe. Why describe? Just destroy. Replace.

Can you picture the future? That one day not too far when all this will amount to less than nothing? Picture the you that you'll become. See him laughing? He's thinking: what a sad little shell that boy was, carrying around all that angst like any of it mattered. He's learned to stop asking the wrong questions. He looks in the rear view mirror of his Porsche and sees no traces of a past worth remembering. He likes his life just fine.

Go, Legion. Don't be afraid.

Just go.

# 6. WORKSHOP

"I know I sound like a total asskiss, but it's an *honor* to know the person who wrote this."

The girl named Poughkeepsie was talking. She had catwalked into the room twenty minutes late and purred her hellos to the others. Tall, fish-netted and punk chic, with chiseled cheekbones and spiteful eyes, she seemed irritated to be sitting down. Somewhere, Randall thought, a line of coke had been laid out on a mirror for her, if only she could remember which VIP room she'd just taken a cab from. The others looked at her, awestruck. "Poughkeepsie's an actress," J'nai, the strawberry-blonde beside him, whispered in his ear. "She's done *several* commercials." Randall nodded, like he too understood how important this was.

They normally rotated apartments each week, but Randall had opted out of his turn, considering that his hovel wasn't large enough for seven people. The evening's duties fell to Bob instead, at his quasi-palatial studio in Gramercy, which Bob reminded everyone was rent controlled at $400 a month. He'd laid out a puzzling yet curiously satisfying spread of dried figs, ranch-flavored soy crisps, chopped liver with Melba toast points, and an oblong bowl of candied pecans.

"Poughkeepsie's right." Across the table to his left, Caramel spoke up. Her skin tone and constitution synonymous with her name, Caramel was sweet and smooth and never disagreeable. Still, too much Caramel makes your stomach sick. "Bob's piece is near perfect. It knocked the wind out of me."

"It's so great to hear you both say that!" Zeeandra said, thrusting her hand into the pecan bowl. "Now who'd like to explain to me *what* Bob did and *how* he did it so we can *understand* why this piece moved us *so* much."

Slowly Randall was acclimating to Zeeandra's inexplicable need to emphasize half the words she spoke. He'd leave class and for the next few hours every thought he had would filter through Zeeandra's voice. The only way he'd manage to free himself was to sing Celine Dion's version of "All By Myself," a song so awful it obliterated everything in its path. Still, Zeeandra was a good teacher. She had spunk, and the class trusted her, despite some dubious ideas, such as beginning each workshop with a prayer. *Non-denominational*, she said. *A little something for the muses floating in the air.* This, along with her restricted font list—she insisted certain fonts had bad karma—gave Randall pause.

Eventually they'd get to his piece, once the coronation of Bob's piece was over. Bob was head lion of this pride, the bright sun that the rest of them, apparently, were lucky enough to orbit. No one criticized Bob's stuff. Randall sat seething as his classmates drooled over works he considered cold and half-hearted. Even Zeeandra seemed to be pulling punches.

At least Bob had a bit of talent. Had the flower petals been reserved for him alone, Randall could have tolerated it. But the main players in the workshop seemed to have developed a self-sustaining fan club. They enthusiastically patted each other on the back, leaving him, the ingénue, exposed and vulnerable to attack. When the criticisms of his first submission came in, he accepted, even appreciated them. He was there to learn, after all. But a few weeks in he wondered why he was the only person to receive any "constructive" criticism. He thought he was being paranoid, until J'nai submitted a story about a woman who unironically falls in love with a grapefruit, and everyone told her it was daring and brilliant, when it was nothing short of ridiculous. He'd hinted at this disparity to Zeeandra during their one-on-one "gab session," but she brushed it off with one of her trademark summations. "Isn't this class *astonishing*?" she asked him. "You, especially, are getting such great feedback, don't you think?" Randall loved it when people constructed questions in the negative. The easy answer was neatly laid out for you, and it was rude not to just go along.

An hour and enough hot air to fill a sky full of zeppelins later, Zeeandra said it was time to discuss his chapter. She picked a section and asked Poughkeepsie to read it aloud. Randall watched Poughkeepsie's eyes roll with every spoken word. She managed, in two minutes, to reduce his novel into a second-rate drugstore paperback, the kind with Fabio clenching a rose between his teeth on the cover.

"So this is the final chapter?" Coleather asked.

Randall looked up. Perhaps it hadn't been the best idea to offer up the last chapters of his novel to the class, instead of the first few. But he didn't need advice on how the story started; it was the end that was murky.

"What Coleather means is," J'nai said, "There's nothing coming after this one?"

J'nai's talent for clarifying the obvious was legendary. Randall turned to Zeeandra; they'd been instructed not to speak until the end. She smiled and spoke for him.

"Randall *believes* this is the last chapter, yes. The *question* is, do *you* believe it? Your thoughts? Bob?"

"Well, accepting that premise, I'll say I dig the open-endedness of it and how through that open-endedness we can derive a more objective ending, if endings can ever be said to be objective. Even discussing the term 'ending' is pointless, since there is no end really, is there? It's more about completeness and in that sense, the opposing forces are juxtaposing well. Vinnie as Raymond's doppelganger, if you will, that perfect means of self-destruction through which he can test himself. Very Burroughs, and yet very anti-Burroughs. So I'm not unsatisfied. Pencil me in as questioning."

"Gosh," Caramel said. "That's profound. Right? Why hadn't I thought of that!"

"Hold up." Poughkeepsie tossed his manuscript onto the table with gusto, much befitting a celebrated star of commercials. "I don't buy any of this. Rich kids in New York are callous fucks. So he lost 50K, big deal. That's mouse droppings! He'd probably just ask for another 100 and lose that too. And the whole getting his tutor to take the test for him thing? Come on, couldn't he tell the kid was using him?"

"Well I think the *point* was that he *could* tell but did it *anyway*," Zeeandra said. "You *know*, like when you're in *love* and you do something *incredibly* dumb to prove something to your partner, like eat a praying *mantis* on a dare?" Zeeandra started blushing. "My boyfriend did that for me one night in Albuquerque. We were *so* wasted. Good times."

A loaded pause took over the room. Randall surveyed the others, most of whom were burying themselves behind their manuscripts. Looking through Bob's ten foot windows, Randall spotted the moon, and empathized: it was hard up there alone, laboring to provide light and inspiration to an unappreciative, barbaric world.

Zeeandra cut through the silence. "Okay...so! What *choices* has Randall made that are either working or not working for you?"

"What's with this walk to the zoo?" Poughkeepsie apparently believed all questions were directed only to her. "Talk about anticlimactic. What am I supposed to feel?"

Bob massaged the scraggly tips of his organic beard. "Sometimes anticlimaxes are better than climaxes, if you think about it. I mean, pardon the clichéd sex analogy, but you're not going to get up and walk out of the room right after you finish, are you? There's gotta be some cuddling, right? The question is, how much anticlimax is necessary? Because if there's too much post-play someone's gonna get antsy for round two and want to get off again. And that may be happening here, I think, because the real climax may not be when Raymond takes the test but rather when he *agrees* to take it, in which case by this chapter we're already expecting another cum shot—excuse my language, ladies."

"Cum shots. Yes...thanks, Bob," Zeeandra says. "I'm wondering if we can talk about some good choices for a few minutes. Something that really worked for you?"

After a few awkward seconds, Coleather spoke up. "Well, I really like the word 'beatific' on page seven. I think it speaks volumes about Raymond's self-delusions."

"Me too. Beatific is a cool word," Caramel said.

Poughkeepsie sighed. She raised her arms into the air and cracked her knuckles vociferously. "Listen. I dig scandalous as much as the next girl. Jailbait sex? So there with you, dude. But what's with the sloppy emotional shit? This Raymond guy is worse than any woman I know. It's like, get a *clue*, he's using you. We knew that two hundred pages ago, so why should we care? Something's got to happen."

"Like what?" Zeeandra asked.

"How should I know? I'm not the author."

Randall wanted to gouge her eyes out with a corkscrew. She wasn't the author, but apparently she knew how to shit on him well enough.

"Yes." Zeeandra paused to take in the wisdom of Poughkeepsie's statement. "We are not the author. Say it with me, people: We are not the author."

The back and forth continued for several minutes. Randall found himself summoning up the rest of Celine Dion's oeuvre to ease the pain. Why did Celine tear up whenever she talked about the children? What was that jerky neck-spasm chest-pounding thing she did at her concerts? Was it some sort of secret Quebecois signal?

"To sum up," Zeeandra had spoken the magic words. Randall's ears sprang to attention. "I think it's *crucial* how we leave our readers. What kind of *goodbye* are we offering them? It can mean *everything*. You can have 364 amazing pages and then page 365 comes around and it's like, uh, no you did *not* just do that, Mr. Novelist. Because if you think about it, what the author is doing with an ending is *breaking up with you*. You've had your little romance and at the end he has to say, OK, Trixie, we had our fun, but it's time we both find some other distraction. He has to convince you that it's really for *the best,* that you *grew* from the experience and are now ready to go out into the world without him. And so I wonder, Randall, are you doing the right thing? Don't leave me this way, no no no no no no. Oh my God, isn't that the *greatest* song? Think about it, this was no overnight *fling*; these were some of the best hours of our lives we've given you. Let us remember the good times and not the fact that you're a pansy-ass fucktwat that breaks up with someone via email, like Martine my ex—eight years later you'd think I'd get over it, but no *here* I am bringing his sorry ass up again. That's the *dilemma*. Some people *never* get over a bad breakup. They'll tell their friends about it and then *no one* will buy your book. Think about it. It doesn't have to be pretty. Just satisfying. Do you understand?"

Randall nodded his head like someone who deeply appreciated understanding.

"Ok. Your turn. Let us have it, Randall."

He laughed, looking around the room. He felt hopeless and heavy, like he was trapped in one of those spinning rotor rides and his face was plastered to the wall. How could he speak? What on earth could he say, anyway? Defending himself would be uncouth. And against what? It was like playing Whack-a-Mole: the second he'd smack down one charge, another would just spring up in its place.

But he had to say something. He had to let them know they knew nothing, that he *knew* they knew nothing, but was going to pretend, *for their sake*, that they had helped him. "Gosh. Thanks. So much to think about."

"Any questions?" Zeeandra insisted. "Come on, Randall."

"You've answered them all, really. Even many questions I didn't realize I had. So much to chew on. Chewy fudge. Delicious, chewy fudge and...delicious! Thank you!"

"It needs work," Poughkeepsie said. "But you know, nothing a few vital shifts in your plot and characterization couldn't fix."

"You know what? Just tighten it." J'nai said. "Make it *more focused*."

"Oh, that's totally it," Caramel added. "It just needs more focus."

"There you go. I just have to focus!" Randall shouted, delighted with the world.

Zeeandra clapped her hands together. "That was *amazing*. Wasn't that the most *ridiculously* amazing workshop ever?" Her eyes ran accusingly past each of them. When they landed on Randall they lingered; he felt he had to smile or else. "I'm feeling zippy. That's the word. Zippy. You guys totally energize me. It's like, post-coital. Seriously."

A round of laughter filled the room, Randall's extra friendly. They passed the marked-up manuscripts to him, and Randall made a concerted effort to thank each person individually. His brain felt squishy, as if a jar full of maggots had been emptied into his ear canal. Maggots, maggots, everywhere. He needed to get out of that space. He needed to feel human again.

Someone tapped him on the shoulder. He turned around to face Poughkeepsie's Palmolive Dishwasher Detergent face. "We're headed out for a drink. You coming?"

Randall wondered how they could still be thirsty after all the blood they'd sucked on. "I've had a really long day."

"You sure?" Bob asked.

"Don't be mad." Poughkeepsie said. "You can't be mad."

"I'm not mad!" he shouted, madder than ever. "I'm *very* happy!"

He grabbed his messenger bag and ran out. Outside the wind propelled people down the street. He glided down Twentieth, past the fancy cars and smug trees and snotty Gramercy Fucking Park, every bench turning his nose up at him, every bush pretending he didn't exist. Everywhere he went in New York, conspicuous displays of prosperity always at arm's reach, reminders of how possible it was to be successful there if you only had the balls to grab it. But his balls weren't big enough and were perpetually blue.

It wasn't all that bad. Yes it was. The common thread ran through everyone's commentary: the chapter simply *wasn't working*. But he already knew the ending was a problem. Was the beginning a problem too? And the middle?

These people didn't know shit. But what if they did? What if they fucking did? Christ, there had to be some purpose to his life. Something that would make all the sacrifices and humiliation worthwhile. How crazy that he'd allowed everything to ride on this. The bill collectors were already calling. The Repo man was sending out feelers. Should he push old clients for referrals? Go back to CATPEE and beg Chantilly LaFontaine for his job back? Who was he kidding? He couldn't tutor for the SAT anymore. No more dewy-eyed boys with Ivy League dreams. No more shaping young minds. They only end up destroying him.

So what, find a new job? He had no skills. Or experience. He had nothing to put on his résumé. Randall Miller — *BA, MA, pedophile*. He couldn't even wait tables. He'd have to return to Jersey. Grow his hair long, stud his left ear with a cubic zirconium and talk to his neighbors about the best way to rust-guard patio furniture. On weekends he'd meet his boys at a Perkin's somewhere on Route 9. They'll all be wearing track pants, and someone will suggest the buffalo wings, and someone else will sigh and say *too fattening*, and they'll pass and discuss a weekend trip to Philly that will never materialize.

Kill him now.

*Dear Moon*, he prayed, as he walked down Third Avenue. *Send me a sign. Something. Anything. A shooting star. A homeless person with a glinty smile. Eclipse yourself, honey. I'll even take a passing cloud. I need a new ending.*

At Thirteenth, he turned east towards his building. Should he go to a bar instead? Drown his sorrows in cheap beer? No. He couldn't spare the money. All he needed was a little direction. A smidgen of good luck. He was talented, gosh darn it. He just needed inspiration. Where was his inspiration? Not in the hallway of his building that's for sure. A single anemic bulb was all that kept him from the mugger-friendly darkness. Not on the creaky six flights that he had to haul up to his apartment, his daily workout substitute. Not inside his sad, lonely, stale apartment. Not likely.

Unless the light blinking on his answering machine meant something...

# 7. GABRIELLE

Brunch on a weekday morning usually meant somewhere on Lex with dainty tablecloths, oxidized mirrors and a vaguely foreign soundtrack. But Dakota lived in Hell's Kitchen. And Dakota decreed the French toast at the bar around the corner from her shared two-bedroom walk-up on Forty-sixth to be the most sublime she'd ever had. *That, and a mean Bloody Mary*, she'd said over the phone, summoning Gabrielle over. *We can't begin our day without it.*

They sat in a dive on Eighth Avenue, in a vinyl upholstered booth mottled with rips and tears, college basketball occupying the three TVs perched above the bar. Dakota wore the same blouse she'd had on the night before. Sleepy became her. Her blonde mane had been pulled back and partially covered by a beret, which still didn't manage to tame it. Thirty-four and never married — not even close, she liked to say — the faith she had in her independence was infectious.

The night before Dakota had managed to squirrel an invitation to the gala opening of a celebrated video installation artist in a gallery in West Chelsea. In between sips of dirty martinis, she shoehorned her way into any conversation involving at least one, but preferably several, convincingly attractive unattached males.

She introduced Gabrielle as "my soon-to-be-divorced friend Gaby" and would then proceed to chew on one of the olives in her glass, allowing for a pause to consider the implications. It wasn't easy for Gaby at first, adjusting to the rhythms of small talk, to the cool air floating across her breasts, which the new top that Dakota insisted she buy left amply exposed. Not quite as exposed as Dakota's, nor as perky, but still, there was something thrilling about having them be on the receiving end of men's eyes, to hear these men craft innuendo that women like her had long given up on hearing.

"You should have left with the Greek," Dakota said, twirling the ice in her glass.

Gabrielle rolled her eyes. "His name was *Dionysus*."

"Exactly. Imagine the depravity, darling! You're overdue for depravity."

Gaby chuckled. The thought of her being depraved seemed absurd.

"Thursday night." Dakota took the celery stick out of the glass and pointed it accusingly at her. "You and I are going to Venom."

"My daughter's play is on Thursday."

"Afterward, silly. We can't show up before eleven anyway. How is Adrianna?"

"Arianna. She's well," Gaby said, and then began to wonder what that meant. "I think. She's very involved in things."

"I can only imagine. Such a tough age. So much power and so little control."

"I'm not sure how she's processing what's going on between Morty and me. I'm trying to be open and communicative."

"You sound like your therapist."

Gabrielle winced. "I'm seeing him after we're done."

Dakota wiggled her glass. "I find these to be far more effective."

"And after therapy, my mother."

"Christ. Better order another round then."

"I'll be fine. Carl will prescribe a benzo and I'll take two before I see her."

Dakota laughed. "I hear you, honey."

"She just doesn't get how isolated I am. *I* didn't even get it. I woke up one day and realized most of my friends are actually Morty's friends. He calls them *our* friends, but really they're just people he knows from the office or from college. It's always been this way."

When she hung around Dakota, it was like learning to speak

Gabrielle for the first time.

"You're coming out of your shell, honey. It's a good thing."

"Is it? I might not have the energy for life's little lessons anymore."

"You're just allowing yourself to be who you are. Isn't that more honest?"

"Now you're sounding like my therapist."

Dakota swooshed her glass. "We drink the same brands."

Later that afternoon, Gabrielle lay on the leather recliner in Carl's office, mentally redecorating. His sense of taste was exasperating. Danish chairs from the 70's mingling with funeral urns from Tibet and tanzanite statues of Malawi goddesses from Indonesia. Exquisite carpets from Turkey shamed by generic paintings of extinct musical instruments, straight from the Pier 1 Catalog.

"Hire someone, Carl," she said.

"Excuse me?" he said.

She tried to phrase it gently. "You should consider redecorating."

Carl's left eyebrow cringed. "I'll let my wife know."

"Ex-wife, Carl. It's OK to let go."

"Are we delaying, Gabrielle? Is that our strategy today? Or do we want to talk about what's bringing out this judgmental side?"

"I'm offering an opinion, Carl."

"Tell me what's wrong."

Gabrielle shifted in her seat and sighed. "Nothing, on the surface. Arianna sent out the application to Princeton. She's busy, as always."

"And the problem?"

"That *is* the problem. I'm not buying this façade of normality. She should be acting out more. She's not expressing her anger, so clearly she's plotting."

Carl chuckled. How she hated his condescending chuckle. "That's a dubious conclusion, Gabrielle. Perhaps you're projecting your methods of reacting onto her?"

"She *is* my daughter. She gets pissed off and then shuts down just like I do. Meanwhile I'm positive. I'm cheerful. I ask her every day: *Arianna, is there something on your mind?* And she looks at me with this hideous indifference and says everything's fine and shrugs. She's concealing something. You think I don't know how this works? I did this for years with Morty."

"Be patient. She will understand. These transitional phases are always hard on the children. You are mutating, my dear. Soon you'll emerge from your pupa stage and see the new colors of your world."

Gabrielle winced. "For Christ's sake, Carl."

"I'm serious, Gaby. Only when you let your family see the real you will they be ready to forge true intimacy with you."

"And what about the resentment, Carl? If I'm myself now, then who the hell was I for the past seventeen years? What if she likes the old me better?"

"You should give her more credit than that. You think she wants you to wallow in an unfulfilled marriage just to preserve the semblance of happiness for her sake? You are a slave to your guilt, Gabrielle."

Gabrielle snorted. "Hmm, I wonder where that came from."

Carl sighed. He tapped his pen against his doodling pad. "I've already told you what I think about this afternoon. You shouldn't fall back into old patterns."

"I'm telling her this afternoon."

Carl put down his pen. "That you've discussed divorce with Morty."

Gaby sighed. "The discussion lasted all of ten minutes. But yes."

"Last time you said your husband would never say the word out loud unless he was seriously considering it."

"Yes. But we were raised the old-fashioned way. We don't give in to divorce so easily. We were taught to think about the children."

Carl hunched over and held his chin in his left palm. "Tell me, Gaby. Is that how you still think?"

Gaby tossed her arms into the air. "I think. I think. I think too much, Carl. Now I don't know what to think. Divorce sounds so liberating and then once it happens—"

"Once it happens, you're alone. And you're afraid of being alone, is that right?"

"I'm forty years old, Carl. For men, forty is the prime of their life. But I don't care what those bitches on *Sex and the City* say. Single women are not glamorous at forty."

"So how do you explain your life lately? Has it been miserable? Unsatisfying?"

Gabrielle bit her lower lip. "Point taken. But how long will that last?"

"You continue to hold on to this ball of fear, Gaby, like your life depended on it."

"Time's up, Carl."

"If only you were as forthright with others as you are with

me."

She pointed repeatedly at her watch. "It's just we're both such busy people."

"How considerate of you. But if just this once you allow me the last word?"

"By all means."

"Stop wasting your time dodging and deflecting, Gaby. The process you've begun is irreversible. You have to stop resisting and allow it to take you where you need to go."

Gaby was already halfway out the door. "Get rid of those infantile paintings, Carl. Shall I give you the number of my decorator?"

She arrived fifteen minutes late to Mediteraneo. The hostess showed her to the table and Selma said nothing. She didn't need to; the look on her face had already wilted the frisee in her salad. Gabrielle sat down, summoned a smile, and ordered quickly. For several minutes the conversation dabbled exclusively in trivialities. But Gaby knew it wouldn't last. A snake sees a hamster and sooner or later the fangs come out.

The food came, and they ate in silence. When the waiter asked about dessert, Selma ordered a cup of mint tea; the meal was clearly not over yet. She dropped the smile she'd been affecting, clapped her hands and folded them together. "So we've enjoyed the meal. And now, it's time."

Gaby sighed. "What do you want me to say? Morty and I are not reconciling. We've discussed divorce."

A busboy arrived with the tea. Selma sat frozen while saucer, cup, and pot were arranged around her. She then poured the tea, dropped two squares of sugar into the cup and twisted the teaspoon at an alarming speed.

"I'm not going to comment. Suffice to say you opened your big mouth and see how far it got you. You should be begging his forgiveness."

"Your perspective is so refreshing, Mother," Gabrielle said. "As usual you're completely off the mark. Morty didn't care about the miscarriage."

"Of course he cares, pasta-for-brains. You think he's going to cry on your shoulder about it? He knows you're pushing him away."

"Perhaps I am. And perhaps he has issues with me. Maybe it's not so one-sided."

"Your husband is as complicated as sheet of loose-leaf paper. You did this to him, not to mention what you're doing to your poor daughter."

"What exactly am I doing?" Gaby's voice was rising, despite all intentions to suppress her anger. "People change. Is that so bad? We learn from our experiences and evolve. Those who truly love you allow for that..."

"That's where you're wrong, *tatele*... True love isn't about evolving. It's about sticking it out when things aren't 'evolving,' as you say. You think your father was perfect? You think there wasn't a thousand times when I wished he'd disappear? I learned to accept."

"Here's your chance, then, Mother," Gabrielle said. "Start accepting."

Selma shook her head. "Darling, I'm old, and I deserve to relax. Even if I were to accept you now, who's to say you won't find yourself again in six months? Self-delusion is the New Jersey turnpike, Gabrielle. A long stretch of road with very few exits."

"Oh, that's rich. Coming from you. And you live where? Park Avenue?"

Selma took a slow slurp of her tea, the contempt hardening her face into a near perfect scowl. "So you're giving up on your marriage." She leaned in closer and whispered. "You hear that rumbling, Gabrielle? That's the sound of your poor father rolling in his grave."

"Considering you sent him there you can probably hear it better than I do."

Where that comment came from, Gabrielle didn't know. Instantly, she regretted it. Even if her mother would never understand, she had to be patient, never cruel. "Scratch that last sentence, Mother, I'm sorry," she spat out.

Selma looked at her as if an earthquake had struck right down the center of their table. Her voice dropped two octaves, to a jittery murmur. "So this is how we speak now." She turned to rest her gaze on the farthest wall. "To the woman who *birthed* you." She faced forward again, threw her napkin onto the table. "I've had it. All the therapy in the world will not cure you, Gabrielle. There's stubbornness and then there's sheer spite. What I did besides love and sacrifice for you, I don't know. But no good deed goes unpunished. I'll say no further. When you come to your senses, give me a call."

And with that, Selma stood up and walked out of the restaurant.

Morty's laughter greeted her when she got home. Arianna's voice too, both coming from the den. She took off her coat. Her husband, home at five o'clock!

She found him with his sleeves rolled up, a glue gun in his hand. On the table was a large model, a representation of Manhattan apparently, albeit an awfully sloppy one, with lines running through it both horizontally and vertically in all manner of pastel magic marker. What on earth was this? Mr. Crafty, all of a sudden, toiling with his daughter. How could she not know about this project? How come *he* knew? But why was she so surprised? Naturally Arianna would favor her father now. Of course they would join forces against her.

The sight stung her. She was superfluous. Dispensable. Her body shook. She wrung her hands like wet towels. She wanted to scream, but no, she needed to be calm. She needed to approach them without violence in her eyes. "What a surprise! What are you two up to?"

"A topographical study of New York's fault lines for my geology class," Arianna said.

"Pass me the lavender sharpie," Morty said.

"You didn't have to bother your father with this, darling. You know I would have helped you."

"Who's bothered?" Morty asked. "I'm enjoying time with my daughter."

*My* daughter, he said. Gabrielle turned to Arianna. "Why didn't you mention this?"

Arianna shrugged. "You seem busy lately."

"I'm never too busy to help out, honey." She was trying her best to keep her tone even. Meanwhile, Morty was making a mess, and Arianna was allowing for it. Even if it wasn't up to her standards, Arianna was going to stand behind it, just to piss off her mother. "Well, I'm here now. May I join you?" Morty looked at his daughter.

"We're almost finished," Arianna said.

"Oh," Gabrielle said. "Almost finished. I see."

Morty sighed. "It'll be fine."

"Of course it will be *fine,* Morty. But if you just allowed me—

Arianna moved in front of her. "Mother, please. Let us finish."

Gabrielle looked at her daughter. This was new, this physical response. This deliberate refusal of help. "Of course. By all means."

"Mother," Arianna repeated. "We're fine."

Gaby looked at Arianna, then at Morty, who caught her glance for a second and then turned back to his coloring. No more would be said, and this too she could add to her list of betrayals.

She could feel the rage brewing. But she didn't say anything. She simply stepped out of the room.

It was too much for one day. She closed her eyes, trying to remember the last moment she had that didn't involve defending herself. Would it always be this hard? *Pupa stage,* Carl said. She thought about Dakota, sitting at a dive bar drinking Bloody Marys at noon. It wasn't so much to ask, a second chance. Painters did it all the time—they'd finish a canvas, and then, unsatisfied, paint over it. Obliterate what wasn't working and replace it with something better. Why can't lives be like that? Why couldn't people understand? Decisions aren't always subtle. Evolution isn't always gradual.

Or was it really only her? Were they all upset with her because she still hadn't fully committed to her change? *Stop resisting,* Carl said. *Let the process take you where you need to go.* Perhaps that was it. Perhaps it was her indecisiveness that was so troubling. Perhaps there was no Gabrielle yet to recognize.

## 8. KEN

It's a good thing my old man is dead. He would've clocked someone real hard once he heard the news. Then he'd force me to send Legion to military school and a whorehouse. The fucking priesthood, if neither of those did the trick.

Listen, I'm not stupid. I know those things won't work. But don't ask me to get it. I don't *get* it. There's nothing to *get* about being attracted to a beautiful woman. It's a fucking *a priori*, like the existence of God. In fact, if it weren't for women, I'd have a hard time believing in the Big Guy. But then I picture Veronica in the garters I bought her, the dimple in the small of her back and the silky perfection of her thighs, and I know someone's up there, mighty proud of his work. How can he not love a woman's scent?

People expect me to empathize because we're all the other somehow. Even I, Ken Cartwright, have been the other. Growing up in the flat death of Indiana, not broad enough to play football, not smart enough to do math tricks, I used my mouth to survive. I was a wheeler and dealer, a diplomat and all-around clown. But you know what? It ain't the same. There's different, and then there's queer. Queer is another planet entirely, and it's not something I'm apt to think about unless it's part of some punchline or insult. That's my context, and I hate having to reflect upon it, I hate having to pretend like we're all walking in each other's moccasins and trying to get along. Bullshit. We *don't* get along. Sure, we can do business, grab a beer after work and invite each other to barbecues, but that ain't *connecting;* that's just lubricating the valves.

You think I'm some racist classist homophobic ignorant fuck? Think again. I just don't worship at the altar of P.C. delusion like the rest of the world does. For Chrissakes, do we not have Mexican maids? When we call technical support, do Hindus not pick up the phone? Smell the fucking coffee, people. It's picked in Ethiopia by illiterate peasants making four cents an hour. That sweater around your neck that you love so much? Ling Ling in Cambodia would like to thank you for buying it. Her seven year-old fingers may smart, but after a handful of ninety hour weeks she was happy to finish it so she could save up enough money to throw some day-old squid on her rice for a change. Some people hear this and shake their heads and think, how sad. Me, I'm not fazed. I accept that the world is a heaping pyramid of shit with a gorgeous glass elephant riding on top, and that precious few of us get to sit on that elephant. I'm just damn lucky to be one of them. Nothing I'll do is going to change the rules of the game.

Maybe that's what so upsetting. Queer ain't part of the rules of the game. There's something intrinsically wrong with them, and yet there's also something wrong with saying there's something intrinsically wrong with them, because jeez there are so many around nowadays. I guess there were plenty in my dad's day too, they were just more quiet about it, like people were more quiet about things in general, but I'm not a quiet guy, so I don't begrudge them their openness or pride or whatever. Let 'em dance in the fucking streets for all I care. Let them get registered and buy Subarus together and attend the company softball game and, fuck, let them even beat us at sports if that's what it comes to, but when the sun sets and it's time to say *sayonara*, I want to go home without them. And now I can't.

Am I gonna have to meet the kid's boyfriends now? I don't want to play nice with some wispy Classics major named Chad or some Lacrosse Bruce. Fuck, he's good looking, too. Which means he's gonna slut around like his equally good-looking old man, except I didn't have to worry about AIDS in my day. What the fuck am I gonna do, give him a pep talk about safe sex? Ridiculous. And they're gonna fall for his baby blues just like that faggot tutor did — twenty-nine years old this cradle-robbing cock-sucker, can you believe that?

I called him yesterday. Randall. Even his name screams buttfuck me. I tried to keep it civilized with this fucker who's raped my son, and even though I know it's not rape if Legion wanted it, I wonder if the kid really knows what he wants. Then again, I knew exactly what I wanted at seventeen, and damn, it sure didn't have stubble or a penis. So I'm getting beyond the "phase" bullshit and trying to deal with reality. Bottom line, the guy's got to scram. He's got to scram exactly the way I tell him to, follow my instructions to the last dotted i on how to turn himself forever into dust I wouldn't be able to recognize if it blew right into my face. This is *my* son. *I* raised the boy. Did I fuck up? Sure. But don't tell me I set him loose on the pansy wagon. I'm a busy guy. I did what I could, which is more than anyone could say about his mother, God bless that loopy witch, and when I say "witch" I mean it literally, because she's Wiccan now.

Anyway, the tutor-fag. Boy was he surprised to hear from me. His voice got rubber-duck squeaky whenever he caught his breath enough to use it, and he stammered in that new-guy-fucks-up-his-first-presentation way that I've warned everyone in my company to get over. Nothing stinks worse than the stink of fear on someone's breath.

The idea was to relax him enough to agree to meet me, which meant dangling carrots on sticks. I told him there were a few things we needed to smooth out, a few loose ends he could help us with now that the application process was in full swing. I said I'd pass on his name to some people. I even offered to buy him lunch down where he lives—Gramercy Tavern makes a burger that'll change your life, I said.

*I haven't tutored your son in months,* he lisped. *You've never been involved before. I'm a little...uncomfortable.*

Fuck I hated the way he said that. Like he thought I was a fucking car salesman trying to hard-sell him on the sunroof. You're fucking uncomfortable, you fucking pedophile? How the fuck do you think I feel?

Then I mentioned he'd be paid his usual hourly. Suddenly, Tuesday at noon opened up. He said, *See you then, Mr. Cartwright* and I said, *Call me Ken, OK?* And he did and it was hard, so hard. He called me Ken and I really, really wanted to say, you child molesting cunt, you've stolen my son from me. You've taken him away to that awful place, the land of leather daddies, dykes on bikes, drag queens and bath houses. You see what's popping in my head? There was no space for all these images before, and now I have to make room, because you fucked my son.

But I didn't tell the cocksucker anything. I just said goodbye. I'll save my choice words for later, when we meet face to face and I get to see him squirm and watch him unravel. Then he'll understand what humiliation means. He'll know the price to pay for the fruits he's picked off my tree, and no matter how juicy or sweet they may have been then, nothing's worth the pain going down. It's his own ass he's fucked.

I'm trying not to get angry. I keep reminding myself that as hard as this whole thing is for me, it's so much harder for Legion. At least the kid was smart enough to get straight to the point when we had our "talk": we had business to take care of, an imminent threat. Sure, I was pissed off. Sure, I was scared as to what it all *means*—still am. I'm hardly sleeping lately. But shit, it took steel balls to come to me and say what he said. I admire his guts. Setting up that tutor? That's what we call shrewdly exploiting a weakness. Once he got what he needed and things started spinning out of control, he was wise enough to come get help from his old man. Steel fucking balls *and* smart.

The kid thinks about things too much. And I know he thinks I'm a jackass. But it's not that simple. I mean, we have breakfast together every morning. I call him every day to see what's going on. I don't pry. He tells me as much as he's willing to. But don't call me absentee. Sure, I crack jokes and sometimes they can turn a little purple. But you gotta have a sense of humor in this life. You gotta be able to roughhouse with your boys, give and take like a man—it's how people learn to accept you. Maybe I could have been a bit more sensitive. But fuck, I didn't know he was queer.

Hell, I know they have their good sides. They're upwardly mobile, savvy, pretty clean outside of all that anal sex. Plus, they have a knack for making neighborhoods pop—go where the gays are and watch the prices soar. Worked for me a few times. So maybe the kid's gonna get made fun of. People will talk behind his back and call him a flamethrower. If he's a true Cartwright, he'll navigate the waters just fine.

At least he'll never have to worry about that fucker again.

# 9. MANDELA

Vacuum-sealed cold cuts, McIntosh apples, Swanson's frozen dinners: new items had invaded the refrigerator. Gone were the artisanal cheeses, the bottles of Hefeweizen. No more shiitake mushrooms, olive oils imported from Spain. The glitzy bags of the gourmet shop on Eighty-sixth had been replaced by the sturdier browns of Costco.

Mandela grabbed an apple and closed the refrigerator door. These small measures killed him; if they'd only let him, they could eliminate the biggest expense of all. He'd tried to breach the topic, but his mother shushed him after the first sentence. *Your tuition is already paid*, she said, shooting him a look of death. *We won't discuss this again.* But how long before these small measures would become bigger ones?

Mandela grabbed a knife from the cutlery drawer. Sarafina needed her apples peeled and sliced, with a pool of honey for dipping. He guessed it would be good for the spoiled runts to get a taste of going without. But Christmas was coming soon, and Tyrese wanted an Xbox and Sarafina a new bike, and instead of denying them, Joe and Deidre would find a way, go into more debt.

He wished he wasn't home. He felt guilty about it and stuck

around solely because his father had asked him to, which was happening more often given the circumstances. Still, now that he was a senior and had so much to tend to, they tried to leave him be. Do what you gotta do, his mother kept insisting, but he knew she said it with an asterisk, the subtext being: you better stick around. And yet he couldn't.

Grandma Lucille's condition was a thick fog over a small rowboat lost at sea, swooping in and settling over them with no signs of clearing anytime soon. Three doctors were called in, with a trio of incompatible diagnoses, speaking in hesitated tones about the black hole of recovery time, the loss of motor skills, the possibility of permanent brain damage. They discussed experimental drugs, avant-garde procedures, highlighting the high cost and risk. Occasionally, when prodded, they'd mention the body's miraculous will to recover. There's hope, they said. But there were so many other things besides hope.

Two weeks prior he'd gone down to visit. The hospital reeked of disinfectant and the measured melancholy of the dying. Still deep in her coma, his grandmother lay withered and yellow, and yet there was an ethereal beauty to her, like autumn leaves frozen in a pond. They stood over her and invoked soothing memories, tales carefully selected to remind a body of its will to live. He wanted to take pictures of her then, but didn't dare suggest it; they'd never allow memories of her this way. Still, her profound quiet mesmerized him. There was a great painting there.

His mother sighed and sighed. Everything that could be done would be, this was a given. In the meantime, silence became a permanent house guest. Even Sarafina and Tyrese had retreated to their TV shows and video games.

Mandela returned to the living room with the apple slices. Joe Robinson huddled over his younger son at the dining table, reviewing the geography of southeast Asia. On the couch, Sarafina was mouthing out the words for a vocabulary quiz the next day; he'd spent close to an hour reviewing with her. He handed Sarafina the plate and looked at his watch. His mother should have been home ages ago. She had taken an indefinite leave of absence from her job.

He wished he could paint, but couldn't fathom putting up a canvas at home; it would come across as frivolous. But the tension only made him want to paint more, which meant more time in the studio at school, more time away from them. He hoped they understood, but he wasn't sure they did.

"When your mother gets home, we'll head out to Boston Market."

His father's comment shook him out of his haze. "OK," he said.

Joe cleared his throat. "You don't have to stick around if you don't want to."

Mandela didn't reply. Earlier that day, he and Lauren had talked about a movie. He'd warned her they'd have to play it by ear. But fuck he needed to get out.

"If you're going, then you and I need to talk."

Mandela shrugged. "About what?"

"Don't fret. You didn't do anything wrong."

"I know. About what?"

"Something," his father said.

His mother arrived at ten after eight. Mandela watched his father kiss her forehead and remove her jacket. Deidre accepted the kindness without comment. No one asked if there was any progress because her face showed that there wasn't.

"You're exhausted," Joe said. "I got home later than expected, otherwise—"

"It's alright, Joe," she said.

"Mandela and I will pick up some Boston Market."

"It's ten blocks away and delivery's free, Dad."

"Let's go," Joe said. "Weren't you in the middle of telling me something?"

"Right."

An early chill had settled in overnight, after a week of warm November weather. Mandela kept his hands in his pockets. He wished he'd taken a hat; his new buzz cut left his head naked. Joe was oblivious; the man didn't understand cold, like he was a polar bear in a past life.

They walked south on Second Avenue. Joe said nothing for three blocks, staring straight ahead. But his father's eyes were already speaking for him. Mandela knew. He studied people's eyes for his portraits. People justify their thoughts with their mouths. But their eyes can't lie for them.

"It's damn cold," Mandela said, blowing air into his hands.

"Son, we've got a situation on our hands," Joe said. "We've been trying to stay out of your hair as much as possible."

"I know, Dad. I get it."

"I'm not sure you do. Your mom may have to quit JP and... forget it, this isn't about that. You have a lot to think about now and we don't want you to lose focus."

"Please, Dad. You shouldn't have to worry about me with all

this stuff going on."

"That's where you're wrong, Mandela. We're dead worried about you starting to get these chivalrous ideas of sacrifice in your mind now that things are a bit tough."

"Why can't I take a year off? What's the big deal? Think about all that money —

"No, Del. Let us worry about that. Now listen to me, because I have a proposition. I know you're pretty set on not applying anywhere Early Decision."

Mandela stopped in his tracks. "Dad, we talked about this."

Joe raised an index finger. "Just listen. Your mother met someone at the hospital. One of the doctor's brothers has connections with admissions at Princeton."

Mandela grabbed the back of his neck with both hands. This couldn't be happening. "Do I really have to say it again?"

"Mandela, it's different this time. Your Mother told the doctor's brother about your painting. He's sure the admissions board will review your portfolio. You're going to get a chance to get into the top school in the country because of your *art*, son. You want to paint and we want you to go to the best school possible. Why not get the best of both worlds? They have scholarships reserved for this stuff."

Mandela paused, letting the words sink in. What exactly was he supposed to say now? That he couldn't apply to Princeton because of Gabrielle Levy? It was ludicrous.

"I don't think I'd like it there," he said, meekly. "Seriously. I just won't."

"Boy, you're going to have to do better than that. We'll take you down this weekend so you can see for yourself."

Mandela looked up at the sky. He felt like the doomed hero in a science fiction movie with the aliens hot on his tail and the portal of escape getting smaller and smaller. There was nowhere left to run in this argument. Of course his parents preferred Princeton. His grandparents lived minutes away. The hospital was nearby. They could move back to Jersey. His father was saying all of this with his eyes.

"Just apply," Joe said. "It's not even Early Decision. It's early action. So you still can opt out. This is a real opportunity. Give me one good reason why you shouldn't."

He was seventeen, and he wanted his freedom. Wasn't that a good reason? But then, the circumstances. The sacrifices being made. The sadness in his mother's eyes and the opportunity, in some small way, to make that sadness a drop smaller. He never understood why it mattered so much to them until now. But they had done it: piece by piece, they'd taken away all the good arguments against applying.

He could not reasonably turn them down. Once again, there was no choice. He was used to it by now. And what about the promise he'd made to Gabrielle Levy? They hadn't spoken in months. She had dissolved their contract in not so many words last time they met. She might not even care. Princeton could accept or reject them both. It wouldn't matter if he applied. All the schools insisted each application was reviewed solely on its merits. Gabrielle insisted otherwise, but what did she know? Nothing. She was just hypothesizing.

They turned the corner onto Ninety-sixth. His father turned silent again, and Mandela didn't know what to say. He didn't want to think about any of it. So instead he thought about Lauren. Her wide, guileless smile. Like his grandmother's. Sometimes he wished he could shut off his brain and smile like she did. He had to try to bring that smile to his face and answer his father. He had to try, even though he knew he was going home to eat this sad meal with his family, stay home and clean up, help Sarafina with her homework, put Tyrese to bed, take out the trash. Lauren would have to wait.

"Ok, Dad," he said. "I'll apply."

# 10. EXCERPTS FROM ARIANNA LEVY'S JOURNALS

October 15th

Grandma called a few minutes ago. She insisted we get together next week since I haven't seen her in like, forever. We used to rely on Friday night dinners together, but apparently even that's no longer sacred lately. Last week, Mother and Daddy came to me separately to excuse themselves out of family night, and yesterday I saved them the trouble by telling them I was invited to Sharon's.

The two of them rarely speak. Apparently they've reached the no-point-in-arguing phase; they're simply *over* their marriage. Besides, Mother is out living her new life. She takes off most evenings before seven, and by the time she gets back I'm ready for bed. She comes to my room and tells me about her evening, and I smile and act like I appreciate all this fucking sharing. I know I'm supposed to be happy for her, but I just can't. She expects me to reciprocate, but I won't, not anymore. It upsets her, but only a little because the "new" Gabrielle doesn't push or prod. *When you're ready to talk, you will,* she says. She thinks she's giving me space, but really it's all selfish narcissism. I look into her eyes and I see nothing — just a glassy hardness, an absence of my mother.

On the upside, I've been spending more time with Daddy. I'm learning so much about him: how he liked to collect stamps when he was a boy and how much he hates turnips because one summer in Delaware his great aunt Irene forced them on him every day. He's told me about the man who changed his life when he was twenty-two, some Joe whom he met when stuck overnight at the airport in Des Moines because of a bad snowstorm, and how this Joe gave him the piece of advice that allowed him to start his business: *Make them need your product, not want it.* I like the way that sounds. I like picturing my father as a young man selling things, making housewives believe they need it. I'm sure he was charming.

Daddy's always been a good listener, so I'm glad to offer my ears lately. I guess we've become each other's crutch. He takes me to the movies and never complains, even when it's a chick flick. He asks me all sorts of questions I've never even thought about, like which of my friends I think I'll stay in touch with after high school ends and which I won't, which really got me wondering. But as nice as it's been, it's also terrible. Because sometimes there's this moment between us, a moment when we realize it's just the two of us, and I look into his eyes and he forces a smile and tells me *Your mother's just going through a phase* like he means it, like he wants me to believe it too. He doesn't want me to see him in pain. So he lies and says everything will be fine, when of course it's not and won't ever be. The two of us were being fed an illusion.

Does she think she can just come and go from our lives at whim? It's so selfish. No wonder I've been raiding her medicine cabinet lately. Yesterday morning she practically accused me of as much, gently reminding me as I was rinsing out my contacts that she was seeing Dr. Carl later that day, and how much it would mean "for us" if I'd go to mother-daughter therapy with her. Ha. I met Dr. Carl once and that was more than enough. The man is greasy and over-tanned. Let Mother swallow up his quack platitudes. If this is supposed to be her getting better, I'd rather she be sick.

I'll give him one thing, though. The man does give good prescription. Apparently the truth can only get you so far on the road to recovery; you need Prozac to take you the rest of the way. Ah, the pleasures of self-medicating. Aside from the occasional Adderall to pull an all-nighter during finals, I've been kind of sheepish about pill-popping. But now I say bring it on: Xanax, Vicodin, Wellbutrin, Klonopin. Percocet is the best—it's an out of body experience. It's like I'm in four places at once.

I'm trying to keep it together. The final SAT is on Saturday and with that gorilla off my back there will be nothing left to do aside from filling out a few applications. But now that it's pretty much over, queasy thoughts are creeping into my mind. Thoughts about Mandela opening his mouth. Thoughts about what life is going to be like after the divorce. Thoughts about how long I can keep up this imitation of a life while everyone around me is living a real one. I don't know how much more I can bear.

November 4th

Wednesday night Bridget, Karynne and I are walking down Columbus on our way to Isabella's when we run into Lauren and Mandela, exuberant and affectionate as puppies. Now that they're like, a couple, I can no longer get annoyed by his presence outside of school. Somehow he's planted himself inside our social circle—the snake. So Karynne asks them to join us and what am I supposed to say? Still, I *can't* hang out with him. I won't fake witty repartee with this *cancer*. So I imagine the excuse I'll make when I go to the bathroom and text someone to get myself out of this pronto.

Isabella's is buzzing; it's warm for November and they've opened the French doors so the tables spill out onto the sidewalk. The crowd is dazzling: women with glowing skin, their bodies hard and accessorized, their hair perfectly pulled back. Men sporting salon stubble and seductive smiles. We love it there. We see ourselves there with our boyfriends in four years, our husbands in eight, owning the world like they do.

Mandela and Lauren have come from some random art show where, Lauren explains to us, Mandela had a long discussion with the gallery owner. She was thoroughly lost, she said, with all the terms swirling about in the air. Bridget looks impressed and asks inane questions. Mandela, for his part, seems slightly peeved, like he and Lauren were heading to her house and now the handjob was going to have to wait. Before I can excuse myself, he excuses himself to go to the bathroom. While he's away we talk about applications and Lauren asks me if I sent mine out yet so I say duh, a few days ago, and she says she did too and we're lucky to have it over with unlike "some people." So I take the bait and say, really, like who? Mandela? And she says, yeah, his parents are really pushing Princeton early, and then I laugh and say I thought he decided against Princeton, and she says he might have to just to get them off his back. So I sigh and take a sip of my cappuccino and change the topic, trying my best to swallow the bile filling my mouth, trying to press it down until Mandela comes back and I can get up and go to the bathroom and get sick—so sick I won't have to fake an excuse to leave.

So the shyster not only took my mother's cash—he didn't even keep up his end of the bargain. Scumbag! Vile, evil *scumbag*. And of course he's going to get away with it. It's not like Mother can ask for the money back. Fuck! He's just biding his time. He's going to get them to adore him and then wham, out comes the whole fiasco.

Meanwhile I'm standing over a toilet watching green mush spittle out of my mouth into a bowl not accustomed to such honesty. I see my face reflected in the glare of the bowl, my swollen, teary face, and I wonder how things have come to this, why I've been chosen for such arbitrary acts of cruelty. I sneak out the side and call Karynne. I just seriously hurled, I tell her. She asks what she could do and I say go out and have fun without me.

Once I got home I thought the solitude would placate me. But left alone with my thoughts was worse than being with friends. It only reminded me that Mother was out on one of her soirees and Daddy was at a basketball game, and they were both getting in touch with their independence, something I would be denied. Around midnight I heard doors opening downstairs. Mother was parading around, assuming she was the first back, singing herself up the stairs. Daddy followed twenty minutes later. I imagined Mother hearing his return and turning the TV up, I imagined him hearing the TV and rolling his eyes, finding solace in a sandwich made in the kitchen, grabbing a quilt from the linen closet and heading for the den.

These are the sounds I need to get used to: the quiet rage, the gaping indifference, the silence of life passing me by. Around 2am I couldn't take it anymore, so I called Penelope. She had been at a cousin's wedding in New Jersey. Without thinking, I begged her to come over. We met in the lobby of my building, and I did what I once thought impossible: I confessed everything. I left nothing out. It was like the final retch of food poisoning, when there's nothing left in you but you still hurl just to get out the pain. I couldn't believe how liberating it felt. I swore her to secrecy and her eyes stared at me with this bedrock intensity, this look that makes we want to believe I can trust her.

Really I'm not so sure it matters, now that the floodgates have released. Maybe I *want* the whole fucking school to know.

So what if I'm the laughing stock? I just can't pretend anymore. Why not go public? WHAT THE HELL'S THE DIFFERENCE? I'm finally seeing things clearly. Maybe Mother's right: the truth shall set me free. Hallelujah. Praise the Lord. It worked for her, so why shouldn't it work for me?

That's it. It's time to write a nice, long letter. An open letter: to the admissions at Princeton, to Principal McKinley, to Carlotta Piper. What the hell, to Mandela's parents — they're probably clueless too. They all have a right to know. Why not? Why the hell not? Do I really have that much to lose? Why should I have to spend one more Goddamn second tormenting myself about the miserable actions of others? Let the chips fall where they may. This agony has to end. I'm tired of being the rock. I'm tired of being the fucking goody-two-shoes stick-in-the-mud. Everyone else is moving and I'm stuck in neutral. No more.

It's my turn to act. Get ready for the truth, Mother. You asked for it.

## 11. LEGION

Wednesday right before second period, normally the worst time of the worst day, and yet all's good at Valhalla High. Perky teachers don't depress him. AP Psych doesn't make him want to bolt for the door. He's even managed to go the entire week without smoking up in school.

No reason to dwell on the present when the future was looking that much brighter. His college search had broadened to include a handful of schools that just last year cunty Carlotta Piper had told him were impossible. Suddenly he's sporting a 1460 and now she's all sunshine, like she knew it all along. Not that he's going to hold any grudges. She's useful, much as the teachers who wrote him off as mediocre and are now eager to write him recommendation letters are useful.

None of this would matter if Ken hadn't done his part. They never spoke about it, other than that one time two weeks ago when his dad took him to The Palm and in between bites of Kobe beef Ken had said, *That tutor guy? He's not going to be a problem for us.* And then, chewing slower, he dropped his smile and his fork and added, *Of course you won't be seeing him ever again.* It wasn't a suggestion. This was the deal they had brokered. He and Ken weren't going to talk about it again. They were going to forget about it the same way you forget about a cockroach you squashed with a shoe and flushed down a toilet. He kind of wished he could call Randall and say goodbye, but he knew he wouldn't.

And Ken was making inroads, in his own small way. The double whammy of the pregnancy and the wayward son seemed to have a sobering effect on him. Veronica was chasing after him with catalogs full of layettes and cribs and all things baby. Under different circumstances Ken would've retreated to later nights at the office and even more visits to the lap dancers at the midtown Scores. Instead he took on the role of expectant father without the slightest trace of irony, lavishing the kind of attention on Veronica he never did before she was carrying his child.

Likely Ken was blaming himself as all parents do when their children might be gay, keeping his fingers crossed for a boy, so he could show the world he could get the formula right. Sometimes Legion would notice his dad flipping through channels, and some show with a gay subplot would be on, and instead of flying past it like usual, he'd stop and linger. This meant: see, I'm trying here. This was communication, and even if it wasn't an *I'm proud of you* speech, it was fucking something.

Even high school was bearable now that the end was in sight. He would treat the last few months like school fucking rocked, like being a senior was the coolest thing ever, like his classmates were awesome people. Easy as hitting a switch in your brain.

Legion took a swig from the water fountain. Looking up, he spotted Mandela and Lauren tucked into a corner near the biology lab. Lauren's eyes were bugged out and her hands were flying every which way. Shit. Legion was pretty sure he knew what this was about. Yesterday a rumor had tumbled down the halls of Valhalla like an avalanche. Legion wished he'd had a chance to discuss any of it with Mandela, but they hadn't been hanging out as much lately. If it was true, and Del really had sheisted big bucks from Arianna's mom, then Legion wanted to give him a big round of applause. *Dude, we're both fucking con artists*, he'd tell his friend. He didn't realize Del had the balls to pull something that hard core. Maybe it was bullshit. But Christ it wasn't Arianna's style to pull this kind of stunt. Something went down, and he needed to know what.

Mandela made eye contact with him, but it was sharp and fleeting. He didn't need any hint to stay away. Lauren was tight with Arianna, and wasn't going to like picking sides. She was pretty chill, so it was strange to see her get so frustrated. Legion watched her cross her arms, whisper and then walk away without looking back.

"Shit," Legion said, approaching his buddy. "That looked rough, dude. Is it the Arianna thing?"

Mandela stared back at him murderously. "I need to get the fuck out of here, man. It's like that bitch put fliers in everyone's lockers or something."

"Word travels fast. You know that."

"You'd think Lauren would give me the benefit of the doubt."

"Her and Arianna are tight."

"Fucking poseurs at this school. The whole thing makes her look super shady, but do you see anyone shunning that bitch? No, it's pick on the black boy time."

Legion smirked. "You thought these people were your friends, dude? Come on."

Mandela looked stricken. "No, but…whatever."

"Is there anything I need to know or is it just bullshit?"

Mandela sighed. "My parents are going to disown me. We have a meeting with the school board on Tuesday. I think they're going to expel me."

Legion nodded his head. He could tell that Mandela was gauging just how much he felt like sharing.

"Listen, only because it's you and I know you don't gossip. Some of it's true. Some isn't. Let's leave it at that. But I can't believe she did this. It's fucking suicide."

"Sometimes people get desperate, dude. You have no idea what's going on behind the scenes. Who knows what kind of shit's going down between her and her mom."

"Her mom's not crazy, dude. Trust me on that."

"Oh shit." Legion laughed. "Did you fuck Arianna's mom?"

"No." Mandela paused. "I probably should have though, considering."

Legion kept laughing. "It might have been hot. She's kind of a MILF."

"Dude, not funny. I'm totally screwed."

"Sweat it out. It may turn out better than you think. You gotta throw the blame where the blame will stick. You can get out of this blemish-free, if you play it right."

"Whatever, man."

"No, Dude. Really. Between you and Arianna's mom, who do you think they're gonna blame? She's a grown woman. Just play the naïve teenager who got in over his head. Say you were scared and confused and, shucks, high school is so hard and the pressure was too much and one thing lead to another…"

Mandela nodded skeptically. "Damn. Sounds like you got the whole thing planned out. Like you have experience with this shit."

"It's not rocket science, dude." Legion looked down to the ground, then looked back up. "Always play the cards you're given. I learned that early."

"Really? Is that how you managed to pull a 1460?" Legion chuckled. He'd trained himself not to take the bait. "Natural genius, my friend. And a good tutor doesn't hurt."

"Yeah. I bet he helped you out a lot." Mandela's face turned blank and stony. "You took the SAT out in Brooklyn, dude. Anything you want to share with me?

Legion patted his friend on the back. "You're a good guy. Hang in there."

He could tell Mandela wanted a different answer, especially now. He wanted someone to commiserate with. "Maybe things aren't what they seem," Mandela said.

"Things are never what they seem."

Mandela extended his hand and placed it onto Legion's shoulder. It lay there, awkwardly, for a few seconds. "Maybe you'll tell me about that one day."

Legion looked hard into his friend's eyes until he slowly retracted his arm. They didn't interact this way, and it wasn't going to start now. "Listen, Del, in the end, none of this matters. It's your life, so do who you have to do, period. You don't owe anyone any explanations."

"I guess. I don't know. I'm sick of fronting, you know?"

"It's not fronting, dude. It's living. We're friends. That's all you need to know."

"Cool. But if you did tell me stuff, we'd still be friends. That's all I'm saying."

Legion nodded his head. "I'll keep that in mind. But think about what I'm saying before the meeting. You owe more to yourself than you do to those assholes."

"Yeah. I guess."

"You're just a kid, Del, remember? We're both just kids."

He tried to keep it casual. It was weird watching Mandela struggle with his integrity at this stage of the game. Hadn't he learned anything? Do anything out of the ordinary, and people talk. The more people talk, the more they form opinions, and those opinions are all that matters. One day you're in like Flynn, and the next you've got your own table in the lunchroom. That was life. It didn't change. Adapt, or die.

Like he'd ever come clean to anyone in this school. What happened to Mandela would happen to him, only ten times worse. Bringing people down to size: the favorite sport of high school. Not just high school. Life. People need to feel superior all the time. Tell Mandela the truth? Not a chance. Not because he didn't want to, or didn't trust him. It wasn't about trust. It would've been nice to just blurt it out. It would feel pretty fucking awesome. But even your best friend will bring you down. He'll talk, because that's the currency of the world, that's power right there. Open yourself up, and the fabric starts to tear. No. He was in control. It was his life, no one else's. He decided what was said, when it's said, how it's said. If they wanted to talk, let them, but not with the power of truth to support it.

Still, it hurt to look into his friend's eyes and have to shut him down like that. Mandela meant no harm. He could handle it. Maybe they all could. Maybe nobody gave a shit about whether anyone was gay, straight or bi anymore. Maybe, or maybe not. Maybe he wanted to be an astronaut, a movie star, a professional golfer, a model or lawyer. Maybe he wanted a wife and three kids. Maybe a boyfriend *and* a wife, and maybe he wanted them to both know about the other and maybe they'd all fuck each other. He wished his friend well. From now on, he was staying positive. College was around the corner. Life, around the corner. His life. Not Ken's. Not Randall's. Not anyone's.

His.

## 12. RANDALL

What a difference a month can make. How wonderful New York seemed when everything was on the up. Five dollar hot chocolate at City Bakery? Why not. ABC Carpet and Home sale? Let's browse! Emporio, Club Monaco, Otto Tootsi Plohound — *ain't nothing gonna break my stride, oh no, I got to keep on moving.*

That day, Randall decided to cab it uptown. He couldn't remember the last time he took a cab. For the past few weeks, he even tried to avoid the subway, opting to walk everywhere within a three mile radius. Fortunately, he'd been holed up in his apartment most of that time working on the book.

He looked out the window and took in the rhythm of New York, the snap and crackle of destinies fulfilling themselves. It was important he start opening his eyes. Start savoring. The city was so alive with the now, with success and progress begetting more success and progress. Soon, his progress, his success. Soon, life would begin. Because he had a winner.

*We have a winner here.* That's what Mandy Schulz of the Black Dove literary agency told him. Winner as in his four hundred pages, the monster which had plagued him for the last year and a half, that record of his life cleverly disguised into fiction. Winner as in come and sign the contracts right away; he was headed there that very minute. Mandy Schulz had the most appropriate name. She sounded *Schulzy*. Randall imagined an unfiltered Pall Mall between her middle and index fingers, glasses dangling around her neck by a twisty gold chain, auburn perm rising above her rouge-laden, pluck-browed face. Her pantyhose matched her hair color. She preferred her Rolodex to her Palm Pilot. She liked to drop names, do lunch at gilded institutions like the 21 Club, Tivo *Young and the Restless.*

After one four minute conversation, Randall had rearranged his life. Had called his parents, told them not to bother sending the next check. Had sent out an email to everyone in his online address book, including people he hadn't spoken to in six years: *Beside myself, y'all! An agent has agreed to take on my novel. Will keep you posted on the release date. I can only hope life is treating you as well. Keep in touch! Randall.*

So what if he hadn't met Mandy Schulz yet? In less than an hour, he'd be under contract. She'd left a message on his machine two days ago: *Randall Miller? Mandy Schulz. Read the opus. Can I tell you? Loved it. Loved. Not a little. A lot. Cleared my afternoon to finish it and I don't give up facials for anything. Special stuff, mister. I feel it in my bones. A few problems. Nothing major. OK, a few major. We'll work together. Build some bridges. You have faith, Randall? Mandy Schulz is gonna get you a sweetheart deal. We have a winner here. Call my office ay-sap. Set something up with Francine.*

He had called back and spoken to her. Listened, rather. She was a steamroller. She had three minutes; she had to be somewhere. She tossed around the word genius. Tossed around the even more important words: movie rights. She bragged about her track record. *Mandy Schulz gets sweetheart deals.* She talked about the authors she represented *and if you only read the genre you'd know how bigshot these people are. Not every book gets sold,* she said. And then, guffawing: *Just every book represented by Mandy Schulz.*

It had been dizzying. Hypnotic. Surreal. He wanted to reach into the receiver and hug her. Offer her sex if that's what she wanted. Whatever. He'd do it. Because where was his life headed before that call? On the express to Fucking Nowhere. Every cent he had went to paying minimum balances on his over-drafted credit cards. The stench of eviction had gotten so bad around him that the other tenants in his building recoiled when they ran into him in the hall. The other week he'd even resorted to "personal directional advertising," seven hours pacing the corner of Twenty-ninth and Lex with a two-sided billboard around his neck. Tedious? Exhausting? Humiliating? Yes. Yes. Yes. But at ten fifty an hour, he couldn't afford to complain.

At Thirtieth and Sixth, traffic came to a grinding halt. His cab driver, a man with a Q and two apostrophes in his first name, was shouting into his cell phone. Randall wished the guy would hurry off the phone. He wanted to tell the man about his book deal, share his tale of dark days and perseverance.

It had gotten so bad lately that Sylvia and Saul Miller had started using the dreaded "m" phrase. *You might have to move back in with us,* his mother had said, her disappointment practically screaming at him through the receiver: Didn't the gays make money? Weren't they good with fabrics? Didn't they cocktail and throw theme parties and have lots of air-kissy friends with connections? Gays are *fabulous*. They have *life partners*. They adopt Shih Tzus and go to Paris once a month to browse antiques and pick up *marrons glaces*. They do not return to Fairlawn, except on holidays, when they come toting perfumes and handbags and Prosecco.

Finally he could eviscerate these thoughts. Finally he'd show his parents that fairy tales do come true, even to schnooks like their son. He'd go to the workshop next week and rub the contract into Poughkeepsie's face. *How's that for an ending, Beatch?* But no, he won't be so petty. He'll be gracious, humble. *Rise above, Randall.*

All thanks to Ken Cartwright. If it wasn't for Ken Cartwright, none of this would be happening. Certainly not the first thought that crossed his mind that afternoon five weeks ago when he'd walked out of Gramercy Tavern after having "lunch" with Legion's father. *Nothing ever happened between you and my son. Nothing,* Ken had said. *He doesn't exist to you, and after this conversation, you don't exist to me. Capiche?*

What was there to say? Was it possible to say something to this man at that point, to a father of a son, look into his eyes and see reflected in them the disgust and shame of fathers everywhere? It's not the same when it's family. It's not the same with a seventeen year old, and he understood that then, understood it in a way he never did before. Even if Ken didn't say it, it was right there on the man's face. Only then did things crystallize: how selfish, how delusional, how moronic he'd been. The question never spoken out loud, but which certainly was on Ken's mind, was *why?* Not why did you want my son. Not why did you break the law or why did you let it get so far. Ken's why was a lot simpler, and yet, the one that shamed Randall the most: Why didn't you know better?

Forty-eighth and Sixth, and little progress. He had splurged for a cab when the subway would have been faster. Why was every car in the Goddamn city on Sixth Avenue all of a sudden? Why couldn't pedestrians stop acting like they own the street and obey the rules of traffic? He was going to be late.

*There are other options, Raymond,* Ken had gone on to say, *But I'm pretty sure prison orange's not your favorite color. It's the smart choice, if you think about it. To stop existing. So much better than being a pedophile. Right, Raymond?*

Randall kept nodding his head, never once correcting the man. Ken was right. There was nothing to save between Legion and him. He would've liked to see the boy one last time maybe, tell him in person how he never had any intention of revealing anything, but it seemed ridiculous now.

The loss wouldn't destroy him; he had mourned that already. It was more the impression that would be left with Legion. He had gotten past the walls and broken into Legion's core. The boy *had* developed feelings for him. And now all that would be rationalized away, forgotten. Legion would retreat into his father's world, a world he had once heroically resisted.

Approaching Columbus Circle, he had six minutes. Q" was still shouting obscenely on the phone. At a woman, Randall suspected. Women exasperated the Q-double-apostrophe Man. In his distracted state Q-double was going to foolishly take Broadway up instead of Central Park West. There was no way Randall would let that happen. He leaned forward against the glass partition.

"Excuse me, sir," Randall said, loudly. "Go up on CPW."

"You said Eighty-two and Broadway," the man said.

"Trust me. Central Park West, and then back to Broadway."

The surprise came after the meeting with Ken, the little things that stayed in his mind, little things which changed everything. Ken calling him "Raymond" repeatedly. The whole tone of the speech, how scary and charming it was, how polite and yet how lethal. Suddenly a crack opened in his mind, and then a door, and then the floodgates: Randall had his ending.

He wrote for three weeks straight, fourteen hours a day. It was as if there were powerful magnets in his ass and the seat; he couldn't do anything but write and eat. He spoke to no one, saw no one, avoided his mail, his hygiene. It felt strange. Wonderful.

When he was done the story was different, but somehow the same. The new twist was genius; Ken Cartwright was not only unrecognizable, but also an obvious work of fiction. Now that the man was the head of an Italian mafia family, who'd ever think the story was real? It was too juicy. Too large. It had to be fake.

Simultaneously he had both removed any connections to reality and made his book more marketable. Sure, it required a bit of research, but his guess was that mafia dons and Wall Street hot shots had more in common than not.

Certainly Mandy Schulz seemed to think so. He'd sent out his book eight days ago and she'd been the first to respond. He knew this was unusual. Most agents took months to respond to unknown writers. He had braced himself for the long haul. He'd expected a slush of form letters, a lot of thanks-but-no-thanks. Instead, Mandy Schulz. God bless her.

On Seventy-ninth, Q" turned left. Smart man; the lights ran quicker on Seventy-ninth. Randall was only two minutes late. He jumped around the backseat, effervescent, like a freshly opened bottle of seltzer. He couldn't help but play out scenarios in his mind: Would Mandy Schulz offer him a cigar? Would they talk book jacket photos?

Q" pulled over at the corner of Eighty-second and Broadway. Randall tipped him generously and said, *Peace Be With you.* Q-double nodded and said, *Thank you, brother.* Randall stepped out of the cab. The sun's rays embraced him. A brisk wind edged him forward. Mandy Schulz's office was across the street, on the same side as the Barnes and Noble. Randall took it as a sign.

Approaching the crosswalk, he looked at his watch. 12:06. Not too bad. As he was waiting for the light to change two teenagers with yarmulkes on their head stood beside him; there was a private Jewish school nearby. Randall stared. Both of them strapping. Varsity Basketball team no doubt. Seniors by the size of them. The shorter and fairer of the two was talking up the finer points of a new Lexus, while the other one nodded along. Sigh. Straight boys and their cars. Randall tried not to look at the taller one's moist lips. Thirty seconds for a light to change you'd think he could resist. But no. Soon they were both naked, and he was down on his knees, the taller one positioning himself behind him while the fairer one...

"Would you like a picture?"

Randall's eyes regained focus. "Excuse me?"

"You heard me," the tall one continued, defiantly. His friend was snickering.

Randall's whole body tensed. He said nothing and looked down to the ground. Once the light changed he sprinted ahead, but not fast enough to avoid hearing one of them say, *pervert.*

## 13. SHIT HITS THE FAN

The clock above Dean McKinley's head read 7:30, the meeting having been called long after school hours so as to avoid arousing suspicion. Mandela canvassed the room, trying to gauge everyone's state of mind. McKinley was taking deep breaths and picking imaginary lint off his suit jacket. Vice President Struthers had pulled her hair into a severe bun and wore prosecutor's glasses. She cupped her hands in front of her and oscillated her head slowly, accusing everyone with her eyes. Carol Negroponte, co-chair of the Board of Trustees, was at least attempting a smile, albeit a smile directed exclusively at his mother and father. In between smiles she jotted down notes on a yellow pad. The other three—two men, one woman—looked vacant and distressed, likely the school's legal advisers.

He and his parents sat on one end of the opposite side of the table, the Levys on the other. They had showed up, instead of sending their lawyer, which was what his mother expected they'd do. Gabrielle's look confused him. The severity which normally occupied her face was present, but had made room for other emotions now, ones he couldn't quite characterize. Her husband was another story. Easily the most uncomfortable person there, he kept shifting in his seat, massaging his eyebrows and sighing.

He expected Arianna to be gloating, but instead she looked stoic, subdued. There was no point in trying to understand her anyway. Did she really believe, when all was said and done, that she'd look like the hero?

His mother, meanwhile, had prepared diligently: probing similar cases for precedent, carefully researching school policy. As appalled as she was, Mandela knew in some way this was a beneficial distraction. She'd taken all her bottled-up stress of the last month and redirected her energies. And Joe Robinson seemed eager to go along. They'd found the lens to view this fiasco through, and were sticking to it: His father's eyes said it all: *That* woman wasn't going to get away with this. How *dare* she.

Three days prior his parents had sat him down, after Tyrese and Sarafina had been put to bed. *You were confused*, his mother said to him. *Shocked*, his father continued, both nodding their heads like hypnotists, hoping, it seemed, to trick him into believing that things really had been that one-sided. The further their narrative spun, the more Mandela realized how much it fit in with their general coziness with self-delusion. What was he supposed to do, argue for the truth? Tell them that when Gabrielle approached him in her car that day that he'd felt a stirring in his cock? Or better yet, that in the months that followed he'd grown to *like* her? This wasn't an option. There was no room for nuance in this all-too-familiar tale of white oppression. Especially now, with Grandma Lucille in a coma. What would his clarifications say about the way Deidre raised her children? He couldn't be a disgrace. *Their* son knew better than to take bribes.

"I'd like to thank both families for coming," Dean McKinley began. "I realize that much of what will be said in this room tonight will likely be contentious. I want to assure you that we at Valhalla have taken every precaution to ensure that this matter be handled with the utmost discretion. No one, short of the people in this room, has any knowledge of what has allegedly transpired, nor do we have any intention of speaking about it. I'm sure all of you have similar concerns and are also taking such measures."

"That depends on the outcome of this meeting," his mother interrupted. "We haven't spoken to the press as of yet."

"Most judicious of you, Mrs. Robinson," Ms. Negroponte said, her left eyebrow raised to match her forced smile. "It's our opinion that keeping this matter private will serve the best interests of both families."

"And the interests of the school," Deidre said. "Let's not forget that."

Dean McKinley cleared his throat. "Mrs. Robinson, I won't sit here and pretend that we aren't concerned about Valhalla's reputation. But let me be clear: we're here tonight to reach a consensus that will be agreeable to all parties. We are, first and foremost, interested in protecting the interests of our students."

"We appreciate your concern, Dean," Joe said. "But exactly what do you mean by a 'consensus agreeable to all parties'? We're not negotiating a Solomonic split-the-difference truce here. Your statement suggests both parties are equally responsible."

"Forgive my interruption." Ms. Struthers raised her hand gently, letting out a quick, tension-breaking chuckle. "But before we venture too far into interpretation, perhaps we can start by acknowledging the particulars upon which we agree? For the record, six days ago, both Dean McKinley and I received the same letter from Arianna in which she claims to have uncovered—for lack of a better word—a 'plot' by her mother to attempt to bribe Mandela in order to coax him out of applying to Princeton. We have since spoken to both parties separately about this. Let me start by asking you, Arianna. Do you stick to the story as presented in the letter?"

"I do," Arianna said, flat as ice.

"And can you please clarify why you sent this letter to us?"

"I sent the letter because my mother's actions were immoral. I wasn't sure how to handle it at first, but bringing it out in the open felt like the honest thing to do. Dean, Vice President, I believe I have the credentials to get into Princeton on my own terms, and I didn't ask nor need to have the playing field tilted in my favor."

Mandela sighed. Arianna was an expert at performances, and this one would be no different. Levelheaded, poised, articulate. And a total sham. She knew about this *ages* ago. If it was all about fairness, why didn't she say something then?

"Very well," Ms. Negroponte said. "And what did you expect *us* to do about this when we got your letter?"

"She wanted to tell the truth," Gabrielle said. "That's all."

"The truth? Yes, let's discuss the *truth*, Mrs. Levy," Deidre's left index finger shot into the air. "The truth is, after inviting my husband and me to a party to fish information out of us, you then attempted to bribe my son based on an irrational, not to mention, overtly racist perception of the college application process."

"She did not just *attempt*, Mrs. Robinson," Arianna said. "She *succeeded*."

Deidre stared across the table at Arianna. "Your mother is an *adult.* She accosted a sixteen-year-old boy. She convinced him he had to take that money or else she'd get him into trouble."

Mandela snorted. Deidre's neck jerked in his direction. Her nostrils were flaring. Much like Arianna, his mother wasn't going to step out of character today.

"Mr. Robinson, is that true?" Ms. Struthers asked. "Did you feel forced to take the money?"

Gabrielle spoke up before he could. "He was confused. I left him no choice."

Mandela looked over to Gabrielle. She looked stricken and determined at the same time, the emotions battling inside her coloring her face. He had seen that face before when he and Gabrielle had walked through the Lower East Side together, a face of realizations arriving too late, of reckoning, a fear of things that couldn't be corrected.

His mother's lips were practically mouthing the answer for him. Twenty eyes stared him down. He could lie. It wouldn't be much of a lie, really. She *had* been intimidating. And yet. No. It wouldn't be right, setting up Gabrielle as the fall guy, just because she was willing.

"I took the money," he said. "I could have said no."

"Mandela!" Deidre shouted. "I'll have you know my son tried to return the money to her, Dean."

"He did," Gabrielle said. "But I wouldn't let him."

"No. You offered it again and I took it again. This is bullshit."

"Please everyone," Gabrielle said. "I don't see the point in splitting hairs. This is clearly my fault and I'm willing to take full responsibility."

"It is your fault," Arianna said. "It's also *his* fault. His hands aren't clean."

"And yours are?" Mandela's jaw was shaking. It was time someone stood up to the weasel. "You're doing this out of spite, Arianna, and you know it. She knew about this months ago, but did she say anything then? Suddenly I'm dating one of her friends and her star's shining a little less bright, so it's time to bring justice to the world."

Arianna looked around to the others, all smiles. It infuriated him how she refused to look over to his side of the table. "I'm not going to qualify such a remark. Mandela can interpret my actions any way he wishes, but the bottom line is he accepted a bribe."

"Arianna, please." Gabrielle's voice rose. "*Don't* persist with this." She turned to face the panel. "It doesn't matter how this came about. It happened, and I should have known better. Having said that, my daughter shouldn't suffer for speaking up. She had no idea what I was doing behind her back."

Joe Robinson let out a snort. "She opens up her mouth and thinks she can get off Scott-free? That's not how the world works. Sometimes there are consequences."

"If I may say something." One of the suits sitting next to Negroponte began whispering in her ear. She scribbled something down as she spoke. "This brings us back to my question to you, Arianna. I asked what you expected us to do with this information. I assume you thought we'd take some form of disciplinary action against Mandela?"

Arianna shrugged. "I didn't think anything." *Yeah, right,* Mandela thought.

"Surely you expect us to do something," Dean McKinley said. "Do you think we should expel him?"

"That's not for me to decide, Dean. If you feel such punishment is commensurate to his offense, then who am I to argue? I did what I did and now it's up to you."

"Arrogant little snot!" Deidre stood up and banged the table.

"Mrs. Robinson, please." Ms. Struthers lowered her glasses. Mandela turned to his mom. Joe took her hand and guided her back to her seat. She released his hand, said *I'm fine* and nodded to Ms. Struthers to continue.

"Arianna, it's your belief that your mother and Mandela share blame in this matter. So let's assume for a second that we felt expulsion was appropriate. But if your mother is equally to blame, and we cannot de facto expel *her,* doesn't that leave us with no other choice but to remove you from our school as well?"

"School policy reserves expulsion based on the actions of the student alone, Dean," Arianna said. "I've scrutinized the guidelines fairly carefully."

Joe Robinson raised his hands in frustration. "Hello? Are we still part of this conversation? If you think you're going to expel my son—

"Mr. Robinson," Ms. Struthers said. "I was merely suggesting a hypothetical argument to Ms. Levy in order for her to see the absurdity of her suggestion."

"I haven't made *any* suggestion," Arianna said.

"Her suggestions are irrelevant, as far as we're concerned," Deidre said. "Ladies and gentlemen, *we* are the wronged party here. *My* family, *my* son. Now I know we're not one of the 'prestigious' families here at Valhalla. We haven't given thousands to the alumni fund. We're not permanent presences at the auctions.

We don't have a chauffeur-driven Mercedes or houses in the Hamptons and the south of France. But if you think we're going to roll over and play dead, you are gravely mistaken."

Mandela's chest burned. This had to be one of the circles of hell, all this grandstanding. His mother didn't have a Mercedes, but she sure as hell wanted one. And now she was seconds away from calling Al Sharpton.

Dean McKinley looked pale. He glanced to his left at Suit #2, and then back at Ms. Struthers. Mandela wondered if they had developed some sort of secret code between them before the meeting. "Mrs. Robinson." He seemed to be searching for the right words. "I understand in moments like this one might say things that are not entirely judicious. Let me assure you, if I must, that under no circumstances could contributions to the school have any *shred* of influence on today's outcome. We are not, nor ever have been, in the business of coddling our benefactors. It is on this bedrock of integrity that our entire reputation rests. Perhaps you have misjudged our line of questioning. So let me ask you, what do *you* expect us to do now?"

"I expect that woman to take full responsibility."

"I have!" Gabrielle said.

"I'm not finished, Mrs. Levy." Deidre practically shouted. "I expect her to write a letter to Princeton exonerating my son of any whiff of impropriety on his part."

"I will write that letter," Gabrielle said.

"You will *not*," Arianna said, her voice for the first time betraying anger.

"I *expect*," his mother continued, "that disciplinary action be taken against the Levys and that Ms. Levy rescind her application to Princeton."

Arianna cackled. "Not likely."

"If I may." Arianna's father had finally decided to speak up. He had the look of a camp counselor caught in a lunchroom food fight. "I'm a man of few words, so excuse my silence so far. But it seems like we're going in circles. Listen, what my wife did was wrong. Dead wrong. I was as shocked as anyone when I heard about it. My own daughter turning my wife in! It's a disgrace. So even if you can't see it from where you sit, I want you to know it's not easy being on this side. And Gaby, well, I think she regrets it. I really believe she does. That may matter squat to you, but I don't think we need to get vicious. Let's think about the children and doing what's best for them. That should be the only agenda. Arianna did the right thing. She shouldn't get punished for it. And your son, well, I don't know much about him, but Gaby approached him first and that counts for a lot. So if we can just accept that and try to work through it, I think we'd be a lot better off."

"Well said, Mr. Levy," Ms. Struthers looked relieved to finally agree with someone. "Arianna, you've put us in a bind. Your coming clean presents us with no simple solutions. Your mother has repeatedly stated she alone is the responsible party. Her actions were disgraceful. They made a mockery of our community and our ideals. Customarily such an egregious act would require us to expel you as a result.

"As for you, Mr. and Mrs. Robinson, it's true Mandela is a minor and as such can be susceptible to influence. But I doubt either of you will sit here and tell me that in situations like this that the person offering the bribe should be punished more than the one accepting it. Forgive me when I say that it was entirely possible for Mandela *not* to have accepted. He could have refused and reported it to us immediately. He did not.

"Those of us here will review this matter carefully and get back to you shortly with a decision. Whatever our course of action, I assure you that both families have rights outside of this forum, and clearly may choose to exercise them. But if I can offer a few words of caution: the more protracted this situation gets, the more our hands will be tied. We are, all three of us, graduates of Valhalla ourselves, and we hold this institution sacred. Never have we ever come across a scandal such as this one. Indeed this is a sad day. I can only hope that everyone involved will learn something from the gravity of this situation. Are there any further comments or questions?"

Everyone was surprisingly silent.

"Then I wish you all a good night."

"We'll see about that," Mandela heard his mother grumble. His father nodded in agreement. They stood up and put on their coats, avoiding all eye contact, embalming themselves in their ball of anger.

"Look, I just wanted to apologize for all this." Mandela turned around. Arianna's father had come within striking distance of his parents. "I know you think we're bad people." His earnestness was unsettling; up close he had the face of a sad clown who no longer needed to fake it.

Deidre held tightly to the lapel of her coat while Joe pressed his arm against her back to escort her to the door. They would not look back or respond to Mr. Levy, who made a mild gesture of resignation with his hands. Mandela felt sympathy for him as he watched the man walk back to his family. He watched Gabrielle lift her husband's coat off his chair and help him into it, and as she did, her eyes shifted and fell on his for a hot second, and Mandela tried, really tried, to understand what that look was trying to tell him. Because it wasn't sympathetic, despite how much she had defended him earlier. And it wasn't sadness, or at least not the kind her husband was displaying. There was a hardness in her gaze, a hardness approaching defiance, as if her mea culpa was part of the plan, as if she'd weighed it and found it worthy. Looking at Arianna, he found the same steely resolve in her eyes, the same refusal to compromise: Gabrielle's stubborn determination passed on and perfected. Two women doing what they needed to do, the rest of the world be damned. He dreaded his ride home, but could not imagine theirs.

## 14. MORTY'S LETTER TO GABRIELLE

You know I'm not the type to do this, Gabrielle. But let's be honest our conversations have left much to be desired, and my therapist—that's right, I have one now—tells me I need to "unpack" my feelings and share them with you. So here goes.

I've wondered, over the past few weeks, if I can call myself a good man. I thought I was a good father, but a good father, no doubt, would've been more in touch. He would've known what's going on, put an end to it before the shit hit the fan. I've tried not to get too distracted. But Gaby, the one rock I thought I could hold on to was your devotion to our daughter. Arianna was your carbon and hydrogen, the building blocks of your universe. No matter what your feelings were for me, I was sure you'd always place our daughter above everything, including yourself. Maybe that's naïve, but I had good reason to be naïve.

I still remember your face in the delivery room when Riri was put on your belly. They say motherhood changes everything for a woman. You *became* Gabrielle that day. Up until then you were shapeless and skittish, barely an adult. When we met I saw some of what I'd given up not too long ago in your eyes, some of that frantic fire. I wanted to relive it, I guess, the uncertainty, the recklessness. You were stretching yourself in so many directions, testing boundaries with your wild, artsy friends. And let's face it, you were a knockout. Still are, which destroys me. I'd reached thirty and colors were beginning to look the same. Suddenly here you were, this kaleidoscopic goddess. Your deep hues were just the challenge I needed.

I was tired of the pussy-footing my parents called living. So much air and not enough breathing. They never cared much for you when they were alive. You were passé, a relic from a forgotten neighborhood, the same neighborhood they could trace certain cousins to not thirty years before. My mother used to water my doubts like the begonias in her garden. *What do you know about her*, she pleaded with me, when I announced our engagement. *She's exhausting, rebellious, hard-headed. She doesn't understand our world. Why make it so difficult on yourself?* I didn't tell my mother about the pregnancy and miscarriage until after the wedding. I couldn't risk the cruelty of her logic wearing me down. She would've cried blackmail, boycotted the wedding. Now, twenty years later, my mother's fears have been confirmed.

I think you expected me to get angry when you told me the truth. You wanted me to scream divorce, tell you to go to hell. You needed some overreaction on my part, some blowup to make you feel that all those years of secret-keeping was worth it. But I didn't give you that. Sure, I was mad, for a couple of hours. But how could it matter now? Even grudges have statutes of limitations. So a few days later I told you I would have married you anyway. Oh, the hatred in your eyes! I was a cockroach. A dog eating its own feces. I was pathetic and weak because I wasn't man enough to hate you. You were *revolted* by my love for you. No, it was more than that—that disgust you could have forgiven. The disgust you had with yourself: *that* was unforgivable. You weren't mad I married you. You were mad *you married me*.

If only I'd seen signs of it sooner. But who could see the cracks in your facade? Were there hints I overlooked? Therapy sessions? Every woman in New York sees a psychiatrist. Sexual frigidity? Believe me, that works both ways. After so many years, it's normal for two people not to make an effort. Stress? Are you kidding? Who isn't stressed here? You kept a lovely home and raised a spectacular daughter. That you were high-strung at times, dramatic, neurotic—was all part of the bargain.

I hate that I'm pleading ignorance here. But I wonder if even you knew what you were capable of. The extent to which you took things, that's what I can't wrap my head around. Bribe a sixteen year-old boy—you never thought of the consequences? You never considered the ways this could backfire? I keep asking myself, why take such a risk? Why prepare, devote and sacrifice for sixteen years, then turn around and risk all that hard work on a bet with no guarantee of success, that was more likely doomed to fail? To this, I have no good answer. The answers that pop in my head, I want to destroy them they're so awful. Because to me only a mother who hates her daughter could do that. A mother who's jealous, who wants something she feels she deserves but can't have.

How else to explain your sudden "discovery" of yourself this past year? Where were you missing? Under a pile of boxes in the closet, between the cushions of our sofa? Who said you were even lost? I can't bear speculating about what happened between you and the Robinson boy. Those meetings you had with him were not right. They did something chemical to your brain, changed its composition.

I don't blame Mandela, though. Those poor people. We invaded their lives. So tragic. So unnecessary. Even when they were calling for Arianna's head I felt for them. They didn't ask to be there. They didn't want to sit across the aisle from us evil white folk. Because that's what you reduced us to: just a bunch of over-privileged white jerks who think money can buy them everything. I tried to study the boy while we were sitting there. I wanted to see what it was that had so affected you. I wanted to *understand*. Every now and then he'd look at you. What could this boy possibly have to say to you?

Remember when I sat you down after that meeting at the school and asked you how you could hate us both so much? I'm still waiting for an answer. For months I've tried to be patient. I'd sit and listen to your spiel: your life was a noose, a cage—looking at me like *I* was the noose, *I* was the cage. I tried to talk to you about it, even when it stung. At this point, I've had enough. I'm tired of understanding.

I suppose I should thank you for your level-headedness that afternoon. I watched you sit still for a few minutes, not crying, not reaching for my hand, not even trying to justify yourself, and for that, at least, I'm grateful. When you spoke, it was with heroic resignation: *You're right. It's over.* I was shocked to hear it, but what else could you say?

Please, let's try to keep this process as smooth and painless as possible. We'll buy you a studio somewhere; even downtown, since that's where you already are now. I'm trying not to resent that. I'm trying not to dismiss this capriciousness as some kind of mid-life crisis. What do you expect to find down there, searching for the remnants of a life that never existed? You should look in a mirror instead. Look in a mirror and *see*, and *accept*. What was wrong with who we were? We weren't selfish or smug snobs cut off from reality. We were a family. A stable, healthy, functioning family.

The house feels empty. It's been feeling empty for a while, but it's different, now that we know you're not coming back. I know she isn't returning your calls, so let me fill you in. Arianna hasn't been expelled. Thank God for small mercies. Of course she's not going to Princeton, but honestly, so what? We're weighing our options, and I'm going to use whatever pull I have. I'm there for my daughter, Gaby. I get home early almost every night so we can eat dinner together. I get tickets to shows, to movies. I'm trying to focus on the positive: I'm getting to experience things a lot of fathers probably don't get to experience. There's no time to waste on the trivial anymore. This is my opportunity to make things a little bit better. To give some semblance of normalcy to my daughter.

I don't know how she's going to move on from this, though. The bond you two shared, it pains me to think about it. You can't just divorce your mother. Creating bitterness in our daughter, I can't forgive you for that. But I must. And I will. I can only hope Arianna will forgive you too, eventually. She's strong, I know that. What our daughter did, it wasn't just courage. It was a shout into the void. We weren't listening. Sure, I blame you, but I wasn't listening. I had plugs in my ears, only heard whatever matched my expectations. Like a shmuck, I told myself I wasn't going to meddle because I wasn't a meddler. I was the nice one, the one she turned to when you pushed too far. I thought I was the moderator, but it turns out I was just negligent.

I was blind. I was deaf. But I'm trying now, to be there for my Baby Girl. I'm trying to understand what the world is telling me. I can only pray you are listening too, and finally gain some clarity.

Morty

# 15. ARIANNA'S FINAL ENTRY

April 10, 2001

Brooke McAllister stopped me in the hall today to ask me how I was doing. It's become common now, especially among the underclass, to come up and ask me how I'm doing. I'm sure some people wish I had just left Valhalla. Certainly a lot of the teachers do. Anyway, pocket-sized Brooke McAllister — everything about her is small, from her tiny head to her narrow circle of friends — wants to know how I'm doing, see, because she's already been deemed next year's presumptive valedictorian, and wants some pointers on how to avoid screwing it up from the girl who wrote the how-to-screw-it-up manual. *What lessons have you learned*, she wants to ask me, not that she'd actually dare to. I almost tell her to go ask Roger Kornblower how he's doing, since he's our new valedictorian, but since Roger got picked by default, no one's giving him props. Poor Roger. Here he thought the allure of being the BMOC would win him a few friends, maybe even some lip-locking with a confused, status-conscious sophomore, but no.

So Brooke asked and I tried to respond respectfully, because I understand she's just a sheep and the flock must continue to graze. Then out of politesse or curiosity or just plain chutzpah, she asked what my plans were for next year. I could have lied, said something vicious like *Why, stalk you and ruin your chances of getting in anywhere, of course,* but instead I went with the truth. I said I might go to NYU. Or take a year off; it's all up in the air. Which it is. Brooke flashed this hideous, Midwestern PTA mom smile at me and said, oh, that's cool, which really meant, oh gosh, your life is so sad, and I didn't spit at her, because I know where she's at; I was her last year and would've felt the same way in this situation. There's nothing wrong with girls like Brooke McAllister. I'm just not one of them anymore.

Daddy's pushing NYU hard. They'd be thrilled to have me, he says. He knows a lot of big shots there, having attended himself eons ago. I don't want to disappoint him after all he's been through. I can't imagine what it's like to separate from someone you've been married to for twenty years. He's doing his best to be chipper, but losing a wife is not like losing a wallet or a car or even a house to a fire; it's more like losing a limb. It's disorienting, all these adjustments you never thought you'd have to make.

Still, I can't bring myself to say yes. How do I explain to him that college just isn't that important anymore? It's not that I'm ruling it out; I just want to understand *why* I'm going. Plus there's Danger. It's sad to admit this, but here goes: I may put off college to be with a boy. Pathetic but true. Even more pathetic, we've been together what, four weeks? Daddy will kill me when I mention it, so I'm propping up all my other excuses before I hit him with this one. But it's a good excuse! I'm not saying I *love* Danger but when I think of him my stomach gets seasick. We've spent every day of the past two weeks together. He's *so* in touch with his feelings! Our chats have totally blown my mind. It's a little scary, giving so much of myself to someone, telling him things I didn't think I could tell anyone. I'm better about that now, thanks to him. Plus he's very romantic. He holds my hand wherever we go and he's bought me cards. Cards! He writes silly lyrics in them to these songs he's writing about me. Did I mention he's gorgeous? I never thought I'd get into the tattooed rocker look, but God he is *hella* hot. Seriously, girls' mouths hit the floor when we walk by.

Last night Clarissa and I went to see the Cornish Game Hens play at this dive bar out in Williamsburg. I was wearing a Smiths t-shirt! Danger and the boys played six songs and I swear the world around me stopped existing: all I could see were those taffy lips, the moppy hair, the reflecting pool eyes, the majestic thrust of his hips. I actually kissed Clarissa on the lips, I was so lost in the moment. *So you like the art mutant crowd now, hunh?* she said, poking fun at me. Yes, I do. I really do.

Sooner or later reality will set in. But maybe it's not like that. Maybe we get to decide what our reality is. It's so easy to dismiss Danger just because he plays in a band. But what's wrong with being in a band? What's wrong with having a passion for something and following it no matter what anyone says? I respect Danger for that. Yes, his name is kind of silly. (His real name's Nate.) He *is* silly, sort of way too full of blue skies and fuzzy dreams, but why not just go with it? What was my passion for four years? Getting good grades? It's sad to think that's what I wanted, to be the best at everything. I didn't care what I did so long as I was good at it. What kind of passion is that?

Maybe Mother's right. Maybe it's about finding your way whatever that way may be. She took one twisted path to figure it out, but I get what she means now. I was playing it so safe in high school. Sending those letters was the first bold, clear-headed thing I did. Not safe. Not smart in the conventional sense. But why look at things conventionally? I like myself better now that I did it. And I'm fine with the consequences. Penelope told me the other day that she thought back to our lives in November, to the weeks right before it all went down, and she can't believe that's who we were. That those kids roaming the halls of Valhalla, thinking they were so cool and untouchable, that those kids were *us*. It's like the mirrors stopped lying, she said. And if Sharon and Karynne no longer walk among us, then so be it. Friendships need to be tested and ours failed the test. I don't hate them. I don't think they hate me either. It just wasn't meant to be.

Anyway, Chapel Hill's a great school, Daddy must know that. And it's not like Danger's a delinquent. So maybe I'll follow him to North Carolina. I can do that because he truly knows what he wants and right now I don't. I mean there's acting, but when I look at Danger, I know I'm not anywhere as sure about that as he is about music. It's not like I'm going to sit around on my ass. I can get a job. Maybe that's what the universe is telling me: to get the hell out of my head and sell something or be someone's assistant. All I know is I want to be with him. I want to see him become this great musician. When he plays his eyes get dizzy like he's giving up everything to be in the moment. I know there's something like that out there for me, something I'll love with such totality that I'll want nothing more than to drown in it. It's OK if I don't know what it is yet because there's no expiration date on dreams. When it happens, I'll be ready.

All my life I've quantified, dissected, compartmentalized, expected. Forgive me for getting Zen, but there's something to be said about living in the moment. Why do you think people in New York take so many yoga classes? It's hard to live in the now, so much harder than regretting the past or anticipating the future.

Speaking of moments, Grandma, Mother and I went out to lunch the other day at an Indian restaurant downtown on Curry Row. Mother picked the place, and normally I'd say she did it on purpose, because she knows Grandma doesn't like ethnic food and she wanted to force her new persona upon us. But when we sat down, and I saw the look on my mother's face — the softness in her eyes, the generosity of her smile — I thought, perhaps this isn't about us. Perhaps this is just a place she likes to eat at now, and she's just sharing that with us. So this thought takes over my mind while we're sitting there chatting, you know the usual family shtick you're only half-tuned into, but this time it's like, *pow!* I'm watching them talk, listening to the way the two of them communicate with each other and I *see* it, what I've always missed, see what it is my mother needs and isn't getting, see why my grandmother wants to but cannot give it to her.

And because I see it too, I can't just sit there and say nothing. I can't. So when Grandma makes some comment about Mother's earrings and Mother snarks back, suddenly I scream, STOP IT, like really loud. *You need to forgive each other and move on,* I say. *You need to do it now, or I'll get up and leave.* I say it so forcefully they look at me like I'm on crack. But then they don't say anything, so I get up from the table.

*Say it. I forgive you. Both of you,* I say. *Or it's sayonara.* Grandma laughs and tries to stop me, but I just turn around and finally mother says it, quietly, and I can tell she means it too, by her voice. And then Grandma sighs and she says it and sure, it's not the greatest, sure it's sort of childish and pointless, but they *did it.* At least I got them thinking outside the box. At least, for a second, they stopped and wondered.

Because you know what, I don't have to hate my mother anymore. I don't have to see her as calculating and cruel. I can open my mind to other interpretations. Grandma hasn't reached that point. She's still struggling with the changes. I understand that she wants things to be the same, but they aren't. They never will be. People think they understand things. They forecast their futures as if they were sunrises, but that's just not possible. Our lives hold so much randomness. We aren't charts or processes. We are animals with fickle brains and even more fickle hearts.

We are all a little crazy and weird and maybe that's a good thing. Maybe that's how it should be.

Some people don't get it when they see Mandela and me talking in the hall. Aren't we sworn enemies? For the longest time I saw it that way; my journal entries from the past year are like an epic poem of loathing. But we both had to finish out the year at Valhalla, and every day I'd see him the anger that filled my lungs started to feel less suffocating, until one day I thought, why *not* talk to Mandela Robinson? Why not go up and ask him about Lichtenstein or complement his shirt? He didn't want to talk at first. He thought I was making fun of him. Or maybe he thought he should hate me too. But I wore him down. Every now and then, we shoot the breeze. No one understands it. I'm not sure I do either, but it feels right, for us to move on. For it not to be stupid and stale.

Anyway, this is getting long and I guess I'm just trying to avoid the inevitable. Not that it's much of a surprise since I've written here like, twice in four months, but after much thought I've decided this will be my final entry for a while. (God, it's like I'm *breaking up* with my journal. Like the journal cares!) I'm not saying forever because I know better than to predict, but it's time to put down the pen for a while. I know I won't stop analyzing things just because I stop writing them down, but maybe I'll stop *over*analyzing. I just want to try being for a change. Letting events happen and processing them as they come instead of wringing every drop of meaning out of everything.

It's kind of like the first summer day at the beach. Some people sit on the sand and look out at the ocean, feeling themselves get hot and sweaty as they ponder the waves. They think about taking a dip, weighing it in their minds until they finally walk over to the water, letting the tide run over their toes before retreating a few steps back. Then they reconsider, and go in to the ankle, then the knee, and then maybe, just maybe, after all that, they jump in.

In the meantime, other people just get up from their blanket and dive in headfirst.

I think that's what it's like with me. My whole life I've pondered the ocean. I've tested a thousand waters with my toes. When I write everything down I'm just not jumping in headfirst. My words are like floaties, causing me to circle perimeters, protecting and limiting me at the same time. Sure, the water's going to be cold. Sure, it'll be uncomfortable for like, six seconds, but don't we all get used to it? Does anyone ever get out of the water and say, God that sucked, I really shouldn't have went in? Hell, no. So why delay it?

I'm ready to start diving.

## 16. PEN-ULTIMATE

The humidity of that late July afternoon was greasy and suffocating. He'd tried to escape it by driving out to the mall, wandering around for almost two hours, presumably to pick up a present for his mother's upcoming birthday; there were a few shops where he thought he'd find a darling vase or tea set.

He walked into the Starbucks at 2:15. The girl behind the counter greeted him with a too familiar, "Hey." He grabbed his latte, found a seat by the window, and waited. Lingered, actually. The high school was two blocks away.

He had played out the fantasy so many times in his mind that he could recite it line for line, like a favorite movie. Still, he wondered how long time would allow him to wallow in these delusions. Wasn't it stubborn of him to expect closure in his life? What exactly did he expect would happen to somehow make things better?

At 3:11, he was ready to succumb to this logic and walk out of that coffee shop one last time. About to, when he looked up, out into the parking lot, and time suddenly stood still.

It was him. Definitely him. Looking the same, with minor adjustments: his hair shorter, a loop spun through the top of his left ear. But the same watery eyes, the familiar t-shirt, Dickies and sneakers – the perfect way they hung on his body. And yet, his demeanor had changed. He seemed self-possessed. Lighter. Almost weightless.

His body felt so tight. He reminded himself to breathe. He headed for the door then turned when he realized the boy was coming inside. Oblivious, the boy joined the line forming by the cash register. He took a deep breath, walked over in a studied attempt to seem casual, and tapped the boy lightly on the shoulder.

The boy cocked sideways. He seemed confused. His eyes dilated and then quickly settled. "Hey."

"Hey," he said back.

"So," the boy said. "Kinda weird. Running into you here."

"Yeah," he said. His could think of nothing else to say.

"I'm going to Harvard," the boy said, excitedly. Proud, but not arrogantly so. No doubt the circumstances still weighed on his mind.

"Wow. That's great," he said, trying to mean it.

"Hard to believe, right? Me at Harvard?"

"A new chapter in your life." He hoped he wasn't sounding angry or bitter.

"I know," the boy said. "I'm due for a change."

They looked at each other, and Raymond felt as if they were each searching for something missing in the other's expression, something that would allow for more than the conversation had so far permitted.

"It's funny." Vinnie's eyes rolled slightly upward, suggesting a memory had struck him. "I sorta figured this would happen someday."

He laughed. "So did I. At least I hoped it would."

"The way things left off." Vinnie looked down to the ground. "I kinda owe you an apology."

Raymond nodded, looked at the boy, then away. He found it hard to be present.

"Anyway, here goes." The boy sighed, holding his palms out in front of him. "I was stupid. I was selfish. A friggin prick. Sometimes I still am, but I'm learning, ya know? I'm more aware than you think."

Raymond chuckled. "I've tried not to think, actually."

"There ain't much I can do about it now." Vinnie's eyes darted around the room nervously, then fell back upon him. "But say I'm sorry. It's all I can do. Probably stupid, but there you go."

"It's not stupid." Raymond shook his head. How much did he want to reach for Vinnie's hand right then. He knew the boy wouldn't resist. He wanted to convey so much in that one final touch, forgiveness and tenderness and pride, the sorrow and the joy and the everything. Everything. But he couldn't.

"Apology accepted," he said, keeping his hands by his side.

"Good," Vinnie said. "I'm glad."

They each nodded a few times, until Raymond realized the boy was *waiting for permission to leave.*

"So, I'll see ya around," he said.

"Sure," Vinnie replied, patting Raymond on the shoulder. "See ya." There it was, over in five minutes. Vinnie walked out the door. They'd probably never see each other again, and yet Raymond felt curiously happy, happier than he'd felt in a while. He could sense his longing pulling away from him, the weight of so much regret releasing itself into the air and disappearing. One moment, a radical undoing of time, and now, finally, a chance to rewrite his memories. Here was his happy ending, and even if it was anything but, even if it was goodbye forever, at least it was real. It promised him nothing, nothing except the chance for him to start over, to set off on a different path, a better path, a new beginning. What more could anyone hope for?

Randall closed the book and kept his eyes lowered for a few seconds. The back sleeve stared back at him, with its brash, hard-earned quote from Jonathan Franzen: "Miller's novel is a relentlessly engaging *tour de force* and one of the most promising debuts of the new millennium." He could hear clapping. Not of the standing ovation kind, but no smattering either. He forced himself to look up and smile. And lo, people were smiling back at him. Many unfamiliar faces, some even holding copies of his book. Apparently they had read the damn thing.

He canvassed the room for faces he knew: his parents, huddled together in one of the back rows, not comfortable with public performances. Dana and Bo, and Miriam from CATPEE, his rabble-rouser contingent, whooping it up in the third row. Mandy Schultz sitting next to Carrie Pepper, the representative from Knopf, in the front, both wearing smart pants suits and encouraging expressions. Zeeandra was also there, her face about two seconds away from tears, with Coleather sitting beside her. He couldn't spot any of the other writers from the group. Jealous motherfuckers.

And Wilder? Yes, him too—fourth row, second person in, with his mellow eyes and lopsided grin, looking around the room in a state of bemused bliss. Turns out Wilder's name was Harold, and while Randall wasn't entirely sure this was *the* Wilder, he had a feeling the last three weeks were only the beginning. He was keeping his fingers crossed.

As for those people he didn't want to see: CATPEE spies ready to hear something worthy of litigation? Irate parents of former students, Ken Cartwright himself? So far, not a single one.

Only one person was missing.

The clapping subsided and Claire, the studiously sexy Barnes and Noble rep, came and stood beside him.

"Thank you all for coming. Randall will now take some questions."

Ah, the moment of truth. He steeled himself and put on the most self-possessed smile he could muster. Six people had their hands up; he chose the least threatening-looking of the bunch. "Yes, the young lady in the third row." He pointed to a dark haired, kind-eyed woman wearing a retro hippie top.

"Forgive me for starting with the obvious, but is it true that you were once an SAT tutor? If so, what do you make of the recent decision by many schools to make the test optional? Doesn't that call into question the validity of standardized tests in general?"

Thank goodness. A real softball. "I was expecting that," he said, lifting an eyebrow and offering a friendly smirk. A few people laughed: *Score*. "Yes, I was an SAT tutor for a few years. I worked for one of the big test-prep companies, and also privately with clients. As for the validity of standardized tests, I'm glad more universities are asking hard questions…"

\*

He stood way in the back, leaning against one of the cases in, of all places, the Study Aids section. Oh, the irony. His attempt at a disguise—a baseball cap pulled low across his eyes, a button down shirt and tie—was lame, and probably pointless, since he wasn't close enough to be seen. Not yet. His eyes kept darting around the room.

Two weeks before, on his way to the Virgin Megastore on 14th, Legion had passed by the Barnes and Noble window and come face to face with Randall's mug on a sign announcing an upcoming reading. He had to backtrack to make sure his eyes weren't fucking with him: It really was Randall, his head tilting down, his mouth open in a half-laugh. Not exactly the Randall he knew, except for the eyes—the same jumpy, lost eyes.

He wasn't sure what to feel. He walked inside the store and found it, nestled among the other titles in the New Fiction section. He picked it up and flipped through it, thought about buying it. Instead, he put the book down, went back over to the sign, and jotted down the time and date on his hand.

It was impossible not to be curious. Why not hear about his alter ego? Why not say hi for old time's sake? Still, he was nervous. Too nervous to take a seat up front with the rest of the book-loving dorks. Too nervous to raise his hand and ask Randall a question: *Uh, Mr. Miller. Vinnie? Pretty lame name, dude. You owe me better than that.*

Of course he wouldn't do that. He was to remain fictional. Besides he already got his prize. Vinnie may not be going to Harvard but he was going to UCLA, which was pretty fucking sweet. So now it was Randall's turn. The guy deserved the spotlight, after all he'd been put through. Now Legion wouldn't have to feel guilty about how things turned out. Not that he did. People do what they have to, to survive; that's all he ever did. If anything, Randall should thank him.

\*

"A lot can be said about the fact that…"

*Holy fuck.* Mid-response, Randall's eyes zoomed in on one corner of the room. A high-pitched squeal escaped his mouth. He coughed, cleared his throat and shook his head before managing to finish his thought. "Sorry. As I was saying…"

*Jesus H. Christ. He's here. Loitering in the back of the room.* Sure, Randall knew it was possible. It had long been one of those variables floating around in the back of his mind. But he wasn't Raymond, for God's sake, desperately hanging out at coffee shops. He hadn't even prepared a reaction.

"Yes, um, striped shirt over there. Thanks for coming…"

He'd just be gracious. Water under the bridge and all that. Smile, say *good to see you* and *tell me what's been going on*. Mention Harold straight away. Let the boy know he's moved on. A bunch of small talk and pleasantries because none of it really mattered anymore, did it, with all that time and perspective? *Why hello, thanks for the material, kid. You don't mind?*

But if it was that easy, then why did his throat feel like he'd just swallowed a gallon of sand? Perhaps because he did think about running into Legion. Perhaps because of his lingering hope that one day this would in fact happen. But why? Did he just want to see that everything was alright with the boy? Of course it would be; boys like him always turn out just fine.

\*

Randall had moved on. This was a big moment for the guy, a dream come true. It'd probably be a bit weird at first, but they could laugh about it and reminisce and who knows maybe even grab a coffee together, like Vinnie and Raymond. Not that he'd apologize like Vinnie. There wasn't any reason for that. No, they could just talk about stuff. He wanted to tell Randall about UCLA. He wanted to tell him about a lot of things actually, stupid things, like the new Dashboard Confessional album and how Ken rented *My Own Private Idaho* and sat down and watched it with him. He wanted to tell him about his baby brother Ian, prune-faced Ian with Ken's green eyes, how happy and rosy Veronica was. He wanted to tell Randall that he thought about him occasionally, and that the thoughts were never sad or angry.

*

"One last question, yes, the tall gentleman with the tie."

Randall swallowed hard. He had to concentrate on the question. He had to give a pithy, witty response, send his fans out satisfied. Knopf wasn't going to send him touring around the country if he was a dud at this reading. He had to be charming. He had to concentrate on this man, this question. Not on Legion. *Christ. Why the fuck was he here?*

*

Once it's all over, he'll go up and say hi. Of course Ken would kill him if he knew about this. Why was even here? He didn't know. He just came. He expected something. What?

Randall announced the last question. The man seemed happy it was almost over. A brunette walked up and officially brought the Q&A session to a close. People clapped. So did he. What next? Should he just join the line and get his book signed? That would be sorta weird. Surprise! Art meets Life. Surreal.

Or maybe not. Why would Randall want to speak with him anyway? Who was he kidding? The guy was gonna be famous or something. He probably had met someone. Had probably moved on. Isn't that what the book was about, putting the whole thing to rest? Of course. Randall hated him. Why *wouldn't* he hate him? He had fucked with the guy really bad.

His father had threatened to ruin him. *Why would he want to see you again, you stupid fuck?*

*

"Mazel Tov." Mandy Schultz pulled him into a fierce bear

hug. "You knocked it out of the park."

"Thanks," he said.

"Stop by the office tomorrow morning. We need to talk paperback rights. I'm not saying, but it might be good news."

He looked across her shoulder. Carrie and Claire were chatting like long lost friends. Several members of the audience were forming a line by the bookshelves to his right. Could they really want to meet him? To talk to him? How ridiculous!

"Hey, big shot."

Harold reached over his shoulder and kissed him on the cheek. Randall turned to his boyfriend.

"You killed it," Harold said.

"It might have killed me."

"Nonsense."

Harold took his hands into his own and looked up at him. His eyes said faith, enthusiasm, love. Randall wanted to bottle up the look Harold was giving him. He wanted to bottle it up so he could enjoy it when he wasn't distracted, because right then, even with this look, even with everyone rushing up and the beautiful chaos surrounding him, he wasn't in the moment. He *couldn't* be. He looked beyond Harold and felt his stomach collapse. His hands were twitching. Legion was still in the back. *Still there.*

\*

What, you're just going to embarrass him? In front of his friends and family? What's the point? They probably know shit and he wants to keep it that way. He doesn't want to see you. You have no reason to be here. This is not your occasion. You're just Vinnie now. That's all. You never wanted to be anything else. You just wanted to get into a good school, show Ken Cartwright you're not a fuck-up. And now you did. You never wanted Randall's love.

Maybe you should just escape now.

\*

Zeeandra rushed over, her palms poised in prayer in front of her trembling mouth. "I'm *tremendously* proud of you!" she said. "There just aren't *words* to describe how I *feel* right now!"

"Tremendously proud works," he said, offering her a kiss on the cheek.

Coleather also came over, with Miriam not too far behind. His mother and father were slowly making their way forward, oddly deciding to join the line instead of coming straight to the front. Dana waved at him, and he waved back, half-heartedly. He was happy for these congratulations, but his eyes kept canvassing the room. They kept wandering, across every corner, until he found Legion, still loitering in the back, flipping through a copy of the book. It looked like he was smiling. He looked up. And for a split second, their eyes met.

\*

He saw me. He knows I'm here. I guess it's okay now, I should just go up to him and talk. And say what, exactly? There's nothing to say. He saw me. Maybe that's enough. Maybe that's all. He'll understand if I leave. He'll understand that I came and saw him and smiled and that will be it. It needs to be enough; let it remain our memories. Our past. Our novel which you've written, Randall, printed words on a page, bound and safe, something that can no longer be revised. Final draft.

Let's keep it at was. Not is. No more is. Because if I go up there, there will be an is. So I won't. I just won't.

\*

Shit, he's moving. He's going to join the line. Fuck! Maybe I'll pretend I don't recognize him. Maybe I'll act confused. I can do that. I can pretend this doesn't matter. It doesn't matter. I'll keep it brief. Can't keep the fans waiting. If he wants to talk more once everyone leaves, I'll just avoid him. If he suggests we meet up sometime, I'll just say, gosh, I'm kinda busy right now, what with the tour and all. Maybe some other time. Yes that's it. Some other time.

I've learned my lessons. I'm not interested in rehashing the past. I don't owe him anything. What does he want, acknowledgment? Recognition? I don't owe him shit. We did what we did. It doesn't matter if it was wrong or right, it just was. And I wrote the book. I fucking wrote this book. With my own tears practically. He won't understand that. He's a kid—he won't get it.

He'll be here soon. Don't even look down the line. Don't. Just wait... Smile. Just let it go, Randall.

Shit. He's coming.

He's coming.

## 17. CODA

The cab driver pulls over at the corner of Twenty-fourth and Eleventh, shakes his head and asks if she's sure. Gabrielle laughs. "No, but I'll take my chances," she says.

She steps out of the cab. The fires of August are simmering down, ushering in days that are at once more gentle and elastic. A soft wind breezes through her hair as her eyes survey the area. Industrial buildings, abandoned lots, and an elevated railroad track, once operational, now shrouded by the jungles of time. Who could see the future in such a derelict landscape? But she knows: life will return here. It will push and persist like the stubborn shrubs and weeds covering her destination. New York is all about reinvention.

The invitation surprised her. A text message so many months later, a minor lifetime in his years. A year ago she wouldn't have been caught dead in this area. Now, looking around, she feels serene. He chose this place as if he still understood her. A place of transition, a frontier; how right he is, again.

She follows his directions and turns into an alleyway on Twenty-fourth, where she sees him standing by what seems to be an altogether unpromising stairwell going up. He smiles. She waves. He's wearing a white beret on his head, sunglasses, jeans, a vintage t-shirt—more stylish than she's used to. He looks both thinner and more substantial, as if his body has grown comfortable with itself.

"You're late," he says, lowering his sunglasses playfully.

"How did you know I'd even show up?"

"I had a feeling," he says, biting his lower lip. "That you'd be curious."

Gabrielle laughs. "Touché, Mr. Robinson. So where is it?"

"Right this way." He motions her up the stairs.

\*

He knew she'd look different. Her hair is shorter than he'd expected. And darker. She wears crème silk pants and a wispy, feminine top with an abstract mélange of colors. Her smile is looser, calmer. She looks, not exactly relaxed, more like someone who's trying on relaxed to see how it would fit. It does.

"So you've heard of this Nami guy?" he asks, as they walk up the stairs.

"I read the same article you did in *The Times*," she says. "I'm more interested in seeing how he's using the site."

"They say they're going to turn this whole thing into a park. Get some major architects to fix it up."

"Don't hold your breath," she says. "But yes, eventually, things will change."

When they reach the top there's an unlocked gate with an orange flier posted to it: "Nami." He opens the gate and follows her inside. A morass of wild vegetation greets them on all sides, but a path has been flattened out.

"So," she asks. "How have you been?"

"Great," he says. "You?"

"Great," she says. "Really great."

She's likely wondering why he invited her here. But she won't ask, yet. He's thought about it a lot. He wants to be ready with an answer, but it's not clear in his mind. He'd been flipping through the contacts on his cell one day and his thumb somehow stopped at her name. He wondered why he had never erased her number, which led to more wondering, about how she was doing, and suddenly it didn't seem so absurd to find out. Suddenly he was sending a text. Maybe he doesn't know why he did it. He just did.

\*

Nami's pieces disorient his audience's ideas of place and geography. Some, like the first piece they encounter—two mammoth globes, one a fairly accurate representation of land mass, the other a darker abstract in which the various continents are grossly disfigured to represent their commensurate power on the world stage—stand starkly in the center. Others, mostly paintings, are camouflaged into the surroundings, as if to suggest an unearthing of treasures lost and only recently discovered. Their meaning is altered by their environment, which in turn forces you to think about the landscape.

There are fewer people milling about than she'd expected. Some collectors mixed in with the usual publicity hounds who simply go where the buzz bus leaves them off. Not that surprising on the Friday before Labor Day, when everyone wants one final dance with insouciant Summer. Even Morty has shipped off to the Hamptons.

They stop by a topographical relief of the continent of Africa done with different colored condoms. She watches him take the piece in. They haven't said much to each other yet. She wonders what it is about him that brings out her shyness.

"So how's Arianna doing?" Mandela's eyes turn to meet hers.

"Great," Gaby says. "She's in Boston for the weekend. Her boyfriend's in a band and they're playing some shows up there."

"So everything's cool between you?"

He never did beat around the bush. "We're working on it," she says.

"Last I heard she got into NYU."

"She did." Gabrielle chuckles. "I doubt she's going though."

Mandela tilts his head, curiously. "You don't seem upset about it."

"She'll be fine. What about you? All packed for Princeton?"

"I'm not going," he says. "Well, I *am* going, but next year. I deferred."

Gabrielle takes a second to absorb this. "Really."

"Yeah. We were going to move back to Jersey, but then my Grandma died. So we're staying here."

"I'm sorry," Gaby says. "Were you close?"

"Somewhat," he says, uneasily.

"And what are you going to do this year?"

"Paint, hopefully," he says. "I applied to a few programs in Europe. If I get a scholarship, I'll go."

She shrugs her shoulders. "Of course you'll get one."

Mandela smirks. She's seen this look before, the day she

picked him up outside Valhalla and told him to get into her car. Puzzled, but eager. Ready for a challenge.

"You always talk about me like you know things," he says.

"I know you're talented."

"That doesn't mean shit."

"In the long run, it means everything."

"And you?" he asks her.

"And me?"

"Why do you think you came today?"

\*

They move slowly along the path. His question has taken her by surprise. Good. He wants to upset her balance a little.

"Why do you think you invited me?" she shoots back.

He smiles. "I asked first."

They pause beside a painting of several of the world's skylines superimposed upon each other, resembling, in the end, a soulless mishmash of steel and glass. He looks at her. She's studying it, but her eyes are unfocused, more like she's looking beyond it, seeing something else entirely.

"I visited my father's grave two weeks ago," she says. "It's been a while. What am I saying, it's been five years, which is more than a while. I invited my mother to come along, but she wasn't having it. *Your father never liked visitors,* she said, as if making a joke could somehow excuse her from the shame of not joining me."

Gaby looks at him. Her eyes fidget with fear. The fear of telling or of holding back, he isn't sure which. "Go on," he says.

"It's a modest headstone, which makes sense. He was a modest man. I brought flowers, but then I remembered my father would have wanted stones. We Jews leave stones for the dead on the headstones, did you know that? Why am I telling you all this?"

Mandela laughs. "You can tell me anything you want."

"Not really," she says. "But I'll continue. So I sat with my father in this cemetery, not underneath a tree, not in the swanky part, rather far from the action, actually, sort of dull and dreary. I sat there and told him everything that's happened in the past year."

"And what did he say?"

Gabrielle smirks. "Don't be flippant. I'm being serious. So I started asking for his forgiveness, you know, because I haven't exactly lived up to his expectations. I haven't been the daughter of his dreams. I started feeling sad for myself for all that happened. I told him I'd been selfish and reckless. And then you know what?"

"I haven't a clue," he says.

"Nothing, that's what. He didn't send me a sign. A bird didn't come and rest on my shoulder, the sky didn't cover with clouds; it was just this tragically ordinary moment where everything went on *exactly the same*. And that's been me, in a nutshell, for as long as I remember: the same. Same worries, same fears, same expectations for some grand answer to life's questions."

Mandela nods, amazed that she still opens up to him just like that. "But that's changed now."

"I think so. I hope so. I used to approach life like it was a sacred family recipe: take a set of ingredients, follow the instructions and things will come out perfect every time. But it's not true. There are too many ingredients. You can kill yourself trying to incorporate them all. You just need to ask yourself what you feel like eating, and whip it up on the spot. I never did that before, but I'm OK with it now. Why am I telling you this?"

"I don't know," he says.

*

They reach the last piece. Appropriately, it's a painting, of a group of spectators seemingly looking out at them. Only their heads have all been replaced with oversized, head-shaped mirrors. The spot has been carefully chosen — while some of the mirrors reflect the people looking at the painting, others reflect parts of the city you may never have noticed, but now you do.

"So what do you think?" she asks him.

"This one's cool, like the city's looking at itself. The mirrors make me think about vanity. But some of what reflects is beautiful. Sort of, like, vanity is necessary here."

Gabrielle nods. "Hmm, maybe you're right. This city promises us too much. It's hard to settle for less when you see what's possible here."

"Sometimes it's harder not to settle. Trust me."

"You know what?" she says. "I'm feeling older. It's a strange feeling. A happy feeling."

"How so?" he asks her. They are standing by a clearing at the edge, facing west. The familiar hum of traffic echoes up from the traffic flowing down Twenty-seventh Street beneath them. A warm wind brushes past, carrying with it the smell of the trees.

"I don't know. I think I might move to Europe."

"I thought you loved New York."

"I do," she says. "I'll do it because I love New York. I want to feel what it's like to rediscover her. Come back and see her with new eyes."

"Perhaps I'll see you there," he says. "Searching for answers at the Gaudi."

She flutters her eyes. "I'll join a collective in Berlin and do guerrilla street art to protest neofascism."

"Meanwhile, I'll be in Rome, shit out of cash, forced to do charcoal recreations of Michelangelo's "Creation of Adam" on the steps of the Basilica of St. Peter. You'll walk by and accidentally drop your gelato on God's nose."

"Not accidentally. Deliberately. Artistic commentary," she says. She stares at him. "Wouldn't that be something, the two of us bumping into one another?"

"It would be," he says. He looks back at her, and sees, now, what he must say. "You're very beautiful."

Gabrielle smirks. "You need to get your eyes checked."

"Seriously. I've always thought so."

"Thank you," she says. She looks amused.

"I've always wondered what it would be like to kiss you."

Her eyes do not flinch. "You flatter me," she says. She half-turns her face, and he can see a faint blush in her cheeks. "Alright to wonder, I guess."

"I think you've wondered too," he says.

She sighs. "You've made me wonder about so many things, Mandela. I wondered and wondered and I even did something about it. And now I'm done wondering for a while. I'm going to linger in this moment I've created for myself."

"You sound happy," he says. "Are you?"

Gaby rolls her eyes. "Happy is on my radar. What about you?"

"I'll figure it out," he says. "Time is good that way."

"Yes. There's something to that."

\*

They walk back to the gate together in silence. Have they said what they needed to say, she wonders. He couldn't have asked her here just to tell her she's beautiful. What a strange thing to admit to now. Almost as strange as expecting anything to come out of this awkward moment. And yet it doesn't feel strange. He begins to walk down the stairs but she hangs back, not wanting to continue just yet. He stops and turns towards her.

"Goodbye," she says to him. "Nice seeing you."

He shakes his head and smiles. "Goodbye for now," he says. "Until Barcelona."

She laughs. She wants to believe. "Yes. I'll be waiting."

He doesn't smile. Instead he claps his hands together and bows his head. Then he turns around and continues his descent. Gaby stands still. She hears him whistling to himself. She closes her eyes and listens. In her mind she watches him fade away from her, out into the street, back to the familiar city.

A breeze kicks up behind her, sending wisps of hair into her face. She brushes them away and looks out into the horizon. She can see the edge of Manhattan, the Hudson, and the continent beyond. A shiver runs through her. How strange to be standing there, on this abandoned strip of the city. She could have never anticipated this moment. Her mouth slips into a grin. She feels lightheaded, euphoric.

The water is calm and gray. Beyond, New Jersey looks hazy and unfinished. She thinks: Funny how people ruminate when they see the immensity of water. The vastness floods their heads with dreams and possibilities. Instead, she closes her eyes and imagines herself outside, looking in. She is out on the river, she *is* the river, and she is staring back at herself, at her chosen spot, so small, and yet so precise, so significant. Because this spot, this moment, is everything. It must be everything.

This, she tells herself, is the only way to see. Not out, but in.

She takes a step down.

# SHOPTALK WITH THE AUTHOR

*I sat down with Randall Miller a few months ago at his newly acquired loft studio in Tribeca. Over a pot of oolong tea and zucchini-oatmeal cookies, we chatted about Barcelona couches, Marilyn McCoo, the death of Irony and, of course, his first novel, "Tutor to the Mob," currently in its third printing and still lingering in Amazon's top twenty. Here are some highlights:*

*If you had to boil it down to its essence, tell me what "Tutor to the Mob" is about.*

Oh Gosh. I hate that question! It's about so many things. Culture clashes. Learning hard lessons. Coming of age. It's about how we learn to cope when life doesn't meet our expectations.

*Tell us about your earliest memories of writing. What inspired you?*

Believe it or not, commercials. I loved commercials when I was a kid. It always bothered me how short they were. I wondered about the people who inhabited them. Who were they? What were they doing after the thirty seconds were over? You remember the one for that perfume En Jolie? Where the woman sings *"I can bring home the bacon, fry it up in a pan"* and so on? I wrote my first short story about her when I was eight. Apparently her husband really *did* forget he was the man.

*I'm sorry?*

(Laughs) What can I say? I've always had a vivid imagination. My mother — she still wants me to go to law school, by the way — recently reminded me that when I was five years old I had a habit of going around the house seizing all the pencils. I was *obsessed* with pencils. I'd hoard them in a special drawer and give each of them names and magical powers. Each day I'd choose one, grab my notebook and a flashlight, lock myself in our hallway closet and write down a string of nonsense words. I believed a Native American shaman was channeling me, and I was writing down his prophecies in code.

*That's so bizarre!*

I know! I can't believe I'm sharing this with you.

*Like Raymond, you were once an SAT tutor. How concerned are you that people will assume this story is autobiographical?*

There's always that danger as a fiction writer. People — non-writers especially — tend to think every story is based on reality. But often that's not true. Yes, I chose to write about something I'm familiar with. But real life isn't nearly as interesting, I'm afraid. I know it's hard for many people to imagine fashioning an entire book out of the tiniest morsels of truth, but that's what I did. It's what the vast majority of fiction writers do. Something strikes a spark, and we run with it. Around that spark, we construct our story. I've come up with an analogy which I think encapsulates it well: Imagine a thousand piece puzzle, and starting with just a few pieces — some on the edges, some in the middle — and then having to create all the pieces around it so that they'll not only fit together, but also result in a full picture that's cohesive and satisfying.

*So, for the record, you're saying there is no real life Vinnie.*

Hear this, all you mothers and fathers of my former students: I did not sleep with your children. Vinnie is not real. He's not a composite of several Vinnie-like boys either. He's simply a product of my imagination.

*There is always controversy when writing about sex between teenagers and adults. Some people are immediately turned off by it, even when it's in a gray area. You've chosen to handle things a bit differently, by making the teenager more of the sexual predator.*

I think as a country we tend to fetishize the innocence of teenagers. Fetishize? Is that a word? But really, it's such a cliché nowadays, how little parents know about what's going on in their children's lives. Junior goes out and mom and dad construct these quasi-acceptable versions of their son's escapades to fill in the gaps of their ignorance. Better than considering the real truth, which would be too shocking. Even when most of us know we weren't so innocent ourselves at sixteen. Can a sixteen year-old boy wield such power? I think so. Not that that excuses Raymond's actions.

*But as a parent, I found the character of Vinnie more than a little disturbing. How concerned were you about portraying a character that many people may find unlikable?*

Did you really find Vinnie unlikable? I sort of like him. It was always a fine line with him. I felt he needed to express to us, in his chapters, why he is the way he is and still not have it seem too psychologically neat. He's a complicated young man. His father, after all, is a mafia don.

*Tell us about that. How did you research that lifestyle? Were you ever afraid of pissing the wrong people off?*

(Chuckles) Well, if any of it were true, I suppose I'd be afraid. As for the research, it wasn't exactly difficult to find information about the mafia.

*New York City plays a major role in your novel. What are the challenges of writing about such a prominent and well-known quantity?*

It's hard to come up with something new to say. Everyone already has their own idea of what New York means to them. I needed to touch upon the universal idea while at the same time offer some fresh perspectives, mostly by having the particular descriptions characterize and illuminate upon Raymond and Vinnie. It's when you want the reader to go "Yeah, that's true," and let it still seem surprising rather than hackneyed.

*You alternate between Raymond's and Vinnie's point of view in the novel. What particular kinds of challenges did alternating POVs present to you?*

I suppose I could get highfalutin and talk about how since there's no absolute truth within human experience, we can only attempt to close in on it through an accumulation of subjective perspectives. But the real answer is that the challenge of alternating POVs is nothing compared to the freedom it provides. One POV can get claustrophobic awfully fast. Whenever I felt trapped in one person's head, I had the luxury of jumping into the other. It all boils down to my having a short attention span.

*The novel mixes in names and events that are fictional among well-known places. How important do you think it is for a writer to be factually true to the time and place he's writing about? Does the writer have license to play around with these truths, even at the risk of losing the reader's trust?*

Wow. That's a great question. It's far more important, I believe, with the kind of novel I've written, for the writer to remain true to his story rather than to the actual events on the ground, so to speak. Giving references to places that exist can provide some sense of "chosenness" to certain readers in the know, but these readers must remember that they're not in the real world, but rather in the author's world, and in that world, my reality rules supreme. I suppose what I'm saying is that readers who pause on certain stretches of truth may be losing sight of the point. That being said, it's still my job to convince them of "my" reality, despite illusions to the contrary. Am I making any sense?

*Sure, sure. So what's next for you?*

I don't know. Sleep? Lots of it. And sex with underage boys, of course.

*You're incorrigible!*

Always ;)

# Acknowledgments

I started *Admissions* — then called "Valhalla" — back in 2001. Seeing this book in print, all these years later, feels surreal to me, especially as the road to publication has been a rocky one.

I completed a first draft in 2006. It clocked in at a monstrous 216,000 words, roughly 730 pages. That June, at the New York State Summer Writers' Institute in Saratoga Springs, Darin Strauss was the first person to read the book in its entirety. He was very encouraging and generous, and I can't thank him enough for his support. Kathryn Harrison, my instructor that summer, and her husband Colin, were also very obliging. They helped my naïve younger self understand that novels need to earn their length. The book has since shed 80,000+ words.

In 2007, I was fortunate enough to meet Julia Fierro and take my first Sackett Street class. I was coming off a particularly unpleasant group experience, and here was Julia, who was unabashedly enthusiastic about my writing in a way that no one ever had been. Julia, you are a force of nature and of good in this world. You have nurtured thousands of writers.

I've been involved in several writing workshops over the years, and had the pleasure of working with dozens (if not hundreds) of other writers who have helped me improve my work. Thanks to all of you for your advice, support, and commitment to your craft.

Friends and family: what can I say? You've been my rock, and you've helped succor me through my lingering doubts, the fallow years of form rejection letters, all the near-misses with agents, and the folding of my first publisher. Thanks for listening, and always being there.

Special shout-outs to these individuals:

For almost a decade, my dear friend Loreena White and I exchanged pages of our work. We challenged and encouraged each other through frequently brutal periods of doubt and discouragement. Thanks for always being there, Loreena.

Lynne Frye Bamberger, your edits helped make this book tighter and smoother.

Erin Harris, agent extraordinaire, thanks for telling me you'll represent me no matter what I write.

Elana Seplow-Jolley, you are rare. And you write amazing jacket copy.

Jeff Condran, I was about to give up on this book. Thanks for making this happen.

Lastly: for many years I was an SAT tutor, first for a test prep company and then on my own. I'm grateful for the many ways those experiences inspired me, but also thankful that my real life experiences were far more pleasant (and certainly less scandalous) than Randall's.

Happy reading!

Eric Sasson's short story collection *Margins of Tolerance* (Livingston Press, 2012) was the runner-up for the Tartt First Fiction Award. His stories have been nominated for the Robert Olen Butler prize, the Pushcart prize, and one is in *The Best Gay Stories 2013*. For three years, he wrote "Ctrl-Alt," a column on LGBT culture for the *Wall Street Journal*, and he is a frequent contributor to *Vice*, *The New Republic* and *GOOD magazine*, among others. His articles have been featured on *Meet the Press* and *Morning Joe Scarborough*, and in 2017, he was part of the team that was awarded the National Magazine award for Personal Service. He was born and bred in Brooklyn, where he still resides.

*Photo credit: Martirene Alcantara*

CPSIA information can be obtained
at www.ICGtesting.com
Printed in the USA
FFOW02n0521090618